DRAGONLANCE DESTINIES

DRAGONS
OF
ETERNITY

DRAGONS
OF
ÆTERNITY

DRAGONLANCE DESTINIES:
VOLUME 3

MARGARET WEIS
& TRACY HICKMAN

3 5 7 9 10 8 6 4 2

Del Rey
20 Vauxhall Bridge Road
London SW1V 2SA

Del Rey is part of the Penguin Random House group of companies
whose addresses can be found at global.penguinrandomhouse.com

Penguin
Random House
UK

First published in the US by Random House Worlds, an imprint of
Random House, a division of Penguin Random House LLC, in 2024
First published in the UK by Del Rey in 2024

www.penguin.co.uk

A CIP catalogue record for this book is available from the British Library

Hardback ISBN 9781529101775
Trade paperback ISBN 9781529101782

Illustrations from stock.adobe.com by the following contributors: Chapter 1: nurofina;
Chapters 2, 3, 6, 12, 24, 35, 41 and 43: Danussa; Chapters 4, 25 and 37: Rawpixel.com; Chapter 5: intueri;
Chapter 7: Marina; Chapters 8, 10, 13 and 31: jenesesimre; Chapter 9: Dmitriy Vlasov; Chapter 11:
Oleksandr Pokusai; Chapter 14: annbozhko; Chapter 15: martstudio; Chapter 16: Eugene; Chapter 17:
Curly; Chapter 18: asiah; Chapter 19: cgterminal; Chapter 20: Yahor Shylau; Chapter 21: t_dalton;
Chapter 22: Artem; Chapter 23: swillklitch; Chapter 26: artbalitskiy; Chapter 27: Rashevskyi Media;
Chapter 29: warmtail; Chapter 30: bioraven; Chapter 32: PikePicture; Chapter 33: Olga; Chapter 34:
Annika Gandelheid; Chapter 36: Christos Georghiou; Chapter 38: Vector Tradition; Chapter 39:
arkadiwna; Chapter 40: Rustic; Chapter 42: alhontess. Additional chapter illustrations courtesy of
Wizards of the Coast by the following artists: Chapter 28: George Barr; Chapter 44: Crystal Sully

Endpaper maps: Jared Blando, © Wizards of the Coast

Book Design by Alexis Flynn
Printed and bound in Great Britain by Clays Ltd, Elcograf S.p.A.

The authorised representative in the EEA is Penguin Random House Ireland,
Morrison Chambers, 32 Nassau Street, Dublin D02 YH68

www.greenpenguin.co.uk

To Gary Gygax
Who loved to play games and shared
his love with the world.

MARGARET WEIS

50th Anniversary Dungeons & Dragons
40th Anniversary *Dragons of Autumn Twilight*

For Joe Manganiello
Who showed me the peace we all share in
traveling this road together.

TRACY HICKMAN

The Current

By Michael Williams

From this height, on dragonback
Aloft in a swift sirocco of wings
The river unfolds itself like a shy god
Intuited by sunlight
In a spindrift of reeds,
Flowing to one horizon
And one only, as the proverbs say.

And yet, in a slow descending
To the languor and stink of marshlands
The river complicates,
Its gray and linear flow
Becomes a tortuous current
Emerging, baffled by light
Into a branching country.

Fly lower still, the ruffle of wings
Disturbing the water now,
And see the river bristle
With strider and minnow and fly
All things teeming and tending downstream
Begetting and dying and always devouring
As the current descends toward nothing.
Floating down to die.

But there in the midst of the current
In the possible flow of waters,
The backflow, obstruction of towheads
Pools of hope behind rocks,
The great complexity is a promise
That what might be the meaning
The design we had always expected
Arises, then rides downstream.

DRAGONLANCE DESTINIES

DRAGONS
OF
ETERNITY

CHAPTER
ONE

anis Half-Elven arrived at the Inn of the Last Home in the morning just before noon. He had flown on griffinback through a storm, and although he was wet and chilled, he looked about with pleasure. Autumn was his favorite time of year to visit Solace, when the vallenwood trees burned with golden flame. Even now, when dark clouds filled the sky and a steady rain seemed to try its best to quench the fire, the trees still brightened the dreary day.

Tanis had traveled from Palanthas, where he and his wife, Laurana, were trying to arrange a meeting of the Whitestone Council. Tanis was glad to be able to leave, get away from the talking and arguing, scheming and bargaining. The work he and Laurana were doing was good and would mean peace for Ansalon for many years. But the talks were tedious, frustrating, and slow-going.

The free people of Ansalon—humans, elves, and dwarves—were represented on the Whitestone Council: an alliance that was credited with winning the War of the Lance. When the war had ended, the council had disbanded. But now minor disputes among the races were threatening the peace. The dwarves of Thorbardin wanted new trading agreements with the humans and were threatening to close the mountain if they didn't get them. The governments of Northern and Southern Ergoth were demanding tariffs on goods entering their countries. The Silvanesti complained of minotaur raiders from Mithas, while the Qualinesti were angered over humans encroaching on their lands.

To address these concerns, the Solamnic knights had proposed that the Whitestone Council be called back into session.

Laurana had been the leader of the Whitestone Forces during the war, and now she represented the elven nations in the negotiations. The Lord Mayor of Palanthas led the Solamnic delegation. The hill dwarves and the mountain dwarves both sent representatives, as did the gnomes and the Ergothians. The kender of Kendermore were represented by their energetic and intelligent young leader, Balif the Second, who claimed to be a descendant of the great kender military hero.

Tanis had no formal role in the proceedings, but all the parties respected him, and he was occasionally called upon to act as mediator if the discussions grew contentious. He was thankful he did not have a formal role, for this meant he could slip away from the meetings to pay a visit to his friends Tika and Caramon, to congratulate them on the birth of their second child.

He was soaked through and dispirited by the time he reached the inn, but the familiar surroundings lifted his spirits. The inn was warm and crowded and noisy. Tika greeted him with a smile and scolded him for traveling through the storm. She took his cloak to dry by the fire, then led him to his usual table, which was located near the bar so that Caramon could join in the conversation while he worked.

Tika and her husband, Caramon, were the inn's proprietors, and she waited on customers while her husband reigned over the bar.

"Shouldn't you be resting?" Tanis asked, seeing her carrying four plates of spiced potatoes, balancing two on her forearms and holding one in each hand. "You just gave birth!"

"I had a baby, not the plague," said Tika. "Young Sturm's down for his nap or I'd let you meet him."

She moved among the tables, delivering the plates and mugs of ale, then came back to sit down beside Tanis.

"Any word from Tas?" Tanis asked.

"No," said Tika, sighing. "I miss him. I'd give most of the spoons to have him back. I'm sick at heart with worry that something has happened to him. I never did trust that woman!"

"What woman?" Tanis asked, unable to follow the leap in Tika's conversation.

"That Rosebush woman," said Tika. "Wearing that horrid, ugly gem around her neck."

"Destina Rosethorn," Caramon called from behind the bar. "You sent us that letter telling us about how you met with Astinus and found out that Destina had gone back in time to the Third Dragon War and taken Raistlin and Sturm and Tas with her."

"You've heard nothing of them since?" Tika asked.

"I haven't," said Tanis. "Truth to tell, I've been so busy, I hadn't thought about it. I guess I assumed that since I hadn't heard any-thing, all was well and everyone had come back safely."

Tika shook her head. "We haven't seen hide nor hair of Tas, and you know he would have come here to tell us his adventures."

"True," said Tanis, troubled.

"I'll go see if your food's ready," Tika said, rising.

She returned with a full plate and set it down in front of him.

"Otik's spiced potatoes—crispy, just the way you like them. Do you need anything else?" Tika asked.

"You were going to bring me a mug of ale . . ." Tanis reminded her.

"So I was!" said Tika, sighing. "I'm that worried, it slipped my mind. Maybe it's the gloomy day, but I feel like trouble's coming. Terrible trouble, and I don't know what or why. I'll fetch the ale."

Caramon handed the mug to Tika, who carried it back to Tanis. She was starting to sit down when a customer spoke up from the back. "Tika, I ordered the chicken stew and you brought me potatoes—"

"And you'll eat potatoes and like it, Hal Miller!" Tika shouted.

"Yes, Tika," Miller said meekly and began shoveling potatoes into his mouth.

Caramon silently brought a plate of stew from the kitchen, set it down in front of Miller, and removed the potatoes. Carrying them back to the bar, he picked up his little son Tanin and began to eat the potatoes himself, sharing them with his son.

Tika sighed and looked out the stained glass windows. A group of kender were loitering about outside the inn, laughing and talking, heedless of the rain.

"They're hoping to be able to sneak inside before I catch them," said Tika. "Every time I look out, I expect to see Tas with them."

"How are the negotiations for the new Whitestone Council coming, Tanis?" Caramon asked, changing the subject.

Tanis sighed and shook his head. "We were close to having everything settled, with the elves and knights sharing leadership, when an elf lord suggested adding a minor provision. One of the knights trotted out some obscure passage in the Measure that prohibited it. The hill dwarves sided with the knights, and the mountain dwarves with the elves, and they nearly came to blows. We have spent three days on the matter, and they were still arguing when I left."

Hearing a baby crying, Tika jumped to her feet. "He's awake from his nap. I'll introduce you. You should eat those potatoes before they grow cold."

Tanis enjoyed the potatoes as he gazed out the window. Solace was located at a crossroads in Abanasinia, and people from all over Ansalon stopped here. Despite the rain, travelers were still arriving at the inn, hastening to find shelter from the storm.

As he watched people hurrying down the road toward the inn, he remembered a time when he would have looked out that window to see the ground far below him. The first proprietor, Otik Sandeth, had built the inn among the branches of an enormous vallenwood tree. Most of the houses in Solace had been built in the treetops to keep them safe from marauders during the lawless years after the Cataclysm.

But the trees had not kept the people safe from the dragons that had attacked Solace during the War of the Lance. The dragons had burned the beautiful trees, but they had not destroyed the inn. It had been lowered to the ground and survived more or less intact. The trees had grown back to their full, magnificent height. Some said the god Paladine had performed this miracle, and there had been talk of hoisting the inn back into the trees, but Tika had refused to allow it. That time had passed, she said, and could never come again. Best to move on.

More customers entered, for today was bread pudding day at the Inn of the Last Home. Tika's bread pudding in brandy sauce was almost as famous as Otik's spiced potatoes.

Tika brought the baby to show Tanis, who smiled to see the fuzz of red hair that covered the baby's head, a match to Tika's own red curls.

"Meet our little Sturm," she said. "We thought we would name him after our dear friend."

"A fitting tribute," said Tanis.

Tika cradled the baby in one arm and picked up Tanis's plate. She was heading to the kitchen when she suddenly gasped and dropped the plate on the floor as a column of shimmering air, like waves of heat rising off a sunbaked road, materialized in the center of the inn.

Customers saw it and bounded to their feet in alarm. Some of them ran for the door. Others remained, either too hungry or too curious to depart.

Tanis jumped up from the table, his hand on the hilt of his sword. Caramon handed Tika their older son and stood in front of his family, prepared to defend them.

A door seemed to open in the middle of the shimmering column and an elven wizard wearing black robes stepped through it. Dalamar snapped his fingers and the column disappeared, then he turned to face the patrons.

"Get out! All of you!" he told them.

They gaped at him, but no one moved. Several elves seated around a table scowled in anger and looked defiant. An elven woman said something to him in their own language. Judging by her disparaging tone and the curl of her lip, it was not a friendly greeting.

Dalamar made a sweeping gesture. His black robes swirled about him. He held a sparkling, sizzling ball of blue fire in his hand.

"I said, get out!" he repeated.

Customers scrambled to obey. Some fled, while others grabbed their pudding or their ale to take with them. The elves left but took their time, giving Dalamar poisonous looks that he returned with equanimity. The inn emptied out rapidly, though the curious lingered outside, peering in through the windows, hoping to see what was going on.

Baby Sturm was screaming, and Tanin wailed. Tika's best friend and cook, Dezra, had heard the commotion and came rushing from the kitchen. Tika handed Tanin to her, gave the baby to Caramon, and strode over to confront the wizard.

"What do you mean, Dalamar the Dark, sweeping in here like a whirlwind, threatening to set fire to my inn, driving away my customers, and frightening my children?" Tika shook her fist at him. Her red curls seemed to blaze with anger. "You'd better have a damn good reason! Wizard or no wizard, I'll tie those black robes of yours into knots and stuff them down your throat!"

Dalamar paid no attention to her. Muttering a few words, he waved his hand. The shutters that covered the stained glass windows flew closed and latched. The door slammed shut of its own accord, and the bolt dropped across it.

Dalamar turned to Dezra. "The inn is closed. Take the children to your house and stay there."

Dezra tossed her head and stood her ground. "I do not take orders from you."

"Do as he says, Dez," said Caramon. "Go home and take the children with you."

"But first bring me my skillet!" Tika said furiously.

"Just take the children, Dez," said Caramon, handing her the baby. "Leave by the back door."

Dezra cast Dalamar a baleful glance, then carried Tanin and the baby away.

Caramon placed a calming hand on Tika's shoulder, then turned to Dalamar. "I think you had better explain yourself."

Dalamar snapped his fingers and the ball of sparkling blue fire disappeared. "The fireball was an illusion. There was no danger to the inn or your children or your customers. I need to speak to all of you—including you, Tanis—in private. For I bring dire news."

"About Tas?" Tika asked, her voice trembling. She took hold of Caramon's hand.

"About all our friends. I told you when I was here last that Destina Rosethorn and the Graygem went back in time with the Device of Time Journeying and took Sturm and Raistlin and Tasslehoff with her. The device was destroyed, leaving them stranded in the time of the Third Dragon War. An artificer created a new device and Brother Kairn, a monk of Astinus, went back to bring them home.

"But Chaos had other ideas," Dalamar continued grimly. "And now history has been upended. To make a long and terrible story short, a traitor killed the silver dragon, Gwyneth, and assassinated Huma before they had a chance to fight Takhisis. The Dark Queen and her armies seized the High Clerist's Tower, and Solamnia fell to her might. She soon conquered all the other nations of Ansalon and, after that, the world."

Tika had listened with growing impatience and now she gave an incredulous snort.

"You expect us to believe such a kender tale? Not even Tas could make that up! I don't know what game you're playing at, Dalamar, but you can take yourself out of my inn! And next time enter through the front door like a normal person."

Caramon squeezed her hand. "Let him finish."

Tika stared at him. "You don't believe this ridiculous story, do you?"

Caramon steadily regarded Dalamar. "I'm not sure what to believe."

Tanis had remained silent and now Dalamar turned to him.

"I came to fetch you, Half-Elven, to take you to meet with Astinus. The possibility exists that we can undo what has been done, but we have only a short window of time to 'fix' history before the river rises and drowns us. We require your help."

"I'll go," said Caramon, starting to take off his apron.

"You will not!" Tika cried, grabbing hold of him.

"You should not leave your family, Caramon," said Dalamar. "If we fail, and the darkness closes over us, the people of Solace will need you—your strength and your courage."

"You're serious, aren't you?" Tika faltered. "Oh, Caramon, I said I had a feeling something was terribly wrong."

"I don't understand—" Tanis began.

"And I don't have time to explain," Dalamar said impatiently. "You can ask your questions of Astinus."

Tanis looked at Caramon. "What do you think?"

"I've known Dalamar a long time. He helped when Raistlin . . ." Caramon pressed his lips together, then said quietly, "He helped me when I needed help. I trust him."

Tanis was still not convinced. He did not entirely trust Dalamar, but he did trust Astinus.

"I left my belongings on the griffin," said Tanis. "I'll go fetch them."

"Be quick about it," said Dalamar. "Time passes and the river rises higher every moment."

Tanis had no idea what he meant about a rising river, but he doubted Dalamar would explain. Tanis put on his still-wet cloak and went to where he'd left the griffin. Most of the crowd in front of the inn had dispersed, although several kender were still loitering about in the rain, probably still hoping for more excitement or at least a free helping of bread pudding.

Tanis took his pack from the saddle and spoke to the griffin, ordering it to return to its stables without him. The wind made a mournful sound as it blew through the vallenwoods. The driving rain knocked the golden leaves from the trees, and the mud squelched beneath his boots. When he again entered the inn, he found Caramon and Tika standing together, their arms around each other. Dalamar was pacing back and forth.

"I'm ready," said Tanis. At least traveling by magic, he reflected, the trip would be dry.

"Not a word of this to anyone," Dalamar warned Caramon. "Live your lives as usual."

Caramon gave a rueful smile. "Trust me, Dalamar. No one would believe us anyway."

"Answer one question before you go, Dalamar," said Tika, reaching out to him. "Did Tas do something back in the past to cause this calamity? Is this his fault? Because, if he did, you know he wouldn't do it on purpose. He wouldn't mean for this to happen ..." She couldn't continue, but broke down, sobbing.

"From what I understand, Tas did his best to save Huma and Gwyneth, as did Sturm and Raistlin and Lady Destina," Dalamar answered gently. "But they were pitted against a foe they could not possibly fight—Chaos."

Tanis shook hands with Caramon, and Tika gave him a fierce hug.

"Take care of yourself! And if you see Tas, tell him to come home right this instant. No more gallivanting about with Rosebush women and ugly gray gemstones."

"I'll tell him," Tanis promised.

Dalamar drew a circle on the floor with a bit of charcoal from the fireplace and told Tanis to step into it.

"Nuitari, I ask your blessing," said Dalamar and spoke the words of the spell. *"Triga bulan ber satuan/Seluran asil/Tempat samah terus-menarus/Walktun jalanil!"*

Magic swirled around them, and the next instant, Tanis found himself standing in the Great Library of Palanthas outside the master's office. Bertrem was there to meet them.

"The master is expecting you," he said, subdued.

Tanis found Astinus writing, as usual. The master did not look up from his work but motioned Tanis and Dalamar to chairs.

Tanis did not take a seat but walked straight up to the desk and put his hands on it. "Is it true what Dalamar told us, Master? That Takhisis is now ruler of the world?"

"Sit down, Half-Elven," said Astinus. "I do not like to have to crane my neck to look up at people. All will be explained. We wait for one more."

Tanis was tempted to snatch the pen from Astinus's hand, but he contained himself, though he did remain standing. Within a few moments, Bertrem opened the door.

"Brother Kairn," he announced.

Tanis had met the young monk before, but he almost didn't recognize him. Kairn had changed out of his monk's robes into traveling clothes: boots and breeches, a long-belted coat, vest, shirt, and hat. He was carrying his quarterstaff and rested it against the wall as he greeted Tanis.

Tanis glanced at Dalamar. "I thought you said Brother Kairn had gone back in time to rescue the others."

"I did, sir," said Kairn somberly. "I brought them to the year 351, to the Inn of the Last Home the night of your reunion. But I was the only one who arrived at the Inn. The others are in Solace somewhere. I just have no idea where."

"In other words, he has lost Destina and the Graygem in Solace in 351 Chaos Time," said Dalamar.

"Chaos Time. What does that mean?" Tanis asked.

"Our time is now Chaos Time. Takhisis is the ruler of the world," said Dalamar.

Tanis was the only one still standing. He folded his arms over his chest. "Is this true, Astinus? Does Takhisis rule the world? This world in which we now stand?"

"She does," said Astinus in his dispassionate voice.

Tanis was confounded. "But . . . how?"

"Sit down, Tanthalas, and all your questions will be answered," said Astinus. He continued to write. "Or you may leave."

Tanis sat down.

CHAPTER
TWO

"Show him the passage in the book, Brother," said Astinus.
Kairn lifted an enormous book from the master's desk and opened it to a page that had been marked with a gray silk ribbon. He offered the book to Tanis.

"Please read this, sir," Kairn said. "It is the record of the night of your reunion in the year 351."

"I know what happened," Tanis said tersely. "I was there!"

"Please read it, sir," said Kairn.

Tanis shook his head in exasperation but began to read. He skimmed through it once, then read it again, more carefully. Finally, he slammed the book shut.

"This is nonsense! All of us attended the reunion that night in 351 *except* Kitiara. Yet according to this account, she was the only one who came!"

"Astinus wrote what he saw, Tanis," said Dalamar. "I told you, time has changed. Those events happened in 351 in the Age of Chaos."

"But if time has changed, as you say, then why don't I remember it that way?" Tanis demanded. "I remember my friends, Raistlin and

Sturm and Flint and Tas, and how we rescued Goldmoon and River-wind and the blue crystal staff and took them out through the kitchen!"

"The floodwaters rise slowly, Half-Elven," Astinus said.

"What flood?" Tanis almost shouted in his frustration.

"As a river floods, the rising waters flow downstream," Astinus said. "In like manner, the rising floodwaters of the River of Time are moving toward us. The events of the past have yet to affect our present. When they do, Tanis Half-Elven, you will look into the sky and see Her Dark Majesty's dragons."

Astinus spoke calmly, but Tanis heard the sorrow in the master's voice. He looked at Kairn and saw grim determination. He looked at Dalamar and saw grave concern. Tanis was shaken, unable to comprehend the awful enormity of the possibility that his world had been cast into darkness.

"Let us say I believe this, Master," Tanis said after a moment. "Dalamar spoke about being able to 'fix' time. How?"

"I have the Device of Time Journeying. I proposed that Destina and I go back to the Third Dragon War again to try to prevent the assassination of Huma," said Kairn. "Astinus has granted me permission."

"If that is even possible," said Tanis, "what has this to do with me?"

"I first have to find Destina and the others. I know they are in Solace and you know Solace well. . . ." Kairn faltered, flushing in embarrassment.

"There is another reason," said Dalamar. "One Brother Kairn is loath to mention. We need you as bait."

"Bait?" Tanis stared at him.

"Takhisis is searching up and down the River of Time for the Graygem. As long as Chaos is in the world, she is not safe. She could lose everything she has won. The Dark Queen was present when Brother Kairn and the others fled to Solace, and she must know or suspect they arrived in the year 351 Chaos Time. In that year, Paladine and the gods rose against her. They fought what is known as the Lost War. As the name implies, they were vanquished. But Takhisis fears that this time, with the help of Chaos, they might succeed and defeat her."

Dalamar handed Tanis a book. As he took it, he saw that the cover was stained with blood. "You can read Astinus's account of the Lost War. And while you are reading, I must leave on an errand of my own. Brother Kairn, give me your rucksack."

Kairn clutched it to him. "I cannot! The Device of Time Journeying is in here!"

"I am aware," said Dalamar. "I plan to ensure that it remains there."

He snapped his fingers and the rucksack flew to his arm. He spoke a word of magic and vanished.

"Be easy, Brother Kairn," said Astinus. "He will return."

Tanis looked down at the book in his hands. He could feel the darkness and despair and sorrow seeping out of the pages. And he had only to look at Astinus to see the same on his ageless face.

He began to read.

CHAPTER
THREE

Dalamar went directly to his library in the Tower of High Sorcery. He checked the wizard lock on the door to make certain it was still in place, then he took Brother Kairn's rucksack over to the fireplace. Kairn had told him about an encounter with a draconian who had searched the rucksack. The draconian had found the Device of Time Journeying, but Kairn had passed it off as a child's toy. But Dalamar couldn't risk the Device falling into the hands of the forces of the Dark Queen, and he had devised a spell to protect the Device from being discovered.

He tossed the rucksack into the fire. Flames swirled about the bag and then vanished. Dalamar removed the bag from the grate. The flames had not harmed it. The rucksack was cool to the touch.

Dalamar summoned an apprentice and handed him the rucksack.

"Open it and tell me what you see inside."

The apprentice rummaged through it. "A shirt, linen, stockings, dried meats and fruit."

"Nothing else?" Dalamar asked.

"No, Master," said the apprentice and returned the rucksack.

Dalamar looked inside and saw the Device of Time Journeying, its jewels sparkling in the firelight.

"I am bidden to tell you, Master, that the gods of magic have summoned you," said the apprentice.

"I expected as much," said Dalamar.

He climbed to the very top of the central spire and entered a room he had built himself after he had become master. He had named it the Chamber of the Three Moons, and he was the only person who had access to it.

The room was small, round, and windowless, with a domed ceiling. An altar made of black, red, and white striated marble stood in the center. The only objects on the altar were three pillar candles—one black, one red, and one white.

Dalamar would have lighted the candles to summon the gods, but the candles were already burning. The gods were here, waiting for him.

Three moons shone from the domed ceiling above him: one white, one red, and one black. Three robed figures stood before him. Solinari was dressed in white from head to toe with only his eyes visible. Lunitari wore red robes that matched her flaming red hair. Nuitari was a disembodied face, round as his moon.

The three gods of magic were cousins—the children of the gods. Solinari was the son of Paladine and Mishakal. Lunitari was Gilean's daughter, and Nuitari was the son of the Dark Queen and her consort, Sargas. Unlike their parents, who were eternally at war with one another, the three cousins stood united in their dedication to the magic and to the mortals who wielded power in their names.

Dalamar bowed before them.

"You are aware of my meeting with Astinus."

"We are aware you met," said Solinari. "But not of what was said."

"We presume you spoke of the Graygem," said Lunitari. "And thus Astinus would keep the meeting secret."

"I have read the account of the Lost War," Dalamar said. "Is Astinus's account accurate? Did Takhisis win the battle and vanquish the gods? It's not that I doubt the master," Dalamar hastened to add, glancing at Lunitari, Gilean's daughter. "But there might be some mistake."

"No mistake," said Lunitari sorrowfully.

"The flames of the Cleansing Fire that ravaged Ansalon shone bright in our eyes," said Solinari.

"And by its terrible light, we saw my mother's dragon armies claim victory," said Nuitari. "And now the River of Time is rising and a tidal wave of destruction is rushing toward us."

"Then we must find a way to stop it," said Dalamar. "Astinus has given Brother Kairn permission to go back to the Third Dragon War with Lady Destina Rosethorn and the Graygem to attempt to restore time."

"The plan offers hope," said Lunitari.

"A forlorn hope," said Nuitari.

"The danger is very great," Solinari added. "Takhisis knows that since Destina is still in possession of the Graygem, she might go back in time to try to undo what was done. The Dark Queen will be watching. If she discovers Destina—"

"We must make certain she does not," said Dalamar. "And thus I propose we keep her attention focused elsewhere. Takhisis has no idea where to find the Graygem. For all she knows, it could be present during the time of the Lost War. If so, it could change the outcome of the battle. We need to play upon her fears. Tell me more about the final battle in Neraka. Astinus's account led up to it, but he did not leave a record of the battle itself."

"Because we were too busy losing," said Nuitari with a bitter laugh.

"Silence, Cousin," said Solinari, frowning.

"By giving you the key to altering time, we could make matters worse."

"Takhisis is coming to enslave us all," said Dalamar in scathing tones. "I do not see how matters can get much worse!"

The three exchanged troubled glances. Solinari's eyes glittered silver. Lunitari's eyes flamed. Nuitari's empty eyes were unblinking.

"If you know something that might help us defeat Takhisis, you need to tell me," Dalamar persisted.

"We cannot," said Lunitari.

"The danger is too great," said Solinari.

"We have seen the end," said Nuitari.

Dalamar looked from one god to the other.

"You're afraid!" he said, awed.

"We have reason to be," said Solinari.

"After her victory in the Lost War, Takhisis banished us from the heavens," said Nuitari.

"But that is all the more reason to fight to change the outcome!" Dalamar insisted.

"You do not understand, Dalamar the Dark," said Nuitari with an unpleasant smile. "We fear we *will* change the outcome. Instead of banishing us, my mother could destroy us. We would cease to exist."

"Listen to me—" Dalamar began, but he spoke to no one.

The candles on the altar flickered, then a blast of wind swept through the room and doused the flames. Dalamar remained at the darkened altar for a long moment after the gods had gone. He was disappointed and troubled and wondering what to do, when he became aware of empty, unblinking eyes gazing at him from a round moon face.

"You have returned to help, after all!" said Dalamar gratefully.

"I have returned to tell you that you do not need my help," said Nuitari. "You will find all you need to know in Astinus's account of the Lost War. The answer is there. Or rather, the answer is not there."

"I am tired of everyone speaking in riddles!" said Dalamar, frustrated. "Just tell me!"

"I have told you and I risk much telling you that," said Nuitari. The unblinking eyes closed. The god disappeared.

CHAPTER
FOUR

anis closed the book containing the account of the Lost War. Or rather, he read about the beginning of the war the gods had launched to try to overthrow Takhisis. Astinus had not recorded the terrible end. The last words he had written were burned into Tanis's mind.

I put down my pen to take up my sword.

He looked up to see that Dalamar had returned. Tanis had been so engrossed in his reading he had not noticed. Dalamar handed Kairn the rucksack. Kairn almost snatched it from his hands and opened it and peered inside. He sighed in relief.

"The Device is still there!"

"Along with your shirt and socks," said Dalamar. "Which is all someone will see if they open it."

Kairn appeared dubious, but he closed the rucksack and kept fast hold of it.

"You read about the battle?" Dalamar asked.

"I did," said Tanis. "A battle that was lost years ago. I do not know how you expect me to change the outcome?"

"The Heroes of the Lance are in the right place but the wrong time," Dalamar explained. "Takhisis remembers that you and the others defeated her in the War of the Lance. She will worry that you have the power to do so again. If you travel to the autumn of 351 Chaos Time, you will attract her attention. Her eyes will be fixed on you, Tanis. And if—the gods forbid—Brother Kairn and Lady Destina fail to change time, winning the Lost War is our last hope."

"But how can we win if we lost?" Tanis asked, exasperated. "We cannot change what happened!"

"But we can," said Dalamar. "The Graygem is in the world. It is in Solace in 351 Chaos Time, and the very fact that the Device took Raistlin and Sturm and Tas from our time to Chaos Time means that the Graygem has already changed the course of the river."

"Let us say I go back with Brother Kairn," said Tanis. "What happens to me if he and Lady Destina succeed? If Huma defeats the Dark Queen as history tells us he did?"

"The River of Time will once more flow in its proper course, and your life will be what it has always been," said Astinus. "You and I will never hold this conversation."

"But it is possible that Brother Kairn and Destina could fail, as Dalamar says."

"It is, sir," said Astinus, continuing to write. "If that happens, you will be stranded in the past, in the year 351, in the Age of Chaos."

"Then find some other bait for your hook," said Tanis firmly. He laid down the book on Astinus's desk and stood up. "Dalamar, use your magic to take me back to the inn."

"I will, if you insist. But first I want to ask you a question," said Dalamar. "What do you think will happen to your wife under the Dark Queen's rule, Half-Elven? Takhisis can see both streams of time. She sees the War of the Lance and—no matter what time she is in—she will never forget that Laurana, the Golden General, defeated her armies, brought down her empire, and banished her to the Abyss. You can read the account of what happens to Laurana in that book—though I warn you, it is not for the faint of heart."

Dalamar indicated the bloodstained volume.

Tanis regarded him, his expression grim. "Before I decide, I need to discuss this with Laurana. She is staying with Lord Gunthar at his home on the Isle of Sancrist."

"You would put them both in danger," said Astinus. "Takhisis finds Laurana through you."

"The Dark Queen draws closer with each passing breath," Dalamar added. "So what is your decision?"

"Don't rush me, Dalamar! I still have questions," Tanis said brusquely. "If I go back into the past, will I find two of myself?"

"No," said Brother Kairn. "According to Alice—"

"Who is Alice?" Tanis interrupted.

"Alice Ranniker, the artificer who made the new Device of Time Journeying," Kairn explained. "Since you are present in 351 Chaos Time, you replace the Tanis that is there. This is a fail-safe measure that prevents you from traveling back in time and suddenly changing into the Tanis who would have no knowledge of the fact that he traveled through time and would thus be unable to return.

"You will retain your memories of this time, even as you step into the body of the Tanis already in Solace in the year 351 Age of Chaos. By the same token, if the Tanis of that time traveled to this time, he would step into your body. It is only when you go to a time in which you are not already present that you will be your original self."

"I suppose that must make sense to someone," said Tanis. "Which leads to my next question. How do you know that the Tanis of that time is even in Solace during this Age of Chaos?"

"According to Astinus's records, when you and your friends were forced to flee Solace for your own safety, you swore an oath to meet in the Inn of the Last Home in five years' time," said Kairn. "Nothing would stop you from keeping that oath. Not even Takhisis. All your friends will be there. Tas and Sturm and Raistlin will be there from our time. Flint will be there, although he will be from Chaos Time. That means the Tanis he knows will be the Tanis from that time."

"Flint and Sturm ..." Tanis murmured.

These two had died years ago. Both had been dear to Tanis, and he still missed them. The thought that he might have the chance to walk with them again helped ease the burden of his decision.

"If this plan to restore time fails, how am I supposed to win this war we lost?" Tanis asked.

Astinus laid down his pen. His gray eyes fixed on Tanis.

"By being yourself, Tanthalas. By following your instincts. By choosing to do what you know to be right. That is how you will win the battle."

"And, according to Nuitari, the answer is there, only it is not there. I think what he means is that we need to figure out what was present during the War of the Lance and is not present now," said Dalamar.

"Why can't gods ever give a straight answer?" Tanis demanded.

Astinus faintly smiled. He picked up his pen and resumed writing. "Because your mortal mind would never understand."

Tanis went over everything he had heard in his mortal mind. The logical, reasoning side of him—probably his elven side—told him the very idea of an Age of Chaos was ridiculous. But then the illogical, emotional side of him—his human side—looked down at the bloodstained book. He knew what Takhisis would do to Laurana if she ever laid hands on her. If there was even an infinitesimal chance that his wife might be in terrible danger and he could save her, he would risk everything.

"Very well, I will go with you, Brother. What must I do?"

Kairn took hold of his quarterstaff and opened the rucksack. He took out a silver globe studded with jewels. "This is the Device of Time Journeying. Place your hand on the device. I will do what is needful to cast the spell."

Tanis made certain his sword was buckled securely to the belt at his waist and hefted his pack.

"Tell Laurana . . ." He couldn't think what to say. His heart was too full.

"I will tell her," said Astinus.

Kairn spoke the words to the spell. "'And with a poem that almost rhymes, now I travel back in time.'"

Magic swirled around Tanis, caught him up, and swept him into the river.

CHAPTER
FIVE

The Device of Time Journeying dropped Tanis onto a road
he immediately recognized, though he had not walked it in
many years: the road he had taken when he had arrived for
the reunion years ago. The time of year was the same: autumn. The
vallenwoods in the valley were ablaze in the season's colors, brilliant
reds and golds. He could see thin columns of smoke curling among
the treetops now as he had seen them then. But the spreading haze
should have carried with it the sweet aroma of home-fires burning.
Instead, this smoke was thick and black. The smell was acrid and
stuck in the throat, causing him to cough.

"The smoke is from the logging camps," said Kairn as he placed
the Device in the rucksack.

"What logging camps?" Tanis asked, startled.

"Verminaard's armies are cutting down the vallenwoods and
shipping the logs to Northern Ergoth, where he is building a new
fortress. First the loggers set fire to the brush to clear the forest, and
then ogres wielding enormous two-man crosscut saws bring down
the trees."

"Cutting the vallenwoods!" Tanis repeated, sickened. Smelling the noxious smoke, he began to actually believe he was in a world ruled by the Dark Queen.

"What do we do now?" he asked.

Kairn slung the rucksack over his shoulder. "I was thinking we should first go to the inn. Raistlin might be there with news. And while we walk, I will tell you what I have learned from Astinus's writings about this period of time."

Tanis was uneasy. The thick smoke obscured the sun, but he could tell it was still daylight, and they should have encountered other travelers. Yet the road was deserted, no one about.

"Dragon Highlord Verminaard rules Abanasinia and regions to the west," Kairn was saying. "His headquarters are in Pax Tharkas, so he can supervise the mining operations there. He rarely visits Abanasinia, but has placed his underling, Highmaster Toede, in charge."

"Toede." Tanis grimaced. "I had forgotten about that slimy hobgoblin. How did he get elevated to Highmaster? He was only a Fewmaster when I knew him."

"Verminaard required slaves to work in the mines and Toede supplied them. Verminaard rewarded him by making him Highmaster. Toede has grown wealthy and powerful in his position, for he has teamed up with Hederick, the High Theocrat, to run a criminal empire. Toede extorts people, demanding payment to keep them from being sent to the mines, while Hederick sells religious artifacts that have supposedly been blessed by the Dark Queen. Up until now, no one has dared challenge either one of them, for they have Verminaard's backing. But now Kitiara's arrival has thrown Toede into a panic, for he fears she is here to take his job."

"Tell me about Kit," said Tanis.

It seemed strange to speak her name again. He had not thought of her since her death during her ill-fated attack on the city of Palanthas. Tanis remembered her last moments, when the death knight Lord Soth came to claim her. He thought of her with regret. His regret was not for her, for she had chosen to walk a dark path and Tanis was fortunate she had not dragged him into the darkness with her. His regret was for lost youth, lost innocence. For he had loved her once. Or thought he had loved her.

He remembered his unhappiness when he had learned that Kitiara would not be coming to the reunion. She had sent a letter, saying she was serving a new lord. As it had turned out, that lord had been Queen Takhisis.

"The circle is broken," Flint had said. "The oath denied. Bad luck."

"Kitiara is Dragon Highlord of the northern part of Ansalon," Kairn continued. "Her headquarters are in Solamnia. By traveling to Solace, she has encroached on Verminaard's territory. Toede sees enemies lurking behind every bush and he fears she is here to supplant him and take Abanasinia. He has been sending frantic messages to Verminaard, pleading with him to come deal with her."

"You said my friends and I had to flee for our own safety. What was I doing in Solace?"

"You were the leader of the resistance," Kairn replied. "The people of Ansalon were not strong enough to challenge the Dark Queen's armies openly, so they formed resistance groups to wage covert war on her forces. You and your friends formed the resistance movement in Solace, based out of the Inn of the Last Home.

"Five years ago, you and your companions were trying to free a group of slaves who were being transported in a caravan to the mines when a force of draconians ambushed you. You and the others barely escaped with your lives. You decided it would be safer for you and your friends to leave Solace for a time, hoping to find some sign that the gods of good had returned to challenge Takhisis."

"In the other time, we left to seek the true gods for almost the same reason," said Tanis, marveling.

"Dalamar says, 'History is the same, only not the same,'" said Kairn.

"What happened to my friends during this period of time?" Tanis asked.

"Sturm went to Solamnia to find his father and to assist in the uprising known as the Second Rose Rebellion. Raistlin traveled to the Tower of High Sorcery in Wayreth to take the Test, and Caramon went with him. Flint sought refuge among the hill dwarves, and Tasslehoff set out for Kendermore to find out what had become of his people."

"I notice you did not mention Kitiara," said Tanis. "Was she a part of the resistance? Were she and I . . ."

He paused, not sure where that question was leading.

"You two were very close," Kairn replied diplomatically. "Kitiara refused to be involved with the resistance, saying she had no intention of risking her life for a worthless cause. She left Solace when you did. She traveled to Neraka to join the dragonarmies, although none of you knew that at the time."

"Where did I go?" Tanis asked with the odd feeling he was discussing a stranger.

"You went home to Qualinesti for a time, but you were angered by the elves' refusal to fight the Dark Queen and you left. You grew a beard to hide your elven features, then spent the remaining years traveling Ansalon, helping where you could and searching for some sign of the return of the gods."

"What happened when I came back to Solace for the reunion?" Tanis asked.

"You were eventually captured and killed," said Kairn.

Tanis stopped walking. "You neglected to tell me that part of the story."

"Because the Graygem is now involved, and the pages of the future are blank." Kairn went on to explain, but Tanis was only half listening.

He had caught sight of a solitary figure seated on a moss-covered boulder. The wind rose, blowing away the haze, and he saw the fading light of the setting sun glint off a metal helm with a horsehair tail.

Tanis knew that helm and the dwarf who wore it, and he felt his heart constrict with both pleasure and pain. Flint refused to admit the mane was horsehair, for he always swore horses made him sneeze. He said that the tail was "the tail of a griffin," and it was no use telling him that griffins did not have such tails. Flint refused to be convinced.

The dwarf was seated on the boulder, carving a piece of wood as he was wont to do, for he had worked all his life and scorned to sit idle. Engrossed in his carving, he had not yet noticed them. Tanis was glad, for he needed a moment to overcome his emotion upon seeing his longtime friend—his dearest friend. Tanis was grateful for the beard that hid his elven features. It also hid his tears. They slid into his beard and vanished.

Kairn noticed his attentive gaze and looked down the road.

"Is that Flint Fireforge?" he asked.

Tanis nodded, not trusting himself to speak.

"One of the Heroes of the Lance. I will be honored to meet him," said Kairn.

Flint was as Tanis remembered him. The dwarf's beard and hair were both white. His long hair flowed down his back as his beard flowed over his chest. He was wearing a coat of mail—iron rings attached to leather—that he had undoubtedly forged himself. His coat was belted and extended to his thighs. He wore tall leather boots and a leather harness for holding his axe. Flint was built along the lines of the boulder on which he was sitting—stout, sturdy, and solid.

The dwarf heard them approach and swiftly rose to his feet. He tucked his knife into his belt, then drew his axe and stood, prepared for trouble. He watched them warily, his brow furrowed.

Tanis grinned at him. "Flint Fireforge! After all these years, are you going to behead me?"

"Tanis?" Flint stared at him. "Is that you?"

"The same," said Tanis. Coming up, he clapped Flint on the shoulder. "I would embrace you, old dwarf, but not while you're holding that axe."

"Embrace me! We've no time for such foolishness." Flint gave a derisive snort, although Tanis could tell he was pleased. "Who's your friend?"

Tanis performed introductions, remembering at the last moment to refer to the monk only as Kairn, not Brother Kairn.

Flint eyed the young man and edged near Tanis to ask in a low voice, "Can he be trusted?"

"He can," Tanis replied, smiling.

Flint lowered the axe and held out a rough and calloused hand. "If Tanis vouches for you, that's good enough for me."

Kairn shook hands warmly. "I have heard a lot about you, sir."

"I'm not 'sir,' young man," said Flint gruffly. "Just plain Flint is good enough."

"I am glad to see you, old friend," said Tanis.

"I wish I could say the same," Flint said, scowling at him. "It's too dangerous for you around here. Oath or no oath, you shouldn't have come back."

"You came back yourself," Tanis pointed out.

"Because I knew you would be fool enough to come back, and someone's got to look out for you!" Flint stated triumphantly. "Good thing you grew that ugly beard."

"Why is that?" Tanis asked, laughing.

"Kitiara's in town," said Flint dourly. "She arrived with a troop of draconians, and Tika says she's been asking about you. Kit won't recognize you with that beard."

Tanis was thoughtful and didn't immediately answer.

"You're not still carrying a torch for her, are you?" Flint asked, regarding him with concern.

"I doused that flame many years ago," said Tanis.

Flint grunted. "Good! Because Tika told me it was Kit who betrayed us to Verminaard and damn near got us killed. Did you know?"

"I did not. But I could have guessed," said Tanis. "Don't worry about me, old friend. I've grown up a lot since those days."

"About time," Flint muttered, but he looked relieved.

"What else is going on in Solace?" Tanis asked.

"You remember that hobgoblin, Toede? When he heard Kit ask about you, he flew into a rage. Seems Highlord Verminaard blamed Toede for the havoc we caused around here—freeing slaves, raiding supply wagons, harassing his troops. The hobgoblin would like nothing better than to send Verminaard your head in a sack, and he'll be doing his best to try to find you."

"I'll keep that in mind," said Tanis. "Are Caramon and Raistlin here?"

Flint grimaced. "They came with Kit. They work for her now. Raistlin is her pet wizard and Caramon is her bodyguard. Raistlin took that Test, seemingly, and is now wearing the black robes. Not surprising. You know I never trusted him."

"What about Sturm?"

Flint shook his head. "No one's heard from him in a long while, Tanis. My guess is that he was killed when Kit and her armies crushed the Solamnic uprising. I heard the knights fought valiantly, but they were no match for the legions of blue dragons."

Tanis would have asked more, but he noticed Flint peering nervously up and down the road.

"Speaking of Toede, we should leave the main highway. Goblin patrols are everywhere these days and it's going to be dark soon."

He had no sooner spoken, however, than they heard hoofbeats, and a horse and rider came into view. The rider was a hobgoblin, large and flabby, sporting red armor in imitation of Dragon Highlord Verminaard. The hobgoblin's big belly protruded from beneath the armor and jounced as he rode. He was wearing a leather helm and carried a sword at his side.

"Toede! Of all the cursed luck!" Flint scowled and hefted his axe.

"He's seen us. Put the axe down. We don't want trouble," Tanis cautioned.

"Maybe *you* don't!" Flint growled, but he lowered the axe.

"And get rid of your staff, Brother!" Tanis warned softly.

Kairn looked at him, puzzled, but then understood. He let his staff fall to the ground, shuffled some fallen leaves over it, and then stood on top of it.

Toede caught sight of them and kicked his horse in the flanks, spurring it toward them, shouting orders to a small force of sullen-looking goblins that were trailing after him.

Toede came riding at Tanis and the others at full gallop, and Tanis guessed he was hoping to see them flinch. Tanis rested his hand on the hilt of his sword and calmly waited. Flint planted his feet solidly and scowled. Kairn stood his ground next to Tanis.

Toede checked his horse just before barreling into them, kicking up a cloud of dust and almost upsetting his beast. He glared at the three of them and, seeing that Tanis and Flint carried weapons, turned his head to bellow at the goblins.

"You're supposed to be my bodyguards! Keep up with me, you slugs, or I'll take my lash to you!"

The goblins took note of Tanis's sword and Flint's axe and slowed to a crawl. Toede fumed but decided to ignore them and turned back to Tanis.

"Who are you?" Toede demanded. His small eyes almost disappeared into the folds of his face. "Where are you going?"

"My friends and I are bound for Solace, Highmaster," Tanis replied respectfully. "We are looking for work. Why have you stopped us?"

Toede puffed himself with importance. "I have orders directly from Dragon Highlord Verminaard himself to search for a blue crystal staff. It is dangerous contraband."

"As you can plainly see, none of us are carrying a staff of any sort," said Tanis mildly. "Certainly not one made of blue crystal. Wouldn't such a staff would be impractical, likely to break? Why does the Dragon Highlord want it?"

"Supposedly it has healing powers," Toede said dismissively. "His Most Exalted Lordship received information that some toothless old hag of a goddess called Mishakal thinks she can challenge Her Dark Majesty by bringing healing back into the world. Takhisis will soon make her pay for her mistake."

"No doubt," said Tanis gravely. "Are we free to go now?"

"After I've searched your packs," said Toede.

Flint glowered. "I'll see you in the Abyss—"

Toede's pudgy face creased in a scowl, and he reached for his sword.

"We should do as the Highmaster says," Tanis advised, stepping on Flint's foot. He tossed his pack onto the ground.

Kairn, looking uneasy, did the same with his rucksack. Flint grumbled, but he took his pack from his back and dropped it. Toede's goblin escort had caught up by now, and Toede ordered them to search the packs.

The goblins eagerly picked them up, undoubtedly hoping to loot them.

"Your pack isn't booby-trapped this time, is it, friend?" Flint asked Tanis. "Likely to explode? I'll never forget what happened to those poor fellows that last time. Spread over half of Ansalon."

The goblins looked alarmed and flung the packs as far away as they could and then backed off. Kairn stifled a laugh and Tanis was glad his beard hid his smile.

"What do you think you're doing, you louts?" Toede yelled at them from the safety of his horse's saddle. "I gave you an order! Bring me that pack!"

One of the goblins gingerly picked up Tanis's pack and held it up for Toede to inspect, then did the same with the other two. Toede rummaged through each of them, removing anything he thought might be useful or valuable. He tried to pull one of Tanis's shirts over his head. Finding it didn't fit, he tossed the shirt into the dirt. He removed a flask from Flint's pack and tucked it into his belt. He picked up Kairn's rucksack, rifled through it, ate the fruit, then dumped it onto the ground.

"Are we free to go now?" Tanis asked.

"After you've paid the toll for the use of the highway," said Toede. "You each owe a steel coin."

He leaned down over the saddle and held out a large, hairy hand.

Tanis saw Flint eyeing Toede's hand and fingering his axe.

Kairn hurriedly intervened, drawing out his purse and giving the hobgoblin three coins. "Allow me to pay the toll for all of us, Highmaster."

Toede studied the money and rounded on Kairn. "These are counterfeit! I've never seen such coins in my life."

"They are silver, minted in Solamnia," said Kairn. "They are quite real, I assure you, Highmaster. Worth more than steel."

Toede put a coin in his mouth, licked it, then clamped his sharp teeth down on it. The coins must have passed his test, for he closed his fist over them and stuffed them into a money pouch.

"I'll be keeping an eye on you lot," he said, then galloped off, yelling for his goblin escort to accompany him. The goblins traipsed disconsolately along behind him.

Flint thrust his axe back into its harness. "The wretch kept my flask of dwarf spirits! I should have chopped off his swelled head."

He eyed Kairn, who was picking up his staff out of the leaves.

"And how did you know he'd be searching for a staff?" Flint asked.

"I heard rumors about a blue crystal staff," said Tanis. "I figured Toede might be willing to take any staff, and we didn't want trouble."

"At least he didn't recognize you," said Flint. "Are you still planning to go into Solace? Even knowing Kit's there?"

"We took an oath to meet there in five years," Tanis reminded him. "Besides, I am curious about this blue crystal staff. If it is blessed by the goddess Mishakal and has healing powers, it could be the sign we were looking for—that the true gods have returned to fight Takhisis."

"Bah! There's been no healing in the world for centuries," said Flint. "As for the old gods, I doubt they're even still around. Let's get off the road in case that hob comes back."

Flint led them along a narrow path through the woods. Tanis noticed that his old friend moved stealthily and kept his hand on the hilt of his knife, darting sharp glances into the shadows that were starting to gather as the sun sank down behind the vallenwood trees, lighting the sky with streaks of pink and orange.

"Where have you been all these years?" Flint asked, glancing over his shoulder at Tanis. "Did you go back to Qualinesti?"

"For a time," said Tanis.

"Is Solostaran still the Speaker?" Flint asked. "Will he support our cause?"

Solostaran had been the Speaker of the Sun, the leader of the Qualinesti people, in the original timeline. Tanis had no idea if he was now and looked at Kairn for the answer.

"Solostaran is still Speaker. I have heard that the elven nations of Qualinesti and Silvanesti both pay tribute every year to the Dark Queen to leave them in peace," Kairn replied. "Thus far, she has honored the agreement."

"That won't last long," Flint predicted. "Sooner or later, she'll turn on them. You must have explained this to Solostaran. I take it, then, that he wouldn't listen to you.

"He and I never did get along," said Tanis. "What did you find when you returned to your people?"

"The hill dwarves were packing up to leave," said Flint. "They're moving into the mountain kingdom of Thorbardin."

Tanis stared at him in astonishment. The mountain dwarves and hill dwarves had been feuding since the days of the Cataclysm, which had sundered the continent, bringing death and destruction. Evil creatures had roamed the land and driven the hill dwarves from their ancestral homes. Starving and besieged by deadly foes, the hill dwarves had sought refuge inside the dwarven kingdom of Thorbardin. But the mountain dwarves had also suffered in the Cataclysm and the king had to conserve what few resources he had left. The king had shut the gates, refusing to let his fellow dwarves inside.

Flint was a hill dwarf and had always hated the mountain dwarves. He had nursed his grudge against them for years. Tanis was amazed to hear him speak in almost grudging admiration of his longtime foes.

Flint saw Tanis's questioning look. "It seems I may have misjudged them. When King Hornfel saw the hill dwarves being threatened by the Dark Queen's armies, he opened the mountain fastness and urged them to seek refuge.

"Not only that, Hornfel told our elders that when the time was right, our people will emerge from the mountain and Reorx himself will lead us to war against Takhisis. Until then, they would keep safe and build up their strength. The hill dwarves rallied around him and, once they were safely inside the mountain, Hornfel sealed the entrances. The Dark Queen herself, with all her dragons, won't be able to get in."

"You could have gone with them," said Tanis. "Why didn't you?"

"Me? Hide under a rock?" Flint gave an indignant snort. "I'd pull my beard out by the roots first!"

"The mountain kingdom of Thorbardin is an awfully big rock," said Tanis, smiling.

"But it's too small for me," said Flint. "I wouldn't be able to catch my breath. Besides, like I said, I knew you'd come back to Solace and that you'd need me."

Tanis was deeply touched, and he realized just how much he had missed his old friend. Although Tanis had grown up in Qualinesti, the elven people had never truly accepted him because of his human heritage. He had met Flint when the dwarf came to sell his wares to the elves, who valued his fine work. Flint had been drawn to the lonely boy, and the two had developed a friendship that not even death could sever.

When the lights of Solace came into view, Tanis stopped to gaze down into the valley. He remembered his other life, how he had come home after five years of wandering to see those lights shining from the homes built in the sheltering branches of the vallenwoods.

Looking down into the valley now, Tanis saw only a few lights glimmering and, even as he watched, they were almost immediately extinguished. He wondered if the residents had closed the shutters in the hope of closing out the darkness.

Tanis was saddened and angry. He couldn't bear to see his homeland swallowed up by fear, its people living in terror. He often complained about his work as a diplomat. He was annoyed by the bickering and arguing among the various races. But seeing a world enslaved, ruled by fear, he now realized his work had value. The Ansalon he had left had not been an idyllic place. Nations still had their differences and went to war over them. The Dark Queen would never stop trying to claw her way out of the Abyss. But in that world, the lights of Solace shone brightly in the night.

Kairn touched Tanis on the shoulder, jolting him out of his reverie. "I thought I heard rustling in those bushes!"

"I heard it, too," said Flint, reaching for his axe.

Tanis cursed himself for not paying attention. Such a lapse would have cost him his life in the old days. He heard rustling and thrashing as if whatever was out there was coming straight for them.

"Who goes there?" Tanis called, drawing his sword.

"I go there!" said an excited voice.

A kender came dashing out of the shadows, waving his hoopak.

"Flint! You're not dead!" Tasslehoff cried.

He flung his arms around Flint and burst into tears.

CHAPTER
SIX

Flint tried to divest himself of the kender, but that proved difficult because Tasslehoff's enthusiastic hug had pinned both the dwarf's arms to his sides and he couldn't move. Tanis at last managed to rescue Flint, who was sputtering in indignation. Tas wiped his snuffles with his sleeve and then started to give Tanis a hug.

Tanis grinned and fended him off. "I'll keep my belongings, thank you!"

Tas, not the least offended, turned to regard Kairn with suspicion.

"Do I know you?" he asked.

"Yes, you know me," said Kairn. "I'm glad I found you. It's me, Tas! Brother Kairn."

"Is it?" Tas was dubious. "Brother Kairn wore gray robes."

"I changed clothes," said Kairn. "But it's still me. Do you know where I can find Destina—"

"I do know you! You brought us back through time and then you lost me!" Tas said in accusing tones.

"I know I did," said Kairn. "I'm sorry. I didn't mean—"

"And you lost Sturm and Destina," Tas continued. "I put my hand on the Device and you said the rhyme and magic began whirling and tossing me about and I didn't know if I was on my head or my heels and then, plop, I landed in a hayfield. After I spit hay out of my mouth, I went to search for everyone else. I found Destina and Sturm, but I couldn't find you or Raistlin. So you lost him, too."

"I am truly sorry," said Kairn earnestly. "I didn't mean to lose any of you. Where are Sturm and Destina?"

"Destina's with me and we're both with Sturm. He's hurt really badly. Destina is afraid he might be dying," Tas said, downcast. "She sent me to look for Raistlin, but I couldn't find him. Do you think Raistlin might be dead again? He wasn't looking good when we left the temple, but then he never really looked all that good when he was alive, so it's hard to tell."

"I know where Raistlin is," said Kairn. "Can you take us to Sturm and Destina? Are they somewhere safe?"

"Safe enough," Tas said cautiously. "We're hiding in the old mill. I can take you to them. It's this way."

Tas headed into the woods and they set out after him. The sun had set, and night's shadows were deepening. Solinari was rising. His light was feeble and weak, however, and they could barely make out the path.

"So when I couldn't find Raistlin, I decided to see if I could find Tanis and Flint, since it's the night of the reunion," Tas was saying as they walked. "I waited by the road like I did in the other past and I found you! Here you are now like you were then!"

Tas peered intently at Tanis. "You look like the Tanis from the present that's really the past, or maybe it's the future. I'm all muddled. Are you that Tanis? Or are you the Tanis from this past, which may or may not be the present?"

"The kender's more addled than usual," said Flint. "What's he talking about?"

"I'll explain later," said Tanis, though he had no idea how he was going to. "I am the same Tanis you've always known, Tas. I came with Kairn to help him find you and Destina and the others."

"Then I'm glad I found you first and I'm truly glad I found Flint and that he's not dead," said Tas. He paused to rummage about in his pocket. "I got you this gift, Flint."

Tas handed the dwarf a very fine knife with a bone handle. Flint stared at the knife, then he looked at the empty knife sheath attached to his belt and then back at the knife.

"That's my own blade, you doorknob!" Flint roared, snatching it from Tas.

"Well, of course it is. I just gave it to you," said Tas. "And it's polite to say 'thank you' when someone gives you a gift."

"Where did you say you were taking us?" Tanis asked, restraining Flint from throttling the kender.

"I told you. The mill that was on Mill Creek," Tas replied. "Do you remember, Flint? You'd go there to mend pots and I'd go with you, and Mistress Miller would feed us fresh baked bread—"

"I know the place," Tanis interrupted, fearing this story could go on for hours. "I am worried about Sturm. You said he is dying. What is wrong?"

"When Destina and I found him, he was all covered in blood and he was really weak. But he said he could walk and he made it as far as the mill before he collapsed. I was hoping the Millers were still there and that they could help, but I guess they're gone because the mill was deserted, and the door was locked. I had to leave my pouches behind with the knights when we were back in the past, but I kept my lockpicking tools in my sock and I opened the door and Destina and I carried Sturm inside and built a fire in the fireplace to keep him warm. Destina is staying with him."

"How is Destina?" Kairn asked.

"I don't think she feels very good, either," said Tas. "You remember when that bad man, Tully, cut her with his knife before I hit him with my hoopak? The cut is an ugly red color. And then she's worried about you. She thinks you lost us because of the—" Tas sneezed. "Drat! I wish I could stop these!"

"Because of what?" Tanis asked.

Tas started to reply and sneezed again.

"He means the Graygem," Kairn said in a low voice. "He wouldn't stop talking about it and we feared the wrong people might know

Destina carried it. Gwyneth cast a spell on him so that he couldn't tell anyone."

"Every time I try to say . . . It . . . a sneeze sneaks up on me," Tas explained. "Wait until you see the . . . It, Tanis. It gives you a squirmy feeling and not the good kind."

"Graygem!" Flint snorted. "Next he'll be telling us he's found a woolly mammoth! This is Mill Road."

They had arrived at a dirt trail, and Tanis recognized it from the ruts left by the wagons loaded with wheat, carrying it to the mill to be ground into flour. Instead of proceeding, Flint came to a sudden halt, crossed his arms over his chest, and turned to face them.

"I'll not stir another step, Tanis Half-Elven, until I find out what's going on. Who is this Destina? How did Sturm get himself wounded? And what does that doorknob of a kender mean about me being dead? Do I look dead?"

"I'll tell you, Flint!" Tas offered, raising his hand eagerly. "It's one of my best stories. It all started when Destina found out that her father had died at the Battle of the High Clerist's Tower during the War of the Lance, which hasn't happened yet and maybe never will—"

"Tas, why don't you run ahead and tell Destina we are coming," said Kairn. "We can find our way from here."

"But I was telling Flint my best story," Tas argued.

"You said Destina was worried," said Kairn.

"I guess my story will keep. And Destina will be really happy when I tell her I found you and Tanis and that Flint's not dead!"

Tas gave Flint another hug before the dwarf could stop him, then ran off down the road.

Flint frowned at Tanis. "There he goes again. Me being dead. I'm waiting."

"I promise I'll explain everything, but right now I am worried about Sturm," said Tanis. "Let's tend to him first."

Flint looked stubborn for a moment, then gave grudging agreement. "Very well. But tell the fool kender that I'm not dead now and never was." His voice softened. "There's the dear old Inn. You can see it from here."

Tanis saw light gleaming from the inn's stained glass windows. He thought something seemed different and then he realized the light was shining on the branches of the vallenwood that was holding the inn in its arms.

"It's still in the trees!" he said, speaking before he thought.

"Where else would it be?" Flint demanded.

"Do goblins patrol Mill Road?" Tanis asked, changing the subject.

The dwarf shook his head. "They don't bother. Since the mill closed, no one ever comes this way."

"Why did the mill close?" Tanis asked.

Flint gave him a strange look. "Don't you remember? Verminaard ordered Miller to deliver all his flour to the army. Miller refused, saying if he did that, the people in Solace would starve. Verminaard sent his soldiers to arrest Miller, only you saved them and helped smuggle them to safety in Southern Ergoth!"

"I recall now," Tanis said. "I'm glad to know they're safe."

"Maybe they are and maybe they're not," Flint replied glumly. "You and I both know there is no safe place in this world."

They continued along the trail, trying to avoid stumbling over the wagon ruts. Tanis looked up at the sky and remembered the night years ago when Raistlin had noticed that two constellations—the Queen of Darkness and Paladine—had gone missing.

She has come to Krynn, Raistlin had told them. *And he has come to fight her.*

Takhisis had lost the War of the Lance and had been forced to return to the Abyss. Her constellation and Paladine's had both returned to the sky. But in this world, she had won, and the stars of her constellation flared brightly in triumph. Tanis searched for the constellations of Paladine and Mishakal, his consort, but could not find them. Perhaps once again, Paladine and Mishakal had come to do battle.

As they continued walking, Tanis noticed Flint had developed a hacking cough and he would absently massage his left arm as though it pained him. Tanis remembered the dwarf had done the same in the days before his untimely death when his heart had given out.

Time had changed, Tanis reflected, but apparently not enough.

The mill came into view, silhouetted against the stars. The huge wheel and the adjacent buildings were dark shapes against the trees. The moonlight glinted in the swift-running creek that had once powered the wheel.

The house itself was dark. Destina had closed the curtains to keep the light from shining into the night, which could have alerted enemies to their presence. But Tanis could smell the odor of burning wood and remembered Tas saying they had built a fire. It was important to keep the wounded Sturm warm, but he worried that if he could smell woodsmoke, so could others.

A rectangle of light suddenly appeared in the darkness—a door opening—and he could see the silhouette of a woman with the firelight behind her. She was holding a lantern, peering into the night. Tas was with her, talking animatedly, and Tanis assumed the woman must be Destina—the "Rosebush woman," as Tika had termed her.

Kairn caught sight of her and broke into a run, calling her name. Destina dropped the lantern and he dropped his staff to gather her into his embrace.

"Good to know love still survives in this world," Flint remarked, his gruff tone softening. "Takhisis can't stamp that out, although I've no doubt she would if she could."

"Love has always been our best hope," Tanis agreed.

By the time they arrived at the house, Kairn and Destina were standing decorously apart, looking flushed and self-conscious. Kairn had apparently told Destina why Tanis was here, for she greeted him graciously.

"I know the sacrifice you make to come," she said. She would have added something else, but Tas interrupted her.

"And this is my friend Flint," said Tas, grabbing the dwarf's arm and dragging him forward. "He's not dead!"

Destina looked a little startled, but she shook hands with the dwarf and then invited them to enter. Kairn picked up his staff and retrieved the dropped lantern. When they were all inside, he closed and barred the door.

Tanis remembered the mill from the days when he had lived in Solace. He had often accompanied Flint here to peddle his wares or make repairs to the milling equipment. The family house was large, commodious, and practical. The door opened onto a single room known as a great chamber, with a low, beamed ceiling and windows on three sides. The bedchambers and the kitchen were located in the back. A single fireplace in the center provided heat to the entire dwelling.

Sturm lay on a pallet near the fire. His eyes were closed. He seemed to be sleeping, but sleep brought him no comfort. His breathing was labored, and he grimaced and shifted as though in pain. Sweat gleamed on his forehead and face.

Tanis knelt beside his friend and clasped his hand. "Hello, Sturm. It is good to see you again."

Sturm didn't respond, and Tanis sighed and lowered the limp hand to his chest. Flint shook his head bleakly.

"Fool knight! I knew he'd get himself killed someday!" Flint brushed his hand across his eyes, then picked up the bucket. "The well's around back. I'll go fetch more water."

"I'll come with you," Tas offered. "I have to make certain you don't die on me."

Flint stomped out the door, muttering into his beard. Tas was about to follow him, when Kairn called him back.

"I need to talk to you and Destina about what has happened," said Kairn. "You know that when we left the time of Huma, I was taking us to 351 AC. But that's not where we ended up. We arrived in 351 Chaos Time."

Destina slumped in despair and put her hands over her face. "So it's true. Takhisis won the war."

"I am afraid so," said Kairn. "And now time has changed."

"It's all my fault," Tas said unhappily. "I flipped the switch on the dragonlance. But I had to save Knopple! I didn't know I was going to change time!"

"The Graygem changed time, Tas," said Kairn. "You are not to blame."

"No," said Destina in a low voice. "I am."

She put her hand to her throat and clasped hold of a jewel she was wearing around her neck. Faint gray light welled from beneath her fingers; Tanis guessed that must be the infamous Graygem.

"We can discuss this later," said Tanis. "But for now, what is important is that Sturm is badly wounded. I need to know what happened to him. Destina, perhaps you could tell me."

Destina drew her hand away from the Graygem and went over to kneel beside Sturm. She drew aside the blanket to reveal his wounds.

"He was stabbed in the chest," she replied. "I tried to bandage the wound to stop the bleeding, but, as you can see, the bindings are soaked with blood. According to Raistlin, the sword was magical, and that was how it penetrated his armor. Tully used the same sword to kill Huma and the silver dragon."

"Sturm tried to save Huma," Kairn added, kneeling down beside Destina. "The sword would have killed Sturm, too, for it pierced his breastplate, but his armor turned the blade."

Kairn indicated the knight's breastplate, which lay nearby. Tanis remembered it well, for the armor and helm and sword had been Sturm's only family legacy. Tanis touched the hole in the bloodstained steel. The armor was decorated with a rose, symbol of the Knights of the Rose. It had defended its own.

"He has lost a lot of blood," Destina said. "And he is burning up with fever. He was delirious before he sank into this stupor."

Tasslehoff stood beside him, looking down on him sadly. "Sturm didn't know me. He thought he was back at the tower and he kept shouting to Huma, trying to warn him about Tully, but Tully stabbed him and then he killed Huma and Gwyneth. He was going to kill Destina. He held a knife to her throat, but since I'm her bodyguard, I couldn't let him hurt her, so I hit him with my hoopak. And then Raistlin lit him on fire."

"He did what?" Tanis asked, shocked.

"Raistlin wasn't responsible. The Staff of Magius acted on its own to avenge Huma's death," Destina said.

"Tully was a very bad man," Tas added firmly. "He called me a thief and he ruined the song."

"What song?" Tanis asked.

"The *Song of Huma*," Tas replied. "Remember that long poem Sturm used to tell us, about how the white stag led Huma to the silver dragon and she led him to the dragonlances? I was worried when we first met Huma because he'd never heard of dragonlances—"

"That's the answer, Tanis!" Kairn cried, springing to his feet.

"The answer to what?" Tanis asked.

"To Nuitari's riddle!" said Kairn. "In 351 Chaos Time, the gods tried to defeat Takhisis and her armies in battle and failed. Dalamar asked the gods of magic if the war could be won, since the Graygem was in this time. Nuitari refused to tell him, but he gave him a hint. He said that we would find all we needed to know in Astinus's account of the Lost War. 'The answer is there. Or rather, the answer is *not* there.'

"During the Lost War, the knights had no weapons that could kill dragons and the dragons slaughtered them. They had no dragonlances!" Kairn concluded. "That is what Nuitari was trying to tell you!"

"But we left dragonlances in the High Clerist's Tower," said Destina. "Even though time changed, and Huma and Gwyneth both died, the dragonlances still remained on the altar of Paladine."

"Perhaps Takhisis destroyed them," said Tanis.

"She could not," said Kairn. "The dragonlances were blessed by Paladine. In the original time, Huma struck Takhisis with a dragonlance and wounded her so grievously, she was forced to return to the Abyss."

Tas raised his hand. "I found a dragonlance. It was made by the gnomes. It didn't look much like a dragonlance, but when I flipped the switch, it began belching and whistling and then it blew up the dragonarmies and Immolatus flew back to the Abyss. Maybe we could find that one."

"Maybe we could," said Destina, smiling at him.

"I know one way we might be able to find out," said Tanis. "We can ask Flint."

Tas scrambled to his feet. "I'll go find him! I wonder if death cured him. Death didn't cure Raistlin of his cough, but it did get rid of Fistandoodle. So maybe being dead fixed Flint's heart."

Tas left, slamming the door behind him.

"What is wrong with Flint's heart?" Destina asked.

"In the original time, Flint died when his heart gave out," Tanis replied. "Tas was grief-stricken. Sturm had died that winter and then Flint in the spring. The loss of his friends affected Tas deeply."

"I am sorry for he has grown dear to me," said Destina. "I used Tas shamefully when I first met him, but he has a generous heart and forgave me. I know what it means to lose someone you love and I am glad he has found his friend again."

Tanis had heard a great deal about Destina Rosethorn, the woman who bore the Graygem. The firelight shone on her face as she knelt beside Sturm. She had twisted her black hair into a knot at the nape of her neck. Her eyes were large and dark. Her complexion, warmed by the fire, should have been warm mahogany, but it was gray, ashen. Her face was drawn and haggard.

Tanis found himself liking her—not only for the tender care she was giving Sturm, but for the almost sisterly affection she seemed to feel for Tasslehoff.

"What are we going to do to make him stop talking about Flint dying?" said Tanis. "Flint's asking questions."

"I am sorry, but you can't answer them," said Kairn.

"I would trust Flint with my life," said Tanis sternly.

"I have no doubt he would never intentionally betray our secret, but we dare not risk it," said Kairn earnestly. "And how would you explain?"

Tanis understood. Now that he considered it, he had no idea what he would have told Flint. The River of Time, the Graygem of Gargath, the War of the Lance. Tanis gave a rueful smile.

"You're right, Kairn. Flint would think I'd pickled my head in a vat of dwarf spirits," said Tanis, sighing.

Destina was bathing Sturm's forehead with water, trying to break the fever that was ravaging his body. Tanis noticed the injury to her neck. The cut was red and inflamed, oozing blood.

"That wound appears to be badly infected, Destina," said Tanis.

Kairn regarded her worriedly. "I've been thinking the same."

"Tully barely nicked me with the blade," said Destina dismissively. "The cut stings a little, but that is all."

She started to rise, but as she did, she staggered and nearly fell.

"You should rest," Kairn said, helping her to a chair.

"I just need to sit down for a moment," said Destina, and she sank back in the chair and closed her eyes.

Tanis regarded her in concern and motioned to Kairn to come join him by the door.

"Destina said that Tully cut her with the knife. I don't want to alarm you, but is it possible the knife was poisoned?"

"Poisoned?" Kairn gasped, horrified. "I don't know. I suppose it could have been. As Tas says, Tully was a bad man. If she has been poisoned, what do we do?"

"Raistlin would know," said Tanis.

"But he's back at the inn," Kairn said. "And Destina and I are supposed to return to the past."

"She is too weak to walk across the room," said Tanis. "Much less travel through time."

He thought Destina might have fallen asleep, but he saw her hand reach up to clasp the Graygem. She closed her fingers over it, and he wondered what would happen to it if she died.

Kairn must have been thinking the same. "Raistlin said the Graygem would not let any harm come to her."

"We need to find him," said Tanis.

Flint returned, carrying the water bucket, and they had to end their conversation. Flint set the bucket on the floor, then went over to stand beside Sturm.

"I've put in a word to Reorx for you, lad," Flint told him. "The god's not known for his powers of healing, bless his beard, and some say he's not around anymore, but, if he is, maybe he can help."

"Did you see Tas while you were out there?" Tanis asked.

"No. Did we manage to lose him?" Flint asked in hopeful tones.

"He went to look for you," said Tanis. "Brother Kairn and I were discussing the Third Dragon War. What do you know about it?"

"That Takhisis won it," said Flint. "Her foul clerics won't let us forget. They're always preaching about how she defeated the knights at the High Clerist's Tower and vanquished the other gods. She has ruled Krynn to this day."

"A knight called Huma fought in that war," Tanis said. "Did you ever hear of him? Or a weapon called a dragonlance that could kill dragons?"

"You're daft, lad," said Flint. "No weapon that was ever made can kill dragons. Not even those forged by dwarves."

Kairn and Tanis exchanged glances.

"Although I don't see how this helps us," said Tanis grimly. "We may have the answer, but we don't have the dragonlances."

"What are you talking about?" Flint demanded.

"An interesting point in history, that's all," said Tanis.

Flint glanced around the room and scowled. "You're talking history and no one's keeping watch! A goblin patrol could be sneaking up on us right now and we'd be none the wiser. Tanis Half-Elven, have you forgotten everything I taught you?"

Flint stomped over to a window and peered out into the night. Tanis smiled and walked over to stand beside him.

"Did you see any signs of goblins when you were out there?"

"No, but I could have missed them," Flint said grumpily. "My eyes aren't what they once were. Although they're good enough to see that dratted kender coming back."

Tas came bursting through the door, carrying a flour sack. He looked accusingly at Flint. "Here you are! I thought you'd been nabbed by a bugbear!"

Tas flourished the flour sack. "Look what I found! It was in the root cellar. There's a lot of interesting things down there. No sausages though."

Flint glared at him. "Did you shut the door to the cellar when you left?"

"Yes, no, maybe," said Tas warily. "Why?"

"Because I found it standing wide open. I nearly fell into it and broke my neck!" Flint said.

"Then I'm sure I shut it," said Tas. "A bugbear probably opened it again. What's wrong with Destina?"

"You remember when Tully held a knife to her throat?" Kairn said. "Tanis thinks the knife might have been poisoned."

Tas stared at him in dismay. "What are we going to do? We can't let both her and Sturm die!"

"There's not much we can do for either of them," said Flint, shaking his head. "The healers and clerics vanished when the old gods fled."

"Goldmoon is here and she's a cleric," said Tas. "Kairn said he saw her at the inn. We could go get her and Riverwind and the blue crystal staff and bring her back here to heal Sturm!"

"And we need to find Raistlin," Kairn reminded them. "Not only do we need his help, we need to let him know where we are."

"I'll go," said Tanis.

"Now wait just a dang moment," said Flint, glowering. "This Goldmoon isn't the only person in the inn tonight. Kitiara is there as well, with a troop of Bozaks. As for Raistlin, he used to work for the resistance, but now he's wearing the black robes and he's here with Kit."

"I haven't seen Kitiara in a long time," said Tas. "Ever since she was dead. I'll come with you."

"We have to hope that Raistlin is on our side," said Tanis.

"More to the point, lad," said Flint dourly, "you'd better hope we're on Raistlin's side."

CHAPTER
SEVEN

anis set out for the inn, taking Flint and Tasslehoff with him. Tas had been torn between wanting to go with them or staying behind with Destina.

"Since I am her bodyguard," Tas had stated.

Kairn had promised that he would take care of her, and Tanis had settled the question by stating that he needed Tas.

"You're an important part of my plan," Tanis said to the kender. "But you have to leave behind the flour sack."

"I don't think I've ever been part of a plan before," said Tas. "Unless you count people saying, 'I plan to call the sheriff.' And it's not a flour sack. It's my new pouch. Admittedly it needs a few alterations and a lot less flour, but—"

Tanis was firm. "The last thing we need is for you to get in trouble over something you borrowed and dropped in your pouch. The flour sack stays."

Tas sighed and handed the flour sack to Kairn, who promised to look after it. Tas was downcast for a moment but cheered up when Tanis asked him to scout the road ahead.

"Maybe there'll be bugbears!" Tas said eagerly as he dashed out the door.

"Don't get too far ahead of us," Tanis called after him. "Don't go inside the inn, and don't talk to anyone!"

Tas waved his hoopak in response and disappeared into the night. Tanis and Flint followed more slowly. The stars of the Dark Queen's constellation shone brightly, illuminating the road.

Flint eyed the stars grimly. "She's not doing us any favors, you know. She lights up the night so she can spy on us."

Tanis did have the strange feeling that they were being watched. He left the open road to walk in the shadows beneath the trees.

"Can you see Tas?" Tanis asked.

"No," said Flint. "Not that I'm looking. Bugbears! What kind of a plan do you have that involves that doorknob?"

"I'm still thinking about it," said Tanis.

He couldn't very well tell Flint that Tas's value lay in the fact that he knew everyone in the inn this night, from Kitiara and Raistlin to Goldmoon and Riverwind to Tika and Fizban.

Although Tanis did have to admit he was worried about Tas's inability to be quiet about his adventures in a past life—*all* his past lives.

As they proceeded along the road, Tanis matched his longer strides to the dwarf's shorter ones, as they had done when they had traveled together in the other time, another world. They were nearing the inn when Flint began to wheeze and seemed to be having trouble catching his breath.

"Let's stop to rest a moment," Tanis said. "I've had a long journey and I'm not as young as I used to be."

"I thought you were looking winded," said Flint. "It's that human blood of yours. Makes you weak. But I suppose we could stop for a few moments, if you insist. We'll sit down on that stump over there."

The loggers had been in this part of the forest, and Tanis grieved to see the stumps of young vallenwood trees, their fallen branches left to molder and decay. He and Flint sat down on a stump near the road.

"You've changed a lot in five years," said Flint abruptly. "I don't just mean the beard. You're not the Tanis I knew, and neither is that doorknob of a kender. Keeps talking about me being dead. And the sick lady wearing that strange jewel. What's going on?"

"I can't tell you," said Tanis. "The secret is not mine to share. I doubt you'd believe me if I did tell you the truth. I find it hard to believe, and I'm living it."

Flint eyed him. "So when that doorknob of a kender blubbers over me and claims I'm dead, he's not telling tales?"

Tanis didn't know how to respond. He had thought he had recovered from his grief over Flint's death, but memories of that sorrowful time flooded back to him. He saw himself desperately gripping Flint's hand as though he could stop him from leaving on that final journey. He remembered listening to Flint's faint words. *And now hope has come into the world. I hate to leave you, just when you need me. But I've taught you all I know, lad. Everything will be fine. I know . . . fine.* Tanis remembered holding the sobbing Tasslehoff in his arms in the sacred place called Godshome. . . .

He was aware of Flint's keen scrutiny and knew he should deny it, but he could not lie to him.

"I see by that long face of yours it's true," said Flint. "I hope I died on my feet with my axe in my hand."

"You died a hero," said Tanis. He rested his hand on Flint's shoulder. "I've missed you, old dwarf."

"Bah! Don't you start blubbering," Flint said, elbowing him in the ribs. "But if you must know, I've missed you, too."

He pulled out a handkerchief and loudly blew his nose, then stuffed the handkerchief away, straightened his belt, and adjusted his axe in its harness. He slapped his hands on his knees and stood up.

"If you're rested, we should be going."

"I'm rested," said Tanis.

They had just resumed their walk when they saw Tas dashing down the road, apparently in search of them.

"Tas! Over here!" Tanis called, stepping out of the shadows.

"There you are!" Tas exclaimed. "I've been looking all over for you. We're close to the inn. You can see the lights in the windows. The inn is still up in the tree branches. The dragons haven't knocked it down. But the front door is being guarded by two draconians. They're searching everyone who comes in, which is probably why I didn't see anyone going in. I went around the back to talk to Tika—"

"I told you not to talk to anyone!" Tanis said, exasperated.

"I didn't talk to *anyone*," Tas protested. "I talked to *Tika*."

Tanis sighed. "I hope no one saw you."

"No one did. Unless you count Otik," Tas said as an afterthought. "He saw me when I climbed up the rope into the kitchen. I gave Tika quite a scare when I popped up through the floor. When she got over being scared and decided she wasn't going to whang me on the headbone with her skillet, she said she was glad to see me and gave me a hug."

"Did you tell her about us?" Tanis asked.

"I told her you were here in Solace for the reunion and she got really angry and said you and Flint were the biggest fools who ever lived and that Solace is crawling with draconians and you're both wanted men and you're putting yourselves in danger."

"Was that all?" Tanis asked.

Tas considered the question. "Tika began to cry and hugged me again and said to tell you she'll be so glad to see you, but not to go in the front door, but to come around to the back. She'll meet us on the ground down below the kitchen. I'll show you the way."

"I remember how to get there," said Tanis. "Anything else?"

"I don't think so," said Tas. "She did say she was going to count the spoons and she'd know if any went missing. I'm not sure why she said that, since it didn't have anything to do with any of us. I asked her if I was a 'wanted man' like you and Flint. She said I wasn't."

Flint snorted. "As if anyone would want you."

"Some people do," said Tas with dignity. "I had a wife, you know."

Flint's eyes opened wide. "A wife?"

"It's one of my best stories," said Tas. "Her name was Mari and she disappeared in a magical cloud of stardust—"

"Did you see Kitiara?" Tanis asked.

"I didn't see her," said Tas. "But Tika said she is in the inn tonight and she's been asking about you."

"What did Tika tell her?"

"That she hadn't seen or heard from you in a long time and she didn't know if you were coming to the reunion or not, but she didn't think so."

Tanis nodded. "What did Kitiara say?"

"That she would wait," said Tas.

CHAPTER
EIGHT

As they rounded a bend in the road, the lights of the Inn of the Last Home came into full view. Tanis called a halt, saying they had to assess the situation.

"The only thing you've got to assess are those two dracos guarding the front door," said Flint. "And they're Bozaks. Worse luck."

Tanis could clearly see the two draconians mounting guard on the landing at the top of the winding stairs. Draconians were creatures of the Dark Queen. They were born of dark magic that had altered the eggs of good dragons to create these hideous beings— a cross between man and dragon. Their heads, scales, wings, and tails spoke of the blood of dragons, but they had legs and arms like men and walked upright. Draconians were smart, cruel, and cunning. Skilled warriors, they took delight in torturing and killing their foes. And they could deal death even after they themselves had died. Depending on their type, their bones would explode or their bodies would dissolve into pools of lethal acid.

There were five different types of draconians, based on the kind of dragon egg from which they had sprung. Bozaks came from the eggs of bronze dragons, and they were often employed by military commanders because of their intelligence and loyalty. Not only were they fierce warriors, but they could also cast magic spells.

Apparently, Kitiara also employed them, for the Bozaks wore the blue armor with blue helms of members of the Blue Dragonarmy. Each carried a large, curve-bladed sword.

As Tanis watched, a human male wearing blue armor emerged from the inn to speak to the Bozaks. He was strong and well built, with fair hair and a chiseled jaw.

Tas stared at him and gasped. "I know that man!"

"Keep quiet!" Tanis warned, seeing one of the Bozaks turn its head in their direction.

"But I do know him," Tas insisted in a loud whisper. "I just can't remember where I know him from."

The Bozaks didn't greet the man with enthusiasm. "What do you want, Bakaris?"

"That's it!" Tas said. "Bakaris! Ouch—" He glared at Flint, who had kicked him in the shins.

"The Highlord sent me to ask if you've seen any sign of this half-elf or his friends," Bakaris was replying sullenly. "I can't remember their names."

"We have them on a list the Highlord gave us," said the Bozak. "If we see them, we'll report to Her Lordship. We don't report to you."

Bakaris was clearly angry. "You should treat me with respect! I am the Highlord's second, and I can make your lives miserable! You lizards will address me as 'sir'!"

One of the Bozaks shoved its snout into his face and poked Bakaris in the chest with a long, clawed finger.

"You might want to watch yourself, *ssssir*," the Bozak said, hissing the word. "It would be a pity if you fell down the stairs and broke your neck, *ssssir*."

"That's a forty-foot drop, *ssssir*," added the other, crowding Bakaris from the other side. "I bet you'd smash up that pretty face of yours, *ssssir*."

Bakaris glowered at them, his fists clenching and unclenching. He seemed to start to say something, then thought better of it. He reached for his sword, then thought better of that. He muttered something about checking on his horse and left, stomping down the stairs. When he reached the ground, he stalked off into the night.

The Bozaks chortled loudly.

"It seems Kit's still inside," Tanis said. "Let's go around back to find Tika. That man, Bakaris. His name does sound familiar. How do you know him, Tas?"

"Don't you remember? Maybe not, because you weren't with us. Bakaris attacked Laurana and I stabbed him with Rabbitslayer, only now it's Goblinslayer," said Tas, as they made their way around the giant trunk of the vallenwood tree. "You should remember him, Flint. You were with us, except maybe you weren't, because that happened in the past that isn't the past and you couldn't have been because I wasn't there."

"He's moonstruck mad," Flint muttered.

"That's how I know the name," said Tanis, who had heard the story from Laurana. Recalling what she had told him, Tanis was tempted to stab the wretch himself.

As they walked, Tanis kept watch on the rope bridges in the trees above them. The bridges extended from limb to limb of the vallenwood trees in which the town of Solace was built. Serving as roads, the bridges connected the houses and businesses, allowing people to move among the tops of the trees. He was worried that someone walking on the bridges might hear them, for Flint was making enough noise for an army of dwarves. Fondly imagining he was being stealthy, he crashed through the brush with his armor rattling and his harness jingling.

"Dracos, heading this way!" Tas warned, pointing to one of the bridges that ran like the filaments of a spider's web among the branches.

They froze, not daring to move, as two Bozaks emerged from the darkness and strode across the bridge directly above them.

"Kit's damn lizards must be all over Solace," Flint grumbled when the draconians were out of sight. "If this Goldmoon is in the inn, how do you plan on getting her past the Bozaks?"

"We'll go out through the kitchen," said Tanis, smiling at the memory.

"That's what we did the last time," Tas added. "Except in this time there wasn't a last time."

The Inn of the Last Home was nestled in the vallenwood's strong branches forty feet above their heads. The inn's foundation was a large slab of stone that workmen had hauled down out of the mountains and hoisted into place in the tree, wedging it among the tree limbs to anchor it securely. The common room and guest rooms rested on the stone foundation. The kitchen extended out beyond the foundation, for it had a trapdoor built into the floor that provided access to the ground. A stout rope tied around a tree limb extended through the hole, allowing those who worked in the kitchen to raise and lower supplies.

Otik stored full casks of ale in a stone outbuilding that was cool even during warm weather, and stacked the empty casks near the enormous fermenting vat. He kept the sacks of grain he used to prepare his famous ale in another outbuilding, along with sacks of potatoes used to make the dish for which he was known throughout Ansalon—Otik's spiced potatoes.

Tanis could smell the fragrance floating down from the kitchen, and he realized he had not eaten in a long time, ever since he'd begun this strange journey.

"Tika said we should wait down here for her," Tas whispered. "She'll come when she can get away."

They were standing in the shadows of the tree, keeping watch for Bozaks, when they heard the trapdoor open. Light from the kitchen flooded through it and they could see a figure silhouetted against it. They knew it was Tika, for her red curls blazed like fire. She caught hold of the rope and nimbly swung herself down to the ground.

"Tas?" she called softly, peering nervously into the darkness, twisting her apron in her hands.

"I'm here!" Tas called. "I've brought Tanis and Flint!"

Tika hurried toward them. She was the same, only not the same, Tanis thought. Tika in that other world was brisk, bustling, laughing, and joyful. The Tika of this world looked careworn, nervous, and apprehensive. But she smiled when she threw her arms around Tanis and gave Flint a hug and a sound kiss on the cheek, and her smile was the smile Tanis knew.

"I am glad to see you, even though I'm not,"Tika told them. "It's been a long, long time."

"Did you recognize her, Tanis?" Flint asked. "I didn't. The last time I saw her, she was a scrawny girl with freckles."

"I've still got the freckles," said Tika with a laugh. "I wouldn't have recognized Tanis with that beard. But what's this I hear about Sturm? Tas told some wild tale about him dying and needing to find two people named Goldmoon and Riverwind because Goldmoon has a blue crystal staff that has healing powers. Do you know what he's talking about? Is he making this up?"

"No, he's not,"Tas said indignantly.

"He's telling the truth," said Tanis. "Sturm is badly wounded and we need help. Goldmoon and Riverwind are Plainsfolk. Goldmoon has hair the color of the silver moon, and the man who accompanies her, Riverwind, has dark hair and he's extremely tall."

"There are two people who look just as you describe, though I didn't see a blue staff," said Tika, sounding doubtful. "They came in with an old man in gray robes—"

"Fizban?"Tas asked.

"I don't know his name," said Tika. "But he's daft, whoever he is. He started rearranging the furniture."

"That's Fizban! I have to go see him!" said Tas.

Tanis caught hold of the kender by his shirtsleeve.

"You will. Just not now," said Tanis. "Is Kitiara in the inn?"

"She's there," said Tika. "And as if we don't have trouble enough, she's brought her two brothers with her. I was glad to see Caramon, but not that twin of his. I never did trust Raistlin. And now he's wearing the black robes!"

"Not surprising," said Flint. "That pasty-faced, skinny mage, always sniveling and whining and poking his nose where it doesn't belong. If it weren't for his twin brother looking after him, someone would have put an end to his magic long ago."

Tika lowered her voice. "Wait until you see Raistlin, Flint. His skin is a strange golden color. There's something wrong with his eyes and he keeps coughing. You know, Tanis, I always did think he was the one who betrayed you."

"He didn't," said Tanis.

"Are you sure?" Tika was dubious. "Then who was it?"

"Kitiara," Flint answered.

Tika thought this over. "That makes sense. I remember the fight you two had, Tanis. That was the night you refused to go north with her to serve the Dark Queen. She flew into a rage. All her love turned to hate in an instant."

"And yet here she is, asking about me," said Tanis.

Tika shrugged. "She's come back either to forgive you or kill you. Whichever it is, you should stay clear of her. But tell me about Sturm. Where is he? Is he truly dying?"

"He was wounded in a battle and he's badly hurt," said Tanis. "We've hidden him in the abandoned mill outside of town. Two of our friends are staying with him."

"You truly think this Goldmoon and some blue staff can heal him?" Tika asked.

"I hope so," said Tanis. "But I need to see her for myself and make certain it is her."

The trapdoor opened and they saw the pudgy body of Otik Sandeth, the inn's owner, framed in the light.

"Tika! Are you down there?" Otik called. "We have customers!"

"That's a change," Tika said with a sigh. "Business has been terrible. No one comes here these days. I'd better go. What can I do to help?"

"I need a table in the back of the inn," Tanis said.

Tika regarded him in concern. "Are you sure you want to go in there, Tanis? What if Kitiara sees you? She might recognize you, even with the beard."

"I have to risk it. This is Sturm we're talking about," Tanis reminded her.

"Come up the rope and through the kitchen," said Tika. "Otik will be at the bar serving ale. I'll sneak you inside."

Tika climbed deftly up the rope, hand over hand, and disappeared.

Flint was glaring at Tanis. "Are you daft?"

"I have a plan," said Tanis. "It's not a very good plan, but it's the best I can manage. I have to talk to Raistlin. I'm going to need his help."

"Are you sure you can trust him?" Flint growled. "He shivers my skin."

"I am sure. Tas, you would know Fizban if you saw him, wouldn't you?"

"Oh, yes!" Tas said firmly. "He's one of my very best friends, even if he is a god and forever losing his hat when it's on his head. Do I get to climb up the rope and sneak in through the kitchen, too?"

"No," said Tanis. "You and Flint are going to walk in through the front door."

"How do we get past those damned dracos?" Flint asked.

Tanis smiled. "You're going to tell them that you're friends of Kitiara's. Your names are on her list."

aistlin Majere sat at the table in the Inn of the Last Home watching his twin brother eat spiced potatoes. The sight was disgusting. Caramon would shovel a large spoonful into his mouth and chew loudly. Then he would talk as he ate, so that bits of potato dribbled out of the corners.

"Eat with your mouth closed, my brother!" Raistlin snapped. "I've seen goblins with better table manners."

Caramon stopped in midchew to stare at his twin in puzzlement.

"Uh? Goblins?" Caramon suddenly understood and grinned. "Oh, right, Raist! Sorry." He began to eat more sedately.

Caramon was Raistlin's twin, but they were as opposite as a sunny day in spring to the darkest, coldest night in midwinter. Caramon was big and brawny and good-looking, with a genial smile and cheerful disposition. Everyone liked him. Everyone trusted him. Everyone was his friend.

By contrast, few people liked Raistlin—and given that he was a magic-user, no one trusted him. Weak and sickly as a child, Raistlin had been the target of bullies. Caramon had always been there to fight his battles. And for that, Raistlin had never forgiven him.

Back in the original time, the twins had gone their separate ways. Raistlin had died trying to challenge the gods. Caramon had almost died trying to save him, his evil and unworthy twin. Now, in Chaos Time, Raistlin was alive and the two were together again. Raistlin supposed he should have been glad to see Caramon after all these years. He should have been happy to embrace him and his faults. The gods knew, Caramon had always embraced his.

But watching his twin slurping and guzzling, Raistlin felt only revulsion.

Caramon was the sole person at the table enjoying his meal. The smell of the potatoes made Raistlin queasy, and he had eaten nothing but a little boiled chicken. His half-sister, Kitiara, had ordered potatoes, but shoved her plate away half-full, much to Caramon's delight.

"You gonna eat that?" he asked, and when she shook her head, he finished it off for her.

Raistlin was about to make some scathing remark when a fit of coughing stole his breath. His lungs burned and he doubled over in pain, covering his mouth with his handkerchief.

Caramon jumped to his feet, instantly attentive and solicitous. "I'm here, Raist. Should I fix your tea?"

Raistlin nodded, unable to speak. He fumbled for the bag of herbs he wore on a belt at his waist along with his spell components and flung it onto the table. Caramon hurried off to the kitchen, shouting loudly for boiling water and a mug.

Kitiara eyed Raistlin, annoyed.

"I cannot comprehend why you let those old wizards torture you. You look like a freak with that gold skin and those weird eyes, coughing and puking up blood. And what did you get in return? Some old walking stick. You should have killed them. I would have."

Raistlin had no breath left to answer her and knew he would be wasting what little breath he had if he did. He had tried before to explain the reasoning behind the Test in the Tower of High Sorcery, but Kitiara could never comprehend that he would be willing to sacrifice his life for the sake of the magic. Even though his body had been shattered, he had been one of the fortunate. He had survived the Test. Many did not.

Raistlin reached to touch the Staff of Magius, which was never far from his hand, tempted to prove to his sister it was far more than a walking stick. But Kitiara had lost interest in him. She again shifted her attention to the door, waiting for Tanis to walk through it. Raistlin could hear Caramon talking to Tika and see him gesturing toward his brother. Tika had a smile for Caramon, but she cast a baleful glance at Raistlin before going back to the kitchen. She returned with a mug of steaming water.

Caramon carefully carried the mug back to the table, gently shook the herbs into it, then anxiously watched over it as he waited the allotted time, allowing the herbs to steep. When he deemed the brew ready, he handed it to Raistlin.

"Drink it slowly," he warned like a mother nursing a sick child.

By now the spasm had eased enough so that Raistlin could sip the tea. He felt the burning sensation diminish and his breathing improve. Caramon looked hungrily around the table but, seeing there was nothing more to eat, he took the dishes back to the kitchen, undoubtedly hoping for another smile from Tika. Kitiara was still focused on observing all who came through the door. Raistlin was left to his own thoughts.

The gods knew, he had enough to think about.

The River of Time had dumped him here, in the inn, last night. At first, he had thought Brother Kairn had succeeded in returning them to their own time, the autumn of 351 AC. But the moment he saw Kitiara in the inn, Raistlin realized that their journey to the past had ended in disaster. They had altered time.

He had still been trying to comprehend what had happened when he had seen Brother Kairn enter the inn alone. Raistlin had managed to hustle him out of the inn onto the porch so they could speak in private. Kairn had told him that Destina Rosethorn, the woman carrying the Graygem, was missing, along with Sturm and Tasslehoff. Raistlin had advised Kairn to return to Astinus and tell him the world had fallen into darkness, while he remained here to try to find the others.

But in order to find them, Raistlin was in desperate need of information about this world in which he had suddenly found himself. Yet he couldn't very well start asking questions without having some plausible reason for doing so. Even his slow-thinking brother might notice his twin had changed overnight and wonder what was going on. Or worse, openly comment on it in front of their sister. Raistlin had therefore decided to feign a head injury.

After speaking with Brother Kairn, Raistlin had gone back inside to sit down with Caramon and his sister. After Kitiara had retired last night, Raistlin spoke to his brother.

"I tripped and fell down the stairs just now and struck my head—" Raistlin began.

"You did?" Caramon was immediately worried. "Are you hurt?"

"Fortunately, I did not break my neck," said Raistlin. "But my head is fuzzy, and I am having trouble remembering things."

"What is it you don't remember?" Caramon asked.

"How can I tell you what I don't remember if I can't remember?" Raistlin said irritably.

"Oh, yeah, that makes sense," Caramon replied with a nod.

"We are in the Inn of the Last Home with our sister for a reunion," said Raistlin. "We're meeting old friends, seemingly. Who are we meeting? Where have they been? Our sister keeps talking about someone called Tanis. Who is he?"

Caramon lowered his voice and leaned near. "He was our friend when we were growing up. He ran the resistance movement against Queen Takhisis. Do you remember Flint and Sturm and Tas? They worked with us."

"Resistance? To the Dark Queen? Wasn't that dangerous?" Raistlin asked.

"It was," said Caramon. "We were betrayed and nearly died in an ambush. Tanis said we needed to leave town until things cooled off. You and I went to Wayreth so you could take the Test. Flint went home to the hill dwarves, and Sturm traveled back to Solamnia to find out what had become of his father. I don't know where Tas went."

"Do you know who betrayed us?" Raistlin asked.

"I didn't then, but I do now," said Caramon. "Our sister."

Raistlin was not surprised. "I took the Test and then what?"

"You and I earned our living as mercenaries until Kit found us and invited us to serve under her command," Caramon said. "I didn't want to work for her, but you said we could gain valuable information we could pass on to the resistance. So now we're serving in the Blue Dragonarmy under Kit's command. We're hoping to meet Tanis here, to tell him what we've found out. Flint's here. He came today. Tika told him that if he saw Tanis, to warn him that Kit is here asking about him."

"You've heard nothing from Sturm?" Raistlin asked.

Caramon shook his head somberly. "Kit said she looked for him when she was in Solamnia, crushing the knights' rebellion. She couldn't find him. Probably just as well."

Raistlin sighed. They had all placed their hands on the Device of Time Journeying. It would have brought them to same place, the same time. That meant Sturm was somewhere here in Solace and badly wounded. Destina and the Graygem were also here, as well as Tasslehoff, who couldn't keep his mouth shut. Raistlin had promised Kairn to try to find them, but he was starting to realize the enormity of that task.

"Is there anything else you need to know?" Caramon had asked. "If not, I'll go help Tika clear up."

Raistlin sat by himself and wondered what to do. Kairn had promised to report to Astinus, then come back for them. Raistlin could do nothing but wait. He had not thought Kairn's journey would take long, but night deepened and Kairn had not returned. Raistlin had finally gone to his room to study his spells and rest, figuring Kairn would know where to find him.

But the morning of the reunion dawned and still Kairn had not returned.

"Something's gone wrong," Raistlin said grimly to himself. "Or rather, something *else* has gone wrong."

Kitiara had been in good spirits this morning. She informed Otik she was expecting guests and commandeered the largest table in the inn. She had waited impatiently all day for Tanis to arrive. Every time the door opened, she sat forward expectantly, only to fling herself back in her chair in disappointment when someone who wasn't Tanis entered.

Raistlin had not seen Kitiara since their last meeting, when she had visited him in the Tower of High Sorcery in Palanthas. His first thought on seeing her again was that this dark world suited her.

Kitiara Uth Matar was now thirty-three years old and, according to Caramon, she was at the height of her power. She was the Dragon Highlord of the Blue Dragonarmy, which ruled Solamnia, Nordmaar, and all the territory east to the Khalkist Mountains. She was a favorite of Her Dark Majesty and also of Ariakas, the commander in chief of the dragonarmies.

Kit was older than her half-brothers—Raistlin and Caramon—and bore little resemblance to them. She took after her father, with dark curly hair she cut short for comfort, brown eyes, and a crooked smile that could be charming to her friends and merciless to her foes.

Kitiara had been excited and cheerful. She had posted the Bozak draconians who served her at the front entrance with orders to question all those who entered and check their names against a list she had given them.

The first name on the list was Tanis Half-Elven. Kit had waited for him all day today, and now, when night had fallen and she had neither seen nor heard from him, her good mood began to evaporate.

She glared at Raistlin, who was slowly sipping his tea.

"That stuff smells worse than dragon fart," she told Raistlin. "Why don't you throw it out and eat something? You're thin as a wraith."

"I am not hungry," said Raistlin.

"He's still suffering from that blow on the head," Caramon explained as he sat down again.

"What blow?" Kitiara asked, startled. "How did that happen?"

"I fell down the stairs," said Raistlin.

"He couldn't remember a thing," Caramon said cheerfully. "He spent last night asking me questions about our past lives and why we were here and what we were doing."

"I may have need of your magic," said Kit, frowning. "I hope you have not forgotten your spells."

"My memory loss was temporary, my sister," Raistlin assured her. "My spellcasting abilities are unimpaired, and I have my staff, which, as you know, has its own powers. Let us say no more about my fall."

"Speaking of staffs," said Caramon, "I hear that fool Toede is riding around the countryside looking for a staff made of blue crystal."

"I heard the same," said Kitiara. "Supposedly the staff is sacred to some long-forgotten goddess and has healing properties. Is it magic, Raist? Do you know anything about it?"

"I know nothing," Raistlin answered with a shrug. "I have never heard of such a staff."

In truth, he had only to look over at two people seated by the fire to see the blue crystal staff and the woman who carried it. The staff appeared to be quite ordinary—a plain wooden walking staff. The woman who carried it was Goldmoon, and she was accompanied by her guardian, Riverwind.

Raistlin had been observing them with interest since they had entered the inn in the company of a decrepit-looking old man wearing mouse-gray robes and a battered, pointed hat. The two had looked bewildered and confused, and the old man had guided them to the fire, inviting them to sit down and rest after their journey.

"I know the trip was a bit unexpected," the old man had said. "One moment people are throwing stones at you, and the next there's a flash of blue light and here you are."

"How did you know that?" Goldmoon had asked, astonished.

"Because I'm Fizban the Fabulous," the old man had said. "I know lots of things. For example, I know that if a man named Tanis Half-Elven offers to help you, you should take him up on it."

He had then wandered off and gone bumbling about the room until Tika had rescued him and guided him to a table in the back near the fire. He had pulled his hat over his head and appeared to be sleeping, but Raistlin had known better.

"So the gods are going to fight back," Raistlin had said to himself.

Fizban was the avatar of the god Paladine, eternal foe of Queen Takhisis. When Chaos had changed time, and Takhisis had won the Third Dragon War, Paladine and the other gods had supposedly fled. But Raistlin guessed they had been regrouping, gathering their strength, preparing for this night of the companions' reunion when healing returned to the world in the form of a blue crystal staff. But Tanis was not here, and Kitiara was.

The door opened, and Kitiara quickly turned to see who had entered.

"It's no one of importance," Caramon said loudly. "Just Bakaris."

Kitiara grinned, and Bakaris gave Caramon a venomous look.

Bakaris was Kit's aide-de-camp and, according to Caramon, had also been her lover until she had grown tired of him and kicked him out of her bed. He had been sulking ever since their arrival in Solace.

"That's because Kit has been talking about Tanis and how he used to be her lover. Bakaris is so jealous he could chew down a vallenwood," Caramon had said. "He's such a dolt, he doesn't realize she's deliberately teasing him, making sport of him."

Bakaris slouched over to the table and flung himself moodily into a chair.

"Where have you been?" Kit demanded.

"I went to check on my horse," said Bakaris sullenly. "You need to discipline those lizards, Kit. They threatened me, their superior! Damn Bozaks. You should have them whipped for insubordination."

"I didn't ask you for advice on how to run my army," Kitiara said in a frozen tone. "I asked you to find out if the Bozaks had seen or heard anything about the friends I'm meeting here tonight."

"You mean one friend—that half-human, Tanis. And they haven't," said Bakaris. "Or at least if they have, they didn't tell me. Next time, ask them yourself!"

Bakaris shoved back his chair, stood up, and stalked off to the bar. Kitiara watched him go, her lips parted in a crooked smile that boded ill for Bakaris.

"Tanis wouldn't miss our reunion, would he, Raist?" Caramon asked.

"Not being Tanis, I have no idea what he would do," Raistlin returned.

"He will come," said Kitiara. "And when he does, I plan to make him my lieutenant. He made a sad mistake when he left me five years ago. He must realize that now."

"Considering you nearly got him killed in that ambush, I wouldn't be so certain," Raistlin remarked.

Kitiara shrugged. "I didn't try very hard to have Tanis killed. If I had wanted him dead, he would be dead. I just wanted to scare some sense into him."

"You know that Bakaris is expecting you to promote him to lieutenant," Caramon pointed out. "What will you do about him?"

"That depends on Bakaris," said Kitiara.

The door opened again, and again Kitiara glanced up. She nudged Caramon. "Look who's here. The High Theo*crap*."

Caramon guffawed. "High Theocrap! That's funny! Isn't that funny, Raist?"

"Hilarious," said Raistlin.

Hederick the High Theocrat paused in the door long enough for everyone in the inn to be suitably impressed by his magnificence. He was the head of the Seeker religious order, dedicated to the worship of Takhisis, and the nominal ruler of Solace. A middle-aged human, Hederick was balding on top with a fringe of gray hair around his ears. He wore purple robes made of expensive cloth, belted around his large middle, and a capelet embroidered in gold thread with the symbols of his office.

"I am looking for Dragon Highlord Kitiara," he loudly proclaimed. "I bear a message to her from Lord Verminaard."

"Stop bellowing, Hederick," said Tika, walking past him carrying a tray of empty mugs. "Kitiara's sitting at that table right over there, as you know full well, for I saw you look straight at her."

Hederick grunted, then glanced around and gave an affected start. "Ah, there you are, Highlord."

"Here I am," said Kitiara, her lip curling. "What is this message?"

"May I join you?" Hederick asked, and he started to sit down in an empty chair.

Kitiara slammed her booted foot on it. "This chair is occupied. What's the message?"

Hederick drew himself up with offended dignity. "I received an urgent notice that has gone out to all those who serve Her Dark Majesty. It is of vital importance, and I felt it was incumbent upon me to tell you immediately."

"If it's so urgent, stop blathering and tell me," said Kit impatiently.

"A valuable artifact was stolen from the Temple of Luerkhisis in Neraka," said Hederick. "Her Dark Majesty is most eager to recover this artifact and punish the thief who took it. We are to be on the lookout for a human female named Destina Rosethorn, the daughter of one of the accursed knights of Solamnia. The artifact is a gray gemstone known as the Graygem of Gargath."

"The Graygem?" Kitiara stared at him in disbelief, then burst out laughing.

Caramon choked on his ale. "Did you hear that, Raist? The Graygem!"

"I am not deaf," Raistlin retorted. He put his handkerchief to his mouth, ostensibly to cover a cough, but in reality to hide his alarm.

Takhisis was already aware that Destina carried the Graygem. The Dark Queen had entered the High Clerist's Tower in search of it. Kairn had activated the Device of Time Journeying only seconds before Takhisis could catch them. Raistlin had hoped they had escaped her when they had traveled to this time, but now that hope was dashed. Takhisis knew it was here, in this place and in this time.

But if she has ordered people like Hederick to search for the Graygem, Takhisis does not know where it is, Raistlin realized, latching on to a fragment of hope. It was now more imperative than ever that he find Destina and warn her.

Bakaris returned with a jug of dwarf spirits to find Kitiara and Caramon still roaring with laughter.

"What's funny?" Bakaris asked.

"Hederick here says we've been ordered by Verminaard to search for the Graygem of Gargath," said Kitiara, wiping her eyes. "Tell us again what this Graygem looks like, Hederick."

"I'll tell you," said Caramon. "It's gray. And it's a gem."

He and Kit both laughed again.

Hederick was red in the face, sputtering with anger. "Lord Verminaard will hear how you mocked him, Highlord!"

"I'm not mocking *him*, Hederick," said Kitiara, grinning. "I'm mocking *you*."

"Everyone knows the Graygem of Gargath is a kender tale," Caramon explained. "It doesn't exist. Isn't that right, Raist?"

Raistlin drank another sip of tea, though it had long since gone cold. "My brother is right, High Theocrat. The Graygem is a myth. You and Lord Verminaard are wasting your time searching for it."

"So don't waste mine," Kitiara added.

Hederick glared at her. "You would do well to listen to Lord Verminaard, Highlord Kitiara, instead of this charlatan wizard!"

Caramon jumped to his feet, his fists clenched. "Who are you calling a charlatan?"

"Sit down, my brother!" Raistlin ordered angrily. "I can fight my own battles—those that I consider worth fighting. Battles with fat Theocrats I do not."

Caramon looked uncertain, but he sat back down in his chair.

Seeing that Hederick was growing increasingly outraged, Tika came bustling up to their table to placate him. "We don't need any trouble tonight, Hederick. Your table is ready. And I've baked some of that apple pie you like."

"I will inform Lord Verminaard that you *laughed*, Highlord!" said Hederick loftily, then permitted Tika to escort him to his favorite table, in front of the fire.

Bakaris shook his head. "You shouldn't insult the High Theocrat, Kit. He'll report you to Verminaard and, let's face it, you're not supposed to be here in Solace. This is Verminaard's territory."

"I'll be where I damn well want to be!" Kitiara said. "First Verminaard has Toede searching for a blue crystal staff and now he wants me to chase after a gray gem. Next he will be ordering us to bring him the Kender Spoon of Turning!"

Caramon laughed again. Bakaris raised the jug to his mouth, tilted his head, and drank. He handed the jug to Kitiara, who took a drink, and then offered it to Caramon. He shook his head.

"Once I start with that stuff I can't quit," he said. "Raist told me it was a sickness and I should stop drinking it."

Kitiara looked dubious, but at that moment the door opened and one of the Bozak guards entered. He approached the table, his clawed feet scraping the floor.

"What is it, Skrit?" Kit asked eagerly. "Do you have news?"

"There's a dwarf outside who claims he's a friend of yours," said the Bozak. "Name of Fireforge. And he has a kender with him. Name of Burrfoot. They are both on the list. Should I let them inside?"

"Send them in at once!" said Kitiara, her brown eyes shining.

"Even the kender?" Skrit asked doubtfully.

"Yes, of course," said Kitiara. "Flint and Tas are certain to know something about Tanis."

The Bozak escorted Flint and Tas into the inn and pointed to Kitiara's table. Tas dashed toward her, only to stop short. He stared at Raistlin intently.

"What are you looking at? You know me, kender," said Raistlin.

"I know you're Raistlin, but which Raistlin are you?" Tas asked warily. "Are you the Raistlin in the past when the past was the past or the Raistlin from the past that is now the present only it's different?"

"I am the Raistlin who will turn you into a cricket and swallow you whole if you don't stop talking nonsense," said Raistlin.

Tas sighed. "That's no help. Both Raistlins threatened to do that to me."

"Sit down and be quiet," Raistlin said, looking to see if Kit had heard.

Fortunately, she was watching Caramon, who had grabbed Flint in a bear hug and lifted him off his feet.

"Put me down, you great oaf!" Flint roared.

Caramon lowered Flint to the floor. The dwarf took a moment to restore his dignity, adjusting his harness and repositioning his helm, which had slipped over his eye.

"You big lummox! Hoisting me about like a sack of potatoes," Flint grumbled. "Hullo, Kit. I heard you were here."

"It is good to see you again, Flint," Kitiara said. "Did Tanis come with you?"

Before Flint could answer, Raistlin jumped to his feet and grabbed hold of Tasslehoff by the topknot.

"Give that back to me!" Raistlin ordered, shaking him.

"Ouch! My hair!" Tas wailed, clutching at his head.

"I saw you take it! I want it back," Raistlin said.

"I didn't take anything!" Tas protested. "Or if I did, you must have dropped it!"

"Then I'll turn you inside out until I find it," Raistlin said grimly.

Holding the Staff of Magius in one hand and Tas in the other, Raistlin hauled the howling kender to a table in a dark corner near the door. He glanced over his shoulder to see Caramon looking unhappy, Kitiara amused, and Flint watching him with distrust.

Raistlin shoved Tas into a chair and sat down opposite him. He leaned close and said urgently, "I need you to answer my questions! And keep your voice down."

Tas rubbed his head. "You made my eyes go all watery."

"Where is Destina? Do you know?" Raistlin asked.

"I *might* know." Tas eyed Raistlin suspiciously. "But you didn't answer *my* question. Which Raistlin are you?"

"If I were the wrong one, would I know about Destina?" Raistlin demanded, exasperated.

Tas thought this over. "I guess not. All right, I know where Destina is. Brother Kairn is with her. . . ."

"Brother Kairn!" Raistlin repeated, shocked. "What is he doing here? I told him to report to Astinus."

"Kairn went to the future to see Astinus and then he came back to this past to take Destina back to the other past to try to fix the present so that it's not this present it's the right present," said Tas all in one breath. "And Tanis is here, too. The right Tanis. Kairn brought him to this past from the future."

"Tanis!" Raistlin exclaimed. "Why did Kairn bring Tanis?"

"You need to ask him yourself. He tried to explain it to me, but it's awfully confusing," Tas said. "It has something to do with him being bait and Astinus and a war that Takhisis won only now she's worried that we might win it and that means she'll keep an eye on us here in the present and not notice that Kairn and Destina are going back to the past."

"Where are those two?" Raistlin asked, not bothering to sort this out. "Have they gone back yet?"

Tas shook his head. "Destina didn't want to leave Sturm because he's dying, and something's wrong with her now, too. Tanis thinks that bad man, Tully, might have poisoned her when he cut her with his knife. The wound looks really bad and Destina is very weak and wobbly. So I said we should get Goldmoon and the blue crystal staff to heal them. That was my idea!" Tas added proudly. "Tanis usually has all the ideas, but this one was mine. So he and Flint and I came to find Goldmoon. Could I go say hi to Caramon now? That man with Kit is Bakaris, isn't it? Do you think he'll remember I stabbed him, even though I haven't yet?"

"Tanis is in the inn?" Raistlin asked. "Where?"

Tas looked around the room and started to raise his hand. "He's sitting at that table—"

"Don't point him out to everyone!" Raistlin snapped, knocking aside the kender's hand.

Tas sat on his hands, so they wouldn't act on their own. "Tanis is sitting at the table at the end of the bar. He's the one with the beard who keeps his head down and his face hidden in the shadows. He's near the old man. . . ." Tas stared, then gasped. "Is that Fizban? But he looks terrible! I have to go find out what's wrong. And look! There's Goldmoon and Riverwind! I need to talk to them, too. Tanis is going to help them escape."

Tas started to stand up, but Raistlin yanked him back down.

"How much does Tanis know about Destina and the Graygem?" he asked.

"Everything. He knows about the—" Tas sneezed. "Drat! Anyway, he knows about It and about the past that was or is or isn't and wasn't—"

"Quiet! Caramon is walking over here!" Raistlin said. "Go tell Tanis I will do what I can to help Goldmoon and Riverwind escape. But that won't be easy with Kit here."

"Fizban's here, too," said Tas. "He can help."

Raistlin remembered Fizban's "help" from the past. "Hopefully we won't be driven to that extremity. Tell Tanis to be ready to act. Go now, before Caramon comes."

Tas picked up his hoopak and dashed off, dodging among the tables and chairs and customers until he reached Tanis. Apparently, Tas was doing as he was told, because Tanis looked over at Raistlin and gave a slight nod.

"Who's that Tas is bothering?" Caramon asked.

Raistlin shrugged. "I have no idea. What do you want?"

"Kit sent me to fetch you," said Caramon. "She thinks she's found that blue crystal staff. The woman over there has it."

Caramon turned to point directly at Goldmoon.

CHAPTER
TEN

As Raistlin slowly rose from the table, he caught Tanis's eye and inclined his head ever so slightly toward Kitiara, then shifted his gaze to Goldmoon and Riverwind. Judging by Tanis's grim expression, he understood. Raistlin leaned heavily on his staff and began to shuffle across the floor, moving as slowly as possible.

"Are you all right, Raist?" Caramon asked worriedly, reaching out his hand to help. "Does your head hurt? Are you dizzy? Let me help you."

Raistlin flinched away from his brother's touch.

"Stop hovering!" he ordered irritably. "What makes our sister think she has found this blue crystal staff?"

"She's been watching those two Plainsfolk in the corner and she noticed the woman has a staff," said Caramon. "Kit questioned the dracos about the two and asked if they checked the staff, but the dracos didn't even remember seeing the Plainsfolk come in. So now Kit's decided to find out for herself, and she wants you to tell her if it's magic or not. She's in a bad mood and looking for trouble, Raist. Between you and me, I think she's realized that Tanis isn't coming."

Raistlin reflected that she would be in a worse mood if she knew Tanis was here, hiding from her. Kitiara glared at him in impatience and began tapping her foot on the floor, as though that would hasten him. As he approached, Raistlin noticed Bakaris sitting with his head tilted back, holding a bloodstained cloth to his nose.

"What happened to him?" Raistlin asked.

"Who? Bakaris? I punched him," said Caramon. "While you were shaking down Tas, Tika came over and Bakaris tried to pinch her . . . uh . . . backside. I told him to keep his hands to himself. He said he'd put his hands where he liked, and I said I'd put my fist where *I* liked, and that happened to be in his ugly face."

Raistlin smiled. "Sometimes you make me proud, my brother."

"Thanks, Raist," said Caramon, flushing in pleasure. He grew somber and added in a low tone, "Did I hear Tas say something about Sturm?"

"What? No, of course not," said Raistlin, cursing the kender's shrill voice. "Why do you ask?"

"Kit was talking about the campaign in Solamnia after you left with Tas," said Caramon. "I'm glad we weren't with her then. The war must have been brutal. Her dragons decimated the countryside and her armies slaughtered entire noble families and burned villages to the ground."

"Does this story have a point to it?" Raistlin demanded.

"It will," Caramon assured him. "I asked her about Sturm and the Brightblade family. I wondered if he was coming to the reunion. She said she had told the dracos if he did come, they were to arrest him. I reminded her that Sturm was our friend and she just shrugged and said that, as far as she was concerned, one knight was the same as another and all knights were traitors."

"You don't need to worry. Sturm won't be coming," said Raistlin.

"How do you know?" Caramon asked, puzzled.

"I just know," said Raistlin.

He glanced about the room, taking note of who was where and what they were doing. Flint was at the bar, drinking ale and chatting with Otik. Tanis remained at his table, sensibly keeping hold of Tas, who was kicking the rungs of the chairs with his heels. A sure sign the kender was growing bored.

Hederick was seated at his table near the fire, drinking ale and looking important. Tika was on her way to the kitchen with a tray filled with dirty dishes. Goldmoon and Riverwind were talking quietly together, paying no attention to anyone else. The wooden staff, decorated with feathers, rested against the wall.

Raistlin glanced apprehensively at Fizban. He had the same long white hair and long white beard and was wearing the same gray robes that were the worse for wear, but he seemed shriveled and more frail. A puff of wind could have flattened him. The old wizard was also wearing his wide-brimmed, pointed hat pulled low over his ears. He appeared to be entirely absorbed in drinking his ale, but Raistlin saw the glint of his eyes over the rim of the mug.

Paladine and the other gods of good believed in freedom, giving mortals the chance to choose their own destiny; Fizban would not interfere with these mortals unless the situation was dire, and then the gods alone knew what he would do. Raistlin reflected that since the word *dire* accurately summed up this situation, he had to be ready for anything.

Kitiara pounced on him the moment he drew near. "You took your sweet time! Did Caramon tell you? I think I've found that blue crystal staff."

"He told me," said Raistlin. "I thought he was joking."

"I never joke. You know that," said Kitiara. "Look at that staff, the one trimmed with feathers. What do you see with those hourglass eyes of yours?"

"A staff trimmed with feathers," said Raistlin.

Kit was displeased. "Is that all? I thought those strange eyes could tell if the staff was magic or something like that."

"My eyes see time as it passes," Raistlin said patiently, having explained this to her before. "For me to tell if the staff is magical, I must first cast a spell on it. If it is, I will see it glow—"

"Oh, never mind!" Kit said impatiently. "I'll find out for myself. You and Caramon come with me."

Bakaris dropped the cloth from his face and clambered to his feet. He had a bloody nose, a swollen eye that was turning purple, and a split lip.

"Let me come with you, Kit," he said, putting his hand on his sword. "I know how to deal with these savages."

He was forced to speak through his nose, and Caramon laughed. Kitiara regarded Bakaris in disgust.

"You're a mess," she told him. "Go to the kitchen and get yourself cleaned up."

"But, Kit—" Bakaris began.

Kitiara ignored him and walked off, heading for the back of the inn where the two Plainsfolk were sitting.

Bakaris glared at Caramon. "You'll pay for this, Majere!"

"Ooh, I'm scared!" Caramon said, grinning.

Bakaris stomped off toward the kitchen and slammed through the swinging doors.

"Be careful of him, my brother," Raistlin warned. "You made him look bad in front of Kit. He won't forget."

Caramon shrugged. "Bakaris is a snake. I'd rather have him for an enemy than pretending to be my friend. That way I know where I stand."

Raistlin was impressed. "Astute reasoning, my brother."

"Is it?" Caramon was surprised. "I just figured it was common sense."

Kitiara stood in front of Riverwind and Goldmoon and rested her hand on the hilt of her sword. The two had been absorbed in their conversation and unaware of her approach. Seeing her staring at them, they rose belatedly to greet her, looking apprehensive. Goldmoon reached for the staff, which had been leaning against the wall, and drew it close.

The Plainsfolk were both wearing the clothing favored by their people—leather tunics and loose-fitting trousers and boots. They had cast aside their fur cloaks to sit by the fire. Riverwind stood protectively at Goldmoon's side, keeping his hand on the hilt of his sword. He was taller than Kitiara by head and shoulders, but he was gaunt and thin, and looked as though he had recently been ill.

Raistlin spoke quietly to his brother. "Kit asked if I knew anything about a staff with healing powers. I lied when I told her I didn't. If this is the blue crystal staff, it is a sign from the old gods that they have returned to the world. We cannot let our sister get hold of it."

"How are we going to stop her?" Caramon asked. "All she has to do is whistle and her dracos will come rushing in here."

Raistlin had no idea, but he wasn't going to admit that to Caramon. "Just do what I tell you to do."

"Sure, Raist," said Caramon as they came to stand alongside their sister.

"I am Dragon Highlord Kitiara Uth Matar," Kitiara was saying, talking to the Plainsfolk. "I have been ordered by Lord Verminaard to find a staff that is said to possess healing powers. Give your staff to my wizard. Let him examine it."

"The staff belongs to Chieftain's Daughter, Highlord," Riverwind replied, polite but firm. "You have no right to take it."

"Raistlin, seize the staff," Kitiara ordered.

Raistlin remembered vividly the first, last, and only time he had ever touched the blue crystal Staff of Mishakal. The staff was a holy artifact of good and it knew its own. It had flared in anger, and he had ended up with blistered fingers. If Kit saw the staff burn him, she would know immediately the staff was suspect. Raistlin dared not touch it, but he was fairly certain it would not harm Caramon.

"Bring the staff to me, my brother," Raistlin ordered.

Caramon hesitated and glanced at him to make certain he knew what he was doing. Raistlin scowled and Caramon hurried to obey. He held out his hand to Goldmoon and spoke to her in a friendly manner.

"If you'll just give me the staff, ma'am, I'll let Raist take a look at it. He'll give it right back—"

Riverwind stepped protectively in front of Goldmoon. "The staff was given into our keeping. We will not give it to you or this wizard."

"Just step back, big fella, we don't want any trouble," Caramon said.

Hederick, seated at his table, made a derisive, snorting sound. Kitiara heard him and flushed in anger.

"I've had enough of this nonsense!" She drew her sword. "I'll find out for myself."

Raistlin suddenly realized what she intended, and so did Tanis, for Raistlin saw the half-elf jump from his chair. Before they could stop her, she lunged and drove her sword into Riverwind's chest. He stared at the blade in shock, then moaned in agony. Kitiara yanked her sword free and blood gushed from the wound. Riverwind clutched his chest and slumped to the floor. He lay unmoving in a rapidly expanding pool of blood.

Goldmoon cried out in anguish. She dropped the staff and sank to her knees beside Riverwind and gathered his limp body in her arms. She held him close, weeping.

Kitiara sheathed the bloodstained sword and prodded Goldmoon with the toe of her boot.

"The staff has healing powers," said Kitiara. "So heal him."

Goldmoon stared up at Kitiara through her tears. "How can I? I am not a healer! I cannot heal him! No one can!"

Caramon gave Kit a grim look. "Leave her alone, Kit. There was no call to kill him! I'll get the damn staff for you."

As he took hold of the staff, it began to shimmer with a faint blue light.

"It's glowing," said Kit, regarding the staff with interest.

"It's glowing!" Caramon gasped. The blue glow was intensifying, growing stronger. "Help me! What do I do?"

"Drop it, you fool!" Fizban shouted. "It's going to explode!"

Caramon flung the staff away in panic. The staff drifted lazily through the air, spun around slowly, and then landed gently on top of Riverwind. As it touched him, the staff's radiant blue light shone throughout the inn, imparting a sense of love so profound and abiding that it touched even Raistlin.

Riverwind stirred and drew in a deep breath. The dreadful gash in his chest disappeared, leaving only a bloodstained hole in his leather tunic. He sighed, as though he had wakened from a deep and peaceful sleep, and opened his eyes. He smiled at Goldmoon, who was staring at him in shock and disbelief. He spoke to her in their language, seeming to want to know what was wrong. She could not answer; her tears of grief changed to tears of joy. She drew him into a grateful embrace. The staff lay on the floor at her side. Its blue light started to dim.

"I'll be damned!" Caramon said, awed.

"So the staff does have healing powers," Kitiara stated in satisfaction. She cast Hederick a smug glance, then reached down to pick up the staff. "I will take this to Queen Takhisis myself."

"Don't touch it!" Raistlin warned.

Kitiara snatched her hand back. "Why not?"

"Because it's not yours!" Tasslehoff cried.

The kender broke free of Tanis's grip, dashed across the room, ducked beneath Kitiara's outstretched arm, and grabbed the staff out from under her nose. He held the staff behind his back.

Kitiara glared at Tasslehoff. "I'm not playing games, kender. Give me the staff."

"I'm sorry, I can't do that," said Tas. "Well, I'm not very sorry, because I never did like you much, but this staff belongs to Goldmoon and people shouldn't take things that don't belong to them."

Kitiara made a grab for Tas. He jumped nimbly backward, only to bump up against Hederick, who had risen from his chair and planted his solid body behind him.

"It seems I must do your job for you, Highlord," said Hederick. "I will take the staff to Her Dark Majesty."

The High Theocrat plucked the staff out of Tas's hands.

Blue light flashed in anger. Hederick howled in pain and dropped the staff, wringing his burned hand and swearing.

Kitiara laughed, then raised her voice, shouting for the Bozaks. "Guards! To me!"

The two Bozak guards flung open the door and ran into the inn, swords drawn.

Kitiara pointed at the Plainsfolk. "Arrest those two barbarians."

As the Bozaks advanced on Riverwind and Goldmoon, Tanis ranged up behind Raistlin. "Flint and I will deal with the Bozaks. Can you deal with Kit?"

Raistlin nodded. "Remember, Bozaks can use magic spells."

"I'm not likely to forget," said Tanis. "What do we do about Tas?"

The kender was dodging among the furniture, taking swipes at Kitiara with the staff and taunting her, calling her a wide variety of interesting and colorful names including "lily-livered lizard lover." He liked that one so well, he said it twice.

"Someone more powerful than we are is watching over the kender," said Raistlin, nodding toward the old man.

"Is that Fizban?" Tanis asked, alarmed.

"Yes," said Raistlin. "Be prepared to take cover."

"The gods help us," Tanis muttered.

"That's the trouble. One of them is likely to," Raistlin said to himself as Tanis and Flint both ran to aid the Plainsfolk.

"We're on your side," Tanis assured Riverwind, who had turned to confront what he thought was a new foe. "We are enemies of the Dark Queen."

Flint planted his feet and hefted his axe. "You keep your lady safe," he said to Riverwind. "We'll deal with these damn lizards. Caramon, we could use your help."

"Caramon!" Kitiara shouted. "I need your help!"

She was confronting Tas, who had jumped up on a table and was jabbing at Kitiara with the staff.

Hederick was glaring at them both. "Just kill the little nuisance, Highlord, and take the damn staff!"

"You take it!" said Kitiara, giving him a furious glance.

Hederick glowered. Nursing his wounded hand, he retreated to the bar. "I'll see that Lord Verminaard hears about this."

Caramon cast an agonized glance at Raistlin, clearly conflicted. "What do we do, Raist? We can't let her hurt Tas!"

"And we can't let her know we're working for the resistance!" said Raistlin. "Get hold of the staff!"

Caramon ran over to where Tas was dancing on the table and now singing "lily-livered lizard lover" at the top of his lungs. Caramon grabbed hold of the table and upended it, sending Tas sprawling on the floor. Before the kender could regain his feet, Kit pounced on him and seized hold of him by his topknot. She drew her knife.

"Don't cut off my topknot!" Tas wailed. "It just grew back!"

"Give the staff to Caramon or it won't be your hair I'll cut!" said Kit angrily.

"Tas, give the staff to me," said Caramon. "I'll take good care of it."

"It's not yours," said Tas stubbornly. "It's Goldmoon's! And we have to have the staff to save Sturm and Destina!"

Raistlin had been keeping a wary eye on Fizban and now saw

him reach into one of the pouches hanging from his belt. The old man took a pinch of something and held it up for Raistlin to see.

"Bat guano," Fizban said, regarding it fondly. "Now, if I can just remember that spell . . ."

Raistlin was alarmed. "No, Old One—"

"Got it!" Fizban shouted in triumph. *"Ast kiranann kair Soth-aran/ Suh kali Jalaran—"*

A ball of fire burst from the old man's gnarled hand, whizzed past Raistlin, streaked across the room, and struck Kitiara on the breastplate of her armor. The impact of the fiery ball lifted her off her feet and flung her backward. She slammed into a wall, striking her head, and slumped to the floor.

The old man rubbed his hands in glee.

"This next one's a doozy. I call it 'Burning Down the House.' Has a catchy tune to go with it."

He began humming. Taking off his hat, he swung it three times in the air above his head.

An explosion rocked the inn, shaking the huge limbs of the vallenwood tree and causing the building to shift on its foundation. The floor canted sideways. Tables and chairs slid across the room and crashed up against the walls. Thick black smoke came roiling out of the kitchen, and they heard Tika scream.

"Fire! Help! Fire!" Fizban shouted. "This place is a death trap! Run for your lives!"

The branches of the tree shook. Smoke filled the air, choking the Bozaks and causing them to break off their attack. Tasslehoff stood in the remains of the ruined table, coughing and batting at the flames with the Staff of Mishakal.

"We're all going to die!" Fizban howled.

Hederick made a dash for the front door and nearly bowled over two more Bozaks, who had come rushing inside. The smoke immediately enveloped them, and they doubled over coughing. Kitiara was shaking her head muzzily and trying to stand up.

"Save the Highlord!" Raistlin shouted. "Caramon! Save the Highlord!"

"Huh?" Caramon stared at him.

"We must save our beloved sister!" said Raistlin. "Take her back to camp where she will be safe!"

Caramon grinned in sudden understanding. "I've got you, Kit!" He picked her up in his strong arms, slung her over his shoulder, and headed for the door.

"Make way! Save the Highlord!" Caramon thundered. "You dracos! Come with me!"

The Bozaks were coughing so hard they could barely stand. They staggered after Caramon, who had firm hold of Kitiara. She hung upside down over his shoulder, beating him with her fists, swearing at him and ordering him to put her down.

"Cover our escape!" Caramon shouted at the Bozaks. "There's likely more of these scum outside!"

The Bozaks ran after him, their swords drawn.

"Save the Highlord!" Caramon shouted.

He barged through the front door and disappeared into the night. The Bozaks followed, still coughing. The door slammed shut behind them.

Peace and quiet descended on the Inn of the Last Home. The vallenwood tree stopped shaking. The fires mysteriously vanished. Fresh air wafted through the inn, blowing away the smoke. But the floor still slanted at an odd angle, and tables and chairs lay strewn about. They could hear Tika exclaiming in dismay at the state of the kitchen.

Tasslehoff emerged from the ruins, clutching the staff.

"Is my topknot still there?" he asked Raistlin anxiously.

"Yes," said Raistlin.

"Is Kitiara really gone?"

"She is," said Raistlin. "You need to give Goldmoon back her staff."

"What staff?" Tas asked, trying to hide it.

"The staff you are holding behind your back."

"Oh, that staff," Tas said. "I was thinking I could borrow it, just for a little while. I could use it to heal Sturm and Destina. I'd bring it right back."

"Give Goldmoon the staff, lad," said Fizban. He had taken a seat at Hederick's table, which was the only table still standing, and was finishing off the apple pie, which had also miraculously survived the destruction. "How would you feel if someone took your hoopak?"

Tasslehoff sighed. "I'll go give it back to Goldmoon."

Tas carried the staff over to where Riverwind and Goldmoon were standing among smashed chairs and overturned tables. Tanis was trying to talk with them, offering them help. Riverwind was listening, but his expression was one of doubt and distrust. Goldmoon looked drained and exhausted, but she smiled to see Tasslehoff with the staff. Its blue light seemed to linger fondly around him as he handed it to Goldmoon.

"This is yours," said Tas. He added sternly, "You should really take better care of it since it belongs to Mishakal and because we need you to heal our friend Sturm. He's dying and we came here on purpose to find you. It was my idea. Tanis usually has all the ideas, but I had this one. You should hurry before Kitiara comes back."

"I don't understand," said Goldmoon, bewildered. She turned to Tanis. "How did you know we would be here?"

"I don't have time for explanations or to tell you why you should trust us," Tanis told her. "All I can say is that we want to help you, and you need our help. You are both still in danger. Kitiara is not the only one who knows about your staff. Highmaster Toede has orders from Queen Takhisis to find it. His goblins are patrolling the roads. My friends and I can take you to a place of safety."

Riverwind shook his head. "I thank you for being prepared to defend us from the lizardmen, but I think we should go our own way and you go yours."

Fizban suddenly began to sing in a high, reedy voice.

He carries a blue staff
As bright as a glacier:
The grasslands are fading, the summer wind dies.

The grasslands are fragile,
As yellow as flame,
The chieftain makes mockery
Of Riverwind's claim.

He orders the people
To stone the young warrior:
The grasslands are fragile, as yellow as flame.

The grassland has faded,
And autumn is here.
The girl joins her lover,
The stones whistle near.

The staff flares in blue light
And both of them vanish:
The grasslands are faded, and autumn is here.

"There's a lot more where that came from," he added when he finished. "But we don't have time for the whole song."

He wagged his finger at Riverwind and Goldmoon, who were regarding him in bewilderment.

"The staff is a blessed artifact from the old gods, a sign that while we may be down, we're not out. You two are strangers in a strange land with no idea where you are or how you came to be here. I know it's hard for you to trust people, especially a bunch as disreputable looking as this lot, but we're hip-deep in river water, and the only way we're going to save ourselves is to put our trust in each other and our faith in the gods. If we don't, we'll drown, and Takhisis—or Nilat the Corruptor, as your people call her—will win."

"And we're not strangers," Tas added helpfully. "We met you before in the past which is now the present, though not the right present, which means you probably don't remember us so I'll introduce us. I'm Tasslehoff Burrfoot. You can call me Tas, everyone does. This is my best friend, Flint Fireforge, who was dead, but he's not anymore. And this is Tanis Half-Elven and that's Raistlin in the black robes. He and his twin brother, Caramon, saved you from Kitiara. They are all Heroes of the Lance. Some people say I'm a hero, too, but I just went along to keep the others out of trouble."

Riverwind cast a baleful glance at Raistlin, and his expression hardened. "Thank you for your offer, but we should go our own way."

Goldmoon rounded on him. "And where do we go on our own,

Riverwind, when we do not know where we are or how we got here? Do we wander about in the wilderness until the dragonmen catch us?"

Riverwind's expression darkened.

Goldmoon placed her hand gently on his bloodstained tunic. "These people were willing to risk their lives for us. What does it matter how they know what they know? The staff saved us and brought us to this inn, perhaps for this very reason—to meet these people. I know it is hard for you to trust, after what we have been through, but it is time we put our trust in someone."

"The decision is yours, Chieftain's Daughter," said Riverwind. "I will obey your command. I will go with them, if you insist. But I will not trust them."

Goldmoon sighed, then turned back to Tanis.

"We will come with you," she said.

"We'll go out through the kitchen!" Tas said excitedly. "Oops! Sorry, Tanis. I forgot you are supposed to say that. You and Flint can show them how to find the kitchen. I have to get my hoopak and talk to Fizban."

Tanis cast a glance at Raistlin. "Are you coming?"

"I'll wait for Tas," he said.

Tanis nodded, and he and Flint guided Riverwind and Goldmoon past the bar and through the swinging doors that led to the back. Riverwind had at least sheathed his sword, though he kept his hand on the hilt. Tasslehoff recovered his hoopak, which he found lying underneath a broken chair, then went to talk to Fizban.

"Hullo, Fizban," said Tas excitedly. "It's good to see you again!"

Fizban looked suspiciously at Tas. "Where's my hat? Did you borrow it?"

"It's on your head," said Tas, pointing.

Fizban put his hand up to gingerly touch the bent and battered hat and frowned. "Are you sure? Doesn't feel like my hat. I think someone must have switched hats on me."

"It's your hat," said Tas. "I should know. I've found it for you often enough."

"If you say so," said Fizban, sounding doubtful. "You should go with your friends. They need you."

"After all the adventures we've been on together they really should be able to take care of themselves," Tas said sternly. "But I suppose I have to go. They'll get into trouble without me. I came to say goodbye and ask when I'll see you again."

Fizban patted Tas on the shoulder. "I'm not sure, lad. My situation's a bit dicey right now. Dicey. Get it? Gamer joke. But if all goes well, I'll meet you when you bring the . . ."

Fizban bent down to whisper in Tas's ear. "Don't tell anyone. Mum's the word."

"Mum? You just said the word was *dragonlances*," Tas stated, confused. "Where am I supposed to take them?"

Fizban whispered again. Tas listened, then sprang back with a cry.

"No!" Tas shook his head violently. "Oh, no! Not ever again! Not ever!"

The kender ran off, nearly barreling into Tanis, who had come back in search of him.

"What happened?" Tanis said.

"I'm not going!" Tas shouted and disappeared into the kitchen.

"Not going where?" Tanis asked, staring after him.

"I'm not certain," said Raistlin. "Something Fizban said to him upset him."

Tanis sighed deeply. "Of course. As if we didn't have enough trouble."

Raistlin was watching Fizban, who was looking about for more pie. "Where are you taking the Plainsfolk?"

"Do you remember Hal Miller's place?" said Tanis. "The old mill. Sturm is there with Destina and Brother Kairn."

"You and I need to talk privately," said Raistlin. "Send Flint and Tas on ahead with the Plainsfolk. I will meet you down below by the storage sheds."

Tanis looked uncertain, but he nodded and went back into the kitchen. Raistlin and the old man were the only ones left in the common room.

Fizban was wizened, his body stooped and bent. But Raistlin noticed, as he went over to speak to him, that the old man's eyes were clear and keen and sharp.

"I take it you know who I am, Old One," said Raistlin.

"Raistlin Majere, Master of Past and Present," said Fizban. "Or, as Tas would say, master of the past that isn't and the present that wasn't." He leaned back in his chair and made himself comfortable. "I'm up to speed on the Graygem and all its comings and goings. What's on your mind?"

"Takhisis knows the Graygem has returned to this time, and she is actively searching for it," said Raistlin.

"And since she has five heads and ten eyes, she's likely to find it," Fizban said sagely.

"Tanis came back to this time hoping to keep the Dark Queen's attention focused on us while Destina and Brother Kairn return to the past to try to fix what went wrong. At least that is what I think Tas meant. I have yet to speak to Tanis."

Fizban nodded, causing his hat to slip down over one eye. "An interesting plan. Your apprentice, Dalamar, suggested it. Takhisis remembers the War of the Lance, and she won't be pleased to find the heroes who walloped her in the past suddenly turning up here and now when she's about to launch her big war. She won the battle the first time, but now, because of the Graygem, she knows you have the power to change the outcome."

"That is what I wanted to ask," said Raistlin. "If Destina takes the Graygem back to the Third Dragon War, we won't have it with us. How can we change time?"

"You already have," said Fizban complacently.

Raistlin frowned. "I don't understand."

"Try to keep up, son," said Fizban. "The Graygem brought you here to the reunion at the Inn of the Last Home in 351 Chaos Time. You weren't here during the first go-round. Your presence in this time has already changed time."

"But we were already here in this time," said Raistlin.

"The Raistlin of Chaos Time was here," said Fizban. "The Raistlin who fought in the War of the Lance was not, because that battle never happened. In the first go-round, minus the Graygem, Kitiara killed Riverwind and Goldmoon, confiscated the staff, and gave it to Takhisis, and the Dark Queen won the Lost War. Now, thanks to the Graygem, time has changed. You and your friends saved Riverwind and Goldmoon and stopped Kitiara from getting hold of the staff. The gods are still in the fight and that means we still have a chance."

Raistlin pondered this. "I think I understand. The moment we arrived with the Graygem, it began to disrupt the flow of the River of Time."

"And that is how Takhisis realized the Graygem was here," said Fizban. "She is mighty and all-powerful, the ruler of the world, the monarch of heaven and the Abyss, the queen of dragons. You and your friends are an annoying itch—like scale mites. No offense."

"None taken," said Raistlin with a faint smile.

"But the itch has caught her attention and she can't ignore it," said Fizban. He held out his hand. "Now, help me to my feet, son. I need to be going. Got very important god-stuff to do. I had some golden disks on me somewhere. . . ."

Fizban glanced about vaguely. "Have you seen my hat?"

"On your head," said Raistlin.

Fizban took it off and regarded it suspiciously. "If you say so . . ."

"It is good to see you again, Old One," said Raistlin.

"I'm glad you got the chance," said Fizban, shaking hands. "Try not to get yourselves killed in this time, because that would really screw everything up."

He walked off through the wreckage, kicking at broken furniture and appearing to take a great deal of pride in the destruction. When he reached the door, Fizban stopped and turned to Raistlin.

"Always remember one thing, son."

"What is that, Old One?"

Fizban winked. "Wonderful spell, fireball."

And with a wave of his battered hat, he righted the tables and restored the chairs, repaired the broken crockery and shattered mugs and even filled them with ale. Fizban then put his hat on his head and disappeared.

CHAPTER

ELEVEN

Raistlin entered the kitchen to find Otik standing in the middle of the room, staring about in bafflement. Otik Sandeth, the proprietor of the Inn of the Last Home, was a portly man—a walking recommendation of his own good food and famous nut-brown ale. He was somewhat the worse for wear after having taken refuge behind the bar during the fracas.

"You should have seen it, Tika," Otik was saying. "First Kitiara kills that poor man, then a staff glows blue and brings him back to life, then a ball of fire flattens her and the inn almost falls out of the tree. Chairs and tables are all smashed and I come in here and find everything smashed and now it's not anymore. It's a miracle. I think I need to sit down."

Raistlin looked around. The kitchen of the Inn of the Last Home was lined with shelves that held stacks of crockery plates and bowls, mugs and cups, and cannisters filled with flour, sugar, and spices. He had heard the plates smashing on the floor and yet now nothing was broken.

"Miracle? Hah!" Tika sniffed as she flung open a window. She had soot in her hair and black smudges on her face. "We may have dishes again, but the food is ruined—my good beef stew covered in ashes and cinder. And the place will reek of smoke for a week."

She glared at Raistlin. "Did you have anything to do with this disaster?"

"I did not," said Raistlin emphatically. "I came to find out if the Plainsfolk got away safely."

"As far as I know," said Tika. "You can ask Tanis. He said he'd wait for you below. How's Caramon? I saw him carry Kit away over his shoulder. She was fit to be tied! I hope she won't be too mad at him."

"He saved her life," Raistlin said dryly. "Why should she be mad?"

"*She* won't see it that way," said Tika. She snatched up a dish towel and regarded it in disgust. "Look at this, Otik! That blasted Bakaris was back here, bleeding all over one of my best towels! I'll never get the stains out."

"Where is Bakaris?" Raistlin asked, suddenly remembering that Kit had banished him to the kitchen.

"He'd be in the Abyss if I had my way!" said Tika dourly. "He came stomping back here, going on about what he was going to do to Caramon if he caught him. I told him I'd wash out his mouth with soap if he didn't stop using such language. I don't know what happened to him after that."

Otik was sitting in a chair, finding consolation in a mug of his own ale. "Bakaris? When he heard the explosion and that old man shout 'Fire,' he bolted for the trapdoor and shinnied down the rope. I haven't seen him since."

"The coward likely ran back to camp," said Tika. "If you see Caramon, tell him I saved some apple pie for him." She paused to stare at Raistlin, who had walked over to the trapdoor. "What do you think you're doing?"

"I am going below to talk to Tanis," Raistlin replied.

"As if you could climb down a rope with those skinny arms of yours!" Tika scoffed. "Use the stairs—Wait! No! Don't jump! You'll break your neck!"

Raistlin ignored her. Calmly clasping the Staff of Magius, he stepped into the opening and drifted lightly to the ground. He looked back up at Tika and saluted her with the staff. She gave him a furious look and slammed the trapdoor shut, leaving him in darkness.

Raistlin spoke the word, "*Shirak,*" and the crystal globe atop his staff gave off a bright light.

"Raistlin," Tanis called. "Over here."

Raistlin went to meet him. "Did you see Bakaris?"

"The man Caramon punched in the nose?" Tanis asked. "No, why?"

"He came down here when he heard the old man yell 'Fire.' He might have been hanging around, and if he was here when you brought Goldmoon and Riverwind down—"

"He could have been watching us," Tanis admitted. "I didn't see him, but I did hear the sound of horses' hooves."

"There is nothing we can do about that now," said Raistlin. "Did Riverwind and Goldmoon get away safely?"

Tanis nodded. "They are in Flint's care, and he and Tas are going to guide them back to the old mill. I promised Flint I would catch up with them, so I cannot stay long."

He paused, frowning, studying Raistlin in the staff's light. "I see you are wearing the black robes."

"And what color robes do you think a wizard would be wearing in a world where Takhisis is queen?" Raistlin returned irritably. "If you do not trust me, Half-Elven, we part ways here and now."

"Forgive me, Raistlin, I wasn't thinking," said Tanis. "This world is . . . so strange. I can't get used to it. Why did you need to talk to me?"

"Takhisis knows the Graygem is here. She does not know where, but she is searching for it. Hederick told Kitiara. Fortunately, she didn't believe him, but Destina is in peril. She and Kairn should leave immediately."

"They were planning to," said Tanis. "But Destina is not well."

"Tas said she was poisoned by Tully's knife," said Raistlin. "Is that true or one of his tales?"

"It's true that Destina isn't well," said Tanis. "She is weak and dizzy and that wound on her neck has an ugly look about it."

"I should examine it myself," said Raistlin. "I have a magical journeying spell that can take me there swiftly."

"Could your magic take me and the Plainsfolk there?" Tanis asked.

Raistlin gave a derisive snort. "If you can persuade Riverwind and Goldmoon to step into a magical circle and listen to me chant strange words as Lunitari bathes us in red light and the magic whisks us through the ethers, then, yes, my magic can take us there at once."

"Sorry, stupid idea," said Tanis with a rueful smile. "You go ahead. Flint and Tas and I will follow with the Plainsfolk."

The trapdoor swung open and light from the kitchen shone down on them. Raistlin could see his brother's large body silhouetted against the light.

"Raist! Are you down there?" Caramon called.

"I am here. What do you want?" Raistlin called back.

Caramon caught hold of the rope and lowered himself down hand over hand. He dropped the last few feet and ran over.

"Tanis, you're here, too. We've got trouble," said Caramon. "That bastard Bakaris rode into camp and told Kit that Tanis was in the inn and that he was the one who helped Goldmoon and Riverwind escape. Kit is furious. She ordered Bakaris to send patrols to search the roads and she's planning to ride out on horseback to look for you herself."

"Does she know where we are bound?" Tanis asked.

Caramon shook his head. "She asked Bakaris, but he didn't know."

"That's good then," said Tanis. "We can take the forest trails, bypass the roads."

"You go with Flint and the others, Tanis," said Raistlin. "I will meet you at the house."

"Watch out for Bakaris, Tanis," Caramon cautioned. "He hates you and he wants you dead."

"Hates me?" Tanis asked, incredulous. "I never met the man! Why would he hate me?"

"Bakaris used to keep Kit warm at night, if you know what I mean," Caramon said with a lewd wink.

"Don't be disgusting!" Raistlin said.

"Sorry, Raist," said Caramon, contrite. "Kit made no secret of the fact she came to Solace to meet you, and Bakaris is mad with jealousy. He's not above sticking a knife in your ribs if he gets the chance."

"My brother is right, Tanis," Raistlin added. "Bakaris is just stupid enough to be dangerous."

Tanis shook his head in disbelief, then ran off and disappeared into the night.

"It's good to see Tanis again," Caramon reflected. "I wouldn't have recognized him with that beard, and neither did Kit, seemingly. Did you give him the information about the Emperor's Summit?"

"I didn't have the chance," said Raistlin. "We had more urgent matters to discuss. Does Kit suspect you and I are involved with helping the Plainsfolk escape?"

Caramon shook his head. "I don't think so. You know our sister. All she cares about is Tanis and how he made her look like a fool. What should we do? Who's this Destina?"

"Never mind that now," said Raistlin. "Go back to camp. Make yourself seen and heard. If anyone asks, you've been in camp since you brought Kit back."

"Where are you going?"

"Better you do not know, my brother. If I am caught, denounce me as a traitor. Tell Kit you had no idea I was involved with the rebels."

"I could never do that, Raist!" Caramon protested, shocked. "You know I couldn't!"

Raistlin did know and sighed inwardly. "Listen to me, Caramon. Our work is far too important for you to throw it away over silly sentimentality. Promise me you will do as I tell you. You will denounce me. You will say you have no brother. I am dead to you."

"But, Raist—" Caramon began unhappily.

"Promise me!" Raistlin said, his voice grating.

"All right, Raist, I promise," said Caramon. "Take care of yourself and drink your tea. I mix three pinches of those herbs with the hot water. If you add too much—"

"Just . . . go! Quickly!" Raistlin ordered.

He waited to make certain Caramon did as he was told, watching his brother walk disconsolately back toward the inn. Caramon hoisted himself up to the trapdoor. Tika shut it behind him and the light from the kitchen vanished.

Raistlin shone the staff's light on the ground, searching for a clear patch. The damp dirt smelled of hops and yeast. Finding what he sought near the fermentation vat, he scratched a circle in the mud, preparing to cast the journeying spell he had learned from Magius.

When the circle was complete, Raistlin took his place in the center, closed his eyes, and pictured his destination in his mind. Traveling to an unknown place was dangerous; he might find himself materializing inside a brick wall or at the bottom of a lake.

Fortunately, he was familiar with the old mill. As a young man growing up in Solace, he had made a study of herbs and their healing properties and, in the absence of clerics, he had used his knowledge to heal people. Hal Miller had sent for him to treat his baby, who suffered from croup.

Raistlin pictured himself once more standing in the main living chamber of the Miller house. He hoped fervently that the spell would work. He had studied it, but he had never before cast it—at least not in this life.

Magius had prayed to Lunitari when he cast the spell. Raistlin had also served that goddess. He had served all three gods of magic at one time or another in his life. He should probably ask Nuitari for his blessing, for he was wearing the black robes, but, like Magius, Raistlin turned instead to the goddess of the red moon. She had always favored him, even after he had taken the black robes in his other life. He hoped she still viewed him with tolerant affection in this one.

The red moon was almost lost among the blazing stars of the constellation of Takhisis. Raistlin had to search for Lunitari and finally found her—a pale red shadow of herself. He invoked her blessing and her faint light seemed to touch him, burnishing his golden skin with warm radiance.

He spoke the language of magic, hearing Magius's voice in his mind. *"Triga bulan ber satuan/Seluran asil/Tempat samah terus-menarus/Walktun jalanil!"*

Magic swirled around Raistlin, lifted him up, and carried him away.

CHAPTER
TWELVE

Raistlin found himself where he had pictured himself—in the main living chamber of the Miller house. He turned to see Kairn staring at him in shock and fear, and reaching for his staff.

"No need to attack me, Brother Kairn!" Raistlin said quickly. "I am sorry I startled you."

"Raistlin!" Kairn sighed in relief. "You frightened me half to death!"

"I had to travel the paths of magic," said Raistlin. "Where is Destina? Tas said she has been poisoned."

"She is lying down in the bedchamber," said Kairn.

"How is Sturm?" Raistlin asked, though he had no need to hear the answer.

The knight lay on a bloodstained pallet near the fire, and Raistlin could see for himself that Sturm was barely clinging to life. He was pale and gaunt, his eyes sunken and his breathing labored. He was unconscious, oblivious to everything, even the pain that wracked his body.

"Can you help him?" Kairn asked.

Raistlin shook his head. "Only the gods can help him now. But I might be able to help Destina."

Kairn picked up the lantern and led Raistlin to one of the bedchambers in the back. Destina lay on the bed, covered with a blanket. She was shivering. Her eyes were closed, but when Raistlin touched her gently, she stirred and stared at him in confusion.

"Raistlin! What are you doing here?"

"I came to warn you. Takhisis knows the Graygem is in Solace," said Raistlin.

"But how could she?" Destina asked, dismayed.

"I can only surmise that the Dark Queen followed us here. Her cleric, the High Theocrat, Hederick, provided Kitiara with an accurate description of you and ordered Kit to keep watch."

"We should leave before she finds us," said Destina. She tried to sit up, but she was too weak and sank back in the bed.

"Our cause will not be helped if you go back in time to die," said Raistlin. "I am going to examine the wound on your neck. Kairn, bring that lantern over and hold the light for me."

"It stings, that's all," Destina murmured.

Kairn shone the lantern on her neck as Raistlin tilted her head back to obtain a better view. He could see the Graygem hanging on its gold chain around her throat. The gem was dark, subdued, appearing to be nothing but a very ugly rock. Yet he knew it was aware of him. Raistlin was careful not to touch it.

"How is she?" Kairn asked in a low voice.

"Tanis was right. Tully's blade must have been poisoned," said Raistlin, studying the inflamed and festering wound. "Fortunately, he barely nicked her. Where is the well?"

"Around back. But we have water here. Are you sure she will be all right?" Kairn asked anxiously.

"The cut is little more than a scratch, and I can treat it. But even this tiny amount of poison has sickened her. She would already be dead if the knife had gone deeper. Hand me that bowl on the table. I seem to remember the Millers had a root cellar, though I don't recall where to find the entrance. Hal Miller used to distill his own brandy and store it down there."

"Brandy?" Kairn asked, troubled.

"Don't worry, Brother. I am not going to drown my sorrows in strong drink. I need it for medicinal purposes."

"I think the root cellar must be near the well," said Kairn, handing over the crockery bowl. "Flint complained that he almost fell into the cellar when he fetched the water. Do you need the lantern?"

"I have my staff," said Raistlin.

Once outside, Raistlin spoke the command, "*Shirak*," and the globe atop the staff began to glow, lighting his way as he walked to the back of the house. He found the door to the cellar standing wide open—a hazard to anyone coming to fetch water. The cellar extended underneath the house and was large and spacious. He noticed that the wooden stairs leading down into the cellar were cracked and rickety and he trod on them with care, shining his light ahead of him. He found the jugs of brandy still lined up neatly against a wall near the entrance.

Removing the cork from one of the jugs, he sniffed. His nose wrinkled at the smell of the fumes rising from the jug. Hal's brandy had not lost its potency. Raistlin picked up one of the jugs and carried it up the stairs.

He closed the cellar door, so that no one would later take a tumble, then located the well. As he had hoped, the ground around it was wet and muddy. He placed the brandy jug on the ground and began to concoct his potion. He drew the small knife from the thong on his wrist, jabbed the blade into the damp soil, and scooped mud into the basin. When the bowl was about half full, he searched for the herb garden and found it near the kitchen.

The garden had gone wild and was overgrown with weeds, but he managed to find the herbs, dittany and pennyroyal. He plucked some leaves of each, crushed them, and stirred them into the mud. He mixed in some other herbs from his pouches, poured a large measure of the brandy into the mixture, then carried the bowl back to his patient.

Raistlin propped the Staff of Magius against the fireplace and handed Kairn the bowl.

"Hold this for me," he instructed.

Kairn regarded the lump of mud dubiously. "What are you going to do with this?"

"It is a remedy from the old days," said Raistlin. "Before there were clerics, people used it to treat bites from venomous snakes. It should also work to draw the poison from this wound."

He sat on the side of the bed and uncorked the jug. The strong smell of brandy filled the air. He poured some in a mug and held it to Destina's lips.

"Drink this."

Destina sipped the brandy and coughed as the liquid bit into her throat.

"Good," said Raistlin, assisting her to lie back down. "I fear this will burn."

He sloshed some of the brandy liberally over the wound. Destina gasped in pain and started to put her hand to the wound.

"No, don't touch it!" Raistlin ordered. "Brother Kairn, bring me the potion."

Raistlin dipped his fingers into the mud and gently daubed the mixture on Destina's neck.

The cool mud must have felt soothing, for Destina faintly smiled.

"That does feel good," she said.

"Is the remedy magical?" Kairn asked.

Raistlin shook his head. "I made a study of herbs when I was young. Hand me the bandages you used for Sturm."

Raistlin cleansed the mud from his hands, then dressed the wound. Destina closed her eyes as he worked, and he saw the lines of pain on her face start to ease.

"Will she be all right?" Kairn asked, regarding her in concern.

"I think so," said Raistlin. "She was fortunate. Very little poison got into her system. We should let her rest."

He glanced at the Graygem that hung from a chain around her neck and saw it flicker with a gray light. Kairn drew the blanket over Destina and he and Raistlin left the room, closing the door behind them.

"A good night's sleep should help. We will see how she is in the—"

Raistlin was interrupted by the burning sensation in his chest. He began to cough and dropped down into a chair, groping for his handkerchief. He pressed it over his mouth.

"Can I do anything?" Kairn asked.

"Hot water!" Raistlin gasped without a voice.

Kairn hurried to the kitchen to fetch a mug and filled it with hot water from the kettle on the hob. He handed the mug to Raistlin, who drew out a pouch and shook some of the herbs into it, not bothering to measure "three pinches" as Caramon had instructed.

He sipped the tea and the spasm eased. Kairn roamed restlessly about the room, peeping in at Destina, going to the window, pacing the floor.

"You should get some sleep, Brother," Raistlin advised when he could talk. "I will keep watch. It would not hurt you to drink some of that brandy. Or I could always cast a sleep spell on you."

"Thank you, no," said Kairn hastily. "One of those was enough." He sat down in a chair and gave a bleak sigh. "You said the Graygem would not let Destina die."

"It won't . . . unless it has finished with her," said Raistlin. "Be hopeful, Brother. The Graygem does not want Takhisis to find it. Strangely enough, we must rely on Chaos to save us."

Kairn did not answer. His eyes were closed, his head slumped. He had fallen asleep.

Raistlin sipped his tea and stared into the flames of the dying fire. His thoughts went to his brother and, oddly, to a conversation he'd had with Tasslehoff after the Graygem had restored him to life and transported him and the others back through time.

"Caramon still talks about you, even after you were dead," Tas had told him. "Tika scolds him when he does and says you aren't worth him making himself unhappy. But Caramon only shakes his head and goes really quiet and walks off."

"Caramon was a fool to care!" Raistlin had said to himself then, and he said the same thing to himself now.

"You could tell him you're sorry," Tas had said.

A log in the fireplace crumbled, sending up a shower of sparks. Raistlin did not replace it.

The room was hot to suffocating, as it was.

CHAPTER
THIRTEEN

Tanis had walked this path that led to the mill in daylight
and darkness, but he scarcely recognized it now that some
of the vallenwoods had been cut down. Once he would have
looked up to see the enormous trees towering over him, their sheltering boughs forming a canopy above him. Now he looked up
through the interlacing limbs of oaks, maples, and walnut trees, and
they were stark and bare, their leaves rotting on the ground. The stars
of the Dark Queen's constellation shone so brightly they cast shadows, lighting the way for Kitiara's patrols.

Tanis hoped he could elude her, even though he was on foot and
she was on horseback. He had the advantage of knowing where Flint
and the others were bound, whereas Kit would have to search the
entire countryside to find them.

Tanis paused beneath an oak tree to get his bearings. Planning to
use the red star of Reorx as a guide, he looked up through the
branches and was dismayed to see a dragon, its scales gleaming blue
in the cold and glaring light.

Tanis recognized Kit's dragon, Skie, and he swore softly. Kit had
brought reinforcements to help in the search. Dragons had night

vision, which meant that Skie could see his prey in the darkness. The leaves that might have shielded Tanis from the dragon's sight lay moldering on the ground.

Tanis increased his pace, hoping to find his friends before Skie spotted them. He heard them long before he saw them. Flint's armor rattled and jingled as he stomped through the leaves, and Tasslehoff was telling Goldmoon and Riverwind about the time the two Plains-folk had traveled with the Heroes of the Lance to Pax Tharkas and how Goldmoon had healed Elistan and he had been able to read the Disks of Mishakal and this had all happened in the past that might or might not be the future.

Tanis could only imagine what the Plainsfolk were thinking. Nomads who roamed the grasslands of Abanasinia, Goldmoon and Riverwind had undoubtedly had few dealings with kender. River-wind was already distrustful of them, and Tas's tales about past futures and future pasts would not help. Tanis's foreboding proved correct, for he reached the group in time to hear Riverwind arguing with Flint.

"We will travel faster on our own," Riverwind was insisting.

"Not if you don't know where you're going," Flint stated. "And what about Sturm? He's badly hurt, and we were hoping the lady and her staff could heal him."

"They did help us escape, Riverwind," Goldmoon said. "Their friend is dying. We should try to save him."

"They *claim* this person is dying," said Riverwind dourly.

"Are you calling me a liar?" Flint bristled.

"Quiet!" Tas warned. "I hear something. Someone's out there!"

Flint raised his axe and Riverwind drew his sword. Both turned to face the threat, argument forgotten.

"It's me!" Tanis called, hurrying to join them. "You can put your weapons away."

"About time," Flint grumbled, lowering his axe. "Where've you been?"

"Talking to Caramon. Kitiara found out we helped Goldmoon and Riverwind escape and she's looking for us," said Tanis. "Draco-nians are patrolling the highway and Kit has her dragon hunting for us from the air."

He cast a grim glance up through the branches. They could clearly see Skie flying low over the treetops, searching the ground below. As they watched, the dragon went into a steep dive, seeming to fly right toward them.

"Look out!" Tanis warned. "Get down!"

He dragged Flint and Tas to the ground. Riverwind put his arm around Goldmoon and the two crouched in the shadows at the base of a tree. A bolt of lightning struck not far from them. Thunder crashed, and they heard falling branches and the crackle of flames.

"He missed us!" Goldmoon breathed thankfully.

"He wasn't trying to hit us," said Flint, getting to his feet. "That was a signal. The dragon's just told every draco within ten miles where to find us. Now what do we do? If we head for the mill, we'll lead Kit and her dragon straight to our friends."

"But we have to go to the mill! We have to save Sturm!" said Tasslehoff. "He can't die now because this is the wrong past, and in the right past he has to fight Kitiara at the High Clerist's Tower to give Laurana and I the chance to use the dragon orb."

"Huh?" said Flint, staring at the kender.

"Just keep going," said Tanis, urging them down the trail. "We have a good head start, and we know these woods and they don't. Hopefully we will lose them."

They tried to find cover in the meager shadows of the bare trees, but Tanis soon realized that their situation was hopeless. Skie was flying in lazy circles above them, keeping an eye on them. Flint's strength was flagging. Goldmoon and Riverwind trudged on gamely, but it was clear they were exhausted. Even Tasslehoff drooped, dragging his hoopak, too tired to tell any more stories.

Suddenly Flint gave a prodigious sneeze.

"Horse!" he exclaimed.

Tanis could hear muffled hoofbeats galloping up from behind them, and he turned to see Kitiara astride a black horse, bearing down on them. She was accompanied by two Bozaks, who loped along at her side, keeping up by using their wings to hop and glide over the ground.

Tanis halted and turned to face her. Riverwind drew his sword and stood in front of Goldmoon. Flint grabbed his axe from his harness, and Tas plucked his knife from his belt and looked very fierce. Tanis did not draw his sword, but he put his hand on the hilt.

Kitiara reined in her mount and leaned over the pommel. Her lips parted in the crooked smile that Tanis had once found irresistible.

"Hello, Tanis," she said pleasantly. "Bakaris told me you were in the inn. I must have missed you in all the excitement. If you and your friends will put down your weapons, no one will get hurt. As you see, my Bozaks are well armed, and they are spoiling for a fight."

Flint snorted. "If your lizards want my axe, they'll have to take it."

"I could put down Goblinslayer, but it will come right back to me," said Tas, flourishing his knife.

Riverwind did not relinquish his sword. Goldmoon joined him, standing beside him, holding the Staff of Mishakal.

Kit was amused. "Your weapons are useless. Have you ever seen Bozaks cast their magic? Their spells can burn the flesh from your bones."

Tanis unbuckled his sword belt and tossed it onto the ground. "We should do as she says."

Goldmoon said something to Riverwind in their own language. He glowered and threw his sword to the ground. Flint glared at Kit but, after a moment's hesitation, laid down his axe. Tasslehoff dropped his hoopak.

"And the knife, Tas," said Kitiara.

"But I told you," said Tas. "Goblinslayer is magic and it will just come back to me. I'll save you the trouble of taking it, because you'll only lose it again."

Kitiara shifted impatiently in the saddle.

Tanis rested his hand on the kender's shoulder. "Drop the knife, Tas."

Tasslehoff sighed and tossed the knife down beside Flint's axe.

Kitiara eyed Goldmoon. "The staff, as well, lady."

"My staff is not a weapon," said Goldmoon.

"Take it from her," Kitiara ordered the draconians.

One of the Bozaks grinned, revealing razor-sharp teeth, and walked toward Goldmoon.

Goldmoon faced the draconian. She was pale but defiant, keeping fast hold of the staff.

"Seize it!" Kit said impatiently.

The Bozak reached out its clawed hand to take the staff.

"I wouldn't do that if I were you," Tas advised.

The Bozak snarled and grabbed hold of the staff. The moment he touched it, blue lightning sizzled around the draconian's claws and traveled up his arm. The Bozak shrieked in pain and dropped the staff.

"No one listens to me," said Tas sadly.

Kitiara stared at the staff, her brow furrowed. "It did the same to Hederick. How do you work such magic, lady?"

"I didn't do anything," said Goldmoon. "I didn't know the staff would harm either of them."

"I did!" Tas said, raising his hand. "I tried to warn him!"

Kit swung herself down out of the saddle and walked over to inspect the staff that lay amid the dead leaves. The staff's blue light had faded. It looked like an ordinary walking staff.

"You pick it up, Tanis," Kitiara said. She smiled, perhaps expecting to see him balk or hesitate. "Bring it to me."

Tanis took hold of the staff, but he did not take it to Kitiara. He handed it back to Goldmoon.

"Why didn't the staff fry you?" Kit demanded.

"Never mind about the staff. Let my friends go, Kit," Tanis told her. "I am the one you want."

Kitiara laughed. "You certainly do think well of yourself." She walked over to stand in front of him and ran her hand over his face. "I do like the beard, though. It hides those weak elf features of yours."

Tanis drew back from her touch.

Kitiara regarded him with amusement. "Don't tell me you are still mad at me? After all these years?"

"You damn near got us killed!" Flint said angrily. "You were the one who told Verminaard where to find us."

Kitiara shrugged. "I did it for your own good, old dwarf. Verminaard was closing in on you and your little band of rebels. The way I see it, I saved your lives. After that near miss, you had the good sense to leave town."

Kitiara leaned back against a tree trunk and crossed her arms over her chest, settling herself comfortably. "I have a proposition for you, Tanis. I want you to be my lieutenant, my second-in-command. Do that for me, and your friends are free to go to the Abyss for all I care."

"You can't do that, Kit!" a man's voice shouted from the shadows of the trees. "You promised me!"

At the sound of a horse crashing recklessly through the brush, the Bozaks both reached for their curved-bladed swords.

"It's only Bakaris," Kit said, exasperated. "Put away your weapons."

Bakaris rode into view. He cast Tanis a baleful glance, then turned to Kitiara. "You can't make that half-human your lieutenant! You promised that promotion to me! It's mine!"

"What are you doing here, Bakaris?" Kitiara asked. "Were you following me? I ordered you to stay in camp."

"I was in camp when a messenger arrived from Dragon Highlord Verminaard," said Bakaris sullenly, talking through his swollen nose. "Toede told him you were here in Solace and Verminaard is angry. He demands to know what you are doing in his territory."

Bakaris slid down off his horse. "I came to warn you. I told you there would be trouble."

"So Toede ran to daddy to complain about me," said Kit, her lip curling. "Ride back and tell the messenger I'll speak with him shortly."

"Send your new lieutenant," said Bakaris, glaring at Tanis.

"Perhaps I will," Kitiara said, annoyed. She turned to smile at Tanis. "Come back to camp with me. After I get rid of Verminaard's lackey, you and I can discuss your promotion over a jug of dwarf spirits."

"Release my friends, Kit," said Tanis. "Call off your dragon and send away your Bozaks. Then I will come with you. But not as your lieutenant. I won't serve your Dark Queen."

Kitiara struck him across the face.

"Let's see how boldly you talk when I hang you and ship your friends off to the mines. You Bozaks, cast a web spell on all of them. Bind them up good. Bakaris, you may as well make yourself useful.

Confiscate that staff and, once the prisoners are bound, escort them back to camp."

"With pleasure," said Bakaris. As he started to remount his horse, Kitiara grabbed hold of him by the back of his breeches and yanked him off. Bakaris landed on the ground.

"What'd you do that for?" he asked, aggrieved.

"I'm taking your horse," Kitiara said, pulling herself up into the saddle. "Mine is going lame."

"But what will I do?" Bakaris demanded. "How will I get back to camp?"

"Walk," said Kitiara coolly. "And do not ever challenge me again!"

She looked up at Skie, put her fingers to her lips, and gave a piercing whistle. Skie spread his wings, veered off, and disappeared into the darkness. Kit rode away on Bakaris's horse, leading her own horse by the reins. Tanis could see no sign that her horse was limping.

Bakaris waited until Kitiara had ridden out of sight, then he picked up the two swords and Flint's axe and hurled the weapons into the brush.

Tanis and Flint exchanged glances. The Bozaks were preparing to cast their web spells that would bind them in cobweb like a spider binds a fly. Once they were bound and helpless, the draconians would drag them back to camp. Flint edged his way closer to a large tree branch lying on the ground. Riverwind was reaching stealthily toward his boot and Tasslehoff was frantically searching his pockets, probably looking for Goblinslayer. Goldmoon stood calmly beside Riverwind, holding the staff.

The Bozaks extended their clawed hands.

"Stop!" Bakaris ordered. "I want to speak to the prisoner."

He swaggered over to Tanis and stood looking him up and down, with contempt. "I don't know what she sees in you."

The Bozaks chortled. "Whatever it is, Bakaris, apparently she doesn't see it in you," said one, grinning.

"You should be nice to Lieutenant Half-Elf," said the other. "Soon he'll be giving you orders!"

Bakaris flushed in anger and drew his sword from its sheath. "Go ahead and web them. Take the staff and haul these four back to camp, but leave the half-human with me. I'll tell the Highlord he died while trying to escape."

"You're going to kill him while he's bound up in cobwebs?" said one of the Bozaks, sneering. "You're a real hero, Bakaris."

"You damn lizards do as I tell you!" Bakaris shouted, rounding on them in outrage. "I'm in command here!"

"We obey Highlord Kitiara," said one. "Her orders are to bring *all* the prisoners back to her, and that's what we intend to do."

Flint gave a roar, picked up the tree branch, and ran toward the Bozaks. Tanis grabbed a knife from his belt. Riverwind drew a knife from his boot, and they both charged after the dwarf. Tasslehoff dashed behind them, triumphantly waving Goblinslayer and shouting, "I told you it would come back!"

Thick strands of sticky cobweb shot from the Bozaks' talons. Goldmoon raised the staff, as a warrior raises a spear, and called out in her own language. A halo of shimmering blue light enveloped Tanis and the others. The magical strands of cobweb dried up and fluttered away.

Bakaris squinted against the blinding blue light.

"Kill them, you fools!" he was raving. "Kill them all!"

The Bozaks started to draw their swords, then one suddenly pitched forward and landed face-first on the ground. The other Bozak fell on top of him. Both were dead, arrows protruding from their backs. Tanis was staring at them in astonishment when he saw the Bozaks' scaly flesh dwindle and wither.

"I always get draconian death throes mixed up," Tasslehoff was saying, observing the dead Bozaks with interest. "Do Bozaks turn to stone, dissolve into pools of acid, or—"

"Their bones explode, you doorknob!" Flint yelled. "Take cover!"

Tanis grabbed Tas and pulled him to the ground. Flint flopped down belly-first beside them and covered his head and Riverwind and Goldmoon ducked behind a tree. The bodies of the draconians blew up, peppering them with shards of sharp bone, scales, and fragments of armor.

Tanis did not forget that someone had killed the Bozaks, and he hurriedly scrambled to his feet to face the new danger. He saw the forest appear to be on the move, trees and brush shifting and undulating. Parts of the forest detached themselves from the whole, and Tanis saw they were surrounded by elves, holding bows in their hands.

The elves were perfectly camouflaged; their clothes, their hair, and their skin were painted with the browns and greens of an autumn forest. Their leader was a woman, who signaled the others to keep to the trees while she came forward.

Tanis stared at her, so astonished he could not move or speak.

Tasslehoff waved his hand in the air. "Hey, Laurana! It's me! Tas!"

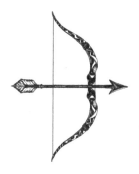

CHAPTER
FOURTEEN

Laurana ignored the kender, glanced at Tanis without recognition, and came to stand in front of Flint. At her signal, the other elves had lowered their bows but kept their arrows nocked, clearly distrustful.

"Are you Flint Fireforge?" Laurana asked the dwarf.

"Maybe I am and maybe I'm not," said Flint, his bushy brows drawing together. "Who's asking?"

"My elven name is Lauralanthalasa," she replied, smiling. "When I was a little girl, you said my name was bigger than I was. You used to visit Qualinesti when I was young. Your fine jewelry is valued to this day. But I remember most the toys. You carved a unicorn for me—"

"Laurana!" Flint gasped, flushing with pleasure. "No wonder I didn't recognize you! You were a child the last time I saw you."

"As you see, I am not a child anymore," said Laurana, and she sounded regretful.

Tasslehoff hurried forward to introduce himself. Wiping his hand on his vest, he held it out to her.

"Hullo, Laurana. I'm Tasslehoff Burrfoot. You don't know me

now, but you will in the future that's the past. I found a dragon orb, you see, and you and I used it to kill the evil dragons that were attacking the High Clerist's Tower. You can call me Tas. Everyone does. And that's Tanis, but, of course, you know him because he's your husband."

Laurana stared at Tasslehoff in wonder, then shifted her startled gaze to Tanis. She studied him intently, as though trying to place him.

"Tanthalas," she said at last. "I would not have recognized you."

Tanis was at a loss for words. She was the same Laurana he had married, the same Laurana he loved more than his life. She was tall and lithe with sun-burnished skin, almond-shaped eyes, and delicate features. But this Laurana had put walnut stain in her blond hair to turn it brown to blend in with the wilderness. She was wearing brown leather breeches and a green-and-russet tunic. Her clothes were worn and rumpled and mud-spattered, as though she was accustomed to sleeping rough. Her boots were scuffed and dirty. She carried a pack on her back, as did the other elves.

"It's good to see you, Laurana," he said at last, lamely.

She regarded him with frowning displeasure. "The kender called you Tanis. So now you have a human name. You hide behind a human beard and you are friends with that Dragon Highlord, Kitiara. I remember hearing about her. She's the woman you used to love."

Tanis was mired in confusion. He tried to concentrate only on this world and not think of the world he had left behind. Yet the Laurana of that world, his beloved wife, and the Laurana of this world were hopelessly entangled in his mind. Add to that the fact that he had no idea what he had done or said to this Laurana or what they had been to each other in this world, and he was left floundering on the banks of the River of Time.

Flint came to his rescue.

"And what's wrong with a beard?" Flint demanded, proudly stroking his own long, white beard, which flowed down his chest. "As for Kitiara, Tanis may have been friendly with her once, a long time ago, but he came to his senses. And speaking of Kit," Flint continued, turning to Tanis, "where is that Bakaris fellow? The last I saw of him, he was yelling at his dracos to kill us."

"Bakaris? Do you mean that human who was with the Highlord?" Laurana asked. "He saw us and took to his heels. Some of my warriors went after him."

"If you find him, put an arrow in him," said Flint.

Laurana smiled at him. "I think the beard looks good on *you*, old friend." She glanced pointedly at Tanis and then shifted her attention to Goldmoon and Riverwind.

"You are Plainsfolk and far from home. What brings you to Solace? And I am curious about this staff. How did you come by it? And how did you perform the miracle? Are you wizards?"

Riverwind frowned and said something to Goldmoon in their own language.

"They saved our lives, I believe that gives them the right to ask questions of us," Goldmoon replied with a faint smile. "A woman more beautiful than the dawn gave the staff to Riverwind. The miracles are hers. I am but the bearer of her gift."

Tas helpfully clarified. "She means Mishakal. The woman who gave Riverwind the staff was a god. At least, that's how the song goes. I can sing some of it if you want—"

"Mishakal!" Laurana repeated, ignoring the kender. "Do you mean Quen Illumini?"

"I am sorry," said Goldmoon. "I do not understand."

"Quen Illumini is the name of the goddess Mishakal in the language of the Qualinesti," Tanis explained.

"How do you know these people?" Riverwind asked, regarding Tanis with suspicion.

"These people are *my* people," Tanis replied. "My mother was Qualinesti. I was born and raised among the elves. And we are all on the same side in this war against the Dark Queen. You are among friends."

But no one was looking friendly. Riverwind was dour and mistrustful, and the elves were muttering among themselves. One said something to Laurana in their language and pointed to the staff.

Laurana responded, then turned back to Goldmoon. "My warriors do not believe the staff came from Mishakal because the goddess fled the world centuries ago. And if she has returned, they wonder why she would make herself known to humans, when all know the elves are Paladine's chosen people. They maintain the staff must be magic. Some want me to take it from you."

"I will never give it up!" Goldmoon said, her eyes flashing.

"You have no right to take it!" Riverwind stated angrily.

"I know that and so I told them, but they still have questions. And so do I," said Laurana. "I suggest that you come with us to our homeland, Qualinesti. My father is Solostaran, Speaker of the Sun. I would like him to hear your story and see this miraculous staff. As you have witnessed, traveling on your own is not safe. We can offer you our protection on the journey."

"But Goldmoon can't go to Qualinesti!" Tas protested. "She and Riverwind are coming with us to heal our friend Sturm. He's dying, and he already died once and that was the saddest day of my life. I don't think I could bear it if he died again."

"What is the kender talking about?" Laurana asked, turning to Tanis. "Who is this friend?"

"Sturm is a Knight of Solamnia," Tanis explained. "He was badly wounded, and it is our hope that Goldmoon and the Staff of Mishakal have the healing power to save him."

"Sturm ..." Laurana repeated. "I remember now. He was your friend when you were living in Solace. He was part of the resistance. Was he in the uprising in Solamnia? We heard about the rebellion, and we honored the knights for their courage, especially since they had no hope of winning. Where is he?"

"Not far," said Tanis. "He and our other friends have taken refuge in the abandoned mill. We have already lost valuable time trying to reach him, so we need to be on our way."

Laurana conferred again briefly with her warriors, and this time, she spoke Common so that Goldmoon and Riverwind and the others could understand.

"A Solamnic Knight is badly wounded, and they believe this woman, Goldmoon, can heal him. I will go with them to learn more about these miracles. Seiveril, return to camp and tell the dragon, Saber, what has happened and where we are going. Tell the dragon to meet us at the mill. And warn him there is a blue dragon in the vicinity. The rest of you, scout ahead to the mill. Keep watch for enemy patrols and for that human, Bakaris. He may be out there somewhere."

The elves melted into the woods, moving through the trees with less sound than the gentle night breeze that stirred the leaves.

"I will accompany you to the mill," said Laurana. "I know a shortcut. We should keep to the cover of the trees. The Highlord has goblin patrols searching for you. After we help this knight, I hope you will consider what I said about traveling to Qualinesti."

"We do thank you for saving our lives," said Riverwind, though he sounded grudging. "But where our road takes us after that, we do not know."

"You are both weary," said Laurana pleasantly. "We will discuss this later."

She led the way through the forest, and Tanis fell into step beside her, as he had done so often. Riverwind and Goldmoon followed, and Flint brought up the rear. Tasslehoff attached himself to Laurana.

"Do you remember me?" Tas asked. "You remember Sturm and Flint and Tanis—"

"I do seem to recall Tanis speaking of a kender friend," said Laurana, smiling. "Especially in regard to other people's belongings which always seemed to end up being your belongings."

"It's sad the way I have to go around picking up after people," said Tas, nodding. "They're extremely careless. But what I really want to talk about is that I heard you mention a dragon named Saber. *I* know a copper dragon named Saber and I'm wondering if he's the same dragon? I can tell you how Saber and I met even though we haven't yet."

"Perhaps some other time," said Laurana. "I need to talk to Tanthalas."

"What about?" Tas asked with interest, preparing to join in.

"I would like to talk to him *in private*," said Laurana.

"You mean you want to talk to him about stuff married people talk about," Tas said wisely. "I know, because I was married once myself—even though Raistlin says I wasn't. I'll go talk to Flint. We have lots of catching up to do. We haven't seen each other since he died."

Tas dashed off to join Flint. Tanis noted that the dwarf was too tired to even grumble at the kender, and he hoped Laurana was right when she said they were taking a shortcut. None of them could keep going for much longer.

"What did Tas mean about you and I being married?" Laurana asked.

"You know kender. Always telling tales," said Tanis, hoping she would leave it at that.

"He sounded very certain," said Laurana. "Did you tell your friends about us? Did you tell them I asked you to marry me and that you spurned me?"

"No, of course not!" Tanis said, startled. "I haven't told them anything. What happened between us was . . . uh . . . a long time ago."

"Two years is not a long time, even for humans," Laurana returned. "If you have forgotten, I will remind you. I asked you to marry me, and you refused. You called me a pampered child who knew nothing of the world. You said that love could not endure in a time of darkness. Now do you remember?"

Tanis did not remember, of course. But he could picture himself saying those words.

"I spoke without thinking," he replied. "I am sorry."

"On the contrary, you were right," Laurana said coolly. "When my father refused to join you and your friends in your fight against the Dragon Queen, you left in anger, and I could not blame you. Did you know the reason why he would not let our people fight?"

"I assumed it was because I was the one asking," said Tanis. "Your father never had any love for me."

"I wish it was that simple. I am ashamed to tell you the truth," said Laurana in a low voice. "I discovered my father had made a secret bargain with the Dragon Queen. He would keep Qualinesti out of the war and, in return, she would agree not to attack us."

"He was doing his duty as Speaker," said Tanis. "Protecting his people."

"It is his duty to lead our people in a war against evil," said Laurana. "I warned him that Takhisis would betray him. Sooner or later, she would turn on him. I told him that I would fight the battle if he would not."

Tanis could see again his Laurana, the Golden General, leading her troops in battle against the Dark Queen's forces. She had worn armor then, not a leather tunic. But her courage and resolve were the same.

"My father said that if I chose to join the resistance, I would have to leave Qualinesti," Laurana was saying. "He feared I would put our people in danger. I asked for volunteers, and there were many who believed as I did. My army is small, but we do what we can. We attack the goblins guarding Verminaard's slave caravans and free the slaves. We disrupt supply lines. We strike the enemy at night and harass them by day."

"Have you gone back to Qualinesti?" Tanis asked.

Laurana shook her head. "I would not be welcome."

"Yet you asked the Plainsfolk to come to Qualinesti with you."

"Because of the miracle of Mishakal's staff," said Laurana. "I was thinking I could convince my father that the old gods had not abandoned us."

"I am sorry you two are estranged," said Tanis. "You and your father were very close."

"I have thought about you a lot since you left, Tanthalas. I wondered where you were, if you were safe."

"I was wrong about love not enduring in a time of darkness," said Tanis. "Look at the two Plainsfolk. Love such as theirs shines the brightest in the darkness. Such love will save the world from evil."

"Personally, I put more trust in arrows than love," said Laurana, smiling. "But then, you always were a romantic."

Tanis returned her smile. Laurana tried to slip her hand into his, but he drew back with the confused feeling that, by having feelings for Laurana, he was being unfaithful to Laurana.

She angrily snatched her hand away. "Are you still involved with that human woman, Kitiara?"

"I am not!" Tanis answered emphatically. "When my friends and I left Solace, we agreed to reunite in five years' time. We did not know then that she was the one who betrayed us. I had no idea she would come to the reunion. She asked me to join the Dark Queen's army, but given that you were hiding in the woods, spying on us, you must have heard her. And if you heard, you know I refused."

"I did hear," said Laurana. "We have been keeping watch on Kitiara Uth Matar. She was the Dragon Highlord who crushed the uprising in Solamnia. Kitiara and her evil dragons swept across the land. The knights had no weapons that could slay the dragons, and they were slaughtered."

Tanis thought about Brother Kairn referring to Nuitari's riddle. *The answer is there. Or rather, the answer is* not *there. The knights had no weapons that could kill dragons and the dragons slaughtered them. They had no dragonlances.*

"Have you ever heard of a magical weapon called a dragonlance? It is blessed by the gods and can kill evil dragons," said Tanis.

"You must mean the dragonlances in the old song *Huma's Lament*," said Laurana. "The song tells how a silver dragon brought the dragonlances to Huma during the Third Dragon War. He and the silver dragon both died at the hands of an assassin. The Knights lost the war, and Takhisis has ruled the world ever since."

"What happened to the dragonlances?" Tanis asked.

"The Dragon Queen discovered the dragonlances when she captured the High Clerist's Tower. She tried to destroy them, but they were protected by Paladine. She sealed them inside the tower and posted undead warriors and one of her dragons to guard it. We heard the knights had mounted an assault on the tower in order to obtain the dragonlances when the Dragon Highlord attacked, but they perished."

"Where are the silver dragons and the other dragons loyal to the gods of good?" Tanis asked.

"According to Saber, the Dragon Queen stole their eggs and promised to leave them unharmed if the good dragons would leave the world. Many of them retreated to the Dragon Isles, but Saber and some other dragons remained. They discovered that Takhisis had perverted the eggs and used foul magicks to turn them into draconians."

"Do the other good dragons know?" Tanis asked.

"Saber says his friend Silvara told them. She is a silver dragon who stayed here to keep watch. According to Saber, the dragons are divided. Some want to hide in safety in the Dragon Isles to protect what they have. Others want to return to declare war on the Dragon Queen. That is why we fight, and if the Plainsfolk speak the truth about Quen Illumini, it seems the gods are now prepared to fight with us. Will you join us?"

Tanis gave the question thoughtful consideration. If Kairn and Destina were successful in changing time, he would return to his other world and never know of this one. But if the two failed in their attempt and he was left stranded in the River's dark waters, he could at least carry on the battle against evil he had started so long ago, even though that was in another world, another time.

Tanis reached out and took hold of Laurana's hand. She was the same Laurana in all worlds, in all times.

"I will fight," said Tanis.

CHAPTER
FIFTEEN

If Bakaris had been plain-looking, he might have grown up to be a better man. But as it happened, the gods cursed him with a handsome face. From his doting mother, he learned that her "beautiful boy" could rely on his good looks to get what he wanted, and his soldier father had taught him that if his looks failed him, brute force could make up the shortfall.

Life had reinforced Bakaris's excellent opinion of himself. He had joined the Blue Dragonarmy at eighteen as a yeoman, and had flattered and schemed his way up through the ranks. He avoided fighting when possible, and if he couldn't avoid being thrown into battle, he would immediately suffer some convenient injury and limp back to the rear.

Bakaris knew how to add charm to his good looks. Women liked the handsome soldier, and he carried on numerous dalliances, deserting his lovers when he grew tired of them. To his mind, every woman should consider herself lucky he bestowed his attentions on her.

But then he met Kitiara Uth Matar. Bakaris was enamored of

her at first sight. She was not only brave and beautiful, she was a powerful Dragon Highlord who could advance his career. Bakaris lost what passed for his heart.

Unfortunately, he was just another low-level officer in the ranks of the dragonarmy, and Kitiara had no idea he existed. He needed a way to attract her notice, so he bribed a superior to have himself assigned to her personal staff. Bakaris was always on hand to run her errands, polish her boots, repair her armor, and regale her with his best stories. Kitiara found him ornamental, charming, and entertaining. She took him for her lover and made him her aide-de-camp.

Bakaris believed his fortune was made. He spent his nights holding this beautiful woman in his arms and his days bullying underlings in her name. He was content for a time, but after several months, he grew tired of being merely an aide. He deserved to be a lieutenant, and he asked her to promote him, thinking she could deny him nothing.

Unfortunately, she denied him this. "If you were a lieutenant, you'd have to fight, Bakaris," Kit told him. "You might hurt that pretty face."

Bakaris had no intention of fighting. He wanted that promotion for the prestige and the money, and he continued his demands, never noticing he was starting to annoy her.

And then came the year 351. Emperor Ariakas dispatched the Blue Dragonarmy to Solamnia to crush the Second Rose Rebellion. Kitiara had ended the uprising with brutal force and gained control of Solamnia. After her victory, she had expected orders to march east to Neraka, but those orders had not come. She and her army were left languishing on the plains of Solamnia, chafing at inaction.

Bakaris was enjoying his breakfast when he received a summons from Kitiara to report to her command tent. He was relieved, for he hadn't seen her in several nights and he'd heard a rumor that she had ordered her guards to deny him entry to her tent. Bakaris had started to worry, but now, she had sent for him, and all was well.

Kitiara was alone in her tent. Bakaris went to greet her with a kiss, as usual, but she turned her head away.

"I have an assignment for you," Kitiara said briskly. "I intend to travel to the town of Solace in Abanasinia. As my aide, you will go ahead with my troops to make preparations for my arrival. Skie and I will follow in a few days' time."

Bakaris laughed. "Come now, Kit. You know you don't want to send me away. You've had your fun teasing me. Let's get down to the real reason you want to see me."

He tried to put his arms around her. To his surprise, Kitiara gave him a shove that nearly knocked him down.

"Do you think my orders are a joke?" she asked with a dangerous flash of her dark eyes.

Bakaris realized she was serious. "You're truly sending me away? Come, Kit, you know you can't get on without me!"

"Since you spent most of the battle in the healer's tent, I think the army can get along quite well without you," said Kitiara coldly.

"I sprained my ankle," Bakaris said, remembering belatedly to limp.

"Then I hope your ankle is better by the time you're ready to leave for Solace," said Kit. "You have your orders. You should go pack."

Bakaris tried a new tactic. "You don't want to go to Solace, Kit. The region is under Highlord Verminaard's command. If you suddenly show up with an army, he'll view that as a threat. He'll think you're trying to muscle in on his territory."

Kitiara shrugged. "Verminaard is far away in the west and, from what I hear, he has his own problems. The slaves in the mines are rebelling in Pax Tharkas, and he's facing a revolt in Southern Ergoth. He won't even know I'm in Solace."

"But suppose he finds out?" Bakaris argued. "Why risk his anger? Solace is nothing special—a crap town in a crap part of the world."

"I was born and raised in that 'crap' town," Kitiara said.

"So let them put up a statue," said Bakaris. "You don't need to pay them a visit."

"As it happens, I want to go. Some friends and I took a vow five years ago to reunite in Solace in the autumn of this year. I want to see my friends again. Especially one of them." Kitiara smiled to herself.

Bakaris recognized that crooked smile and scowled. "Who is he?"

"Not that it is any of your business, but his name is Tanis Half-Elven," Kitiara replied. "Ask around while you are there. See if there is news of him."

"Half-Elven!" Bakaris said, seething with jealousy. "He must be revolting! Half man, half elf."

"Yet he is twice the man you are, Bakaris," said Kitiara, and she laughed at her own wit.

Bakaris was furious at the insult, but he had sense enough to keep his temper. He was sometimes a little afraid of Kitiara.

She turned away from him and walked over to a large wooden map table and sorted through a pile of maps until she found the one she sought. She unfurled a map of Abanasinia.

"Take a squad of Bozaks with you. Set up camp here, outside of town." Kit pointed to the map. "Don't bully the townsfolk. They'll be frightened when they see the soldiers. You need to ease their minds. Tell them I am coming for a holiday and I mean them no harm. And make provision for Skie. He'll require a cave, perhaps somewhere in these foothills, near Crystalmir Lake."

Bakaris paid no attention to the map. He caressed her shoulders and kissed the back of her neck.

"But who will keep you warm at night when I'm gone, Kit?" he asked.

Kitiara turned to face him. She pressed her body against his, and Bakaris smiled until he felt the sharp point of a dagger slide beneath his armor and jab him in the ribs.

"The choice is yours, Bakaris," said Kitiara with her crooked smile. "You can go to Solace or to the Abyss. Which will it be?"

Bakaris stormed off in a murderous rage. Returning to his tent, he flung himself onto his cot. No woman had ever treated him so badly, discarded him like a broken toy!

His conceit would not let him believe Kitiara was through with him, however. He lay on his bunk and eventually convinced himself that she would think twice and rescind her orders. He hung about camp a day or so, waiting for her to come looking for him.

But the only one who came looking for him was the commander of the Bozaks. "The Highlord wants to know when we are leaving for Solace," the Bozak stated. "What do I tell her?"

Bakaris sulked. "Tell her we leave tomorrow. If she needs me tonight, she can send for me."

She didn't send for him, and Bakaris had no choice but to travel to Solace. He arrived in a foul mood and established the camp near some lake—he didn't bother to learn its name—and made preparations for Kitiara's arrival.

Three days later, he saw Skie flying over Solace and was on hand to greet Kitiara when the dragon landed. He escorted her to her rooms in the Inn of the Last Home and was pleased when she asked him to join her for supper. Perhaps absence really did make the heart grow fonder.

But dinner proved disastrous. First Kitiara introduced him to her loathsome half-brothers: Caramon and Raistlin Majere. They had not been with the army in Solamnia but had been off on some secret mission of their own. They were also here for the reunion, and all Kitiara could talk about was Tanis. Tanis this and Tanis that. She and her brothers spent the entire meal reminiscing about their adventures together.

Bakaris decided then and there he would find some way to get rid of this Tanis Half-Elven when he came to the reunion. But Tanis didn't show up. Kitiara was hurt and angry, and Bakaris enjoyed every moment of her suffering.

And then fortune smiled. Bakaris discovered that Tanis had been in the inn the entire time, spying on Kitiara, and that he had helped the Plainsfolk with the blue crystal staff escape.

Bakaris had gleefully informed Kitiara that Tanis had made a fool of her. She was furious, and when she rode off to catch her lover, Bakaris decided to follow. The fortuitous arrival of Ariakas's messenger gave him an excuse. He rode after Kitiara and found her and Tanis easily.

Bakaris waited in eager anticipation to see her gut him. But instead he saw her stroke his face and offer to make him her lieutenant!

Bakaris made the first of several mistakes. He announced his presence. He revealed that he'd been spying on her and he berated her for giving the loathsome half-elf his promotion. Kitiara was already angry at Tanis for spurning her, and she lashed out at Bakaris, taking his horse and leaving him to walk back to camp.

But at least now, Bakaris reflected, he had the opportunity to slay his rival.

Bakaris had been going to kill Tanis once he was safely bound in cobwebs, when he heard the zing of arrows and saw the draconians drop down dead, at which point an army of elves carrying bows and arrows and brandishing swords poured out of the woods.

Bakaris knew when discretion was the better part of valor and immediately took to his heels. He ran and ran, stumbling and falling, getting up and running again. He heard the elves pursuing him, and he ran until he was certain he'd left them behind, and then he ran some more. Finally, he was forced by sheer exhaustion to stop, catch his breath, and consider what to do.

Bakaris was still determined to kill Tanis, but not while the half-elf was armed and surrounded by armed friends. He had overheard Tanis and the dwarf talking about heading for the abandoned mill. Bakaris knew it, for it had once been used by the rebels as a base of operations. The perfect place for an ambush.

He walked to the mill, making good time, his path lighted by the Dark Queen's stars. When the house and outbuildings came into view, he lurked about in the woods, watching for Tanis and his elf friends.

The house was occupied, for Bakaris could see lights and smell woodsmoke, but he didn't see any sign of elves. He left the woods and stealthily approached the house, circling around to the back of the mill, searching for a place to hide. The only places he could find were the outbuildings in the back, and he knew when the elves arrived, they'd likely do a thorough search of the buildings. He was cursing his ill luck when he tripped over a wooden door, stumbled, and fell to his hands and knees.

Bakaris froze, not moving, afraid someone inside the house had heard him. When no one came to investigate and no lights appeared in the back windows of the house, he picked himself up. He could see by the starlight that he'd fallen over the door to the cellar. He heaved it open and peered inside. The cool darkness smelled of dirt and apples. The cellar appeared to be empty, and Bakaris went from cursing his bad luck to blessing his good fortune.

He descended the stairs, leaving the door open until he could find a lantern. He located one hanging on a nail on the wall. The lantern had the stub of a candle inside, and there was flint and tinder to light it. When he had light, he shut the cellar door. As luck would have it, there was even a large, empty barrel in which he could hide if the elves searched down here.

His good fortune just kept coming, for he next came across several jugs of what turned out to be a passable brandy. Bakaris roamed deeper into the cellar, taking the jug with him. He was enjoying a swig when he heard voices coming from the house above and the sound of footsteps crossing the ceiling over his head.

Bakaris had not realized that the cellar extended beneath the main part of the house. He wondered uneasily if they had heard him moving about down here. Again, when no one came hunting him, he realized that they hadn't. He needed to know if Tanis had arrived and listened to try to distinguish his voice from the others. But all the voices were muffled and he couldn't hear well enough to differentiate one from the other. The wooden ceiling was low, and Bakaris came up with the idea to poke a hole in the wood in order to hear better. He thrust his sword into the ceiling, and dirt and rotting wood cascaded down onto his upturned face.

Bakaris spit dirt and hastily blew out the lantern before anyone noticed the light shining through the hole. He was certain this time someone would come. No one did, and he realized he was now stranded in pitch darkness, for although he had the lantern, he had not thought to bring the flint and tinder with him.

Bakaris was cursing his bad luck when he noticed a chink of light shining through the jagged hole he'd made in the wooden planks of the floor above. He could now hear the voices clearly and understand what they were saying.

"How is Destina?" one asked.

"Much better," another replied. "The poultice has reduced the inflammation and drawn out the poison. I believe she will be well enough to travel by morning."

Bakaris recognized Raistlin's irritating hissing voice and was elated. He had long suspected Raistlin and his twin, Caramon, were traitors, and now he had proof. He'd caught Raistlin in a house known to be frequented by rebels, and Tanis was on his way to join his friends. Bakaris could already hear himself telling Kitiara that her lover had died trying to escape and her twin brothers were traitors and should be executed. She would see the folly of her ways and start to appreciate him.

Pleased with his good luck, Bakaris perched on the barrel and settled himself comfortably in the darkness with the jug to keep him company and happily gleaned information that would be like a knife to Kitiara's heart.

CHAPTER
SIXTEEN

Raistlin went to the bedchamber to check on his patient and was glad to find Destina still sleeping peacefully. She did not waken, even when he cleaned off the dried mud and washed the wound. He could see the Graygem around her neck. The jewel was dark, as though it, too, slept. Raistlin was not fooled. Chaos was awake and watchful. He could only hope the Graygem had taken heed of the warning that Takhisis was searching for it and would remain quiet.

He was drawing the blanket up to Destina's chin, hiding the Graygem from sight, when he heard an odd sound seeming to come from below the floorboards. Raistlin paused in his work to listen intently. All was quiet. He didn't hear the sound repeated, and he passed it off as vermin running about in the cellar.

"How is Destina?" Kairn asked anxiously, coming into the room.

"Much better," said Raistlin. "The poultice has reduced the in-flammation and drawn out the poison. The wound is starting to heal. I believe she will be well enough to travel by morning."

They left the bedchamber and were quietly shutting the door

behind them when Raistlin heard the jingle of armor. "Soldiers! Douse the light!"

Kairn blew out the lantern. Raistlin brought the words of a spell to mind and reached into one of his pouches.

Someone tapped on the window and a voice called softly, "It's me, Tanis."

Raistlin let go of his spell. Kairn heaved a relieved sigh and hurried to open the front door.

"We heard the rattle of armor and feared you were the Highlord's troops," said Kairn.

Tanis smiled. "That was Flint. He and the Plainsfolk and Tas are waiting outside. I came ahead to make certain all was well. How is Sturm?"

"Breathing," said Raistlin.

Tanis glanced at the pale figure lying comatose on the pallet. "I hope Goldmoon can help him. What about Destina?"

"She is better. She will be ready to travel by morning."

"At least that's some good news. I'll go fetch the others," Tanis said and went out the door as Tas came bounding in.

"We brought Goldmoon and Riverwind!" Tas announced. "How is Destina? Is Sturm still alive?"

"Destina is much better," Kairn replied. "Sturm is holding his own."

"Good!" Tas plunked himself down in a chair. "It's been an exciting night since we left the inn."

"What happened?" Raistlin asked. "And keep your voice down."

"Fizban blew up the inn. We escaped with Goldmoon and Riverwind, Kitiara's blue dragon found us and then Kit and her Bozaks caught us—"

Kairn gasped. "They caught you?"

"It's rude to interrupt," said Tas, eyeing him severely.

"I'm sorry," said Kairn. "Please go on."

"Kitiara asked Tanis to be her lieutenant and he said no and then Bakaris rode up on his horse and Kitiara told the Bozaks to web us and then she rode off and took her dragon with her." Tas paused for breath. "Bakaris was going to kill us because I haven't stabbed him yet, but then Laurana and her friends killed the Bozaks and they blew up. And so here we are with Goldmoon and Riverwind and Laurana."

"Laurana . . ." Raistlin murmured. "The circle closes."

"What circle?" Tas asked.

"Never mind," said Raistlin.

"I'm always never minding," said Tas, sighing. "I guess I'll go tell my story to Destina."

"She is sleeping," said Raistlin. "Do not disturb her."

Tas sighed again and roamed about, looking for something to do, and caught sight of his flour sack.

He plopped down on the floor and set to work transforming it into a pouch and almost immediately stood up again. "I need rope for the handles. Maybe there's some in the cellar. I'll go look. I might find some sausages, too."

He was halfway to the door when Tanis and Flint entered, accompanied by Riverwind and Goldmoon and Laurana. At the sight of Raistlin, Laurana stopped in alarm and reached for her sword.

"A Black Robe!"

"He is a friend," said Tanis. "His name is Raistlin Majere. He and his brother serve in the Highlord's army, but they work for the resistance."

"I can vouch for him," said Flint, sounding grudging. He glared at Raistlin. "Although if you ever say I did, I'll deny it."

Laurana regarded Raistlin distrustfully, but she returned her sword to its leather sheath.

"And who is this human?" she asked, eyeing Kairn.

"He is Kairn, an exile from Solamnia," Tanis answered.

"I am pleased to meet you," said Kairn.

"You should go sit with Destina. Take your rucksack with you in case you two need to leave," Raistlin advised.

Kairn understood. He picked up his rucksack, bid good night to those in the room, then opened the door to the bedroom and disappeared inside. He shut the door behind him. Raistlin was pleased to see that the room—and the Graygem—were dark.

Raistlin cast an irritated glance at Tasslehoff. "I thought you were going to the cellar."

"I guess I'll stay here," said Tas. "Goldmoon's going to heal Sturm and she might need me to boil water."

Riverwind was gazing down at Sturm. The Plainsman's stern expression softened, and he said something in a low voice to Goldmoon. She nodded and glided past him to stand beside the pallet.

"What is his name?" she asked.

"Sturm Brightblade," said Tanis.

"He is very badly wounded," Goldmoon said with sorrowful pity.

"He is close to death," said Raistlin.

Goldmoon knelt on the floor to examine the wound. Destina had removed Sturm's armor and laid it to one side. Goldmoon glanced at the breastplate, covered with blood, and his helm and his sword in its sheath lying on the floor near him. She put her hand on his forehead and spoke to him.

"Tanis tells me you are a Knight of Solamnia. My people know little about the knights, but we do know that you are devoted to the fight against the Dragon Queen."

"Sturm tried to save Huma, but he couldn't," said Tas. "That bad man killed Huma and then he stabbed Sturm."

"Come with me, lad," said Flint gruffly. "We need to give Sturm some air."

"I'll stop breathing, if that will help," Tas offered.

"It won't," said Flint and he led Tas off into a corner. Tas sat down, clutching his flour sack, his arms around his knees.

Laurana remained standing by the front door, watching Goldmoon with skepticism.

"There has been no healing in this world for centuries, Tanthalas," Laurana said softly. "Do not get your hopes up that she can save your friend."

Goldmoon gently rested her staff on top of the blanket that covered Sturm's body and took his hand in her own.

"I am told the name of the goddess who gave me this staff is Mishakal," Goldmoon said. "I ask her blessing on you, Sturm Brightblade. I ask her to ease your pain, heal your flesh, and restore you to health, if such is her wish."

The staff began to glow with a pale blue light. Sturm drew in a labored breath. He let go of the breath with a sigh and did not draw another.

"We are too late. He is gone," said Tanis. "Paladine has taken him to his final rest."

"Paladine be damned! Sturm cannot die!" Raistlin said angrily. He bent over the knight and roughly shook him by the shoulder, as though waking a sleeper. "It is not like you to give up, Sturm Brightblade! Do not leave us! This is not your time!"

Sturm shuddered and then he drew in a deep breath. He let it out, and this time he drew in another, and another after that. He opened his eyes and struggled to rise.

"I am coming, Huma!" he cried and reached reflexively for his sword.

Raistlin gently eased him back down onto the pallet. "The fight is over, at least for now. That battle has ended. You were badly wounded, close to death. But all is well. You should rest."

Sturm stared at him in confusion and then he saw Goldmoon, who was smiling down on him.

"Goldmoon!" Sturm said, marveling. "What are you doing here?"

Goldmoon drew back, startled. "How do you know me?"

"He must have heard us talking," said Raistlin quickly.

"But he was unconscious," said Riverwind.

"I have treated people who were unconscious, yet still aware of what was going on around them," Raistlin replied. "You are still very weak, Sturm. You must sleep and allow the healing to continue."

Sturm had already closed his eyes. His breathing grew deep and even. His face regained color, and he sank into a peaceful slumber.

As Goldmoon picked up the staff, its blue light faded and it was once more plain and ordinary.

"Thank you, Mishakal," she said softly.

Riverwind's stern face was wet with tears. He grasped her hand and lifted her to her feet. Goldmoon smiled at him, her expression radiant.

"The gods have blessed us," she said softly.

"You both should get some sleep," Tanis advised. "Have no fear, we will keep watch."

"I have no fear," said Goldmoon. "Mishakal watches over us."

Tasslehoff blew his nose on Flint's handkerchief. "Fetching Goldmoon was my idea. Tanis usually has all the ideas, but this was mine."

Riverwind led Goldmoon to a far corner where he spread his cloak on the floor. The two of them sat down and Goldmoon rested her head on his chest, even as she kept her hand on the staff. He put his arm around her and the two of them talked softly.

Laurana had been watching in silence. Tanis saw a glimmer of tears in her eyes.

"Now do you believe the gods have returned?" he asked.

Laurana did not answer him but went to Sturm. Kneeling down, she gently touched him, as though to assure herself he was warm, alive, and breathing.

She gazed at him in wonder, mingled with doubt.

"For many years, my people have waited for some sign that the gods had come to challenge the Dragon Queen. Now it seems the gods are here, but they do not come bearing swords. They bring us healing, and while that is welcome, we cannot fight the Dragon Queen with blue crystal."

"The gods are prepared to fight, as well," said Tanis. "You saw the staff destroy the magic of the draconians."

"I must think about all I have seen this day," said Laurana, frowning. "You and your friends may rest easy this night. My warriors and Saber will keep watch."

"You cannot now take Goldmoon and Riverwind to Qualinesti," said Tanis insistently. "Not if Solostaran is beholden to the Dark Queen."

Laurana cast a troubled glance at the Plainsfolk, who had fallen asleep in each other's arms. Smiling faintly, she raised her hand to Tanis's face. "I do not like the human beard. But I might grow used to it in time."

She left, quietly shutting the door behind her. Tanis stood gazing after her.

"She is Laurana and she is not Laurana."

"This is our world and it is not our world," said Raistlin. "I expect we will get used to it in time."

"I really don't want to get used to it," said Tanis.

"You may have no choice," said Raistlin.

Flint had ventured over to gaze down at Sturm. The dwarf had removed his helm and was holding it in his hands.

"I'm glad to see you again, lad, after all these years," said Flint.

The dwarf's eyes were red, and he scrubbed his face with his sleeve and started to wipe his nose, only to realize he didn't have a handkerchief. He rounded on Tas and snatched his handkerchief from the kender's hand.

"I guess you must have dropped it," said Tas.

Flint snorted and started to stuff it into his belt, then he grimaced and pressed his hand to his chest, dropping the handkerchief.

"Flint, what's wrong?" Tas asked, alarmed. "You're not going to die again, are you?"

"If I do, it will be because you've badgered me to death!" said Flint.

But he sagged weakly down in a chair at the table, breathing heavily.

"What are you all staring at? I'm fine!" Flint said, scowling. "It's those spiced potatoes. They never did agree with me."

"I'll sit with you," said Tanis. He started to pull up a chair, then glanced around. "Where's Tas?"

"Pestering those poor Plainsfolk," Flint said, jerking his thumb at the kender. "As if they didn't have enough trouble."

Tanis turned his head to see Tasslehoff lurking about near Riverwind and Goldmoon. They were both sleeping soundly. The blue crystal staff lay nearby, the guardian of their slumber.

"Don't bother them, Tas," said Tanis. "Let them rest."

"I'm not going to bother them," said Tas. "I just want to look at them. It's been a long time since I've seen them, since I haven't yet."

"Moonstruck mad," Flint muttered, shaking his head. He was breathing easier and rose to his feet. "The blade on my axe is dull. Hal Miller used to keep a sharpening stone in the cellar."

"I'll come with you," said Tanis. "Perhaps I can find some food."

"Maybe there's sausages," Tas said eagerly, sidling over toward them. He was holding the blue crystal staff behind his back and trying hard to look as though he wasn't.

"What are you doing with that?" Tanis demanded.

"What?" Tas asked.

"The staff," said Tanis, exasperated. "And don't try to hide it. The staff is taller than you are."

Tas peered over his shoulder. "Oh, *this* staff. I was going to show it to Flint."

"I've seen it," said Flint.

"But you haven't seen it up close," said Tas. "Like this."

Tas got a good grip on the staff, gave a wild swing, and smacked Flint soundly in his chest. Flint howled in rage and Tas clouted the dwarf again, this time in the stomach. Flint doubled over with a groan, clutching his belly. Tas raised the staff a third time, but Tanis grabbed it and took it away from him.

"What do you think you're doing?" Tanis demanded angrily.

"I'm healing Flint," Tas said in triumph. "He won't die now."

"Tanis, look," said Raistlin, pointing to the staff. It was shining with a bright blue light.

Tanis stared, struck speechless. Flint was clutching his belly with one hand and bellowing and shaking his fist with the other.

"Healing me? I think you broke a rib, you doorknob!"

"It's not your ribs, it's your heart," Tas explained. "And now it won't break and you won't die and you won't have to wait for me under a tree."

"Is it possible?" Tanis asked Raistlin in a low voice. "Did the staff heal him?"

"Flint, how are you feeling?" Raistlin asked.

"Like some fool doorknob of a kender hit me with a staff!" Flint roared. "How do you think I'm feeling?"

But Tanis noted that when the dwarf sucked in an outraged breath, he did so without wheezing. His cheeks were a ruddy color, no longer gray, and he was stomping about with anger and renewed energy.

"What do you think?" Tanis asked Raistlin.

"I think that Tasslehoff Burrfoot is the smartest person in this room," Raistlin replied.

CHAPTER
SEVENTEEN

The house was quiet once again. Riverwind and Goldmoon had gone back to sleep after the excitement with Flint and Tas, and this time, Goldmoon kept her hand firmly on the staff. Sturm slept peacefully, one arm flung across his face. Flint had gone outdoors, saying he was going to sleep in one of the storage sheds, where he wouldn't be assaulted by staff-wielding kender. Tasslehoff had gone searching through the house and found a blanket but was sad to report no sausages. He carried the blanket into a corner of the room and spread it out on the floor. He leaned his hoopak against the wall, divested himself of his flour sack and hung it on the hoopak, then rolled himself up in the blanket and closed his eyes.

Tanis yawned. "Sleep is contagious."

"You go rest," said Raistlin. "I am wakeful anyway. I will keep watch."

"I would, but I need to tell you about why Astinus asked me to come here," said Tanis.

"I sent Kairn to report to the master that the past had changed," said Raistlin. "Knowing Astinus, I wasn't certain he would act. I thought he might just keep writing."

"He does keep writing," said Tanis. "Until the end, when Takhisis vanquishes the gods. And then, as Astinus said, he laid down the pen to pick up the sword."

Raistlin was grave. "As bad as that?"

"Worse," said Tanis grimly. "Let us sit by the fire. This is not a tale for darkness."

They drew their chairs closer to the fireplace.

Tanis lowered his voice, so as not to wake the sleepers. "In 351, this date and this time where we are now, Takhisis discovered that the other gods were planning to rise against her. Emperor Ariakas held a summit of the Dragon Highlords in Neraka. He announced that a 'Cleansing Fire' would blaze across Ansalon. The Highlords and their dragons swept over the land, imprisoning or killing all those suspected of rebelling against the Dark Queen. They destroyed towns and villages that were suspected of harboring rebels. Tens of thousands died. Solace was utterly destroyed."

"Interesting," Raistlin murmured.

"That's all you have to say?" Tanis asked.

"For the moment," said Raistlin. "Continue."

"The gods joined together with mortals to fight the Dragon Highlords in what would be known as the Lost War."

"I assume, from the name, they lost," said Raistlin.

"Takhisis reigned supreme from that time on. She has not yet overtaken the time in which I live, which is 358, but as Astinus says, the floodwaters are rising. She soon will."

"If Astinus is the god Gilean, as many believe, the neutral gods cannot allow the balance to be upset. They must try to restore it," Raistlin said.

"That is the reason Astinus gave Brother Kairn and Destina permission to go back in time to try to change what happened, restore history, and once more banish Takhisis to the Abyss."

"Takhisis knows the Graygem is here," said Raistlin. "Hederick told Kitiara. But why send you back to this time? And why did you agree to come? You must know that if Kairn and Destina fail, we will be stranded here."

"I'm bait," said Tanis, with a rueful smile. "I am here to keep Takhisis's attention focused on us. She knows the Heroes of the

Lance are also here in this time and that, because of the presence of the Graygem, we have the power to change history. She fears we might win the war we lost."

"No wonder the Dark Queen is nervous. Our arrival with the Graygem is already changing the flow of the river," said Raistlin. "According to Fizban, in the original time, Kitiara killed the Plains-folk, seized the staff, and gave it to Takhisis."

"The hope is that she will keep watching us instead of looking back to the Third Dragon War and seeing her true danger—Destina and the Graygem."

"And what will you do if they fail and we are stranded here?" Raistlin asked.

"I do not like the thought of living under the Dark Queen's tyranny. I think we should make her worst fears come true. We win the war that was lost," said Tanis. "But to do that, we must find the drag-onlances. The gods and mortals were defeated because they had no way to fight the evil dragons."

"Caramon told me the same. I remember wondering at the time what happened to the dragonlances that Gwyneth gave to Huma."

"Laurana says that Takhisis tried to destroy them, but when she could not, she sealed them up in the tower. The knights tried to recover them, but the tower is guarded by undead and a green dragon. The knights failed in their attempt."

"And so they are still in the High Clerist's Tower, drenched in Huma's blood," said Raistlin. "We should find a way to recover them. The emperor will be holding a summit of Dragon Highlords in Neraka. That would be the time for the army of gods and mortals, armed with dragonlances, to strike."

He fell silent, thinking. Tanis picked up the poker and leaned forward to stir the dying fire, sending sparks up the chimney.

"Even if we had an army and that entire army was armed with dragonlances, how could we hope to defeat Emperor Ariakas, five Dragon Highlords, and their assembled armies and dragons? Not to mention Queen Takhisis?" Tanis asked glumly.

"We would need the good dragons to join us," said Raistlin.

"According to Laurana, when the good dragons found out that Takhisis stole their eggs and changed their young into draconians, they fled to the Dragon Isles to protect what they have left. Saber does not think they will return."

Tanis flung himself wearily back in the chair. "This is hopeless. I do not know why we are even talking about it. The High Clerist's Tower is far away in Solamnia and the dragonarmies control all the land between here and there."

"Do you remember what I told you once about hope and the carrot?" Raistlin asked.

"That hope is the carrot you dangle before the draft horse to keep him plodding on," said Tanis. "I remember. Although I don't see how that helps us."

"The carrot is in the High Clerist's Tower," said Raistlin. "A dragon orb."

Tanis frowned. His expression darkened.

"Not the orb you are thinking of," Raistlin said, with a twisted smile.

"The orb you used to save yourself and leave the rest of us to die while you went to serve the Dark Queen," said Tanis.

"But you didn't die, did you?" said Raistlin coolly. "You went on to defeat Takhisis at the battle of Neraka, and you couldn't have done so without my help." He stirred impatiently. "Are we going to waste time reminiscing or are we going to try to find a way to change what might be our future?"

"What *might* be our future," Tanis repeated with some bitterness.

"The future is never promised to any of us," said Raistlin. "The gods could drop a fiery mountain down on us this moment. Our goal is to keep Takhisis's attention focused on us. We are a diversion. We must convince her that we pose a danger to her. Remember that the future is not promised to the Dark Queen, either. Not since the Graygem has changed the course of the River of Time. And you can always take comfort in the fact that Astinus is recording all of this in his book."

Tanis gave a rueful smile. "A book that no one will ever read. But I suppose we should at least give him a good story to tell. You were speaking of a dragon orb."

"The orb is hidden inside the High Clerist's Tower. This is the same dragon orb Laurana and Tas used to defeat Kitiara and her dragons during the War of the Lance. The dragon orb has the power to summon evil dragons and lure them to their doom. With the orb and the dragonlances, we could win this battle that was lost."

"That might be true, but, as I said, the High Clerist's Tower is hundreds of miles away. We would have to cross enemy territory to reach it and, if we survived that, we would then have to get past the dragon Takhisis left to guard it," said Tanis. "The battle would be over before we were halfway there."

"We can be there tomorrow," said Raistlin. "The magical journeying spell can take us to the High Clerist's Tower in a heartbeat. Not only that, I can sneak us inside the tower. The dragon will never know we are there."

"You never knew such a spell before," said Tanis. "Did you learn it from that evil wizard? The one that possessed you?"

"Fistandantilus? Apparently death severed the connection," said Raistlin. "Now I have only myself to blame. I learned the spell from Magius."

Raistlin rose to his feet and picked up his staff. "I must memorize this spell and others tonight and then get some sleep. Tomorrow promises to be an eventful day. If you have need of me, I will be in the back bedchamber."

He started to leave the room, then paused to turn back. "There is one caveat. We must achieve this feat without getting ourselves killed, for our deaths would again change the flow of the River of Time. I suggest you also try to sleep."

Tanis shook his head. "You have ruined sleep for me. I will go talk with Laurana."

Raistlin gave a knowing smile.

"I'm going to ask her more about the High Clerist's Tower," said Tanis defensively.

"Indeed," said Raistlin. "Shut the door quietly on your way out."

CHAPTER
EIGHTEEN

Bakaris sat on his barrel in the pitch darkness of the root cellar and cursed his ill luck. He had heard enough to convict Raistlin Majere of treachery ten times over. He had found Tanis here in the farmhouse and could lead Kitiara straight to him. But none of that did him a damn bit of good because he was trapped in this blasted root cellar surrounded by a horde of murderous elves and a copper dragon.

Bakaris was hungry and a little drunk from the brandy and feeling very sorry for himself. He did not dare fall asleep, for he knew he snored (Kit had complained about it) and he feared the elves would hear him. But he kept nodding off and jerking awake, and it was then he heard Tanis tell Raistlin he was going to talk to the elf woman.

Bakaris was instantly wide awake. When Tanis came around the back of the house, Bakaris would throttle the half-human, get him in a choke hold, drag him down into the cellar, then stab him through the heart.

Bakaris jumped to his feet, knocking over the barrel, which fell to the floor. He groped his way through the pitch-dark cellar by shuffling his feet and moving slowly with his hands outstretched, but he still managed to stumble into something and smack his head on a wooden beam. At last he reached the stairs and climbed them slowly, watching and listening.

As he cautiously raised the trapdoor and poked his head out, raindrops struck him in the face. Just his luck. No moon, no stars. He wiped his eyes and climbed out of the cellar, peering through the rain-filled night. How was he going to find Tanis when he couldn't see a damn thing? He moved swiftly to take cover beneath the eaves.

Bakaris decided a prayer to Takhisis would not go amiss.

"Bring the half-human to me, Your Dark Majesty, and I'll do the rest," Bakaris whispered. "That's all I ask."

But the Dark Queen must have had more urgent matters on her mind that night. The rain continued to fall, and Tanis did not appear. No one appeared. Yet the elves were out there somewhere and so was a copper dragon.

Bakaris was now soaked, hungry, and shivering with the cold. He could always go back down into the root cellar, but he had come to loathe it with every fiber of his being. He stood under the eaves, trying to warm himself with the flames of hatred and vengeance, only to find that the rain had doused the fire.

"Maybe I don't get the chance to kill him," Bakaris muttered. "But I'll have the satisfaction of telling Kit that her lover is a damn traitor who's in love with an elf."

He could not see the dragon for the clouds. He could not see the elves for the rain. He was again cursing his ill luck, when it suddenly occurred to him that if he could not see his foes, they could not see him.

"Now is my chance to escape!" Bakaris realized.

The elves undoubtedly had the house surrounded, but he had outrun them once, and he was confident he could do it again, especially in the dark during a rainstorm.

Bakaris drew his sword and set off into the night. He stayed away from the road and headed straight for the forest, planning to find cover among the trees. He had nearly reached the woods when he heard the zing of an arrow and felt something thud into his leather jerkin.

Bakaris was armed, but he had no thought of fighting. He took to his heels and ran blindly through the rain, expecting any moment to drop down dead with an arrow in his skull. He crashed heedlessly into the wet brush, caroming off tree trunks, and slipping and falling in the mud, but he kept running. Finally, he had to stop to catch his breath. He listened for elves, gasped for air, and tried to figure out what to do.

Bakaris had completely lost track of his whereabouts in his mad dash. Clouds still obscured the Dark Queen's friendly stars. He should probably wait here for daylight, but he imagined an elf hiding behind every tree and decided to keep going. He blundered about in the forest, unable to find a path and feeling even more sorry for himself, when the woods suddenly came to an end and so did the rain.

The clouds rolled away. The stars sacred to Takhisis shone brightly, and Bakaris saw the road that led back to camp right in front of him.

Bakaris should have given thanks to Takhisis for saving him, but he was annoyed with the goddess for refusing to help him kill Tanis. He took a moment to search the skies for the copper dragon, but there was no sign of the beast and he walked back to camp, arriving just as the sun was rising.

He smelled breakfast and his stomach rumbled, but he was eager to talk to Kitiara, and he went straight to her command tent. Two Bozaks were standing guard and halted him when he started to enter.

"Where do you think you're going, Bakaris?" one asked.

"To speak to the Highlord," Bakaris said, scowling.

"The Highlord is not receiving visitors," said the other Bozak. "Especially one who looks like dragon vomit."

Bakaris had to admit he was a sorry sight. He was wet and mud-splattered, but he didn't appreciate being insulted by lizards.

"The Highlord will see me!" he said proudly. "Tell her I found Tanis."

The Bozaks exchanged glances, and one of them went inside the tent to inform Kitiara. She came out and immediately pounced on Bakaris.

"Where have you been?" she demanded angrily. "You were supposed to bring Tanis and the others back to camp. I've been waiting all night!"

Bakaris suddenly saw the flaw in his plan. In his obsession with killing Tanis, he had completely forgotten that Kitiara had ordered him to bring Tanis and the Plainsfolk and the others back to camp. He was good at coming up with excuses and he thought swiftly.

"We were attacked by elves, Kit. They killed the dracos and would have killed me, too, but I managed to escape. The elves took Tanis and the others to the abandoned mill outside of town. I followed them at peril of my life, for they're here with a copper dragon."

"Elves and a copper dragon?" Kit gave a snorting laugh. "You expect me to believe this kender tale of yours? No one has seen a copper dragon on Krynn in centuries."

"Well, I saw one," said Bakaris. "I thought you would want to know what Tanis and Raistlin and the others were plotting, so I hid in the cellar and spied on them. I heard everything they said. They're still there, but they won't be there for long. They're talking about leaving this morning."

"Why didn't you say so at once?" Kitiara turned to the Bozaks. "Take a squad to that abandoned mill on the outskirts of town. If you find anyone there, arrest them and bring them to camp. And keep watch for a copper dragon."

The Bozaks looked dubious at this, but they did not question her and hastened off as they were told.

Kit eyed Bakaris narrowly. "You'd better not be lying. Come inside the tent where we won't be disturbed."

He followed her and she closed the tent flap behind them. She went to her desk and sat down.

"Tell me what happened," she ordered.

Bakaris started to bring up a chair.

"Remain standing," said Kit. "You won't be here that long."

Bakaris described the ambush in lurid detail, making himself the hero, telling how he had fought the elves until he was struck on the head and knocked unconscious. When he came to himself, he heard Tanis say they were going to the mill, and he followed them.

"Tanis knew these elves," said Bakaris. "He was very friendly with them, especially one of them, their leader. He talked about marrying her."

Kitiara stared at him, breathing hard. Her dark eyes smoldered and she clenched her fist on the desk. Bakaris enjoyed seeing her suffer. She deserved it, he reflected, after the rotten way she had treated him. He continued on with the story, gleefully twisting the knife.

"The elves escorted those Plainsfolk with the blue crystal staff and Tanis and the others to the mill. Your half-brother Raistlin Majere was there waiting for them. I warned you about him, Kit. I told you he was a traitor. And so is his twin, Caramon. They're both working with the rebels. Maybe next time you'll listen to me."

Kitiara bounded to her feet, her hand gripping the hilt of her sword. She was shaking with rage, and Bakaris feared he had gone too far. He remembered belatedly the old adage about killing the messenger and he sneaked a look to make certain he had a clear run to the exit.

Kitiara did not attack him. Instead, she paced back and forth at the back of her tent as Bakaris watched her warily.

"You said you heard Tanis and the others talking. What did they say?" Kit asked abruptly.

Bakaris fumbled about in his brandy-soaked brain, trying to remember.

"Something about Emperor Ariakas and his plan to wipe out the resistance and how he was assembling all the Dragon Highlords in Neraka. Raistlin said they could take this opportunity to destroy all the Highlords and the Dark Queen."

Kitiara stopped pacing and rounded on him. "Raistlin said that?"

"He did," Bakaris stated smugly. "I heard him clearly."

"My brother said they could fight five Dragon Highlords, Queen Takhisis, and hundreds of our dragons?" said Kitiara, a dangerous edge to her voice.

"Maybe," Bakaris faltered, thinking his story had sounded better in his head. "Their voices were muffled. It was hard to hear."

"You just said you heard them clearly," Kitiara reminded him.

"I could at first, but then they walked off and I couldn't," said Bakaris.

Kitiara regarded him in disgust. "Next time you're out bedding some wench, Bakaris, don't come to me stinking of brandy with some harebrained story to cover for your absence."

She returned to her desk, sat down, and picked up one of her dispatches. "You're dismissed."

Bakaris walked up to the desk, slammed his hands down, and leaned over it to confront her. "I am telling the truth!"

Kitiara glanced up at him. "If you're fond of that pretty face of yours, Bakaris, I suggest you take it out of my sight."

Bakaris hurriedly removed his hands and stepped back.

"I'm telling the truth," he repeated stubbornly. "Raistlin has a plan to defeat the armies using a powerful magical weapon— a dragon spear or a pike or a lance or something like that. He and Tanis talked about them. Raistlin also talked about something called a dragon orb. I remember that because I thought it was odd. What is an orb anyway?"

Kitiara glared at him and he hurried on.

"This orb and the magical pikes are in the High Clerist's Tower in Solamnia," said Bakaris. "Raistlin said that if they had the orb and these dragon pikes, they could launch an attack on the Highlords at the Emperor's Summit. What's funny? Why are you smiling?"

"You had me worried for a moment," said Kit. "Dragon orbs and magical pikes? Even if all this was real, the High Clerist's Tower is hundreds of miles away. They would never get there in time."

"Oh, yeah? Your traitor brother, Raistlin, said he could take Tanis and the others to the tower in a heartbeat. Some sort of magic spell."

Kitiara regarded him, frowning. "You're not smart enough to make this up, are you, Bakaris?"

"No," he said proudly.

"You can go," said Kit, her lips twitching. "But stay around camp in case I need you."

"So you believe me?" Bakaris asked, elated.

"Sure, Bakaris, I believe you," Kit replied. "You're my hero. Not a word of this to anyone."

"Do you want me to arrest Caramon?" Bakaris persisted.

Kitiara fixed him with a baleful look and Bakaris beat a hasty retreat.

By this time, he was starving. Bakaris entered the mess tent and saw Caramon Majere seated at a plank table with several companions, eating breakfast.

Bakaris was feeling good. Caramon would rue the day he'd punched him. Bakaris sauntered over.

"Kit's going to have to find an extra stout rope to hang you, Majere," he remarked.

Caramon continued eating, chewing stolidly. "Why would she hang me, Bakaris? For punching you? I call that a public service."

"They'll hang you because I have proof your brother is a damn traitor!" Bakaris said angrily. "And if he's a traitor, then so are you."

"What did you say, Bakaris?" Caramon asked, rising to his feet, his hand on the hilt of his sword.

Bakaris put the massive wooden table between them, but Caramon lifted it up and heaved it to one side. His comrades rose with him, their hands on their swords.

"You should watch who you're accusing of being a traitor," said Caramon. "What's this proof you have?"

Bakaris belatedly remembered that Kitiara had ordered him to keep his mouth shut.

"You'll find out soon enough," he said and stalked off to the sounds of laughter.

The men liked Caramon. No one liked Bakaris. He knew beyond doubt that Caramon was in league with the rebels, but he couldn't prove it, and no one would believe him, not even Kitiara. She might be willing to believe Raistlin was a traitor. But not Caramon. He was her favorite.

Bakaris grabbed some food and retired to his tent to feel sorry for himself and plot his revenge.

CHAPTER
NINETEEN

After Bakaris left, Kitiara remained alone in her tent, mulling over everything Bakaris had told her—or at least the half she believed.

His accusations against Tanis had the ring of truth, and she was furious. She had offered him wealth and power. She had even offered him herself, and he had spurned her yet again. She pictured capturing Tanis, seeing him on his knees before her, begging for his life. Kit would smile and then kick him in the teeth.

She let herself linger on this pleasant daydream for a moment, then she thought over what Bakaris had told her about orbs and magical pikes. She didn't believe him, but, as she had said, Bakaris wasn't bright enough to make that up, which meant he truly had heard Raistlin talking.

She decided to seek advice, and she turned to the one being in this world she could trust, her best friend and confidant. Divesting herself of her dragonscale armor, she put on a leather jerkin, shirt, and breeches, buckled on her sword, and left camp, taking the road that led to Crystalmir Lake.

When she had been young, growing up in Solace, Kitiara would have encountered fishermen along this road, walking to the lake in the cool of the early morning; women carrying baskets of laundry; children eager for a swim. Today, she was alone. No one dared visit the lake now, for the blue dragon, Skie, had taken up residence in one of the caves in the hills.

The clean, crisp scent of pine trees filled the air. Clouds lingered, trailing long fingers of mist and foretelling more rain. The lake was smooth and slate gray. Kitiara stopped to refresh herself and splash water on her face before undertaking the long uphill climb to Skie's cave.

The dragon's lair was not easy to find. Kitiara had to pick her way among the rocks to reach the cavern, and she was hot and sweating by the time she arrived. The physical exertion had cooled her temper, however, and she was in good spirits when she reached the cave. She stopped to call out before she entered, letting Skie know she was not an intruder.

"It's me, Kit," she said and then walked inside.

"I'm sleeping. Go away," Skie growled.

Kit gave her eyes time to adjust to the dim light and finally located the blue dragon curled up in the back of the cave. His tail wrapped around his legs, touching his nose. His eyes glittered. The dragon did his hunting at night and slept during the day, so now he was grumpy and in a bad mood.

"I have to talk to you," said Kit. "It's urgent."

"Can't it wait? I just finished a big meal," Skie said peevishly.

"It's important." Kitiara found a convenient boulder and sat down. She could see the bloody remnants of several deer strewn about the cave.

Skie did not stir but eyed her glumly.

"Say whatever it is you came to say and let me go back to sleep."

"You have heard me speak of my half-brother Raistlin Majere, the wizard," said Kit. "He's very talented in magic and knows a lot about magical artifacts."

Skie yawned and shifted his body to a more comfortable position. "What about him?"

"According to Bakaris—"

"That dolt!" Skie said, sneering. His upper lip curled, showing his fangs. "You haven't taken up with him again, have you?"

"Not that it is any of your business, but no," said Kit. "Never mind how Bakaris came to find out, but he claims he overheard Raistlin talking to Tanis Half-Elven—"

"So Tanis came?" Skie asked. "How did your liaison with him go?"

"I didn't come here to talk about Tanis!" Kit said angrily.

"So it didn't go well," Skie said.

"He's a damn traitor," said Kit. "Now can we talk about these artifacts? They have something to do with dragons, and I was wondering if you had ever heard of them. One is a weapon. Bakaris couldn't remember exactly what it was called, but it was something like a dragon pike or a dragon spear or lance—"

Skie reared up so suddenly that he grazed his mane on the ceiling of the cavern.

"Dragonlance?" he said in an altered tone.

"I suppose that could be it," said Kitiara, startled by his reaction. "Bakaris couldn't remember."

"He heard Raistlin Majere speak of a dragonlance?" Skie said slowly. "What did he say about it?"

"That he knew where they could find them," said Kitiara. "Is this true? What are dragonlances? I have never heard of them."

"Dragonlances were forged by the silver dragons for one reason only, and that was to give mortals the power to kill chromatic dragons like me," said Skie, his voice grating. "A silver dragon brought the dragonlances to a Solamnic Knight named Huma during the Third Dragon War. Huma was going to use the dragonlances to fight the Dark Queen during the battle of the High Clerist's Tower that took place during the Third Dragon War, but he was slain by an assassin before he could. The tower fell to Takhisis. She tried to destroy the dragonlances, but Paladine protected them. She sealed up the tower and ordered the green dragon Cyan Bloodbane to guard it."

"So that's why the knights tried to break into the tower when we were in Solamnia. They were after these dragonlances," said Kitiara. "I wondered at the time. But these weapons are only lances and a lance would bounce off your scales. Are you sure they are so dangerous?"

"A dragonlance would *not* bounce off my scales," Skie said irritably. "It would cleave through my flesh and pierce me to the heart! That's why Takhisis went to all the trouble to seal them up. But you said Raistlin spoke of two artifacts. What was the other?"

"Something called a dragon orb," said Kit.

Skie sucked in a long, slow breath and let it out in a hiss that crackled with flickers of lightning. "You are certain that's what he said? Dragon orb?"

"Yes, because that fool Bakaris asked me what an orb was. Why? What is wrong?"

"The dragon orbs are the most feared artifacts among our kind," Skie replied. "They were created by powerful wizards centuries ago to lure us to our doom. The wizards used their magic to ensnare five chromatic dragons—red, blue, green, black, and white—and trap them inside crystal orbs. The captive dragons cry to us, their brethren, to come save them, and we are compelled to answer the call, constrained to fly to them in frenzied madness. The wizards would lie in wait, then use their magicks to destroy us."

"Raistlin said that these orbs along with the dragonlances could defeat our armies at the Emperor's Summit," said Kitiara. "If there's the slightest risk . . ."

"There is," said Skie grimly. "And the risk is not slight. Where is this dragon orb?"

"In the High Clerist's Tower," said Kitiara.

"Along with the dragonlances," Skie said. "I keep telling you, Kit, the old gods have returned, and they're taking up arms against us."

Kitiara thought about the blue crystal staff that had healed a man. She didn't mention that to Skie, not wanting to upset him further.

"Let them try," Kitiara said dismissively. "I have more urgent problems. A messenger came from Ariakas yesterday. The emperor has ordered me to return to Neraka immediately, ahead of the summit."

"Ariakas?" Skie repeated, alarmed. "That's not good!"

"Verminaard is behind this," said Kitiara. "According to the messenger, he told the emperor I fled Solamnia because I was losing the battle."

"You weren't winning," Skie pointed out.

"I crushed the uprising!" said Kit angrily. "I hanged the instigators and left troops in Palanthas and other cities to keep the population under control. I could afford to leave Solamnia on business of my own."

"You *quelled* the uprising, but you didn't crush it," Skie retorted. "You never caught its leader, Gunthar Uth Wistan. He and others may have gone to ground, but they haven't given up the fight. And now the old gods are back to help them, and you're being recalled to Neraka. Did the messenger tell you why?"

"Ariakas wants to discuss my future," said Kitiara.

"Which means you don't have one," said Skie.

Kitiara knew well enough what it meant. She and Ariakas had known each other for many years, long before he became emperor. He had wanted to take her to his bed, telling her it would be good for her career. Kitiara knew her worth, however, and she had refused. She planned to rise in the dragonarmies through her merits. She had done so, impressing Ariakas, who made her a Dragon Highlord in the Blue Dragonarmy.

The other Highlords resented her, certain she had slept her way to promotion—particularly Verminaard, who had wanted the rich spoils of Solamnia for himself.

"Verminaard told Ariakas that I wanted to snatch the Crown of Power off the emperor's head and put it on my own. . . ."

Kitiara suddenly fell silent. She gazed into the darkness of the cave, a slight smile on her lips.

Skie eyed her uneasily. "I know that look and I don't like it. What are you scheming?"

Kitiara shifted her gaze and her smile back to the dragon. "Why shouldn't I wear the Crown of Power? Why shouldn't I take it?"

"Because Ariakas would find ten different ways to kill you, each more painful than the last!" said Skie.

"Takhisis won't let him. She likes me," said Kit.

"For the moment," Skie growled.

Kitiara understood what he meant. She knew better than to trust Her Dark Majesty.

"I must do something to increase her favor and gain her support," said Kit. "Then she'll back me against Ariakas."

"You should have never left Solamnia," Skie grumbled. "Or at least you should have come here for a better reason than hopping into bed with a former lover."

"You are right," Kitiara admitted, pacing back and forth. "It was a fool's errand, and Tanis played *me* for the fool. But he'll pay—"

She came to a sudden halt. "Or maybe I did have a reason . . ."

"What would that be?" Skie asked, skeptical.

"I came to Solace because I uncovered a plot by the resistance leader, Tanis Half-Elven, to travel to the High Clerist's Tower to find the dragonlances!" Kit said triumphantly. "I will not only foil their plot, I will seize the dragonlances. . . . Skie! That's it! That's the answer! That is how I destroy Ariakas!"

"Keep your voice down!" Skie hissed.

"Bah! No one is listening! No one would dare spy on me!" said Kitiara, but she did lower her voice. "You said these dragonlances can kill chromatic dragons. I arrive at the Emperor's Summit with these dragonlances, which I pretend to give to the emperor as spoils of war. But instead, when I approach the throne, I use them to kill Ariakas and take the Crown of Power. And after that, I deal with any other Dragon Highlord who dares cross me."

"You are forgetting one small detail," said Skie. "You forget that these dragonlances are blessed by the gods. Takhisis couldn't destroy them. You wouldn't be able to touch one."

Kitiara was stymied. She had to admit what Skie said was true. She had seen a blue crystal staff nearly burn off Hederick's hand. She could only imagine what damage one of these accursed lances could cause. But she refused to give up her plan.

"I'll have Ladonna create some sort of magical gauntlets to protect me. That wizardess needs to do something to earn her pay. How long will it take us to fly to the High Clerist's Tower?"

"Three days," said Skie.

"Three days?" Kitiara was not pleased. "I cannot wait three days! Raistlin said they would arrive tomorrow."

Skie snorted. "That's impossible unless *they* fly."

"Raistlin knows a magic spell," said Kit. "Maybe it has something to do with that staff he carries. He tried to tell me about it once."

"You know very well that I have to stop to rest and hunt for food," said Skie, sounding resentful. "I cannot fly on an empty stomach. Three days. Or maybe you'd rather walk?"

Kitiara drew closer to the dragon, smiling a charming smile. "Skie, there is another way. . . . Dragons know all manner of magical spells. I'm sure you could cast a spell that would take us to the tower in the blink of an eye."

Skie growled, but he didn't say anything.

"You wouldn't have to worry about hunting or sleeping," Kitiara continued in wheedling tones. "You would arrive well rested, well fed. I'll grab the dragonlances and the dragon orb and then you can whisk us away to Neraka."

"I don't *whisk*," said Skie with a vicious snap of his teeth. "And I don't travel by magic. Dragons are meant to fly. I enjoy flying!"

"If you can't cast a spell, I guess I will ask Ladonna," said Kitiara. "She could use her magic to send both of us . . ."

Skie snarled. "I can cast the damn spell! But I can only take us *near* the High Clerist's Tower. I cannot take us inside the tower itself. The magic spell requires that I be able to visualize the location, and for obvious reasons I have never been inside the High Clerist's Tower. And then we have to deal with the green dragon, Cyan Bloodbane. Takhisis left him to guard the tower. You'd have to get past him."

"That great mound of green blubber?" said Kitiara disdainfully. "He does nothing but eat and sleep. I have heard he has grown so fat he can barely fly. He will not be a problem."

She drew near Skie. "Then you will do this for me?"

"I suppose I must," Skie grumbled. "But you must promise me

that if you get hold of the dragon orb, you won't do something stupid like trying to use it yourself. You can keep the dragonlances, but you must smash the orb to pieces."

"I promise," said Kitiara.

"When will you be ready to leave?" Skie asked. "I need to rest tonight."

Kit pondered. "I'd like to leave immediately, but I have to make arrangements for my armies to start marching to Neraka. I need my forces in place before the Summit. I will meet you here when I'm ready, sometime tomorrow."

She placed her hand on Skie's snout and gently rubbed the blue scales. "You are my one true friend; the only being in this world I trust. I need your help and your support. Please stand by me. Picture how well the Crown of Power will look on my head!"

"You're going to get us both killed," Skie muttered. "I'll think about it."

"Good," said Kitiara. She gave his snout a pat.

Skie grunted and lay back down, shifted his bulk until he got comfortable, and then closed his eyes.

Kit was about to depart, then turned back. "One more question."

Skie opened one eye to an annoyed slit. "What?"

"Have you heard of the Graygem of Gargath?"

"I have," said Skie with a yawn.

"What do you know about it?"

"That it flew around the world and changed gnomes into kender," Skie said.

"I know that silly tale. But does it truly exist?" Kitiara persisted. "Is it real?"

"What do you think?" Skie gave a derisive snort. "A gray rock that changes gnomes into kender? Of course it's not real! Now stop asking stupid questions and let me get some sleep."

Relieved, Kitiara left Skie curled up comfortably on the floor of his cave. As she walked back to camp, she went over her plans to send her troops marching east to Neraka. She had to decide what to do about Caramon, as well. She thought it likely that he was a traitor like his twin, since Raistlin led him around like a very large dog on a leash. She could always hang him, of course, but the other soldiers liked Caramon. Morale was already low, for her troops were languishing here in Solace, missing out on the fighting. And the looting.

She shrugged and put Caramon out of her mind. She'd think of some way to punish him. Now she had to concentrate on overthrowing the emperor.

CHAPTER
TWENTY

A gentle touch jolted Raistlin from a deep sleep. He immediately rose to confront danger, the words of a spell on his lips. Destina swiftly withdrew her hand and backed away.

"It's only me, Raistlin! I did not mean to startle you," she said. "Kairn and I thought we should leave early, while everyone is still sleeping."

Raistlin sighed; the words to the magic spell died. He rubbed his neck and grimaced. He must have fallen asleep while studying his spells, for his spellbook lay on the floor. He rose from the bed, picked up his book, and returned it to its case. He had studied the journeying spell last night and had hoped to find the spell emblazoned in his mind this morning, but this time there was nothing but ashes. He glanced at the Graygem and saw it wink.

"What is the hour?" he asked.

"Near sunrise," said Kairn.

Raistlin glanced out the window. Rain had fallen during the night, but it had stopped now. Darkness was giving way to a gray dawn. Everyone else was still deep in slumber.

"I want to say goodbye to Tas," said Destina.

"If you must," said Raistlin. "But be quick about it."

Destina walked over to the kender, who was still asleep, his head resting on his flour sack. She shook him gently by the shoulder.

"Tas . . ." she said.

"I didn't do it," Tas said drowsily. He sat up, blinking.

"Kairn and I are leaving, Tas," said Destina. "I wanted to say goodbye."

Tas was wide awake now. He jumped to his feet. "Goodbye? But aren't you taking me with you?"

"She can't, Tas," said Raistlin. "We need you to find something that is lost. You are the only one who knows where it is."

"I *am* good at finding things," Tas said. "But Destina needs me, too. It's very sad that I can't be in two places at once." He cast a sudden, hopeful glance at Raistlin. "Can I?"

"No," said Raistlin. "Thank the gods."

Tas thought it over. "I'm sorry, Destina. If Raistlin and the others need me for an Important Mission, I guess I should stay."

"I will miss you very much, Tas," said Destina, her eyes glimmering with tears. "Thank you for being my bodyguard and, more important, for being my friend."

She gave Tas a kiss on his forehead. He was afflicted by a snuffle and wiped his nose on his sleeve.

"Are you going to stop that bad man from killing Huma and Gwyneth?" Tas asked.

"I am going to try," said Destina.

"Tell Gwyneth I said hello and say hi to Knopple for me if you see him," said Tas. "And—"

"Enough!" said Raistlin. "Come with me."

"Where are we going?" Tas asked, reaching for his hoopak.

"I was talking to Destina and Kairn, not you," said Raistlin. "You're covered in flour from sleeping on the flour sack. Go take a bath."

"Do I have flour in my topknot?" Tas asked worriedly.

"You have flour all over," said Raistlin.

"I guess I'll take a bath, then," said Tas. "And look for bugbears. And see if Flint's still healed this morning."

Once Raistlin had made certain Tas was out the door, he accompanied Kairn and Destina to a quiet, empty room in the back part of the house. Destina had changed from her bloodstained jacket and skirt to a simple high-waisted linen dress and a hooded woolen shawl, which she had wrapped around her neck and shoulders to conceal the Graygem.

Kairn was wearing a knee-length belted tunic over a linen shirt and homespun breeches with a hat to cover his head. He was carrying his quarterstaff, and Destina wore her sword around her waist.

"We found these clothes in a chest," she explained, seeing Raistlin observing them. "When we arrive at the tower, we plan to tell people we are refugees from Palanthas."

"As good a story as any, I suppose," said Raistlin. "Although I am sure the knights will be curious to know how a refugee woman dressed in homespun comes to be carrying a valuable sword."

"I never thought of that," Destina said.

She glanced at Karin, who nodded. "Raistlin is right. They would at least ask questions and we want to remain inconspicuous."

Destina sighed and unbuckled the belt. She lay the sword on the bed. "The sword was my mother's. My father had it made specially for her. I don't like to leave it behind."

"If all goes well, you won't," said Raistlin enigmatically. "How are you feeling?"

He motioned Destina to a window to examine the wound in the dim light. She had washed away the mud. All that remained was a thin gash, and it was healing.

"Kairn told me you saved my life," Destina said. "I am very grateful."

Raistlin shrugged it off. "Just remember that Tully carries a poisoned knife."

"I am not likely to forget," said Destina with a wry smile.

"I need you to remember something else," said Raistlin. "Take the Graygem back to restore time, but do not use it unless you control it."

"Control it?" Destina was perplexed. "I am not sure what you mean."

"You took control of the Graygem to kill Captain and Mother," said Raistlin.

"I wanted to protect Kairn. I did not know it would kill them," Destina protested.

"Of course you didn't," said Raistlin impatiently. "How can we predict Chaos? And you may be driven by circumstance to use it again. Just be aware that the Dark Queen is searching for it, up and down the River of Time. If she sees the gray light flare, if she hears the blast, if she feels the tremors, she will know where to find you. And the Graygem."

Raistlin eyed Destina. "Chaos is our hope, as it is our despair. That is the paradox. We will do our best to keep Takhisis distracted."

Kairn took the Device of Time Journeying from the rucksack and held it in his hand. The room was dimly lit by the pale light of dawn filtering through the window. The light did not touch the Device. Its jewels did not shine or sparkle.

"Thank you for everything, Raistlin," said Destina earnestly. "I am sorry for involving you, but perhaps the gods were watching over me when I did. I could not have walked this path without your help."

"If you change the River of Time, you and I will never meet," said Raistlin. "I will have no memory of you. I will have no memory of Magius. The river will flow as it was meant to flow and wash away a past that never was. And while that is for the best, I think in many ways it will be a great pity."

Destina took hold of Kairn's hand. She rested her other hand on the Device.

"I am ready," she said.

Kairn spoke the words that activated the Device. "'With this poem that almost rhymes, now we travel back in time.'"

The jewels of the Device glowed brightly, and Kairn and Destina disappeared. The last Raistlin saw was a flicker of gray light, like a wink.

"And so it begins," Raistlin said. "Or ends."

He located the chest containing the miller's clothes and rummaged about until he found some that might fit Sturm, since his clothing was covered in blood. Raistlin carried the clothes to the front part of the house and draped them over a chair.

He then left the quiet house and walked to the creek. The morning was dreary and the clouds threatened more rain. The elves were awake and stirring about their camp, packing up bedrolls and preparing to travel. Several cast dark glances in his direction, and none of them spoke to him. Raistlin reached the stream, took off his clothes, and waded in, gasping at the shock of the cold water. He was shivering when he returned to the house to find Tanis unpacking a basket of food.

"The elves have provided breakfast. Flint is fetching water," said Tanis. "How is Destina this morning?"

"She is well. She and Kairn have started on their journey," said Raistlin. "They left at dawn. We will travel to the High Clerist's Tower tonight, the gods of magic willing. We must recover the dragonlances, make Takhisis believe we are a threat."

"How much time do we have?" Tanis asked.

"Three days, starting now," said Raistlin. "Of course, that assumes Chaos does not meddle with Destina. I, for one, think we should plan on living out the remainder of our lives here."

Tanis removed a large loaf of brown bread, dried apples and pears, figs, raisins, and nuts. "You realize you're going to have trouble with Flint."

"I realize," said Raistlin.

Flint came in at that moment, carrying the bucket of water. The dwarf set it down on the floor.

"What's in the basket?" he asked.

"Breakfast," said Tanis, cutting the bread with his knife.

"Breakfast?" Flint glared at the nuts and berries. "For what? A squirrel? I don't suppose there's any ale."

"We must make do with water," said Tanis.

Flint heaved a sigh, took a hunk of bread and nibbled at it, then shrugged and took another piece. "It's not as bad as it looks."

"Sturm is awake," Raistlin reported in a low voice to Tanis. "I have no idea how much he will remember of what happened to him. And I have no idea how we will explain any of it."

Sturm was sitting up on his pallet, staring at Flint. His bewildered gaze shifted to Tanis.

"Tell me, Raistlin," Sturm said in a low voice. "Do you see Tanis and Flint? Or am I delirious?"

"You are not having fever dreams. They are both here in the flesh," said Raistlin. "Do you remember Destina and Tas bringing you to this house?"

"I remember seeing the assassin slay Huma and I could not save him," said Sturm slowly, thinking back. "And then I remember hearing voices cry that the High Clerist's Tower had fallen. Takhisis came for the Graygem, but we escaped. Destina and Tas and I were in a field. I collapsed, and Destina and Tas brought me here to a world filled with darkness and flame and despair. But then blue light shone on me and eased my pain. A voice told me that the gods needed me and I must keep fighting."

He put his hand to where the gash in his chest had been and found it healed. He shook his head in wonder. "Where is Destina? She cared for me. I would like to thank her."

"She and Brother Kairn have left upon their journey," said Raistlin. "They have gone back to try to restore the River of Time. Takhisis is searching for the Graygem and we need to keep her from finding it. Tanis has traveled from our time to help us accomplish that mission. The Heroes of the Lance have one last battle to fight."

Tasslehoff entered the house, freshly scrubbed and devoid of flour. He came to the table and sat down next to Flint. "I'm coming with you. Raistlin said I was very important."

"We don't need any dang kender!" Flint grumbled. He glanced at Raistlin. "Or mages, either, for that matter."

"You do," said Tas. "You just don't know it yet."

Tas picked up a hunk of bread, a handful of raisins, and Tanis's knife, which he started to drop into his pouch. Tanis retrieved the knife and Tas, munching on bread, went over to talk to Sturm.

"I'm glad we found Goldmoon and that she healed you. It was my idea," said Tas. "Tanis usually has all the good ideas, but I had this one."

"Goldmoon and Riverwind," said Sturm.

His gaze went to them. The two were stirring, waking up. They looked momentarily confused, undoubtedly wondering where they were. Then Goldmoon looked down at the staff in her hand. She said something to Riverwind. They both glanced at Sturm, and Goldmoon smiled.

"They were here last night, weren't they?" said Sturm. "And Laurana . . . Was she here?"

"She is outside now," said Tanis. "But she won't know you, Sturm. You two have never met. This present isn't the past that hasn't happened, as Tas would say."

"A world where the kender makes sense," said Sturm. "I must go for a walk, clear my mind."

"There's a stream out back," Raistlin said. "You can bathe and change into those clothes. They should fit you."

"Watch out for bugbears," Tas warned.

"There are no bugbears, you doorknob!" said Flint.

"But there are elves," said Tanis. "So don't be surprised."

"Nothing would surprise me at this point," Sturm said. "Not even bugbears."

He picked up the clothes and left the house, heading for the creek. Riverwind and Goldmoon packed up their belongings. Tanis offered them some food.

"As you see, Sturm is well," he said. "Do not think him ungracious. He remembers little of what happened."

"Flint is fine, too, aren't you, Flint?" said Tas. "You're not going to die anymore. But you'll still wait for me under the tree, won't you?"

Flint snorted and stood up. "I'm going to go find real food. There might be something in the kitchen."

"I'll go with you," Tas offered. "Maybe there's sausages. Or bugbears."

Goldmoon and Riverwind went outside to the stream. After they were gone, Raistlin sat down at the table and began to eat with a revived appetite.

"I talked with Laurana about traveling to the High Clerist's Tower," said Tanis, sitting down beside him. "I believe we should risk it despite the dragon."

"The risk should be small," said Raistlin. "The journeying spell will take us directly inside the tower. The dragon will not even know we are there."

"Laurana said the tower was also guarded by undead."

"Caramon said the same, but when I pinned him down, he admitted he heard it from some soldiers who heard it from other soldiers, who swore they saw ghosts. My guess is that they saw them at the bottom of a jug of dwarf spirits."

"When can we leave?" asked Tanis.

"I must first study the spell, and that will take some time," said Raistlin.

"What do we do about the Plainsfolk—"

The door banged open and Laurana entered the room.

"We have trouble," she said.

CHAPTER TWENTY-ONE

"I knew it!" Tas cried, rushing out of the kitchen. "Bugbears! I have to warn Sturm!"

He started out the door, but Tanis caught hold of him. "Stay here with me where I can keep an eye on you."

"But the bugbears—" Tas began.

"There are no bugbears!" said Laurana impatiently.

"We know," said Tanis. "Go on."

"One of my people saw that human who serves the Highlord hanging about this house last night."

"Bakaris?" Raistlin asked, troubled.

Laurana shrugged. "I do not know his name. Aleta fired an arrow at him, but he got away. We tried to follow him, but lost him in the rain. He must have gone back and reported to the Highlord, for now Saber has spotted a squadron of draconians on the road, heading for the mill."

"Where did they see him?" Raistlin asked urgently. "Near the house?"

"Yes," said Laurana. "He was coming from the back—"

"I heard a sound last night," said Raistlin. "It came from the cellar. I thought it was vermin. . . ."

Flint hurried out the door, and soon returned to report.

"A man was in the cellar. He left his footprints all over, as well as an empty jug of brandy. I found it next to a barrel right below where you're standing."

Raistlin thumped the floorboards with the staff and, on the second attempt, he punched through the rotted wood.

"Bakaris could have heard everything we said," Raistlin said, glancing at Tanis. "He would tell Kitiara what he heard, if only to worm his way back into her good graces."

"And now he knows you are helping the resistance," Tanis added. "What about Caramon? Will he be in danger?"

"Caramon knows what to do," said Raistlin. "Meanwhile, we must decide what *we* are going to do."

"Saber could deal with the Bozaks, but if they do not report back to the Highlord, she will suspect something is wrong and come to investigate," Laurana said. "I think we should leave now before they arrive. You and your friends could come with us."

"I spoke to you of our plan to go to the High Clerist's Tower last night," said Tanis.

"Then you are determined to go through with this insane venture?" Laurana asked.

"We haven't discussed it with our friends yet, but I hope they will agree," said Tanis.

Laurana appeared displeased. "You are either very brave or very foolish, Tanthalas."

"Probably equal parts of both," said Tanis. "But we need to decide what to do about the Plainsfolk. We cannot take them with us."

"And I cannot take them to Qualinesti. My father . . ." Laurana shook her head. "I do not like to think I cannot trust him, but he has changed since he became beholden to the Dragon Queen. He is consumed with fear. Although he is Speaker of the Sun, he now sees only shadows. I have been thinking—"

Tas excitedly raised his hand. "I know! I know! You could take them to Pax Tharkas!"

Laurana drew back, staring at him in shock. "How did you know? I spoke no word of this to anyone!"

"Because that's where we go in the past that isn't this past, but another past, even though it seems they're both kind of the same only different—"

"Tas, go look for bugbears," said Tanis grimly.

"You said there weren't any bugbears," said Tas.

"I might have been wrong," said Tanis.

Tas went out the door, giving Tanis a reproachful look. "I wish you'd make up your mind."

Laurana stared after him, then turned to confront Tanis. "I *did* come to propose that the Plainsfolk travel with us to Pax Tharkas. Saber brought us news that the people Verminaard enslaved have risen up against the Dragon Highlord and taken over the mines. Verminaard was either injured or killed in the battle. But Elistan, the man who led the revolt, is said to be dying of a wasting disease, and Saber fears the rebellion will fail without him. I told Saber about the Plainsfolk and the staff of healing. The dragon has offered to go with us, provide us safe escort. There are many sick and injured among the people, as well as children. I only made up my mind this morning. How did the kender know?"

"We try not to ask Tas too many questions," said Raistlin. "For then he answers."

Laurana cast him a distrustful glance. "Let us talk outside, Tanthalas."

She walked back out into the morning sunlight. Tanis accompanied her. Riverwind and Goldmoon were walking together with Sturm, coming back from the stream. Riverwind came to a sudden halt and put his hand on his sword. He said something to Sturm and pointed to a dragon, just flying into view above the tree line.

"There is Saber now," said Laurana and she waved her arm.

Saber saw her signal and began to spiral down, landing in an open field not far from the house. The dragon stood twelve feet in height. He had two horns on his head, and his copper scales gleamed in the morning sun. He folded his wings at his side and settled down to wait, not venturing near, for Riverwind had drawn his sword.

"You need have no fear," Sturm told him. "Saber is a metallic dragon, and they are foes to the Dark Queen."

"Saber!"Tas shouted, dashing toward the dragon. "It's me! Tasslehoff!"

Saber regarded the kender in perplexity, then shook his head and turned to Laurana. He said something in elven and gestured to the Plainsfolk with a claw.

"What does the dragon want?" Goldmoon demanded.

"Saber would like to speak with you," Laurana said.

Saber bowed to the Plainsfolk with respect, extending his wings and lowering his head until his horns touched the ground. He spoke to them in Common, assuring them of his protection on the journey to Pax Tharkas.

Raistlin kept his distance, for the dragon was glancing at him. Sturm came over to stand beside him. The knight had bathed and changed into the clothes Raistlin had found for him. They were simple, but of good quality, as befitted the miller. Breeches, shirt, a leather vest beneath a russet-colored tunic.

Sturm was not paying any attention to the dragon. He was watching Laurana. "It grieves me to meet her as a stranger, when she was once my trusted friend."

"And will be again, or so we must hope," said Raistlin. "And now we should be going before the draconians arrive."

"Going where?" Sturm asked.

"Tanis will tell you," said Raistlin.

"Am I going to like it?" Sturm asked.

"Probably not," said Raistlin.

His attention was arrested by Tas, who was talking to Riverwind and Goldmoon. "Tell Elistan I said hello. Oh, and there's a friend of mine named Sestun. He'll need rescuing. And poor Flamestrike . . ."

Raistlin cast a glance at Sturm, who walked over to Tas, gripped his shoulder, and marched him back to the house. Raistlin went to speak to Riverwind and Goldmoon.

"I remind you that time is passing," said Raistlin. "If you are going to leave, you should do so now."

"My people and I will provide you an escort to Pax Tharkas,

which is a five days' journey," Laurana added. "The trip will be dangerous, but Saber will accompany us. I would give you time to reflect on your decision, but we need to set out immediately."

Goldmoon turned to Riverwind and clasped his hands in hers. "I see our path clearly before us now, my beloved. Mishakal asks us to carry her staff and her blessings to this man and to the children. We will honor the past by taking from it the good and the sorrowful that have made us what we are. But the past will rule us no longer. I am no longer Chieftain's Daughter. But I will be Riverwind's wife."

"And I will be Goldmoon's husband," said Riverwind. "We have seen many strange things and met many strange people on this journey. So long as we are together and the gods walk with us, we will go where we are called without fear."

"We will come with you, Lauralantha—" Goldmoon stumbled over the name.

"You may call me Laurana," she said. "The word fits more easily on the human tongue. We are prepared to depart at once, if you are."

"We have few belongings, and they are packed," said Riverwind.

"I'll check the road ahead," Saber offered, and took to the air. The sunlight flashed on his copper scales and shone through his coppery wings.

Riverwind and Goldmoon looked uncertainly back at the house.

"We should tell the others—" said Goldmoon.

"I will say your goodbyes for you," Raistlin offered. "The elves are impatient to leave."

"Please thank Tanis and your friends for helping us," said Goldmoon. "And thank you, Raistlin. I fear we misjudged you."

She reached out to him, but Raistlin drew back from her touch, sliding his hands into the sleeves of his robes.

"May the gods walk with you," he said.

Goldmoon lowered her hand. "And with you."

She and Riverwind joined Laurana, and the three of them set off at a swift pace. The elves fanned out around them, taking cover in the brush.

"Goodbye, Goldmoon! Goodbye, Riverwind!" Tasslehoff shouted from the house, waving his hoopak. "I'll see you at your wedding!"

Raistlin returned to the house and found the others waiting for him.

"I told them where we are going and how we are going to get there," said Tanis. "The Bozaks could be here at any time. When will you be ready to cast your spell?"

"The journeying spell is complex," Raistlin said stiffly. Last night's failure to grasp the spell had shaken him. He was prey to doubt, picturing himself having to face them and admit defeat.

Sturm was not helpful. "Since Raistlin has never cast this spell before, it will be safer to arrive at the tower after dark anyway. The gods know where we'll end up."

Raistlin swallowed an angry retort.

Tanis cast him a concerned glance, which Raistlin pointedly ignored.

"Then we should take shelter in the woods," said Tanis. "Hopefully when the Bozaks search this mill and find it deserted, they'll assume we have gone with the elves and they'll leave. We can return to the house and get what rest we can while Raistlin studies his spell."

"I won't be magicked," said Flint, crossing his arms over his chest.

"It's very exciting, Flint!" said Tas. "I was with Magius when he cast this spell. I didn't know I knew magic, but I guess I do because he said I could help and I did. He and I took us to the High Clerist's Tower. I'll help you, too, Raistlin. Don't worry."

Raistlin sighed deeply. He picked up the case that held his spellbook and the Staff of Magius and accompanied the others into the woods. They kept watch on the house while he sat down alone beneath a tree and drew his spellbook from its case.

He remembered so clearly Magius taking the time to teach him the journeying spell. Few mages would have done so. Most guarded their spells jealously, refusing to divulge them to anyone. But Magius had been generous, taking pleasure in passing on his knowledge.

Raistlin stared down at the words he had written in the language of magic and tried to make sense of them, but just like last night, they seemed to crawl off the page like ants running away to hide. He had to concentrate. He had to master the words, make the magic his own.

He would do so for the honor of his teacher.

CHAPTER
TWENTY-TWO

Destina and Kairn had discussed their plan to return to the High Clerist's Tower during the time of the Third Dragon War, trying to decide when to arrive. They could not calibrate the Device down to the hour, but, as Alice Ranniker had told Kairn, the more specificity as to date and time he could provide, the closer he would come to attaining his goal. Since he and Destina would appear to any onlooker to materialize out of the ethers, they also needed to find a location inside the High Clerist's Tower where no one was likely to observe their unorthodox arrival.

The High Clerist's Tower was a massive fortress designed centuries ago by Vinas Solamnus, founder of the Solamnic Knights. Built in the Vingaard Mountains, the tower guarded the Westgate Pass, which led to the Solamnic city of Palanthas. The soaring complex consisted of sixteen floors containing hundreds of rooms, including offices, a dungeon, a private chapel, bedchambers, a kitchen, pantry, and wine cellar, an armory, an extensive library, chambers for the High Clerist and his attendants, and the beautiful Temple of the High Clerist, on the ground level.

Centuries ago, at the height of Solamnia's power, the High Clerist's Tower had been filled with life. Pilgrims came from all over Ansalon to pray in the temple, where the High Clerist and his staff presided over the religious order of the knighthood. But now most of the floors were sealed off, their rooms dark and deserted. The knights barely had men enough to defend the tower.

Destina and Kairn planned to return to the Knight's Chapel on the date of Immolatus's attack on the temple. That seemed a critical point in time, for the same event had occurred in Astinus's original record. Immolatus had attacked the tower for a different reason then, but he'd suffered the same disastrous outcome. Huma and Gwyneth and Commander Belgrave had fought Immolatus using the dragon-lances, critically wounding him.

At that point in time, the Graygem had caused the River of Time to diverge. In the original timeline, Commander Belgrave had survived the assault, uncovered the plot of Mullen Tully to assassinate Huma, and stopped him. But in Chaos time, Belgrave had died, and Tully had slain Huma. Takhisis had been victorious. The words on the pages of Astinus's account of Huma had vanished, replaced by words written in blood.

Because the words were no longer there, they needed the Graygem to restore the original. And yet the Graygem would start to change time the moment they arrived.

As Raistlin had told Destina, "Chaos is our hope, as it is our despair. That is the paradox."

The Knight's Chapel was located on the second floor. It was a private sanctuary reserved for the use of the knights, as opposed to the main temple, which was open to the public. Since Huma and the three other knights were manning the defense at Noble's Gate, Kairn was confident he and Destina would find the chapel empty.

The Device of Time Journeying brought them safely to their destination and set them down gently outside the Knight's Chapel. They could see stars shining in the darkness and were relieved to find that they had arrived at night, as they had planned. They entered the chapel and closed the door behind them. Sunlight never reached the chapel, which was located in the interior of the tower, yet blessed light, shining through the stained glass windows, illuminated the room, keeping darkness at bay.

Kairn stowed the Device safely in his rucksack as Destina looked around the silent chapel. The peace and tranquility eased her troubled spirit, and she rested her hand on the back of one of the rosewood pews.

"Since we came here last, I have been wondering if my father visited the chapel before his death," she said. "I like to imagine that when he heard from Sturm about the return of the true gods, he sought them himself and found them here. Perhaps he also found the courage to stay to defend the tower, led by Sturm's example."

Destina sighed and ran her hand over the polished wood. "I would have taken all that away from him. I am mortified to think that I plotted to rob my father of his honor and his faith, and I writhe with shame when I see myself trying to give Sturm Brightblade that potion of cowardice. Without Sturm's sacrifice and my father's during the War of the Lance, the High Clerist's Tower might well have fallen to the Dark Queen's might. And now I have seen for myself the dreadful shadow she casts over the world."

Destina clasped her hand around the Graygem. It was dark and cold to the touch, but she could feel it pulse with life.

"I have done so much harm, and now I have a chance to restore what I destroyed," said Destina. "And yet, again, I fear I will fail."

She wished that she had the strength to take hold of the Graygem and command it to do her bidding, as she had done when Kairn's life had been in peril. But even as she considered it, the Graygem grew hot as flame, and Destina was forced to let go.

"It is hopeless," she said despairingly.

"We are here *because* we have hope," said Kairn.

He took hold of her hand and, as he did, she saw the small ring of Chislev on her little finger reflect the gray light. A memory touched her. She reached out to it, tried to hold on to it, for it seemed important. But the Graygem flared and the memory shattered as the walls and floor shook with a violent tremor. A blast of horns sounded the alarm and a call to arms. She heard a triumphant roar, and the dust of ages cascaded down from the vaulted ceiling. A chalice fell from the altar and landed on the floor with a metallic clang.

They could not see, for there were no windows, but they had no need to see, for they both remembered.

"Immolatus is attacking the temple," Kairn said.

The lights suspended from the ceiling on chains were swaying as the walls shook from the thundering blows of the dragon's massive tail and his brutal claws. They could smell smoke and see it rising up the stairs.

Terror gripped Destina, seeming to twist her heart and dissolve her bones.

"Dragonfear!" Kairn gasped, and she felt him tremble. He gripped his staff, sacred to Gilean, his knuckles white.

Destina grasped the little ring of Chislev and held on fast with her failing strength. She couldn't form the words, for her mouth was numb, but they must have been in her heart. The fear of the dragon eased, though the assault still continued.

Kairn took a torch from the wall, and they ran down the hall toward the stairs that were rapidly filling with smoke from the iron-wood gates. Immolatus had first set fire to the gates, then battered down the stone walls to try to enter the temple.

"The stairwell that leads to the courtyard," said Kairn. "The shaft extends through all sixteen floors. The stairs on the first floor open into the temple."

They located the nearby stairwell and began to descend the stairs, moving slowly and clinging to each other to keep their balance as the walls shook and trembled.

"Immolatus smashes the altars of Paladine and Mishakal," said Kairn, recalling what Astinus had written. "He does not know that Gwyneth is aware of his coming and that she and Huma are preparing to confront him. Huma is armed with a dragonlance, and Gwyneth takes her true form, that of a silver dragon, to attack him."

Over the noise of crashing stone, they could hear the dragon howl in pain and outrage. Not far from where they had taken refuge, they heard a man shouting and other men crying out in fear.

"I recognize the voice. That is Commander Belgrave!" Destina said.

They reached the bottom of the stairwell and found the door

leading into the temple closed. Kairn placed the torch into a sconce on the wall and cautiously opened the door a crack so that they could see. Soldiers were running about in confusion, their training and discipline subsumed by the dragonfear.

They could not see Commander Belgrave from their vantage point, but they could hear him try to rally his soldiers.

"But his men are overcome by dragonfear and they flee, leaving him to fight alone," said Kairn. "He picks up one of the dragonlances thrown by Huma and deals Immolatus a critical blow. Immolatus is in terrible pain with no stomach to continue the fight, and he limps away. Belgrave is badly wounded, but he survives and stops Tully—"

Kairn was watching from his place behind the door, when a soldier came running straight toward it. He shoved open the door and then stopped at the sight of Kairn and Destina, crouching in the stairwell. The soldier was frantic with terror, his eyes wide and white-rimmed. Half-crazed from dragonfear, he drew his sword and sprang at them.

Kairn ducked the soldier's wild swing and struck him on the side of his helm with his staff, knocking him to the floor. The soldier lay still.

"He'll be all right, won't he?" Destina asked worriedly.

"He will have a headache when he wakes, but nothing worse," said Kairn.

He started out the door, when Destina caught hold of him and pulled him back into the safety of the stairwell.

"Immolatus!" she whispered.

The red dragon was staggering through the smoke of the burning ironwood and crawling over the wreckage of Noble's Gate. The sun was just starting to rise, and Immolatus squinted against the light. Blood flowed from large gashes where he'd been struck by the dragonlances, and he limped on an injured leg. He could barely see, for Gwyneth in her silver dragon form had attacked him with her breath-weapon—an icy blast of frost that had engulfed his head. Groaning in agony, he managed to fly over the walls of the High Clerist's Tower, his injured leg dangling, leaving gouts and splotches of blood on the walls and the ground below.

"There is Commander Belgrave," Destina said softly, pointing.

"He is badly wounded," said Kairn. "But he will recover from his wounds."

"He has to," said Destina.

Titus was covered in blood, both his own and the dragon's, and his armor was pierced in numerous places. He had attacked Immolatus with the dragonlance, but he had missed the killing stroke and the dragon had seized him in his jaws, picked him up, and hurled him to the ground.

Titus lay where he had fallen, grimacing in pain. The dragonfear was gone. The soldiers who had fled in terror were starting to return. One drew near Titus, who reached out his hand for aid. The soldier took hold of Belgrave by the arm. Destina saw a knife flash and watched in horror to see the soldier thrust his blade into the commander's armpit.

Belgrave stared at the soldier, a look of astonishment on his face. The soldier hid the bloody knife in his boot and rose to his feet. Destina caught a glimpse of his face and recognized him.

"Tully!" she cried. "Help! Seize him!"

Tully heard her, and he shifted to face her. She sprang to her feet and ran toward him, hardly knowing what she was doing, her only thought to detain him. She saw his eyes widen, and at first she thought that he had recognized her, then she realized he was not looking at her. He was staring at the Graygem. Glancing down, she saw it pulse with a strange, eerie light.

He stared at the jewel and then he backed away and melted into the darkness of the temple.

Belgrave was looking searchingly about. His gaze fixed on Destina. He beckoned to her and she knelt at his side.

"Help is coming, sir," she said, clasping his hand.

Belgrave gave an impatient shake of his head, as though that did not matter. "That man, Tully! He is an agent for the dragon! He is plotting . . . to betray Huma! Stop him!"

He gripped her hand so tightly, she winced.

"Promise me, Destina!" he said urgently.

"I promise, sir," said Destina.

Belgrave sighed and fell back. "The light is fading. I cannot see. Where is Sir Huma?"

"I am here, Commander," said Huma, coming to kneel beside him.

Destina drew back into the shadow of the stairwell as the other knights and soldiers gathered around their fallen comrade, their heads bowed in grief and shame for having deserted him. Belgrave struggled to speak again, but he choked on his own blood.

Huma clasped the commander's hand to his chest. "Your watch has ended, sir. Go to your rest."

Belgrave drew a final, shuddering breath, gave a deep sigh, and closed his eyes. He did not draw breath again.

Destina waited tensely for the cries of outrage and for Huma to order them to go in pursuit of the assassin, but the commander's injuries were so numerous, it seemed no one noticed the fatal wound. She was shaking, and Kairn put his arm around her.

"Tully killed him, Kairn! Did you see?"

"I saw," said Kairn. "What did the commander say to you?"

"He told me that Tully was a traitor, an agent of the dragon. The commander made me promise I would stop him. He knew me, Kairn!"

"That is not possible," said Kairn.

Destina watched as Will—the commander's loyal and dedicated retainer—sank to his knees by the body.

"He cannot die, sir," said Will brokenly. "He is not dead, Sir Huma! He will be well!"

Huma listened to him, his expression one of weariness and sorrow. "Commander Belgrave walks with Paladine now, Will. We must let him go."

"'He walks with Paladine,'" Destina repeated. "That is how he knew me. The gods are with us."

Destina was suddenly enraged and grasped hold of the Graygem to yank it from her neck. The gem was blazing hot to the touch, and she was forced to let go of it. But she would not let go of her anger or her resolve.

"I may not be able to control the Graygem, but I will not let Chaos win." Destina tucked the Graygem beneath her blouse and wrapped her shawl around her shoulders, burying it, as though she would smother it. "I will make time my own."

Kairn regarded her in uneasy doubt. "What do you mean to do?"

"I came here to 'fix' time, to restore the original timeline. But that doesn't exist anymore, Kairn. All we know is that Huma and Gwyneth have to defeat the Dark Queen and banish her to the Abyss. I will strive to make that happen. We will save the song, as Tas said. Nothing else matters. I won't let it matter. Not even the fact that Tully saw the Graygem."

Kairn stared at her, appalled. "Are you certain?"

"I could see the gray light reflected in his eyes," said Destina. "I would swear the gem wanted him to see it! We need to find him before he tells Immolatus or the Dark Queen."

"I think we are too late. He knows you saw him murder the commander and he heard you call him by name," said Kairn. "You are a threat to him. He could come after you. We should return to our own time, even if it is consumed by darkness. We will find a way to fight Takhisis—"

Destina clasped his hands in her own. "I vowed I would give my life to fix history, Kairn. I promised the commander as he lay dying that I would stop Tully. I will not run. The gods fight with me. Will you?"

"You know the answer, Destina," said Kairn. "You have always known."

"I know that I love you," said Destina. "And love is our best weapon against evil."

"And there is Sir Reginald," said Kairn in a low voice. "I think he is looking for us."

The knight appeared haggard and shaken, still recovering from the shock of the dragon's attack and the death of Commander Belgrave. Kairn and Destina rose to greet him.

"I am Sir Reginald Homesweld," he said, introducing himself. "I hope you do not think me discourteous, but I need to know who both of you are and how you come to be here."

"I am Destina Rosethorn, and this is Kairn Uth Tsartolhelm. We are refugees from Palanthas. We were returning through Westgate Pass when we were attacked by the dragon. We escaped and have made our way back here to seek refuge."

"You were among those who stayed here?" Sir Reginald asked. "I do not remember you, but there were many at the time. What is in the rucksack?"

"Clothes, food," Kairn replied. He took it off his shoulder and held it out. "You can search through it if you'd like."

Sir Reginald waved it aside. "That will not be necessary. As far as seeking refuge here, I fear you have come at an inopportune time. The Dark Queen's forces are advancing on us. We will find you accommodations in the tower, but you must understand the danger. We cannot vouch for your safety."

"How far away are the dragonarmies?" Destina asked.

"They are within two days' march," said Sir Reginald. "I must insist that you remain inside the tower. I cannot have you interfering with the tower's defenders. The guest rooms are on the sixth floor. I will take you there. I must warn you, though, you will be on your own. No other guests are staying with us—for obvious reasons."

As he was escorting them up the stairs, they encountered a red-robed wizard coming down. He was holding a staff topped with a crystal globe held in a dragon's claw. Both Kairn and Destina recognized Magius. He did not know them, of course, and he paused to stare at the sight of them.

"I see we have guests, Sir Reginald," Magius said.

His gaze was so intense that Destina self-consciously started to take hold of the Graygem to hide it from his sight. But she recalled Raistlin warning her that, when she did, she only called attention to it. She quickly clasped both her hands together.

"They are refugees from Palanthas," Sir Reginald stated.

Magius said nothing to them. He turned his full attention to Sir Reginald. "What was that dreadful commotion? I was rudely wakened from my slumber."

"The dragon Immolatus attacked the temple," said Sir Reginald. "We could have used your help."

"Since when?" Magius asked, with a sardonic smile.

Sir Reginald frowned and did not answer.

"Did you slay the dragon?" Magius asked. "Hopefully before he damaged the wine cellar?"

Sir Reginald was stone-faced. "Lord Huma and the elf woman,

Gwyneth, wounded the beast using those weapons they call dragon-lances. Sadly, Commander Belgrave was slain in the attack."

"A pity," said Magius coolly. "But, after all, you knights live for death and glory."

He bowed to Destina and Kairn. "A pleasure meeting you both. By the way, you might want to concoct a more believable story. Even Sir Reginald here can see through it."

Sir Reginald watched him continue down the stairs and shook his head. "We may live for glory, but he lives to be unpleasant. Your rooms are this way."

"I wish we could warn Magius that he is in danger," said Destina in a low voice as they followed the knight.

"It would do no good," said Kairn. "Raistlin tried to tell him and Magius paid no heed."

When they arrived at the guest rooms, Sir Reginald said he would send a servant with water for washing and asked if they needed anything else.

"As I said, you are on your own," Sir Reginald added. "We don't have men enough to stand guard."

"Where is Sir Richard?" Destina asked.

Kairn cast her a warning glance. Sir Richard had been standing guard the night the Gudlose had abducted Magius. They had slain the knight, garroting him, almost severing his head.

"I met him the last time we were here," Destina added hurriedly. "I was thinking I would like to see him again, thank him for his kindness."

"Sir Richard is getting some well-deserved sleep," said Sir Reginald. "He and I take turns, so that one of us is always on duty."

"Then he won't be here tonight," said Destina.

"Not as weary as he was," said Sir Reginald.

"One more question, sir," said Destina. "Are you familiar with a yeoman named Mullen Tully? Did Commander Belgrave mention him?"

"He did," said Sir Reginald, giving her a puzzled look. "Why do you ask?"

"We have reason to believe he is an agent for the dragon Immolatus," Destina replied.

Sir Reginald gave her a penetrating look. "Commander Belgrave believed the same. But how did you know?"

"I was with Commander Belgrave as he lay dying," Destina faltered, seeing him regard her with suspicion. "He warned me about this man, Mullen Tully. He said he was an agent for the dragon, sent to kill Lord Huma. Those were almost his last words."

"I see," said Sir Reginald, his grim expression relaxing. "We have been keeping watch for him and we will continue to do so, although he might be hard to find. We have many hundred yeomen serving here."

"I understand," said Destina. "We would now like to go to the temple to offer our prayers to the gods. We will not be in the way, I assure you."

"You should know that dragon defiled the temple," said Sir Reginald.

"But the gods are still there," said Destina.

Sir Reginald smiled. "Indeed, they are, Mistress. Offer your prayers and may Paladine grant them."

He told them they could take their meals in the dining hall, which was located on this floor, and then hurried away.

"At least Sir Richard will not die this night," said Destina, relieved. "And they will be keeping watch for Tully. He must have known the commander suspected him and that is why he killed him, hoping no one would notice in the confusion of the battle."

"It almost worked," said Kairn. "If you had not been there—"

"But I was there, as the gods intended!" said Destina. "I know Tully by sight. We must find him."

"Remember he might be trying to find you," said Kairn. "As for now, he has probably fled back to the dragon's camp. We know he goes there to report, and that the wounded Immolatus will give him the greatsword with orders to kill Gwyneth and Huma."

"The dragon's camp . . ." Destina murmured in thoughtful tones. "Immolatus will end up fleeing the battle when the gnomish invention blows up and destroys his army. We must make certain that happens. The gnomes were planning to bring their invention to the knights so they could use it to defend the tower, but it broke down on the road. Tas made it work. You told him he changed history, yet

Astinus wrote that the explosion of the gnomish device destroyed the army of Immolatus."

"Which means that even without Tas, we know something happens to cause the device to explode," said Kairn.

"In truth, we don't know anything because the Graygem could be changing everything," said Destina bitterly. "I would like to make certain . . ."

"And, as a scholar, I would like to know what happened," said Kairn.

"It means we will have to leave the tower without anyone knowing, for if the guards see us, they will try to stop us," said Destina. "Tas sneaked out through the Sacristy. Is what we are doing wrong?"

"The book is now your book, Destina," said Kairn. "It is not mine. Not even Astinus's."

As they were leaving the sixth floor, Destina cast a glance at the room she remembered belonged to Magius. A strange, eerie light shone from under the closed door. Destina paused to stare at it, her brow furrowed. She raised her hand as though to knock.

Kairn guessed what she intended.

"Magius has a dragon orb," said Kairn softly. "He smuggled one out of the Tower of High Sorcery in Palanthas with the plan to use it during the battle. He will hide the orb tomorrow night to prevent it falling into the hands of the Gudlose. Centuries later, Tasslehoff will find this same dragon orb and use it as Magius intended—to defeat the forces of the Dark Queen."

"If I warned him, all of that might change," said Destina. She sighed and lowered her hand, clasped it around the Graygem.

They continued down the stairs to the temple. Men were already at work, attempting to repair the damage done by the dragon, gathering up the pieces of broken statuary and cleansing the dragon's blood from the floor and the walls. Others were preparing to escort the body of Commander Belgrave to the Chamber of Paladine for burial. Torches blazed, and the temple was filled with light. Huma was inspecting the mounted dragonlance, and Destina heard him ask Gwyneth how he could best make use of it when the two were airborne battling the forces of the Dark Queen.

She and Kairn continued to the Sacristy, a room off the temple, located near Merchant's Gate. The Sacristy served as a robing chamber for the High Clerist and the other knights prior to conducting services in the temple. Cloaks and ceremonial robes and other raiment hung from hooks on the walls. Helms and pieces of armor were stored in chests. Books lay on the tables. No one was inside, however. The time for ceremony was over. Everyone was preparing for battle.

"Tas crawled through that window," said Destina, pointing.

"I think you and I could just walk through the door," said Kairn dryly.

They took two hooded cloaks from the hooks on the wall and put them on over their clothes. Anyone seeing them from a distance might mistake them for knights. Kairn cautiously opened the door and looked outside, blinking in the bright sunlight. The door provided access to a courtyard between Merchant's Gate and the main entrance, Noble's Gate. Seeing no one around, they hurried out.

They avoided Noble's Gate, for men were cleaning up the rubble left by the dragon's destructive rampage, and instead crossed over the bridge that led to the Knight's Spur, a small fortress on the east side of the tower.

The knights had pulled their forces back from the Knight's Spur, for they no longer had troops enough to defend it, and it was deserted. Destina and Kairn descended the ramp that led from the fortress to the plains below.

"Tas left the tower to try to find a gnome village that lay to the east," said Destina. "He spent the night in those woods and from there he saw the gnomes, traveling along the road."

They entered the woods where Tas had camped for the night, and from that vantage point they could see the road, barely visible through the trees, and what appeared to be a dark river flooding the plains.

"Armies of the Dark Queen," said Kairn. "They are coming from all parts of Solamnia, converging on the High Clerist's Tower. Takhisis is taking her time, waiting for all her forces to assemble. She is well aware that the knights can do nothing but await her pleasure."

They hastened through the woods, feeling very vulnerable away from the safety of the tower. They almost immediately saw the gnome version of a dragonlance. The contraption consisted of a gigantic ballista bolted onto a large steel box with what appeared to be a castle-like turret in front. Steam belched from a boiler attached to the back. It was supposed to be rolling along on numerous wheels, but despite being wreathed in clouds of steam, the dragonlance had ground to a halt.

A small army of gnomes surrounded it, kicking the wheels, waving their arms, pointing fingers at one another, and shouting accusations.

Destina and Kairn approached the contraption with trepidation, aware that gnomish devices had an unfortunate tendency to explode, especially one that carried several kegs of what the gnomes termed "boom powder." Before they reached it, however, a kender darted in front of them, waving his hoopak and nearly running into them.

"Beg pardon!" the kender shouted over his shoulder. "Frightful hurry!"

The kender was tall, for a kender, and a bit on the portly side. He was wearing the usual colorful and mismatched clothing of a kender, though his was disheveled and covered in soot, as though he had recently been in a fire. His hoopak was charred and trailing wisps of smoke. If he'd had a topknot, it was gone, as were his eyebrows.

"Hullo, hullo, hullo!" the kender called to the gnomes.

When the gnomes caught sight of him, all arguments ceased. The gnomes appeared astonished. They huddled in conference and then one of their number detached himself from the group and hurried over to meet the kender.

"UncleTrapspringer!Whyareyouhere?Youaredead," said the gnome in accusing tones.

"Uncle Trapspringer!" Kairn said, awed. "Of course!"

"Hush!" Destina squeezed his hand.

"I was momentarily incapacitated!" Uncle Trapspringer was saying indignantly. "You lot went off and left me."

"Becauseyouweredead!" said the gnome irritably. "Boom!And thatwasthelastwesawofyou."

"Confound it, slow down!" said Uncle Trapspringer, highly annoyed. "You know I can't understand you when you mash all your words together. I admit that I probably shouldn't have lighted my pipe that close to the boom powder, but live and learn, as they say. You will be glad to hear I have given up smoking. Nasty habit. I see you're having a spot of bother with the contraption there, Knopple."

"We have come to the High Clerist's Tower to make delivery of our invention, which, as you can see, is intended for the impalement and subsequential demise of dragons."

"Not going to be doing much impaling if it isn't moving," said Uncle Trapspringer, regarding the whistling and belching machine with a critical eye.

Knopple waved his hand in a dismissive gesture. "Minor technicality. We plan to refer it to committee. A pity, really, because we were going to test it on a big red dragon we saw flying about."

"I think I might have an idea," said Uncle Trapspringer. "I see a switch there on that panel. It is in the 'Off' position. Perhaps if you turned it to 'On' your invention would work."

Knopple glared at him. "Everyone's an engineer."

"Just try," said Uncle Trapspringer. "It couldn't hurt."

"Oh, yes, it could," Knopple muttered in ominous tones. "Show of hands. Who is in favor of flipping the 'Off' switch to 'On'?"

After some discussion, the gnomes voted to flip the switch. Knopple walked over to the switch and seemed to hesitate, perhaps because most of the other gnomes were backing away.

"Duckandcover," one advised.

"Sound advice," said Uncle Trapspringer, and he jumped behind a tree.

Knopple drew in a deep breath, covered his eyes, and flipped the switch.

Bells rang. Whistles shrieked. The boiler belched and the contraption roared to life. The blades on the ballista began to whirl. The wheels started to turn, slowly at first, then picking up speed. The gnomes raised a cheer and began jumping onto the deck of the contraption as it trundled along.

Knopple climbed into the turret high atop the contraption. "My

Life's Quest. I shall call it a dragonlance since it is a lance meant to kill dragons. I will refer it to the Committee on Trademarks, Patents, and Copyrights."

He pointed and shouted, "Leadmetothedragon!"

The contraption bounced along, jouncing over ruts in the road and sending gnomes flying.

Uncle Trapspringer emerged from behind the tree and stood gazing at the dragonlance as it rumbled along, belching and whistling, headed for the camp of Immolatus.

"My idea, you know," Uncle Trapspringer said proudly. "Especially the addition of the boom powder. Gives it quite a kick. Well, must be going. Opposite direction, of course. Don't want to be in the radius of the blast zone."

Uncle Trapspringer gave Kairn and Destina a jaunty wave and set off down the road.

"At least we know that Reorx watches over the gnomes, and by his grace they survive the blast that destroys Immolatus's army," said Kairn.

"And to think we met Uncle Trapspringer," said Destina. "Tas would be thrilled." Her voice softened. "I hope I see Tas again. But even if I do, I might not remember him. As Raistlin says, none of this will have happened."

"You will," said Kairn. "I don't know how or why, but you will. Tas leaves an indelible mark on the lives of those who encounter him."

The sun was sinking down toward the mountains when Kairn and Destina returned to the abandoned Knight's Spur. They discarded their robes, leaving them in the fortress, then crossed the bridge and returned to the High Clerist's Tower.

All was quiet. Work had ceased for the day. Those on duty walked the battlements, keeping watch on the armies snaking toward them. Those off duty went to get what sleep they could or gathered in the dining hall to talk of the dragon's attack and how Huma had driven him off using magical weapons provided by the gods. But their mood was dark and grim.

"More dragons will come, as well as the Dark Queen herself," said one of the soldiers. "Magical weapons or not, how can we stand against them?"

Kairn and Destina ate supper in the dining hall, though neither was particularly hungry. Sir Reginald saw them and nodded in passing, as though glad to see they were obeying orders. He hastened on, too busy to speak to them.

"We should not go back to our rooms," said Kairn. "Tully might find out where you are staying and come searching for you. And this is the night Immolatus will send the Gudlose to abduct Magius. Our rooms are on the same floor as his."

"And we can do nothing to save him!" said Destina bitterly. "Not without changing history. People wish they could foresee the future, but I think it is far better to live in happy ignorance."

Kairn suggested that they spend the night in the Knight's Chapel. Tully would not think to look for them there. As they entered the chapel, Destina felt the presence of the gods soothe and comfort her. One of the knights had taken time from war preparations to place fresh candles on the altar. Their flames burned steadily, without flickering or wavering. She sat down in one of the pews.

Kairn leaned his staff against the wall and placed the rucksack on the floor, then sat down beside Destina. He put his arms around her, and she rested her head against his shoulder.

"I have been thinking. If we do find Tully, what do we do with him?" she asked. "We cannot accuse him for we have no proof against him. He would simply deny everything, and it would be our word against his."

"Dalamar would say we should kill him," said Kairn wryly. "But even if we could bring ourselves to murder Tully in cold blood, his death might not change anything. Immolatus could simply send another assassin."

"Tully must have a secret way to enter the tower, for he comes and goes between here and the dragon's camp with impunity," said Destina. "Did Astinus mention it in his writings?"

"Tully was little more than a footnote," said Kairn. "Astinus wrote that he was an assassin sent by the dragon to kill Huma and Gwyneth and his mission failed when Commander Belgrave denounced and killed him. History swept him away after his death and forgot about him."

"But Chaos remembered," said Destina.

The stillness of night closed around them, bringing sleep and blessed forgetfulness.

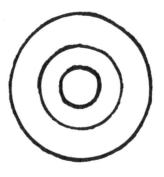

CHAPTER
TWENTY-THREE

Night had also fallen on Raistlin and those centuries away from Kairn and Destina. Yet the two were in his thoughts. He and the others had spent the morning hiding in the woods and watching the Bozaks search for them. The draconians had fanned out, entering the house, searching the cellar, and poking around the outbuildings. They investigated the grounds around the house, then came together to discuss their findings.

"The house is empty, but people were staying there," said one. "And someone was down in the cellar."

"Bakaris," said another who appeared to be the commander. "Hiding from danger. As usual."

The Bozaks all chuckled.

"The stink of elves is still in the air," the commander continued. "Elf footprints are all over the ground and there's evidence they made camp. And it looks like a dragon landed there. Probably that copper we heard about."

"Judging by the traces, the elves went off in that direction, sir," said one, pointing to the west. "We couldn't tell for certain, but it's likely the half-elf and his friends went with them."

"Should we go after them, sir?"

The Bozak snorted. "I'm not tangling with a copper. Our orders were to search for the half-elf and apprehend him and the others if we found them. We didn't find them. So now we go back to camp and make our report."

The Bozaks departed, taking the road back toward Solace. After they left, Tanis and the others returned to the house to make preparations to leave. Tanis started to approach Raistlin, but he made an impatient gesture, waving him away.

The words to the magic remained dark and kept slipping away. He swore softly. The spell had come to him so easily yesterday and today, but when he most needed it, the magic perversely eluded him. He tried to remember the sound of Magius's voice, his intonation, where he placed the emphasis on each syllable, the flow of the words, the rhythm. Raistlin tried and failed and tried again until the words muddled together and he had to clear his head.

He was thinking of Magius and remembered a conversation. The two had been talking about the Test in the Tower of High Sorcery. Mages risked their lives to take it, for failure meant death.

"Have you ever asked yourself why we take the risk?" Magius had asked.

"Most believe we do it for the power," Raistlin had replied.

"I made the same mistake when I was young," Magius had said. "Before I had taken the Test, I reveled in the thought of the power magic would give me. Afterward, I was wiser. Consider what the magic requires of us. We must spend hours every day studying and memorizing spells. When we cast them, they drain our bodies and our minds to the point of collapse. And the next day, we must do this all again. And what power do we gain? The power to cast a spell over a handful of goblins that does nothing more than provide them a restful night's sleep."

Raistlin had smiled. "Then why do you do it?"

"The same reason you do. For the sake of the magic," Magius had said.

Raistlin heard Magius speak, and the words to the spell seemed to catch fire on the page and blaze before his eyes. He knew pure joy in that moment, and it was worth the trouble and torment. For the sake of the magic.

He returned to the house at sunset, weary, but triumphant.

"Do you know our spell?" Tasslehoff asked eagerly. "If you don't, I might be able to help."

"I know it," said Raistlin. "Are you ready to leave?"

"Not me! I won't be magicked!" Flint stated with grim finality. "Especially not by a kender!"

"The choice is yours, Flint," said Raistlin. "The rest of us are traveling to the High Clerist's Tower this night. You can either come with us or wait around here for Kit to find you."

"Or go back to Thorbardin and hide under the mountain," said Tanis.

Flint grumbled, but he seemed to be wavering.

"You know that I dislike and distrust magic, Flint," said Sturm. "I was in a similar situation where I had to choose between trusting in a wizard's spell or abandoning my friends. In the end, that choice was no choice."

"And now that you're not going to die of a broken heart, Flint, you can excerpt yourself all you want," Tas added, proud of a new word.

"You mean *exert*," said Flint.

"What I mean is that you can chase after Berem this time and your heart won't give out," said Tas.

Fortunately, Flint ignored him. "Is there a boat involved?" he asked Raistlin. "I don't like boats ever since that time Caramon almost drowned me."

"No boats," said Raistlin. "I promise."

Flint grunted. "Then I guess I'll come along. I can't let you youngsters go off on your own."

"We should leave quickly before he changes his mind," Tanis said in a low voice. "What do we have to do?"

"Bring whatever you want to take with you and follow me," said Raistlin. "I suggest you and Sturm have your weapons ready, for we might face an unfriendly welcome on our arrival."

Tanis shouldered his pack, which he had restocked with food. He picked up waterskins the elves had left them and a lightweight elven blanket given to him by Laurana. Tasslehoff brought his flour sack, stating it was his new pouch. He was carrying his hoopak and a rolled-up elven blanket that he said he had found and assumed no one wanted. Flint stated that he was taking his axe and needed nothing else.

They had to wait for Sturm, however, for he insisted on wearing his breastplate over his tunic and shirt. He had cleaned off the blood, and Tanis helped with the leather straps, binding it securely to the knight's body. Finally, Sturm put on his helm and buckled on his sword. He lightly touched the gash in the breastplate, as if in gratitude to the armor for saving him, then picked up a bedroll and gravely announced that he was ready.

"You are taking us directly to the High Clerist's Tower," he said to Raistlin, as the mage led them outside.

"The magic will carry us to the same place Magius took us—the entryway at Noble's Gate," Raistlin replied.

"What about the dragon?" Sturm asked.

"Caramon told me the green dragon named Cyan Bloodbane guards the tower. I know Cyan Bloodbane of old. Or rather, I will know him, as the kender says. Cyan is cruel and self-centered, a bully and a coward, but he is also extremely lazy. Guarding this tower for centuries would suit Cyan, for he would have nothing to do except eat and sleep. I am not worried about him, but we might face undead inside the tower—at least according to Caramon."

"I am sorry I did not get to speak to your brother," said Sturm with regret. "How is he?"

"The same now as always," Raistlin said with a touch of bitterness. "Chaos upends history, the Dark Queen rules the world, the River of Time alters course, and Caramon goes on forever. And now stop talking, all of you. I need to concentrate."

Raistlin drew the cowl over his head and led them to a relatively clear patch of ground he had located during the day. He scratched a large circle in the mud with the Staff of Magius, as Sturm and the others watched in silence.

"Stand inside the circle," Raistlin ordered when he was finished. "Do not move while I am casting the spell. We have no idea what to expect, so we must be prepared for anything. I remind everyone to keep quiet while I am casting the spell. Nothing must interrupt my concentration."

Tas jumped into the circle and jammed his hands into his pockets. Tanis entered and stood next to Tas, prepared to throttle him, if necessary. Sturm took his place, keeping as still as the distant mountains. Flint eyed the circle but didn't step inside. He shifted back and forth, from one foot to the other.

"Flint . . ." said Tanis.

"Don't rush me!" said Flint.

"We should leave," said Sturm.

Raistlin raised the staff.

"Wait!" Flint cried. "I'm coming!"

He sucked in his breath, scrunched his eyes shut, and leaped into the circle, landing with a thud. Tanis rested his hand reassuringly on the dwarf's shoulder.

"We're ready," he said to Raistlin.

Raistlin drew back his cowl, raised the Staff of Magius, and gazed up into the sky to seek the blessings of the gods of magic. The time was early evening. The sun had set. The stars of the Dark Queen's constellation shone brightly, lighting the night so that she could keep watch.

Raistlin had to search for the moons of the gods of magic and, when he found them, he was amazed to see all three moons visible. They were very close together, and Raistlin realized that he was witnessing the Night of the Eye—one of those rare times in history when the three moons were aligned in such a way that they resembled an eye, with Solinari the white of the eye, Lunitari the red iris, and Nuitari the pupil.

At this time, even a lowly young wizard like himself would find his power enhanced. Magius had called only on Lunitari, the goddess to whom he was devoted. But Raistlin hoped that all three of the gods of magic were here together for a reason, to wage war on Takhisis. In his time, Raistlin had served all three gods, and he prayed that all three would be with him now.

"Gods of magic—Solinari, Lunitari, Nuitari—I ask your blessing this day. Walk with us as we seek the weapons we need to drive the Dark Queen back to the Abyss."

Raistlin envisioned his destination—the entry hall at Noble's Gate. He recalled Magius collapsing after their arrival, for the spell was draining. Raistlin knew the same might happen to him or worse, but he was glad to take the risk, to feel the magic burning in his blood.

He closed his eyes and saw the words blaze with fire and began reciting the spell. *"Triga bulan ber satuan/Seluran asil/Tempat samah terus-menarus/Walktun jalanil!"*

The magic swirled around them with the force of a whirlwind. It picked them up and carried them into the gathering shadows, then set them down in pitch darkness.

"Don't move!" Raistlin warned. He spoke the word, *"Shirak,"* and the globe on his staff burst into light.

"I thought we were going to the High Clerist's Tower," said Flint dourly. "The mage has brought us to a junk heap."

"We stand at Noble's Gate," said Sturm gravely. "Or what was left of it after Immolatus attacked the temple."

The dragon had torn down the walls, leaving behind shattered stone and fallen beams. The piles of debris were blanketed by centuries of dust and dirt.

The night was still and quiet. Too still. Too quiet.

Raistlin was completely drained. He clutched at his staff to keep from falling. He had a sense of foreboding, and he could tell by their expressions that his companions felt the same. Flint kept a firm grip on his axe. Tasslehoff drew Goblinslayer.

"You might want to douse the light, Raistlin," Tanis said. "I can see the stars through the cracks in the walls, and if we can see out, others can see in."

Raistlin had just strength enough to whisper the command, *"Dulak."* The staff's light went out and darkness engulfed them. He started to collapse and felt Tanis catch hold of him and ease him to the floor. The blazing fire of the magic burning in his blood had consumed him, leaving only ashes. He lay with his eyes closed, listening to the others talking.

"I can usually see in the dark," Flint was saying in a low voice. "Most dwarves can. But I can't see my beard under my nose in this accursed tower. How do we find these lances in this foul murk?"

"We don't," said Tanis. "We'll have to wait until morning."

"You mean spend the night here?" Flint was horrified.

"I am afraid so," said Tanis. "We need to find the dragonlances. Make yourselves as comfortable as you can. Stay together. Tas, don't wander off."

"I guess I'll stay with you," said Tas, gazing bleakly into what seemed endless night. "When Caramon talked about ghosts, I was hoping they would be the exciting kind of ghosts that freeze your blood and shrivel your bones. But these kinds of ghosts only make you sad because you remember how you tried to save the song and you couldn't and Gwyneth and Huma died."

He wiped his hand across his eyes. Dropping his hoopak, he sat down on the floor and put his head in his arms.

"I will take first watch," said Sturm. "I'll be outside if you have need of me."

"Wake me when it's my turn," said Tanis, as Sturm crawled back through the rubble. "The rest of us should get some sleep."

Flint snorted. "I'm not shutting my eyes. We're not wanted here." He raised his voice. "Just so you know it! I've got my axe in my hand!"

His voice echoed through the empty chamber and was almost immediately swallowed up by the night. Raistlin heard the others bedding down, making themselves as comfortable as possible. Someone draped a blanket over him. He did not look to see who it was.

Raistlin tightened his grip on the Staff of Magius. He had felt Magius's spirit with him from the moment he spoke the words of magic, guiding and supporting.

"Thank you, my friend," Raistlin said silently. He started to drift off into an unsettled sleep. The last words he heard were Flint's.

"This place shivers my skin."

CHAPTER
TWENTY-FOUR

The night passed, and the morning sun shone down on a scene of purposeful confusion in the camp of the Dragon Highlord. Kitiara had returned from her visit with Skie yesterday, in the late afternoon, and announced that her forces would be pulling out of Solace and marching east to Neraka. Kitiara issued her orders, then retired to her tent to write dispatches that her messengers would carry to the army in Solamnia.

Caramon was awake early. He hadn't slept much that night, for he had been waiting with trepidation for Kitiara to summon him and accuse him of being a traitor like Raistlin. Caramon was prepared to denounce his twin, as Raistlin had instructed—though Caramon thought it likely he would choke on the words before he could deliver them. He also thought it likely that Kitiara wouldn't believe him. Caramon had considered making a run for it, but he couldn't leave without first knowing what had happened to his brother.

The Bozaks sent to arrest Raistlin and Tanis and the others had returned yesterday to report that they had found the mill empty and signs that those hiding there had gone west with a large party of elves. Caramon guessed that in reality, his brother and the others were on their way to the High Clerist's Tower. Caramon had been standing outside of Kitiara's tent when Bakaris had returned with his report, and he'd heard him say that Raistlin and Tanis had spoken of going to the High Clerist's Tower to find some sort of magical weapons.

Kitiara had scoffed at the notion, but then why this sudden decision to pull out of Solace and head to Neraka?

Caramon didn't have the answers, and now that he knew Raistlin was safe, he was too busy to give the matter serious consideration, for Kit's orders had thrown everything into turmoil. Soldiers began to take down tents, pack up gear and equipment, and load everything into the supply wagons that would soon start the long journey to Neraka. Caramon was an officer and he was supervising the loading of the wagons when he saw Highmaster Toede, accompanied by his goblin escort, ride into camp.

The hobgoblin looked around at the activity in astonishment. He expected someone to hurry to greet him and hold his horse and fawn over him. No one did or even paid much heed to him. Toede was incensed. He sat on his pony, fuming, waiting for someone to take notice. Finally, an officer saw him and came over to speak to him.

"Highlord Kitiara is not in camp," said the officer. "She just left a short time ago, leaving word that she was going to visit her dragon, Skie. I can give you directions to his lair."

"No, no!" Toede exclaimed, highly alarmed at the prospect. "I do not want to trouble the dragon. Actually, I came to speak to her second-in-command, Bakaris."

The officer sent someone to find Bakaris. Toede slid off his horse and paced about impatiently, swearing importantly at his goblin escorts, who paid no attention to him. Caramon sauntered over, hoping to find out what Toede wanted with Bakaris and wondering uneasily if this had anything to do with Raistlin and their friends.

Eventually Bakaris arrived, wearing his most ingratiating smile.

"I am honored by this visit, Highmaster Toede. How may I be of service?"

"Let us go someplace where we can speak in private," said Toede.

He ordered the goblins to stay with his horse, and he and Bakaris left camp, heading into the forest. The goblin escorts immediately abandoned the horse and ran to the mess tent, hoping for a free meal. Caramon gave Bakaris and Toede a head start, then followed them.

Caramon was a big man, but during their days fighting in the resistance, he had learned from Tanis how to move through the woods without making a sound. He kept to the shadows, and when the Bakaris and Toede stopped, Caramon ducked behind a tree to eavesdrop.

"What is going on?" Toede demanded. "It looks like you are breaking down camp."

"We are," said Bakaris. "Kitiara has ordered us to leave for Neraka."

"Interesting," said Toede. "I am worried about the welfare of the Highlord, friend Bakaris. Between you and me, Verminaard is not pleased with her."

"I heard a rumor that Verminaard was dead," said Bakaris. "He was killed in a slave revolt in the mines."

Toede bristled. "Lies! And I think we know who is behind them!"

"Who?" Bakaris asked.

"Highlord Kitiara!" said Toede. "Verminaard would make a formal complaint against her to the emperor for encroaching on his territory, but he fears Kitiara will only wriggle her way out of this by going to the Dark Queen. You and I both know how Her Dark Majesty has always favored her."

"Because she's a female," Bakaris said, sounding wise. "Women stick together. But what has this to do with me?"

"Lord Verminaard has a high regard for you, Bakaris," said Toede.

"He does?" Bakaris was surprised. "I didn't think he'd ever heard of me!"

"Oh my, yes," said Toede. "News of your gallant exploits has reached his ears."

"Which exploits in particular?" Bakaris asked with interest.

"You know ... exploits," Toede said vaguely. "Lord Verminaard would like you to know that, in the tragic event anything were to happen to Dragon Highlord Kitiara, you would be next in line to become commander of the Blue Dragonarmy. He himself would recommend you to the emperor for promotion."

Bakaris straightened to his full height and placed his hand on the hilt of his sword, as though he could already picture himself in blue dragonscale armor. Then reality hit him and his shoulders slumped.

"You and I both know that nothing is going to happen to Kitiara," said Bakaris glumly. "The Dark Queen protects her. Ariakas admires her. I've heard rumors he is her lover. She'll probably be emperor herself one day."

"None of us knows what this life holds for us," said Toede in solemn tones. "Highlord Kitiara is reckless in battle. She always leads the charge in person, and she is the first to attack the foe. She could well be killed in the fighting."

"But we're not fighting," Bakaris pointed out. "There's no one to fight."

Toede glowered at him in irritation. Caramon knew perfectly well what Toede was hinting at, but the hobgoblin was being much too subtle for Bakaris.

"The Highlord might suffer some *tragic accident*," Toede said, laying emphasis on the words. "*Someone* might cut the straps on her dragon saddle, causing her to fall off in midair, or *someone* might see to it that she tumbled down a cliff and broke her neck."

Bakaris finally caught on. "Accidents do happen, don't they, Highmaster? Although I am certain we both pray to Her Dark Majesty to keep Kitiara safe."

"I pray day and night for the Highlord's health," said Toede. "Unfortunately, Her Dark Majesty is so busy, she doesn't always have time to answer our prayers."

"l know that all too well," Bakaris said, brooding. "I asked her for something and she didn't deliver."

Toede was growing annoyed. His small eyes narrowed. "We were speaking of the Dragon Highlord."

"Yes, of course, sir," said Bakaris hastily, hearing a dangerous note in the hobgoblin's voice. "I understand."

"I hope you do," said Toede grimly. "And now I must take my

leave. I am glad to have had a chance to talk with you, Bakaris. Please give Highlord Kitiara my regards when you speak to her and tell her I was sorry to have missed her."

"I will do so, Highmaster," said Bakaris. "Allow me to escort you back to camp. Could I offer you something to eat or drink?"

"Thank you, no," said Toede, adding importantly, "I must be returning to my duties."

The two left, heading back into camp, where Bakaris shouted for men to fetch Toede's horse. The hobgoblin mounted and rode off.

Caramon saw Bakaris smile as he watched Toede ride away, with the well-fed goblins trailing behind.

"You dolt," Caramon muttered, referring to Bakaris. "I'll wager a hundred steel that if you are stupid enough to kill Kit, Toede is the one who plans to step into her boots as commander."

Caramon walked back to camp slowly, wondering what to do to stop Bakaris from murdering Kitiara.

The obvious answer was—nothing.

The world would be a much better place if Kitiara wasn't in it. Unfortunately, in the case of his sister, his decision wasn't that simple.

Caramon owed Kitiara a debt. She was older than her half-brothers, and when their parents died, she could have run off and left them. But she had stayed with them, putting off her own ambitions.

Raistlin had been a sickly child and might have died but for Kitiara.

She had made sure they both had skills to earn a living. She had taught Caramon to use a sword and, seeing Raistlin's talent in magic, had found a mage school for him. She left only when she was convinced that they could survive on their own and she had come back to Solace every so often to check on them.

Kitiara was by far the most capable of all the Highlords. She was a courageous and skillful leader. Her troops and her dragons were loyal to her, and she treated them well. Her death would be a blow to the Dark Queen.

Caramon should walk away and let Bakaris cut the straps on Kit's dragon saddle or whatever scheme he was going to hatch.

Yet Caramon could still remember when he and Raistlin were

little; watching Kitiara hold his brother as he struggled to breathe, battling death to save him. Caramon wished he could talk his problem over with his twin—although he knew perfectly well what Raistlin would tell him.

"We owe our sister nothing or, if we do, we paid our debt to her long ago," Raistlin would say.

Caramon sighed. Still undecided, he went to find Bakaris, thinking to keep an eye on the man. But Bakaris wasn't in the mess tent, even though they were serving lunch and he never missed a meal. Caramon asked around.

"I saw him leaving camp," said a Bozak. "He was heading off in the direction of Crystalmir Lake."

"When did he leave?" Caramon asked.

"Not long after that hob Toede rode out," the Bozak replied. "Trust Bakaris. He never misses a chance to get out of work detail."

Caramon was disturbed. Bakaris could have a perfectly innocent reason for going to the lake, but Caramon doubted it.

Kitiara had said she was going to visit Skie, whose lair overlooked Crystalmir Lake. She could be returning to camp anytime now, and she would be on foot, for the climb to reach Skie's cave was too difficult for a horse. She would be alone.

Caramon still hadn't decided what to do, but he buckled on his sword and set out in pursuit. Bakaris had a good head start and Caramon walked at a rapid pace, keeping watch for him. The road that led to the lake skirted a pine forest. The road was deserted and as the lake came into view, Caramon could see Kitiara approaching from the opposite direction. But no sign of Bakaris.

Caramon halted, keeping in the shadows of the pine trees.

Kitiara reached the shores of the lake and stopped. The sun was hot. The water was cool and inviting. She often bathed in the lake, and now she stripped off her leather jerkin and flung it onto the ground, then pulled off her boots. Fortunately for Caramon's modesty, Kitiara kept her shirt and breeches on.

She sat down on the bank and dangled her legs in the cool water as she gazed dreamily out at the distant mountains. Any other person would have been building castles in the air. Caramon could imagine that Kitiara was probably storming them.

Movement caught Caramon's eye. Glancing to his left, he saw Bakaris emerge from the pine trees and move stealthily toward Kitiara. Bakaris was walking on the balls of his feet, sneaking up on her from behind. Kitiara did not hear him approach.

Caramon stole forward, his heart thudding in his chest, the blood rushing in his ears. Bakaris bent down and picked up a large jagged-edged rock.

Caramon made up his mind. If Bakaris had challenged Kitiara to a fair fight, Caramon would not have intervened. But he could not stomach murder.

"Kit! Look out!" Caramon bellowed and broke into a run.

Kitiara heard him and with the quick instincts of a warrior, scrambled to her feet. She whipped around and saw Bakaris right behind her, poised to strike. She raised her arm in defense, and that probably saved her life. Bakaris had intended to crush her skull, but she deflected the blow and he struck her only a glancing blow on the forehead. She reeled, dazed, and he knocked her into the lake.

Caramon shouted again, but Bakaris was mad with fury and bloodlust. He grabbed hold of Kitiara and forced her head underwater, trying to drown her.

Caramon flung himself onto Bakaris from behind and yanked him off Kit. Bakaris turned on him, his face contorted by rage, his lips parted, teeth bared like a ravenous beast. He reached for his sword. Caramon doubled his fist and struck Bakaris in the face. The force of the blow spun the man around and he fell backward into the water.

Caramon paid no attention to Bakaris. He grabbed Kitiara by the shirt collar and dragged her out of the lake. She wasn't breathing, and he laid her on her belly on the ground and pounded her back until she gagged, spit out water, and sucked in a breath. She lay still for several moments, just breathing, and then rolled over and sat upright. Blood from the jagged cut on her forehead mingled with water and ran down her face.

"Help me up," she said, coughing and wiping away blood and water. She held out her hand to him.

Caramon did as he was told and pulled her to her feet.

Kitiara swayed a little and blinked her eyes and clung to Caramon until she steadied herself. Then she drew in a shaky breath.

"I'm all right now. Let go of me."

Caramon released her and suddenly remembered that Bakaris might be coming at him with his sword, prepared to stab him in the back. Caramon turned to see Bakaris lying in the shallows, staring up at the sky. His eyes didn't blink. He wasn't moving.

Caramon gulped. "Is he ... dead?"

Kitiara kicked Bakaris in the temple with the toe of her boot. His head flopped to one side. "He's dead. You broke his neck."

Caramon looked at his big fist and sighed. "I didn't mean to."

Kitiara shrugged. "You gave him a quicker death than I would have. Why did he try to kill me?"

"Toede put the idea in his head," said Caramon. "He told Bakaris that if anything happened to you, Verminaard would make Bakaris a Dragon Highlord."

Kitiara laughed. "And Bakaris believed him. Talk about being too stupid to live. Now that Verminaard's dead, Toede probably expects to take his place and he doesn't want me in the way."

Blood dripped from the jagged cut on her forehead. She drew her knife, sliced off the hem of her shirt, and handed the strip to Caramon.

"Bind this around the wound. Damn that bastard Bakaris anyway!" Kitiara swore. "He's given me a throbbing headache and made me ruin this shirt."

Caramon bound the crude bandage around the deep gash. The bandage was almost immediately soaked with blood, but at least it wasn't dripping down her face. "You should have one of the sawbones take a look at that."

"Bah, they'd just plaster some sort of foul muck on it," said Kit. She cast Caramon a quizzical look. "Why did you save me? Why not just let Bakaris kill me? I know you and your brother are traitors."

Caramon was taken aback. "I ... uh ... that is ... I'm not ... Raist isn't ..."

"Stop lying," said Kitiara with her crooked smile. "You were never any good at it, unlike your twin. You're a sentimental fool, Caramon. I should hang you, but you did me two favors. You saved my life and rid me of Bakaris. So I'll do you a favor in return."

Caramon eyed her distrustfully. "What's that?"

"I hear your brother and Tanis are traveling to the High Clerist's Tower to find some sort of magical lances," said Kitiara. "Skie and I are planning to stop them, unless by some miracle that sack of blubber Cyan Bloodbane kills them first. I'll give you a chance to join them. You and your twin came into this life together, and you should at least leave it together."

"You're letting me go free?" Caramon asked in disbelief.

"Let's put it this way: I'm letting you live a few days longer," said Kitiara. "I'll even make the trip easy for you. The journey to the tower by horseback would take weeks, and by that time Raist and Tanis will be dead. One of my dark clerics has the power to send you there in moments. The journey won't be pleasant, and it comes at a steep price, but I know you'll pay it to try to save your brother."

"How does this spell work?" Caramon asked. "Who is this cleric?"

"You've probably seen her around camp," Kitiara replied. "She's the elf with the green skin who smells like rotting fish. She's built a shrine to Zeboim on the outskirts of camp—the one decorated with dead fish that stinks to the Abyss."

"I've heard about her. Why is she even here?" Caramon asked, still not trusting Kit. "We're nowhere near the sea."

"Ariakas foisted her off on me. He wanted to be rid of her, and he didn't dare offend Zeboim by banishing her cleric. Doesn't pay to anger a sea goddess who can sink an entire fleet."

"I suppose not," said Caramon.

"The elf tried to convince me that Zeboim can send a waterspout that will suck a person into the air, carry you across continents, and spit you out at your destination. It's supposedly safe, but, as I said, it's probably not a pleasant way to travel."

"So if this cleric can take a person somewhere in moments, why don't you make use of it yourself?" Caramon asked.

"I won't pay the price," said Kitiara.

"What does she charge?" Caramon asked uneasily, wondering if he had enough money.

"Your soul," said Kitiara.

Caramon stared at her. He didn't think he'd heard right. "What?"

"Your soul," Kitiara repeated complacently. "You pledge your soul to Zeboim, and the goddess will claim it after you die. You have to hope she won't be in a hurry for it, but one never knows. As for me, my soul is my own, and so it will be after my death. No one—not even the Dark Queen—is going to claim it."

Kitiara smiled her crooked smile. "So what will you do, Caramon? Will you sell your soul to save your unworthy brother—even though you know he wouldn't so much as lift his gold-skinned little finger to save you?"

Caramon regarded his sister grimly, now understanding her game. Kitiara was adept at tormenting people in unique and creative ways. His reward for saving her life was the loss of his soul.

Kitiara picked up her leather jerkin and slung it over her shoulder. "I'll be in my tent. Come tell me what you decide."

"You know what I'll decide," said Caramon harshly.

Kitiara grinned. "Give Tanis my love. Tell him Skie and I will see him soon. And thanks again for saving my life."

Caramon glanced down at Bakaris. "What should I do with the body?"

"Leave it," said Kitiara. "The vultures have had slim pickings lately. They can use a good meal."

She walked off, heading in the direction of the camp.

On his return, Caramon sent men to the lake to give Bakaris a decent burial. Bakaris had been a worm and a weasel, but he had endured the torments of the damned at the hands of Kitiara. She had broken him, and the least Caramon could do was bury the pieces. Caramon could tell by the soldiers' muttered remarks that they would have been glad to let the buzzards have Bakaris, but Caramon was an officer, and they obeyed orders.

Caramon then went to an encampment the soldiers irreverently called Gods' Alley. Here the clerics who served the lesser gods of the dark pantheon had their shrines. Some, like the clerics of Morgion and Chemosh, were hoping for converts. Others, like the minotaur cleric of Sargonnas, served the needs of their people, although Kitiara had few minotaurs in her army. Sargonnas was the Dark Queen's consort, and Kitiara did not like divided loyalties.

Caramon gave the shrine of Morgion the Plague God a wide berth. Zeboim's shrine was at the very end of the alley, set apart from the others, and when he drew near and caught a whiff of rotting fish, he understood why.

Zeboim's shrine was a mound of sand in the shape of a dragon turtle—a hideous beast that was the terror of sailors, for it could grab a ship in its maw and smash it to kindling. The elven cleric had decorated the dragon turtle with shells and bones and offerings of dead fish in various states of decomposition.

She was busy around her shrine, and when she caught sight of Caramon heading her way, she ran to meet him. The elf was a strange sight. She was taller than Caramon by a head and shoulders, thin and angular, with greenish skin and orange hair. She smiled at him in greeting, and he was shocked to see she had filed her teeth to sharp points to resemble the shark's teeth she wore on a string around her neck. Between the stench and the teeth and the wild, half-mad look in the elf's eyes, Caramon almost lost his nerve.

He reminded himself of the danger to his brother and their friends, covered his nose and mouth, and tried to breathe as little as possible.

"Welcome, stranger, to the shrine of Zura," said the elf. "I am Alaria Shortfin."

"I was looking for the shrine of Zeboim," said Caramon, devoutly hoping he'd come to the wrong one.

"Zura is the elven name for Zeboim," said Alaria with her shark's grin. "A common mistake. How may the goddess serve you?"

Caramon explained that he wanted to travel to the High Clerist's Tower and that Highlord Kitiara had told him that Zeboim's cleric could take him there in moments.

"I can," said Alaria. "A magnificent spell. Did the Highlord also tell you that you must give your soul to the Sea Goddess in exchange for her blessing?"

"She told me," Caramon replied grimly. "What happens to my soul when Zeboim takes it?"

"Zura gifts it to Her Dark Majesty, of course. Takhisis would be angered otherwise," Alaria replied, appearing shocked he would even ask. "She will chain you in the Abyss and tear out your heart with her claws and devour your flesh with her teeth and snap your bones in her jaws every day for all eternity."

Alaria licked her own sharp teeth with her tongue as though relishing this prospect, and Caramon felt his gut shrivel. As a child, he'd been terrified by the Dark Queen's clerics and their tales of eternal damnation. He'd had nightmares about them, and those frightening dreams came back to him. He must have looked ghastly, for Alaria regarded him with concern.

"You're not going to back out of the deal, are you?" she asked anxiously. "If it's any comfort, Zura can't take your soul until you're dead, so why should you care? You'll be dead."

Caramon recalled Raistlin telling him much the same thing when they were children—undoubtedly one reason why the dark clerics had tried to burn his twin at the stake.

Caramon drew in a deep breath and immediately regretted it, for the smell of rotting fish made him gag. "I'm going through with it."

Alaria produced a document written on fish skin and handed him a knife, informing him that he was required to use his own blood for ink. Caramon made a slice on his arm as instructed, and Alaria caught his blood in a small coral bowl. She then mixed his blood with water, dropped the document into the bowl, and waited tensely.

"We have to see if Zura accepts your offering," said Alaria. She closed her eyes and began to pray. "Sea Goddess, this human comes before you to beg your favor and to gift you his soul in return. As you can see, his soul is big and strong and handsome and will undoubtedly please Her Dark Majesty."

Apparently, Zeboim liked the looks of Caramon's soul, for the bloody water began to boil.

Alaria smiled, ecstatic. "Zura accepts your soul. We may now proceed with the spell. I call it Zura's Water Way."

Alaria draped a necklace of shells and shark's teeth around Caramon's neck, smeared his forehead with some sort of fish oil, and then hauled him down to Crystalmir Lake. As he walked past the shrines, the other clerics called after him.

"Chemosh will treat your soul better than she will!" said the cleric of the god of the undead.

"Are you sure you wouldn't rather have the plague?" Morgion's cleric jeered.

Alaria flashed them both angry glances and hurried Caramon past their shrines.

"Pay no attention to them," she said. "They're jealous."

Arriving at the lake, Caramon saw that the burial detail must have completed their task, for Bakaris's corpse was gone.

Alaria took him to the bank of the lake and told him to take off his sword, his armor, and his helm, and strip off his clothes.

Caramon was hot with embarrassment. "I'll do no such thing! I'm not traveling through the ethers naked! And I'm not going anywhere without my sword! The deal is off. I want my soul back."

He started to rip off the necklace.

"No, no, no, please!" Alaria begged, clinging to him. "I am certain that in the case of such a big, courageous warrior as yourself, Zura will make an exception. I will ask her."

The cleric dropped down on her knees in the shallow water and raised her hands to the sky. Her lips moved in prayer, and at last she smiled and stood up, dripping.

"The Sea Goddess is very fond of you," said Alaria. "She grants your request. You may leave on your clothes and your armor and your sword, but you must remove your helm."

"My helm?" Caramon asked. "Why?"

"Zura is full of quirks," said Alaria. "Who can tell? Throw it into the water."

Caramon sighed and took off his helm and tossed it out into the lake. He was considerably startled to see a gigantic fish leap up, catch his helm in its maw, and disappear beneath the water with a tremendous splash.

Caramon licked dry lips. He had not really believed that this mad cleric could truly work the will of Zeboim, but he believed now. He was grateful when the cleric told him to kneel down in the water, for his legs were quivering and he wasn't certain he could stand.

Alaria waded into the water, though she kept her distance from him.

"I don't want to get caught in the spell," she told him.

Caramon did not find that reassuring. He set his jaw and waited.

"Zura!" Alaria cried, again raising her hands to heaven, "I beseech you to grant this human's plea to take him with all speed to the High Clerist's Tower, or at least somewhere in the vicinity, since I am well aware that you will not want to go near the tower, which is sacred to your enemies Paladine and Mishakal—curse their names."

Caramon broke out in a sweat. "Vicinity? What does that mean? Wait a damn minute—"

"If you find him worthy," Alaria continued loudly, ignoring him, "I ask you to bless this human with Zura's Water Way."

The clouds above the lake darkened to an ugly color of greenish gray and began to boil. Thunder rumbled and lightning flashed. A swirling waterspout formed in the clouds and began snaking down toward the ground. Caramon realized in horror that the spout was coming for him.

The cleric leaped to her feet and fled. Caramon tried to run, but a rush of wind caught hold of him and carried him, flailing and screaming, into the spout. Ferocious winds whirled around him, hammered and buffeted and twisted him. His eyes and nose and mouth filled with water and he couldn't breathe and he couldn't see. He realized he was drowning, and at that moment, dying would have been a pleasure.

And then the goddess spit him out.

Caramon landed with a thud that jarred every bone in his body. He lay on the ground more dead than alive and watched the waterspout lift into the air and disappear. The swirling clouds vanished, and the sun shone.

And there in front of him, several miles away, was a building that he hoped and prayed—though not to Zeboim—was the Tower of the High Clerist.

CHAPTER
TWENTY-FIVE

The River of Time flowed on. The same morning sun that shone on Caramon, gazing at the High Clerist's Tower in the present, gilded the mountains that surrounded the High Clerist's Tower during the Third Dragon War in the distant past. The knights were preparing for battle.

Destina and Kairn had spent the night in the Knight's Chapel. They woke to the sound of blacksmiths' hammers repairing armor and honing the blades of swords and pikes and knives. The sounds reminded Destina of the last time she had seen her father before he and his troops rode off to do battle in this same High Clerist's Tower, centuries away in a future that no longer existed.

Destina saw Sir Reginald entering the chapel, his expression dark, and she sat up, groggy and confused.

"How long have you two been here?" Sir Reginald demanded.

Kairn blinked at him. "What is the time, sir?"

"Near dawn," said Sir Reginald.

"Then we have been here since we left you, sir," said Kairn, rising to his feet. "We must have fallen asleep."

Sir Reginald eyed them. "You did *not* go to your bedchambers?"

"As Kairn said, we fell asleep," said Destina. "The chapel was quiet and peaceful, and we were weary from our journey. Why do you ask?"

She had the dreadful feeling she knew the answer.

"The wizard Magius is missing," said Sir Reginald. "We believe that he was abducted in the night. He was alone in his room, which is not far from the guest quarters. We found blood on the floor and evidence of a struggle, but no other signs. The guards swear no one entered the tower through the gates. I was hoping you might have seen or heard something."

Destina could have told him how the Gudlose had entered the tower and used their powerful magic to abduct Magius. She could have told him that a terrible fate awaited the mage, but she did not dare. She felt unaccountably guilty, as though she were responsible.

"What about Sir Richard?" Destina asked.

"What about him?" Sir Reginald asked, puzzled.

"Is he . . . is he well?" Destina asked in confusion.

"Of course he is well," said Sir Reginald. "I told you yesterday that he and I slept in shifts. Why do you ask?"

"We are sorry to hear about Magius," said Kairn, avoiding the question.

Sir Reginald wearily rubbed his eyes. "We assume the dragon's agents captured him. Lord Huma was outraged. He was going to ride to the dragon's camp to save his friend. I had difficulty convincing him to stay. I think he would have gone anyway, but Gwyneth joined me in pleading with him and he finally listened. You should return to your rooms. The servant will bring food and water."

"Is there anything we can do to help with preparations for the battle?" Kairn asked.

"We have done all we can," said Sir Reginald.

A man shouted his name at that moment, and he excused himself and hurried off.

Destina and Kairn returned to their bedchambers. Destina cast a glance at Magius's door, which was standing open, and saw servants mopping up blood on the floor. She turned away, clasping the Graygem.

A servant brought breakfast. Destina felt better after she had eaten. She joined Kairn, and together they went in search of Mullen Tully, even though, as Destina said, such a search would probably be as futile this time as it had been the last.

They made their way to Noble's Gate, where men were continuing to clear away the destruction left by the dragon. Immolatus had battered his way through the main gate, setting fire to the ironwood doors and tearing down much of the outer wall. Men were hauling away the rubble so that the tower's defenders could enter and leave unimpeded. Destina studied the workmen, but none of them was Tully.

She and Kairn walked from the gate into the courtyard, where a crowd was gathering. The sky was clear, though clouds massed in the east. Destina gratefully breathed in the fresh air, even as she listened to the soldiers talk in grim tones about the campfires of the Dark Queen's army, as numerous as the stars in the night sky.

Destina and Kairn joined the crowd to find out what was going on. They saw Huma, Sir Reginald, and Sir Richard standing in front of the tower's main gate, studying the battlements and discussing where best to position archers to defend against enemy attempts to scale the walls. Gwyneth was at Huma's side. She was in her elven form, perhaps fearing her dragon form would intimidate those not accustomed to dragons.

One of the guards atop the battlements suddenly called a warning. "Two riders approaching under a flag of truce!"

Huma and Gwyneth and the others swiftly climbed the stairs leading to the battlements to see for themselves. A throng of soldiers followed, weapons in hand. Destina and Kairn joined them.

Two riders—a man and a woman—were approaching the tower's main gate. The woman carried a white flag, and the man led a packhorse bearing a blanket-wrapped bundle, bound with rope, draped over its back. The blankets were stained with dark splotches.

Destina recognized the two riders as the same members of the Gudlose who had accosted her to try to seize the Graygem. The man was known as Captain. He had called the woman Mother, and she was a powerful magic-user.

Captain and Mother both reined in their horses.

"We are sent by the dragon Immolatus to speak to Lord Huma," Captain called loudly.

Huma thrust aside those who would have stopped him, fearing an ambush. He walked forward, within arrow range, and gazed at the two riders.

"I am Lord Huma. Say what you have to say and be gone."

"The dragon Immolatus sends you a gift," said Captain. "We are returning your wizard, though I fear he is a little worse for wear."

Mother snapped her fingers, and the ropes that bound the bundle to the packhorse slithered away like snakes. The bundle tumbled off the horse to the ground. Mother gave a contemptuous wave, and the blankets vanished, revealing the body of Magius.

They had stripped off his robes and flayed his flesh from his bones. His legs had been broken, bent and twisted, his face battered so that he was almost unrecognizable. But it seemed to Destina, watching through eyes blurred with tears, that Magius still smiled.

"Even in death he triumphed," said Kairn softly. "Immolatus sought information on the dragonlances and the tower's defenses. History records that Magius died without revealing what he knew."

Huma stood silent, gazing down at the body lying on the ground in front of the gate, his fists clenched at his side. His face was cold and impassive, as though carved of marble. But his eyes burned blue as the heart of a flame.

"Let what happened to this man be a warning!" Captain shouted. "Everyone present will share his fate on the day Her Dark Majesty enters the High Clerist's Tower in triumph. Surrender now and she will permit safe passage for all who want to save themselves."

Huma turned to those crowding the battlements and the courtyard below.

"If any man wants to leave, he may do so freely. None here will stop him or shame him," he called.

"We stand with you and the silver dragon, my lord!" a man called out, and the rest of the soldiers joined him in clamorous support.

Huma regarded them with pride and turned back.

"You have our answer," he said.

Captain shrugged. "So be it."

Mother had been carrying Magius's staff. She tossed it down on top of the body. She and Captain turned their horses and rode off slowly and with obvious contempt, knowing that Huma would respect the flag of truce.

One of the soldiers on the battlements raised his bow, arrow nocked, looking to Huma for orders. Huma set his jaw and grimly shook his head. The soldier lowered his bow.

Then someone pointed and cried out, "Look there!"

A woman with flame-red hair, wearing red robes the color of blood, appeared beside the body of Magius. Two men joined her. One man wore white robes that shone bright as the silver moon, and the other wore robes blacker than night, as if a hole had been cut out of the darkness.

Captain and Mother had their backs turned and did not see them. The woman knelt beside the body, kissed Magius gently on the forehead, then picked up his staff and raised it to the heavens.

Red light streaked from the crystal ball atop the staff and struck Captain in the back. He fell from his horse, dead before he hit the ground. Mother stared at him in shock and then swung her horse around to see who had attacked them. She saw the three, standing guard over Magius. Mother's eyes widened in astonishment and fear. She sucked in a hissing breath that would be her last.

White light streaked from the crystal and hit her between the eyes. She toppled backward, her skull cleaved in two. The flag of truce fluttered to the ground. The two horses bolted in terror. Darkness flowed from the crystal atop the staff and shrouded the bodies of Captain and Mother. When the darkness lifted, all that remained of them were two piles of ashes.

The light of the staff faded away. The two men and the woman turned to face Huma. The woman lifted the staff in salute and then the three disappeared, taking the Staff of Magius with them.

Shaken by what they had seen, no one in the tower moved or spoke. And then Huma raised his voice so that it might have been heard in heaven.

"Thus do the gods of magic have their revenge!"

"And thus do the gods punish unbelievers," said Destina softly, remembering Raistlin's words.

Huma walked toward the stairs that led from the battlements. "I will recover his body."

"Let us do that sorrowful task for you, my lord," said Sir Reginald.

Huma shook his head. "He was my friend."

As he descended the stairs, soldiers lined the battlements, armed with bows and arrows. Gwyneth spoke softly to Huma. He pressed her hand and then left her, walking out the gate to the place where the Gudlose had dumped Magius's battered body. Huma knelt at his friend's side and, taking his broken hand, spoke to him in a low voice. Huma took his time, heedless of the danger. The mournful wind carried his parting words.

"You are with your beloved Greta now, Magius. Wait for me, my brother, my friend. You will not wait long."

Huma wrapped Magius in the bloodstained blankets, then picked up his body. Cradling him in his strong arms, Huma carried his friend through the gate. The silence was profound. Soldiers removed their helms and bowed their heads. Some wiped away tears.

Sir Reginald was there to meet him in the courtyard. He had ordered men to bring a litter, and they were waiting to bear Magius to his final rest. Huma gently lowered the body onto the litter and drew the bloodstained blankets over his face.

"I will take charge of the body, my lord," Sir Reginald offered. "We will make all seemly, and then he will be interred with honor alongside Commander Belgrave."

Huma reached out to Gwyneth. She took his hand and stood beside him. Huma's grief was etched on his face, and his tears glistened in the sun. Yet he smiled as he shook his head.

"Magius would not want to spend eternity with a bunch of stodgy old knights. He once told me he hoped to die with the magic burning in his blood. We will build a funeral pyre for him, as was done for the knights in the days of Vinas Solamnus."

"I will make the arrangements," said Sir Reginald.

He began issuing orders, and those men not on duty hastened to obey. The litter bearers carried the body into the temple. Huma and Gwyneth walked behind, holding fast to each other. No one paid attention to Kairn and Destina, for which they were grateful. Destina wiped away her own tears.

"History continues to unfold as it should," Kairn told her. "The gods of magic avenged Magius's death and took away his staff. It was lost to history until, centuries later, Par-Salian would give it to Raistlin Majere."

Huma prepared his friend for his final journey. He refused all help, even Gwyneth's, saying this was the last service he would do for his friend. He cleansed the body, straightened the maltreated limbs, combed his hair, and then dressed Magius in his finest red robes.

The soldiers spent the rest of the day constructing an enormous funeral pyre in the courtyard at the entrance to Noble's Gate, using the wood intended for scaffolding, cooking, and heating. When they finished at sunset, the pyre stood twelve feet high. They doused it with resin, and then the men formed two lines and saluted as an honor guard carried Magius to his rest.

Kairn and Destina stood among those lining the way. Destina had picked some roses she had found on a bush in the garden where the cook grew his herbs. She placed the blooms on the litter as the men carried it past her. Huma and Gwyneth and the other knights walked behind it, their helms beneath their arms.

Destina overheard Huma talking with Gwyneth. "I went to his room to fetch his spellbooks. Magius often told me that if something happened to him, he wanted me to send his spellbooks to the master of the tower of Wayreth. He emphasized they were to go there and not to the tower of Palanthas. Apparently, he had some long-standing grudge against the master of that tower—a man named Snagsby. He said that on no account were his books to go to him. But the books were not there. I searched but I could not find them."

"The gods of magic must have taken them," said Gwyneth. "Since we are under threat, they could not allow such powerful spell books to fall into the wrong hands."

"Of course," said Huma quietly. "I did not think of that."

The honor guard placed the litter bearing the body on the stones beside the pyre. The sun had set. The sky was dark except for the sparkling stars. None of the three moons was in the heavens this night, shrouding their faces in mourning.

Huma climbed a ladder to the top and assisted the men to raise the body and rest it on the pyre. Huma whispered a few final words to his friend, kissed the cold forehead, and then descended to the ground. He and Gwyneth stood with Sir Reginald and Sir Richard and the others near the pyre, holding flaming torches. Drummers beat a mournful dirge. Huma held his torch high.

"Let the fire of the gods carry the soul of Magius to heaven," he cried, and flung his torch onto the logs. The other torchbearers did the same.

The fire flared, roared, and crackled. Sparks flew into the night sky, rising higher and higher in the still air until they seemed to dance among the stars. Smoke spiraled upward, bearing the soul of the departed. The flames burned so fiercely, the heat was so intense, that no one could stand near the pyre.

The flames shone on Huma's face, drying his tears, and then the pyre collapsed in a rush of crackling wood, sending up a cloud of fiery cinders and burning embers. And then the flames died, and soon nothing remained but smoldering wood.

The crowd around the funeral pyre began to disperse. Sir Richard and Sir Reginald quietly ordered the men to return to their duties, for the Dark Queen was expected to launch her assault on the tower tomorrow. Men maintained a respectful silence or spoke in hushed tones, offering whispered consolation to Huma.

He and Gwyneth were the last to leave. The wind rose, blowing from the east, and scattered the ashes on the stones of the High Clerist's Tower.

"Until we meet again, my friend," said Huma.

Turning away, he took Gwyneth's hand, and they walked together back into the temple.

Destina and Kairn had sought refuge from the heat amid the ruins of Noble's Gate. She and Kairn drew back as men hastened past them.

Sir Reginald caught sight of them and frowned. "You two should return to your rooms and remain there for the duration of the battle."

"We want to help, sir," said Destina. "I am the daughter of a

Knight of Solamnia and a warrior woman of the Ackal. I would disgrace the memory of my parents if I hid from a fight."

"I am a knight's son," said Kairn. "I will not shirk my duty to my homeland."

Sir Reginald appeared to be on the verge of refusing, but Huma happened to be walking past them and overheard.

"I honor your loyalty," said Huma. "We will need such courageous hearts to defeat the Dark Queen. I hope you will join the tower's defenders."

He continued on his way through the gate and into the temple.

"He is right, of course," said Sir Reginald. "I would assign you to posts, but I don't think it will matter."

As Kairn and Destina entered Noble's Gate, they could hear the low rumble of distant thunder. They planned to take the stairs that led to the sixth floor and their bedchambers. Soldiers had worked diligently to clear the rubble from the entrance, but there were still piles of rock stacked up around the gate or shoved off into the corners and it was difficult for them to see their way in the darkness.

"We should have thought to bring a torch," said Destina.

"I'll fetch one," said Kairn. "Wait for me here."

He went back outside the gate to where men had stacked torches in buckets to be used in the work of readying the tower's defenses, which would go on all night.

Destina moved back into a corner to keep out of the way. She shivered in the night wind blowing down from the mountains and wrapped her jacket more closely about her. It was then she noticed the Graygem.

The gem had been dark and cold most of the day and she had almost forgotten about it. But now it glowed with gray light, dim at first, but growing stronger. Destina clasped hold of it, and it was eerily warm to the touch. She edged farther back into a corner, hoping none of those passing by would see. But the gray light shone brighter, welling out from between her fingers.

One of the soldiers turned his head and looked straight at her. Gray light illuminated his face, and Destina gasped, recognizing Mullen Tully.

At first, she feared he might recognize her, realize she had seen him kill Commander Belgrave. But he wasn't looking at her. The light of the Graygem glistened in his eyes.

"That is a strange jewel," Tully said. "It must be worth a lot."

He reached out his hand to seize it.

Destina clenched her fist and struck Tully in the jaw with such force that he staggered backward. Kairn returned, just as Destina struck Tully. Kairn tried to seize him, but he ran off and disappeared into the darkness.

"Are you all right?" Kairn asked, worried. "Did he harm you?"

"He didn't attack me, Kairn," said Destina, massaging her hand. "He tried to take the Graygem. Perhaps Immolatus sent him! Or Takhisis!"

"Perhaps ..." said Kairn, sounding dubious. "But I noticed he wasn't carrying the greatsword."

"What does that mean?" Destina asked, exasperated. "He could have hidden it."

"Or Immolatus hasn't given it to him yet," said Kairn. "All we know for certain is that Tully saw a valuable jewel and tried to steal it."

"The Graygem wanted him to see it, Kairn," said Destina, clasping her hand around the jewel that was now cold and dark.

"But Tully doesn't know what he saw," said Kairn, trying to be reassuring.

"He may not know," said Destina. "But Immolatus might."

CHAPTER
TWENTY-SIX

he red dragon, Immolatus, was the Dark Queen's favorite. He was young, at the height of his powers, and took pride in his strength and ferocity. He was the commander of his own army with a host of goblins, hobgoblins, ogres, and human soldiers under his command. But now he lay in his tent, groaning and suffering, his scales blackened and blood oozing from multiple wounds inflicted by a lone knight, a single silver dragon, and terrible magical weapons.

Immolatus groaned and rolled over onto his side in an attempt to find some position that eased the pain.

The ground on which he lay was covered in blood. A trail of blood led from the High Clerist's Tower to his tent. He had managed to fly most of the way back, his blood falling like red rain. He had at least made it to his camp before he'd grown too weak and was forced to crawl on his belly to his tent.

Most of his troops had witnessed his ignominious return yesterday, and officers had run to see what had happened, demanding to know if the battle had started. Immolatus had snarled at them and sent for the clerics of Queen Takhisis. When they arrived, he had ordered them to treat his injuries. They had taken one look at the wounds and told him that the weapon that had struck him was cursed, sacred to Paladine, and that they could do nothing for him. In fact, they had refused to touch him or even come near him.

And so he lay bleeding and suffering in his tent throughout the day, in such pain that he would have given up and let death take him, only that would have robbed him of his thirst for revenge. He needed to know more about these accursed weapons, so he had sent for the Gudlose, a band of cutthroat mercenaries, led by a man named only Captain and a magic-user named Mother. He had sent them to capture a war wizard known to work for the foul knights, figuring this wizard would be able to provide information.

The Gudlose had done the job and brought back the wizard, but their attempts at forcing him to talk had failed. He had gone to his death without saying a word.

"In other words, you bungled it," Immolatus had muttered, but not to the Gudlose. They were a scary bunch and he didn't want to cross them—at least not while they might still prove useful. He'd be damned if he was going to pay them, though. He sent them back to the knights with the body and a warning that this would be the fate of all who chose to defend the tower.

The Captain and Mother had taken the body under a flag of truce, but night had fallen and they had not yet returned. Or if they had, they had not reported back to him. He was starting to think maybe he wouldn't wait; he'd roast them once he was feeling better.

Immolatus had fallen into a pain-filled doze and wakened to the sound of voices outside his tent. One belonged to his guard, and he sounded awestruck and terrified to the point of incoherence. The other voice was a woman's, smooth as dark velvet, cold as black ice.

"No need to announce me," Takhisis told the groveling guard. "He is expecting me."

"Damn right, I'm expecting you!" Immolatus growled with smoldering rage as the Queen of Darkness entered the tent.

The goddess could take many forms in the presence of mortals, depending on what she wanted from them. As Takhisis, Queen of Dragons, she was an enormous and fearsome five-headed dragon. Each head was a different color and capable of delivering different forms of lethal attacks. The blue spit lightning bolts, the green breathed poisonous gas, the black spewed acid, the red shot fire, and the white blasted frost.

When she appeared in this form, enemy armies fled in terror— and sometimes her own armies fled with them. Thus, Takhisis found it more practical to lead her armies to battle as the Dark Warrior: a massive humanoid figure encased in black, wielding an enormous mace she called Crusher of Hope.

But when she wanted something, she appeared in the form of a human woman of terrible beauty, with dead-white skin, obsidian-black hair, bloodred lips, and eyes that were empty and dark as the Abyss. In this form, she confronted Immolatus and stood over him, gazing down on him.

"Why are you here?" he snarled, and then groaned.

"First, I came to see if the report was true," she replied. "That you disobeyed my orders and attacked the High Clerist's Tower."

Immolatus reared his head in ire. "Damn right I attacked the Tower. While you and your armies were meandering across the plains, those blasted knights were growing stronger every day!"

"Their forces consist of a silver dragon, a handful of knights, and an army of draggletailed soldiers who are deserting in droves," said Takhisis in a tone as cold as the darkness beyond the stars.

"They are deserting because I filled their hearts with fear!" Immolatus roared defiantly.

Takhisis sneered. "By nearly getting yourself killed."

She advanced on him, her skirt dragging through the pools of blood on the grass. "Don't lie to me, Immolatus. You planned to seize the tower and keep it for yourself!"

It should be mine, after all my work, Immolatus thought, seething. He didn't dare give voice to his thoughts, however. He decided to shift his strategy, go on the attack.

"Look at these wounds that terrible knight inflicted on me! This is your fault! You should have warned me!"

"Warned you of what? That you might be attacked by a knight inside a tower filled with knights?" Takhisis asked caustically.

"You should have warned me about those horrible weapons!" Immolatus howled. "The knights carried no such weapons when I attacked them at Westgate Pass. I chewed them up and spit them out and then I roasted them alive in their own armor. But now the knights have fearsome lances made of silver that are blessed by their foul gods. You should have warned me about these weapons, damn it! Or at least destroyed them!"

"They are called dragonlances," said Takhisis. "They were forged by Reorx in Silver Dragon Mountain. I cannot destroy them, for they are protected by the gods. I remind you that if you had not disobeyed my orders and attacked the tower, you would not now be injured. I came to tell you I have a mission for you."

"Me?" Immolatus moaned. "What can I do except wallow in agony?"

Takhisis regarded him with disdain. "You are useless, that is true, but you have spies and assassins working for you. Tell them to keep watch for a human female wearing a gray gemstone on a golden chain around her neck. If they find her, they are not to harm her. They are to bring her and the gemstone to me."

Immolatus thought this an odd request. "What is this gray gem? Smoky quartz? It doesn't sound all that valuable."

Takhisis said with a shrug, "It is a religious artifact that was stolen from the Temple of Luerkhisis. The gem is worth nothing to speak of. I plan to make an example of this human, to serve as a warning to others who would dare to steal what is mine."

Immolatus knew better. Takhisis was everywhere at once, yet she couldn't find a hunk of smoky quartz? She wasn't telling him the truth, but that wasn't surprising. She didn't trust him. She didn't trust anyone. Her five heads didn't even trust each other.

"You want me to go to all this trouble over some worthless jewel," the dragon stated. "What are you going to do about these accursed dragonlances? You can see the wounds they inflicted on me. I warn you—they'll do the same to you!"

Takhisis laughed, highly diverted. "No weapon ever forged has the power to harm me. My armies are within a day's march of the tower and, when they arrive, I expect you to be prepared to take part in the battle. Send word to me through my clerics when you have found this jewel."

Takhisis stalked out of the tent, and Immolatus sank back onto the ground, exhausted. His wounds oozed blood and burned and throbbed and ached. The attack had occurred the previous night and, far from closing, his wounds were getting worse. The scales around the gashes were turning black and dropping off.

Immolatus groaned and rolled over. His gaze rested on his treasure horde, which he kept inside his tent, ringed round with all manner of warding spells and trap spells. Admiring his treasure eased his pain, and his gaze roved lovingly among gems and jewel-encrusted golden chalices, chests of gold, and magical weapons.

Immolatus paused to linger fondly on a greatsword. He knew its provenance. The greatsword was forged of steel, made by ogres for Takhisis. The hilt was set with five jewels that looked like five eyes: an emerald, a ruby, a sapphire, a white diamond, and a black diamond. Takhisis had given it to him as a mark of esteem, and Immolatus called the sword Deathdealer, because the blade was enchanted. It could glide through armor and pierce even the scales of his enemies, the metallic dragons.

He had a brilliant idea. This was how he could take his revenge.

"I will give the sword to Tully and send him to slay the knight and the silver dragon," said Immolatus.

But then, admiring the sword, he reconsidered.

The weapon was a thing of beauty. He had coveted it from the moment he saw it. Ogres were known for their skill in forging weapons, and he had always been impressed by the craftsmanship. The greatsword was extremely valuable, and Mullen Tully was devious, treacherous, and willing to do anything for money. All of which made him a decent spy, but not the sort of person one entrusted with a valuable, jewel-encrusted sword.

Immolatus's gaze roved over the rest of his treasure horde and came to rest on a dagger. The weapon was plain and appeared to be quite ordinary. Its value lay in the fact that the maker had impregnated the blade with a magical poison so powerful it could kill a man with a scratch and even kill a dragon, though Immolatus had his doubts about that.

Immolatus decided he would give Tully the dagger. He should

be able to find ample opportunity to slay this knight. A simple nick on the skin would suffice. As for the poison being able to kill a silver dragon, it wouldn't hurt to try. At least, it wouldn't hurt Immolatus.

He shouted for the guard. "Tully is due to report to me tonight. Send him in the moment he arrives."

"Yes, Lord. Oh, and there's a cleric named Mortuga demanding to see you. He just rode into camp."

"He can just ride back out of camp and into the Abyss for all I care!" Immolatus snarled. "Any sign of Captain and Mother?"

"No, Lord," said the guard.

Immolatus lay back down and suffered.

When Tully assured him that the knight and the silver dragon were dead, he might deign to join Takhisis in her battle. Or he might not. Immolatus considered he had done his part by attacking the temple, even though she didn't appreciate it.

Immolatus groaned and rolled over yet again.

Midnight brought no comfort to Immolatus but did bring Mullen Tully. He was still wearing his yeoman's uniform. His jaw was bruised, and he had a swollen lip.

Immolatus eyed him. "I heard you'd been beaten up by goblins."

"That's a damn lie!" said Tully angrily. "I tripped and fell. Never mind about me. I came to tell you that those gold-plated mercenaries you raved about are both dead."

Immolatus raised his head. "Captain and Mother? Dead? How? Who killed them?"

"You know how they claimed they didn't believe in gods?" Tully asked. He added with an unpleasant smile, "Let's just say they are now believers."

Immolatus had no idea what he meant. And on reflection—realizing that now he wouldn't have to pay them—he didn't care.

"I have an assignment for you," he told Tully. "See that knife in that chest? Not the chest with the rubies. The one to the left. The knife's lying next to the sapphire poignard."

Tully located the knife and reached to pick it up.

"Be careful not to cut yourself," Immolatus warned. "The blade is tipped in deadly poison."

Tully eyed the knife but didn't touch it.

"What am I supposed to do with it?"

"I want you to use it to kill that accursed knight and the silver dragon who inflicted these wounds on me."

Tully was appalled. "Me? Kill a knight and a dragon? With nothing but a knife? That lance must have pierced your brain!"

"I told you the knife is poison," Immolatus snarled. "The silver dragon walks about in mortal form. Strike her then. Even a scratch or a deep cut will work. So long as the poison gets into the bloodstream, she is doomed. Same goes for the knight."

Tully gingerly picked up the blade, making certain to touch only the handle. He examined it. His gaze shifted to the jewel-encrusted greatsword.

"If you want me to kill a dragon," said Tully, "give me that sword."

"No knight in the history of knights ever carried a greatsword," said Immolatus. "You'd be quite the spectacle, lugging that sword around. Not at all suspicious."

Tully slid the blade into its sheath and carefully tucked the knife into his belt.

Immolatus lay back down. He closed his eyes, then he realized by the smell that Tully was still hanging around.

"You have your orders," Immolatus said. "Go away."

"Have you ever heard of a gem that glows?" Tully asked.

"No, and neither have you. No one has, because glowing gems don't exist," said Immolatus. "Stop pestering me."

"I saw one today," Tully persisted. "It was ugly and glowed with gray light. I was wondering what it might be worth."

"Get out!" Immolatus sucked in a breath. Flame crackled from his nostrils.

Tully took the hint and hurriedly ducked out of the tent. Immolatus let go of his fiery breath and ended up coughing and groaning, for the cough hurt his fractured ribs. He could feel the bones crunching, and he cursed Tully and cursed knights and cursed his queen. He was drifting off to sleep when, speaking of Takhisis, he remembered she had said something to him about a jewel. Gray in color. She hadn't said it glowed, however. But he should probably tell the guard to go after Tully.

Immolatus thought about the energy required to lift his head and summon the guard and give orders and then explain to Tully . . .

"Bah!" Immolatus snarled. "Let Takhisis find her own damn jewel! I owe her nothing and she owes me plenty. Ungrateful bitch."

The dragon closed his eyes. As he drifted off, he heard the distant sound of whistles and belching. But the sound was far away, and he was in too much pain to care.

CHAPTER
TWENTY-SEVEN

anis woke in the morning after a restless sleep, oppressed by dreams whose terror lingered with him into the dawn.

He and the others had camped out in the shelter of the ruins of Noble's Gate, spending the night wrapped in blankets on the floor. Many years had passed since he had been forced to sleep on cold stone, and he grimaced as he sat up, rubbing his stiff neck. He was surprised to see the sun shining down over the walls of the High Clerist's Tower, wondering why Sturm had not wakened him to take the morning watch. He wished he had wakened him. He might not have had the unsettling dream.

Afraid something was wrong, Tanis rose to go search for his friend.

Sunlight edged its way through jagged holes and cracks in the walls, revealing the full extent of the destruction they had only glimpsed the night before. Chunks of broken stone lay strewn about the charred remains of the great ironwood gates. Dust covered everything, including the sagging cobwebs that spanned the gaps in the wall. Nothing stirred. Nothing lived. Even the spiders had long since died.

"Good morning," said Sturm, coming in from outside, threading his way through the debris. "A terrible sight, isn't it?" he added, noticing Tanis staring at the ruins in shock.

Tanis had been to the High Clerist's Tower many times in his life. Following the War of the Lance, the knights had restored the tower to its former glory. He had been a guest in the tower, and he knew Noble's Gate well, for that was the first gate that led into the temple from the main entrance. He found it difficult to believe he was in the same place.

"Raistlin told me I would find the tower changed, that Noble's Gate had been destroyed. I was prepared for that," Tanis said. "But I was not prepared for the bleakness, the desolation. As if all hope had been crushed and was lying dead among the ruins. I wonder if the dragonlances are even still here."

"They are here," said Sturm. "As hope is here, even in the midst of darkness."

"Did you stand watch all night?" Tanis asked. "You should have wakened me."

"I wasn't tired," said Sturm. "I felt as I did when I was keeping vigil before I was knighted. I prayed to the gods, and they are with us, Tanis. Their temple has been defiled, their altars covered with blood, their statues broken. But Takhisis could not destroy the gods, just as she could not destroy the dragonlances. She is watching us, knowing we are not from this time and we defeated her once."

"Takhisis spoke to me," said Tanis in a low voice. "It was only a dream, yet it seemed very real. She promised death, but I sensed her fear. She will keep her eyes on us and send her servants to try to stop us, though she knows that all she has accomplished is in danger unless she finds the Graygem."

"Then we must make certain she doesn't find it," said Sturm.

His calm and courage were reassuring. The lingering horror of the dream evaporated in the morning sunshine.

The others were still sleeping. Tasslehoff was curled up in a corner, his head resting on his pouch, his hoopak on the floor beside him. Raistlin lay where he had fallen last night, his hand still clasping the Staff of Magius. Flint was sleeping soundly and apparently comfortably. He lay on his back, his hands clasped on his chest, gently snoring.

"Only a dwarf could sleep comfortably on a bed of rock," Tanis remarked.

He and Sturm walked into the courtyard. The sun had risen above the peaks of the mountains that formed a solid bulwark at the tower's back. The peaks were covered with snow. The autumn wind was out of the south, warm as the promise that no matter how deep winter's darkness, spring would return.

"Did you see any sign of the green dragon?" Tanis asked.

"I saw him near the early hours of dawn," said Sturm. "He must have been out hunting during the night. He flew south toward the plains and I lost sight of him in the morning mist."

Tasslehoff came wandering outside as they were talking, rubbing his eyes. "I don't usually sleep this late, because I miss lots of interesting things when I'm asleep, but I was dreaming about Destina. I hope she and Kairn can save the song. How many days until we find out if they did?"

"Three days, according to Raistlin," said Tanis. "Yesterday, today, and tomorrow."

"And then what happens?" Tas asked.

"Either Destina and Kairn succeed and we return to our lives as they were with no memory of this, or they fail and we remain in this world to the end of our days," said Tanis.

"I'd like to go back to my life that was in the past which is in the future, but I'd also like to stay in this present with Flint and Sturm since they're not dead anymore." Tas shook his head. "Only I don't want to stay here in the tower because of the ghosts."

Flint joined them, smoothing his beard and adjusting his helm. "The mage is awake, in case anyone's interested. The kender is right. This place shivers my skin. The sooner we take these dragonlances and leave, the better."

They returned to Noble's Gate to find Raistlin seated on the floor in a shaft of sunlight, his spellbook open in his lap. He was studying his spells, whispering the words to himself.

Tanis had no appetite, but he asked if anyone was hungry.

"Not for squirrel food," said Flint.

"There are too many ghosts. I remember when that bad man killed Gwyneth and Huma, and I have a stomachache here," Tasslehoff said, putting his hand on his heart.

Sturm shook his head. He did not sit down but walked into the temple. He stopped just inside, staring into the darkness. His expression was dark and grim. Perhaps he was seeing ghosts and remembering his failure.

Raistlin closed his spellbook.

"Where are these dragonlances?" Flint asked.

Raistlin glanced over at Sturm. "The knight stands at the entrance to the temple. The dragonlances are inside, on the floor near the altar. We also need to find the dragon orb. If we are trapped in this time, I will require the power of the dragon orb to fight the Dark Queen's dragons. I know it is somewhere inside the tower, because Tas found it here during the War of the Lance. He should be able to remember where it was."

"I remember," said Tas. "But it won't be there because *there* isn't there. I found it on the first level of the High Clerist's Tower in the middle of the dragon traps during the War of the Lance, but it won't be there because either the war has already happened or maybe will happen or maybe won't happen at all. I don't know. I'm getting all muddled."

"Just tell me where you found the dragon orb," Raistlin said.

"It was on top of a stand and the walls were like jagged teeth that trapped the evil dragons when the orb called them and then the knights killed them and they screamed when they were being stabbed," said Tas. "But I'm telling you it won't be there, because the dragon traps aren't there. The Temple of Paladine where Huma and Gwyneth died is where it isn't."

Raistlin was silent.

"What's the matter?" Tanis asked.

"The kender is right," said Raistlin. "The dragon traps were built after the Third Dragon War, after the knights were victorious. They won't be there now."

"So you bring us to this godforsaken tower to find an orb that isn't here," said Flint.

"The orb *is* here," said Raistlin impatiently. "I just don't know where. Tanis, you and Sturm and Flint fetch the dragonlances. Tas and I will search for the dragon orb. He can at least take me to the first level, where he found it. We will meet back here."

"Are you certain you don't want me to come with you, Raistlin?" Tanis asked.

"Why? Because you do not trust me with the dragon orb?" asked Raistlin, his lip curling.

"You are right, I don't trust you," said Tanis coolly. "What do you expect? You used the orb to transport yourself to safety, abandoning your brother and the rest of us to our deaths in the Blood Sea. But, no, I was thinking you might need my protection."

Raistlin was annoyed. "I assure you my magic is powerful—"

"Silence!" Sturm turned his head to look back outside Noble's Gate. "I thought I heard footsteps."

He and Tanis drew their swords. Flint jumped to his feet, holding his axe. Tas grabbed his hoopak.

They could all hear the sounds now. Someone was roaming about in the rubble.

"Raist? Are you inside there?" a voice called.

Raistlin looked astonished. "Caramon?"

"Yeah, it's me." Caramon appeared, climbing over the rubble to reach them. He was scraped and bruised and soaking wet all the way down to his boots. Water plastered his hair to his head and dripped off his armor. His shirt and breeches were soaked. His boots squelched with water when he walked.

"Took me long enough to find you," he said disgruntledly. "I've been walking around this damn tower since dawn. It was like some nightmare. I could see where I was going, but then when I thought I was here, I wasn't. At least now I am."

Caramon glanced around at the destruction and shook his head. "So this is the High Clerist's Tower where Takhisis won the war. I can believe the stories about it being haunted. It makes me feel all twisted up inside."

"How did you get here?" Raistlin eyed his brother disparagingly. "Did you swim?"

"In a manner of speaking," said Caramon, shivering. "It was the worst experience of my life."

"How did you get past the dragon?" Tanis asked.

"Cyan?" Caramon gave a dismissive shrug. "He's sound asleep on the plains in front of the Knight's Spur. I could have walked off with the whole damn tower and he wouldn't have noticed. Once I heard you and Tanis and the others were here, I couldn't leave you to face Kit on your own."

"Face Kit?" Tanis asked, alarmed. "What do you mean?"

"Bakaris told Kit that you and Raist and the others were coming to the tower to get some sort of magical lances, and she's on her way to stop you," said Caramon. "She knows the truth about us, Raist— that we're working for the resistance. She's mad at us for betraying her and she's furious with you, Tanis. She left her army in Solamnia and came all the way to Solace just to see you, and you made her look like a fool."

"So you escaped—" Raistlin began.

"Naw," said Caramon. "She sent me here. And not out of sisterly affection. She sent me to taunt you. I'm supposed to tell you that she's coming to kill all of us."

"She's trying to scare us," said Raistlin. "She hopes we will abandon our search for the dragonlances and flee."

"I'm not so sure," said Caramon dubiously. "She sounded like she was really looking forward to killing us."

"How long will it take her to reach the tower?" Tanis asked.

Caramon paused to consider. "When I left, she was making plans to order her army to Neraka for the Emperor's Summit. Once her army is on the road, she'll come after us. She's riding Skie, and he's fast, but he'll have to stop to hunt and rest. So three days."

"Three days," Tanis repeated skeptically. "She must know we'll be long gone by then."

"She does know," said Raistlin. "Skie is a dragon and a powerful magic-user. He knows any number of spells that could bring them both here in the blink of an eye. We therefore have to assume we don't have much time before Kit arrives. Caramon and I will search for the dragon orb."

"How do you even know for certain it is here?" Tanis asked.

"Because Magius brought it here from the Tower of High Sorcery. He hid it before the dragonarmies attacked using an apport spell. He planned to simply reverse the spell, but he died before he could. That is why the orb will be here when Tas finds it during the War of the Lance," Raistlin stated.

"Which is in the future that's in the past," Tas added helpfully.

"Even if I understood all this, which I don't, I don't see how this helps us," Flint stated. "We could spend months searching the tower for this dragon orb and Kit could be here any moment!"

"Do you know this apport spell? Can you reverse it?" Tanis asked.

"Magius would be the only one who could reverse it," Raistlin said and then paused. "But if we knew where he hid it, we might be able to find it using another spell. And I think I know where it is! The wine cellar!"

"Of course," said Sturm with a faint smile. "He teased that he was going to transport us to the wine cellar."

"Everyone knew Magius was accustomed to visiting the wine cellar. If he hid the orb there, he could easily recover it without anyone suspecting," said Raistlin.

"Do you know where the wine cellar is?" Tanis asked.

"I do. Magius took me there," said Raistlin. "The cellar is belowground, not far from the dungeons. I was only there once, but I believe I could find it again. Caramon, since you're here, you might as well come with me. The rest of you go with Sturm to search for the dragonlances. We will meet back at Noble's Gate."

"Can I come look for the orb, too?" Tas asked. "I know where it isn't."

"You go with Tanis. But I will need to borrow your hoopak," said Raistlin.

"My hoopak?" Tas was pleased. "Is it magic? I always thought it was, you know. Maybe we could switch. You carry my hoopak and I'll carry the Staff of Magius."

"Just give me the hoopak," said Raistlin.

Tas sighed and handed it to Raistlin. "Take good care of it."

"I promise," said Raistlin and handed the hoopak to Caramon.

"What do I do with it?" Caramon asked.

"Nothing," Raistlin replied. "And don't be concerned, Tanis. This time, I won't run off with the dragon orb. Come, my brother. The wine cellar is located in the north part of the tower. We must enter through a different gate."

Raistlin pulled the cowl over his head and walked off.

Caramon hesitated, looking uncertainly back at the others. "I heard the tower was guarded by undead ..."

"I saw a wraith," said Tas.

"Here?" Caramon was horrified. "In the tower?"

"It was in this tower, but not this tower, if you know what I mean," said Tas. "It was during the Third Dragon War. I was walking down a hall—"

Raistlin half turned his head to glare at his brother.

Caramon heaved a sigh, then hurried after. "I'm coming, Raist!"

Flint stared after Raistlin, puzzled. "Who is this Magius he keeps talking about?"

"He was Raistlin's friend," Sturm replied.

Flint snorted. "Raistlin never had any friends."

"He had one," said Sturm.

CHAPTER
TWENTY-EIGHT

anis watched Raistlin and his brother head eastward along the corridor. Caramon stayed protectively by Raistlin's side, one hand on the hilt of his sword and the other awkwardly holding the hoopak. Even after they had disappeared into the darkness, Tanis could mark their progress by the light of the glimmering crystal atop the staff.

"What are we standing around here for?" Flint demanded. "Let's find these dragonlances and get out of here."

"One of us should stay here to keep watch for Kit," said Tanis.

"There are a great many dragonlances and it will take all of us to carry them," said Sturm. "As for Kitiara, let the gods stand watch. We must put our faith in them."

"What gods?" Flint said in a low voice to Tanis. "There's only one, the Dark Queen, and I don't want her anywhere near me."

They made their way toward the entrance of the temple. The sunlight grew feeble as they moved closer, and finally disappeared altogether. Looking ahead, they could see only darkness that seemed as absolute as death, unending as grief.

Tanis had walked in many dark places in his life, but he was reluctant to enter the temple. He was not afraid. He would have welcomed fear, compared to the unbearable sorrow that seemed to wring his heart and crush his soul. He and Flint and even Tasslehoff stopped. Only Sturm kept going, walking toward the temple.

"Sturm, wait! We need light," Tanis said.

Sturm paused, but he seemed to do so reluctantly. "I know where I am going."

"Well, I don't! I saw a lantern on the floor near the entrance," said Flint.

"I wish I had my hoopak," said Tas in a small voice. "I'm not afraid of the dark, but this is darker than dark. It's the kind of dark I felt inside me when Flint died."

Fortunately, Flint was climbing over the rubble and didn't hear. He returned with an iron lantern, dented and covered with rust.

"It still has the stub of a candle, and I brought my tinderbox with me," Flint stated. "I figured we might need it! I'll bet none of the rest of you thought of that!"

"You see now why we needed you, old dwarf," said Tanis, making no mention of the fact that he had his own tinderbox with him in his pack.

Flint placed the lantern on the floor and drew out the box that contained flint, fire steel, and swatches of linen known as char cloth. He struck the flint against the fire steel, producing a spark, lit the cloth, and then touched the burning cloth to the candle's blackened wick. After several tense moments, the wick caught fire. Flint was starting to pick up the lantern when the flame blew out.

Flint glared at Tas. "Did you do that?"

"Ghosts," said Tas, his voice quavering.

Flint sheltered behind a wall and lit another piece of cloth. Once more he held the fire to the candle. The wick caught, but another blast of cold air blew it out and knocked over the lantern. It went rolling across the floor.

Flint grabbed his tinderbox, thrust it into a pocket, and stood up. "I'm leaving. Dragonlances aren't going to help us if wraiths freeze our blood and drain us dry!"

"We do not need light, nor do we need to fear the undead," said

Sturm. "I will guide you, for I know the way even in the darkness ahead of us. Stay close to me."

Sturm was pale, his jaw set. He gripped the hilt of his sword and walked forward toward the entrance of the temple.

Flint hesitated, then plunged after him. "We can't let the fool knight go alone!"

Tas followed, repeating to himself, "I'm not afraid. Kender are never afraid. I'm not afraid."

Tanis brought up the rear, his hand on his sword. The impulse to turn back grew in intensity, yet he did not feel threatened. Whatever ghostly presence was here was not malevolent. At least not yet. It was simply warning them.

Tanis lost sight of Sturm, but he was keeping close to Flint and Tas. Both were moving slowly, and suddenly Tas stopped.

"I tried to save the song!" Tas shouted into the darkness and burst into tears.

Flint sucked in a harsh breath.

"I can't go on!" he said through gritted teeth. He was shivering so hard his armor rattled. "My legs . . . won't work!"

The chill darkness enveloped them, draining their courage, if it did not drain their lives.

Tanis could barely walk, as though invisible shackles were clamped onto his legs. The exertion left him weak and gasping for breath.

"Where is Sturm?" he asked in a hoarse whisper.

"He kept going . . ." Flint said. He sucked in a shaking breath and pointed. "Look! There!"

As Tanis watched in awe, a dragon materialized out of the darkness and towered above Sturm, blocking his way. The dragon was not a living dragon; it was not made of flesh and bone, scale and blood. A living dragon would have been less terrifying. This dragon was a spirit formed of light that was pale and sharp and cold as steel.

"Turn back, mortals," said the dragon. "The living have no place here. The High Clerist's Tower belongs to the dead."

Sturm slowly removed his helm and thrust it under his arm. The spirit's ghastly light gleamed on his haggard face, wet with tears, lined with grief.

"I have no wish to disturb the dead," he said. "I am Sturm Bright-blade and I have come to pay my respects to a noble knight, Huma Feigaard. I was proud to call him my friend. Yet, at the end, I failed him—"

Sturm choked on his grief and could not speak. He put his hands to his eyes and bowed his head. The spirit did not speak. But a silver glow shone from the dragon's eyes and surrounded the knight with holy radiance.

"Sturm Brightblade," said the dragon. "I am Gwyneth, the guardian of my lord's final rest. You have come to honor the dead."

"I have, Lady Gwyneth, although hundreds of years have passed," said Sturm, raising his head. His tears glimmered silver.

"The River of Time flows into eternity," said the spirit. "The passing of years means nothing to the dead. You may enter to do my lord homage and you may bring your companions."

Silver light illuminated the temple, banishing the darkness. Crystal stars sparkled in the domed ceiling, shining on the altars of the gods beloved by the knights: Habakkuk, Mishakal, Paladine, and Kiri-Jolith. Immolatus had torn down their statues and smashed the altars. But on the broken altar of Paladine, four candles burned. The body of a knight clad in armor lay on a bier before it.

The decay of death had not touched the knight. His face was that of a living man who has fallen into a deep and restful sleep. His eyes were closed, his hands clasped over his breast. His helm and his sword were at his feet. His armor gleamed with silver light. The dragonlances lay on the floor below the bier, shining silver in the candlelight.

"I've never seen the like," said Flint, his voice soft with awe. "Maybe Sturm was right and the old gods are here with us, after all."

"They never left," said Tanis, remembering another place, another time.

Sturm approached the bier with reverence and respect. When he reached it, he drew his sword from its scabbard and gave the knight's salute to a noble foe.

"Thus I salute you, Death, even as I defy you. In the end, as you see, you cannot win."

Sturm sheathed his sword and knelt before the bier in silent prayer. He then rose to his feet, made a reverent bow to the dead, and took his place beside the bier as a guard of honor. Gwyneth stood at the head, her silver wings folded at her side.

"Is it my turn now?" Tas asked.

"It is," said Gwyneth gently.

Tas started to walk forward, then looked around. "Flint, you should come with me."

The dwarf looked startled. "But I didn't know him."

"That's all right," said Tas. "I'll introduce you. Come on."

Flint glanced at Tanis, who nodded. "We should all pay our respects."

Flint thrust his axe into its harness and took off his helm. He and Tanis accompanied Tas to the bier.

"Hullo, Gwyneth. I'm Tasslehoff Burrfoot. Do you remember me? You cleaned my face with magical elf spit."

"I remember you, Master Burrfoot," said the dragon, and her silver light seemed to glow brighter.

"This is my friend Flint Fireforge," Tas said, urging Flint forward. "You didn't meet him before because he was dead and waiting for me under a tree. But, as you can see, he's not dead anymore."

Flint, looking abashed, made a bobbing bow. "At your service, ma'am."

"And this is my friend Tanis Half-Elven," said Tas.

Tanis could only gaze at the dragon, overcome with emotion. He honored the valiant knight, but he also honored the love that had endured long after death and imbued the temple with sacred and holy radiance.

"Lady Gwyneth." He bowed with reverence.

The dragon gracefully inclined her head.

"We should go now, Tas," Tanis added softly.

"But we came to take the dragonlances," said Tas. "Don't you want them?"

Tanis felt as guilty as if he'd come to plunder a tomb. "It isn't right, Tas. The dragonlances belong here."

Tas turned back to the dragon. "Could I talk to Huma?"

"My lord would be honored," said the spirit.

"He would?" Tas asked, astonished. "Even though I'm not a knight like Sturm?"

"You are brave and loyal and true, Master Burrfoot, and your heart is free of guile," said the dragon. "Any knight would be proud to possess such qualities."

Tas stood very tall as he walked to the bier and rested his hand gently on the knight's cold, pale hand.

"I want to tell you that I'm sorry I couldn't save the song, Lord Huma," said Tas. "But then it occurred to me that maybe you never heard it. So I thought I'd sing you the little bit that I remember."

> *. . . the night of the full moons red and silver*
> *Shines down on the hills, on the forms of a man and a woman*
> *Shimmering steel and silver, silver and steel,*
> *Above the village, over the thatches and nurturing shires.*

Tas wiped his nose with his sleeve. "That part is near the end. There's a lot more that comes in front of it—all about how you and Gwyneth meet and she gives you the dragonlances and you drive the Dark Queen back into the Abyss, only none of that happened because that bad man, Tully, stole the song. But now we're here to make our own song. And to do that we need to take the dragonlances. I hope that's all right."

"My lord grants you permission to take them," said the spirit. "Go with our blessing."

Tas gently patted Huma's arm. "Thank you, Huma. Have a good sleep."

Flint bowed deeply. "May Reorx grant you rest, sir. I hope the kender wasn't too much of a bother."

"The gods grant you rest eternal, Lord Huma," said Tanis. "And you as well, Lady Gwyneth."

"These are the dragonlances," said Tas, indicating the weapons on the floor.

"Beautiful," Flint said softly as he drew nearer to have a closer look. "Now this is fine craftsmanship! Dwarves forged these, didn't they?"

"Reorx sent his finest craftsmen to Silver Dragon Mountain," said Gwyneth.

Flint started to reach out his hand to touch one of the lances, then glanced apprehensively at the spirit and drew it back.

"You can pick it up," said Tas. "Huma won't mind."

Flint hesitated, but it was clear he longed to hold it. He clasped his hand around one of the lances and lifted it from the floor.

"Well balanced. Lightweight. The edge is finely honed," said Flint, regarding it with admiration. "But I have worked with iron all my life and I've never seen metal so pure. What process did the dwarves use to make such fine quality steel?"

"That is not steel. It is dragonmetal, blessed by Paladine, and it flows in only one place in the world—Silver Dragon Mountain," said Gwyneth. "Reorx himself forged the first dragonlance beneath the mountain, using a silver arm and wielding a silver hammer. Reorx then brought dwarven smiths to the mountain to forge the rest and my people hid them away. The lances lay forgotten for many centuries until I brought them to Huma."

Flint ran his hand over the lance and blinked his eyes very rapidly. "I thank you for the opportunity to see and touch such a marvel, Lady Dragon."

"The dragonlances are yours," said Gwyneth. "My lord and I lost our battle, but we have guarded the dragonlances for the heroes we knew would come in our stead."

"We are grateful, Lady Gwyneth," said Sturm. "We will strive to be worthy of you and your lord."

The dragon dipped her head in gracious acknowledgment, and then the spirit faded away. The bier and the body of Huma vanished and the silver light died. But the flames of the four candles still burned. The dragonlances shone with a faint silver glow.

Tanis and Sturm counted twenty dragonlances.

"We could use many more," said Tanis. "But I am grateful to have any."

Flint and Tas wrapped the lances in the soft sheepskin in which Gwyneth had carried them from the mountain. As Tanis picked up what he thought was the last dragonlance, he was surprised to see more shining in the candlelight. He and Sturm gathered up those, and when those were carefully wrapped, they turned back to find more. The final count was one hundred.

"The question is, what do we do with them now?" Tanis asked, gazing down at the bundles.

"Why are you asking me? I don't know!" said Tas loudly.

"I wasn't asking you," said Tanis, giving Tas a puzzled look. "I was talking to Sturm. We can't take them back to Solace. Not while Kitiara is there."

"They would do us no good in Solace, anyway," Sturm agreed. "We should take them to the knights."

"According to Laurana, Lord Gunthar and the knights who survived the fall of Solamnia are in hiding. Perhaps Raistlin knows—" Tanis began.

"He doesn't!" Tas shouted. "And neither does Fizban! I won't go there!"

He turned and dashed off.

"Tas—" Tanis called, but the kender had disappeared, swallowed up by the darkness.

"That was odd, even for Tas," said Sturm. "Should we go look for him?"

"We'll never find him if he doesn't want to be found," said Tanis. "And I have the feeling he doesn't want to be found."

They carried the bundles of lances to the front of the temple, where they hoped to find Raistlin and Caramon waiting for them. But when they reached Noble's Gate, they saw no sign of the twins.

"At least Kitiara's not here," said Sturm.

"Or Tas, either," said Flint. "He's always around when you don't want him and never around when you do. I'll go find him."

"No, Flint," said Tanis. "Tas needs to work this out for himself."

"Work what out?" Flint asked.

"Tas knows what we are supposed to do with the dragonlances," said Tanis. "Fizban told him."

"That daft old wizard who wrecked the Inn?" Flint shook his head. "I won't even ask how he knew, but if he told Tas, why doesn't Tas tell us?"

"I know this sounds strange since we are talking about Tasslehoff Burrfoot," said Tanis. "But I think he's afraid."

CHAPTER
TWENTY-NINE

Tas had no idea where he was going, but that was all right because some of the best adventures happen when you don't know where you are going.

Sadly, he wasn't interested in adventures just now. He was too unsettled and disgruntled. He traipsed about the wooden benches in the temple and thought about the word *disgruntled* and wondered what it might feel like to be gruntled, and eventually he ended up standing beside the broken altars. The candles on the altar of Paladine were still burning. He could hear Tanis and Sturm and Flint leaving the temple, carrying the bundles of dragonlances to the front of the temple.

"I don't know why they can't just leave me alone," Tas muttered irritably. "Always asking me stupid questions like where to take the dragonlances. How should I know? It's not like anyone told me. Especially not Fizban."

He kicked a chunk of rock and watched it roll across the floor for quite a distance until it fetched up against a booted foot.

Tas was considerably startled to see the booted foot, and he looked up from the foot into the face of a man who was standing in front of one of the altars. The man was wearing the armor of a Knight of Solamnia and bore the symbol of a sword on his breastplate. His armor was very ornate and must have once been beautiful, but it was dented and smashed, as though the knight had been in many battles. His helm rested beside him on the altar. The helm was decorated with long, curled horns, and it was also dented and one of the horns was broken.

The knight was tall and imposing. He had short black hair and long black mustaches, black skin, and black eyes. The candle gleamed on his armor and in his eyes, which seemed warm and understanding.

Once Tas got over being startled, he remembered his manners and held out his hand. "My name is Tasslehoff Burrfoot. My friends call me Tas."

The knight took Tas's hand in a firm grasp. "I am Kiri-Jolith."

"You are?" Tas stared at the knight in astonishment. "Kiri-Jolith the god?"

Kiri-Jolith smiled. "I am honored to meet you, Master Burrfoot."

"You can call me Tas. Everyone does. I know another god," said Tas. "His name is Fizban and he's a great friend of mine—"

Tas stopped, uncomfortable, remembering.

"I know Fizban is your friend," said Kiri-Jolith. "He told me I might find you here."

"He did?" Tas was growing even more uncomfortable and decided to change the subject. "You look like you've been in lots of battles."

"I have," said Kiri-Jolith. "I am the guardian of a sacred place some know as the Gateway to Heaven, for it leads to the home of the gods—all the gods. We came together at the beginning of time to create the Gateway as a monument to the balance of good and evil that keeps the world turning. Takhisis has long sought to close the Gateway to Heaven and raise it as a monument to herself. She has attacked me many times and sent her evil dragons to try to drive me away."

"The Gateway sounds like a wonderful place," said Tas. "I'd love to visit it. Where is it?"

"You know it," said Kiri-Jolith. "For you have been there."

"I have?" Tas asked, amazed. He mulled over what the knight had said. "Home of the gods. Now what does that remind me of?"

And then he knew. And he didn't want to know. He began to sidle away.

"It's been very nice meeting you, Kiri-Jolith, but I . . . uh . . . I have to go join my friends. They need me, you know."

"They do indeed," said Kiri-Jolith gravely. "They need you to tell them where they are supposed to take the dragonlances."

"To the Gateway. Because its other name is Godshome," said Tas in a low voice. He sighed and shook his head. "I won't go back there. Not in this time or any other time."

"Because Flint died there," said Kiri-Jolith gently.

Tas nodded and wiped away a snuffle. "So you see, I can't tell anyone about Godshome because I don't want Flint to die again."

"But you healed Flint," said Kiri-Jolith. "You invoked the blessing of the goddess Mishakal and touched him with her sacred staff."

"I did more than touch him," said Tas. "I walloped him pretty good—twice, just to make certain it took."

"It took," said Kiri-Jolith, smiling.

"But if we go to Godshome, how can I be certain Flint isn't going to die there again?" Tas asked.

"You cannot be certain," said Kiri-Jolith. "When we step into the River of Time, we never know where it will take us. The Solamnic knights will rally under the leadership of Lord Gunthar and ride to Godshome to join forces with the elves and the good dragons to attack Neraka and the armies of the Dark Queen. They will need the dragonlances."

Tas heaved a sigh. "Then I guess I'll tell my friends. Would you like to come meet them? I know they'd like to meet you. Especially Sturm."

"I know Sturm Brightblade well, as he knows me," said Kiri-Jolith. "Farewell, Tasslehoff Burrfoot. You have the heart and soul of a true knight."

"I don't suppose I could have a helm to go with it?" Tas asked, looking longingly at the helm with the curved horns.

Apparently, he couldn't, for Kiri-Jolith—and the helm—disappeared.

CHAPTER
THIRTY

aistlin walked down the corridor, trying to remember the way to the wine cellar. He and Caramon were in a small pool of light, shed by the crystal atop the Staff of Magius, surrounded by a river of darkness. He knew that the corridor encircled the temple, but he had difficulty judging where he was in the corridor, as he had no point of reference—the wall hangings, the tapestries, and the dust-covered statues of the knights standing in the corners were the same in one corridor as in the next. He could mark their progress only when he reached one of the gates that gave access to the temple.

Caramon was uneasy and stayed so close to Raistlin that he was nearly tripping on his heels.

"Put away your sword before you stab me!" said Raistlin. "If anything does attack us, it won't be flesh and blood. And stop fidgeting with the hoopak! It is of vital importance to my spell!"

Caramon had been nervously swinging the hoopak around and around by the leather thong. He sheathed his sword and clasped his hand firmly on the hoopak.

"Sorry, Raist," he said, abashed. He glanced around uneasily. "It sure is dark in here. I almost wish we didn't have light. It makes the dark worse, if you know what I mean."

Raistlin did know, although he wasn't going to admit it. Beyond the circle of light, the darkness seemed darker by contrast. Dark and unbearably empty.

"What are you going to do with the hoopak?" Caramon asked in hushed tones.

"The magic I plan to cast requires a forked twig as a spell component," Raistlin replied.

Caramon eyed the hoopak dubiously. "This is forked, but it's not a twig."

"Try not to be a greater fool than the gods made you, Caramon," said Raistlin. "It will work."

"If you say so, Raist," said Caramon meekly. "Where are we going?"

"To Knight's Gate," said Raistlin.

"I hope it's not in ruins, too," said Caramon.

"It isn't," said Raistlin. "Immolatus tore down only the northern gate. Knight's Gate is on the eastern side of the temple."

They continued down the vast and empty corridor. The floor was carpeted with dust. Apparently, no other living being had walked this hall in hundreds of years. Raistlin could not even see tracks of rodents.

"I'll be glad when we get out of here," Caramon said. "Can I ask you a question?"

"You just did," said Raistlin.

"Well, then another," said Caramon.

"Go ahead," said Raistlin resignedly, knowing Caramon was like a dog guarding a bone. He would never let it go.

"Is this Magius you talk about the Magius who owned this staff?" Caramon asked.

"He is," Raistlin replied. "He gave it to me."

"But you said that a White Robe, Par-Salian, gave the staff to you after you took the Test."

"He did," Raistlin said. "Magius died centuries ago."

Caramon wrinkled his brow in confusion. "But then how—"

"Leave me in peace, Caramon," said Raistlin. "I need to concentrate."

He was beginning to grow uneasy, for he did not remember the corridor being this long, and he wondered if he had passed Knight's Gate without knowing it.

As usual, Caramon read his twin's mind, echoed his doubts.

"How do you know where we are? It seems to me that we've been going in circles."

"In a manner of speaking, we are, for this hall encircles the temple," said Raistlin. "There are other rooms and facilities on this level, however, such as the dungeons in the north part of the tower and—I hope—the wine cellar."

"Wait!" Caramon said, pausing. "I felt a draft. Maybe we've come to another gate."

Raistlin stopped and lifted the staff so that the crystal shone on the wooden double doors set beneath an arched entryway. He could see gashes made by battle-axes that had hacked into the wood, and he remembered the hordes of the Dark Queen's soldiers swarming into the tower when it fell. He searched for a sign to tell him which gate this was, hoping that it had not been destroyed.

"The tower has five gates that lead to the temple. We entered at Noble's Gate," Raistlin said. "Each was marked by a different symbol."

He raised the staff higher until the light shone on the keystone above the door. He could see, carved into the stone, two hands folded in prayer.

"This is Pilgrim's Gate," Raistlin said, relieved. "The next gate should be Knight's Gate."

They continued on, moving faster now that Raistlin knew where he was, and at last came to another gate. Raistlin held the staff high to see the symbol in the keystone: a sword, a rose, and a crown.

"The symbol of the Knights of Solamnia," he said. "This is—"

He was stopped by a fit of coughing. He fumbled for his handkerchief and pressed it to his mouth as the hacking cough tore at his body with such fury he staggered and almost fell.

Caramon hovered near him, anxious and concerned. "Here, Raist, I'll help you. Lean on me!"

Raistlin angrily thrust aside his brother's arm and leaned on the staff until the spasm eased and he could draw a shuddering breath.

"Are you all right?" Caramon asked worriedly.

"Am I ever all right?" Raistlin rasped. He wiped the blood from his lips. "Be quiet and let me think. I need to figure out where we go from here."

Raistlin remembered clearly the time Magius had decided to flout Commander Belgrave's orders and conduct their own interrogation of the prisoner in the dungeons. The prisoner had laughed as he talked about how Immolatus had killed the knights at Westgate Pass, roasting them in their own armor. Raistlin had feared Magius was going to kill the man, and apparently Magius had thought so as well, for he had abruptly left.

I need a drink to get the foul taste out of my mouth, Magius had said, and he had taken Raistlin to the wine cellar.

"We entered through Knight's Gate," Raistlin murmured, talking to himself, and suited his action to his words. "Magius turned to the right from here and we proceeded down a hall—this hall—and down this staircase."

He descended the stairs. Caramon walked at his side, undoubtedly wondering how a man who had been dead for centuries had led his twin anywhere. He opened his mouth, but Raistlin glared at him, so he shut it again. Once they reached the bottom, Raistlin paused to get his bearings.

"This hallway leads north to another flight of stairs and eventually down to the dungeons. We walked up the stairs to the wine cellar, which was at the end of an alcove."

He shone the light of the staff around the corridor. "I thought we came this direction, but I don't see the door to the wine cellar."

Caramon stood fidgeting at his side. He cleared his throat. "What I don't understand is how this Magius—"

Raistlin gave an exasperated sigh. "He came to me in a dream."

"To help you find the wine cellar?" Caramon asked, astonished. He shook his head in admiration. "Must be some damn fine wine."

Raistlin could almost hear Magius's laughter, and he smiled.

"According to Magius, it was. Give me the hoopak and stand over there, out of my way. Be quiet. Do not even breathe loudly."

"Sure, Raist," said Caramon and he sucked in a breath, apparently prepared to stop breathing altogether.

Raistlin conjured up an image of the dragon orb in his mind and focused his attention on it. Holding the hoopak in one hand, he softly spoke the words of the spell that he hoped would allow him to find it.

"*Demanis Ajah!*" Raistlin said beneath his breath.

The hoopak swung around in an arc and then stopped, pointing to a passage that led east.

"We go this way," said Raistlin.

Caramon let out his breath and drew in another. "This is like that game we played when we were kids, isn't it? What was it? Hunt the Thimble?"

Raistlin did not waste his breath answering. He refocused his thoughts on the dragon orb and walked down the hall, holding the hoopak out in front, following its lead. They had not gone far when the hoopak swung violently to the right, almost hitting Caramon. Raistlin held up the light and saw that they stood before an alcove with an arched ceiling. The carving on the keystone above the door depicted grapes and a vine.

"Is this another gate?" Caramon asked.

"This is the door to the wine cellar," said Raistlin, pleased and relieved. "I remember now!"

Guided by the light of the staff, he and Caramon entered the alcove and came to a double door made of ironwood and banded with steel. He shone the light on it and stood staring at the door in grim silence. Or rather, he stared at what remained of the door. The High Clerist had kept the wine cellar locked, and only he had the key. Magius must have thought the dragon orb would be safe here, under lock and key. And given that it was a wine cellar, no one would think to look for a valuable magical artifact.

He had not taken into consideration that the marauding soldiers of the Dark Queen would smash the padlock and batter down the doors to get to the wine.

Raistlin tried not to give way to despair. The magical spell he had cast had brought them this far. Just because they had found the wine didn't mean they had found the dragon orb. He was about to enter the cellar when Caramon stopped him.

"Let me go first, Raist. We don't know what's in there."

Raistlin didn't argue, remembering how he and his brother usually worked together—steel and sorcery. He stepped to one side as Caramon drew his sword and walked slowly through the broken door.

"It's dark as Takhisis's heart in here," Caramon reported. "I can't see a damn thing."

"I'll bring the light," said Raistlin.

He followed his brother, carrying the staff, and stopped to stare in dismay. The light shone on smashed barrels and casks and rows of wine racks that had been torn down. The floor glittered with shards of broken glass.

"What does this orb look like?" Caramon asked.

"A globe made of glass," said Raistlin. He didn't mention that there was a dragon trapped inside.

Caramon gave a low whistle and lowered his sword. "The place has been ransacked. The soldiers must have been overjoyed to stumble across a cellar filled with barrels of dwarf spirits, ale, and wine. Better than a treasure vault. What if they found his orb? I know soldiers, and if they couldn't drink it or sell it, they would have smashed it."

"The orb has a strong sense of self-preservation," said Raistlin, as much to reassure himself as his brother. "It knows how to hide from danger."

"I hope it doesn't consider us dangerous," said Caramon. "Otherwise we've wasted a trip."

Raistlin stared at his twin. Caramon could be annoyingly astute sometimes, and Raistlin cursed himself for not having considered the possibility that the orb might hide from him. If it did, he would never find it.

"We will keep looking," he said.

They continued on, their boots crunching on broken glass. Every time Raistlin trod on a piece of glass, he shuddered wondering if he had just stepped on the remains of the dragon orb.

He pictured the orb in his mind. He remembered what it was to hold the dragon orb in his hands. The glass had been cold, so bitterly cold he had feared his flesh might freeze to it. He saw again the swirling mists, the hands reaching out, trying to drag him inside.

"Are you all right, Raist?" Caramon asked worriedly.

Raistlin didn't immediately answer. He could feel his heart thudding in his chest and the chill of sweat on his forehead. He could banish the memories of the dragon orb, but he couldn't banish the longing, the desire to try once again to gain mastery over it. Once he had gained control, the dragon trapped inside the orb would obey his commands. It could spirit him away from an ill-fated ship that was sinking into the Blood Sea and take him to safety, leaving Tanis and Caramon and the others to drown. . . .

"Keep looking," he said wearily.

He raised the hoopak, still holding the image of the dragon orb in his mind, and the magic led them deeper into the wine cellar. They had to wade through the debris, and at one point the light of the staff gleamed on a human skeleton lying amid the broken remains of a barrel.

"Must have been one hell of a party," Caramon observed.

Raistlin watched for the hoopak to dip or turn or indicate in some way that it had located the dragon orb. It gave no sign, and they kept on until suddenly they could go no farther. They had reached the back wall.

"We've run out of cellar," Caramon said.

"I can see that," said Raistlin.

He had been growing increasingly concerned. Perhaps he had been mistaken about the wine cellar. If so, Magius could have hidden the orb on any of the sixteen floors in any of the hundreds of rooms. He was about to give up when the hoopak suddenly lurched, jumped from his hand, and landed on the floor.

"It's here!" Raistlin breathed. He handed the Staff of Magius to Caramon. "Hold the light for me so that I can see."

"Oh, no!" Caramon did not touch it. "I've seen what staffs like this and that blue crystal staff do to people. It won't fry me, will it?"

Raistlin glared at his brother. "If the staff doesn't fry you, I will!"

Caramon gingerly touched the staff with the tips of his fingers.

He cringed, expecting to be burned. Nothing happened to him, and he grasped it firmly. The crystal's light seemed to shine brighter.

"I think it likes me," said Caramon.

Raistlin gave a derisive snort and bent over the hoopak. He noted the direction the forked end of the staff was pointing and stiffened in bitter disappointment. He slowly crept forward, motioning for Caramon to accompany him with the light.

"Stop!" Raistlin ordered, raising his hand. "Don't move!"

Caramon froze in place. "What is it? What'd you find?"

Raistlin reached out his hand and picked up a piece of glass.

"A part of the dragon orb," said Raistlin.

He found four more pieces and made a pathetic little pile of them.

"How can you tell?" Caramon asked.

Raistlin raised a piece to the light. "The glass of the orb is clear, and the glass bottles are brown. The pieces of the orb are delicate and thin and rounded. The glass of the bottles is thick and crude."

Raistlin wondered what had become of the dragon trapped inside.

"The orb is destroyed," he said, numb with despair. "And so are our chances of defeating Takhisis."

Caramon squatted down beside the pile of glass pieces and poked at one with his finger.

"It's so fragile looking, I'm surprised it didn't shatter. Instead, it broke cleanly into five pieces when it hit the floor. Say, Raist, I bet you could glue it back together—"

"Glue!" Raistlin drew in a seething breath. "You are so stupid, my brother—"

He stopped and stared at the five pieces of broken glass. Five pieces . . . The orb has a strong sense of self-preservation. . . .

"Caramon! You are a genius!" Raistlin cried, ecstatic.

He carefully gathered the five pieces and, as he did so, he noticed that each was a different color: white, blue, red, green, and black—the five colors of the five chromatic dragons loyal to Takhisis. Raistlin held the pieces of the orb in his cupped hands.

Closing his eyes, he spoke the words of the spell.

"Ast bilak moparalan/Suh akvlar tantangusar."

He heard Caramon gasp, and he opened his eyes to find that he was holding the dragon orb, whole and intact. Red mist swirled lazily inside.

"I'll be damned!" said Caramon, awed. "You fixed it!"

"I didn't fix it, because it was never broken," said Raistlin with a sigh of heartfelt relief. "What we saw was an illusion designed to make the looters think it was broken. Thus, the orb protected itself."

He cradled the orb in his hands. "Search for a book, Caramon. Anitra Belgrave gave Magius the book with instructions on how to use the orb and a velvet bag for safekeeping. Both should be close by."

Caramon poked about, flashing the light around the cellar.

"Found them!" Caramon reported. "They were over in that corner."

"Hold the bag open," Raistlin instructed.

Caramon tugged at the drawstrings and opened the bag. Raistlin had purposefully avoided looking into the dragon orb, fearing he would fall prey to the mesmerizing effect of the swirling mists and that the red dragon trapped inside would seize him. Averting his eyes, he dropped the orb into the velvet bag.

Caramon peered down at it and was so startled he almost dropped it.

"Raist! The orb . . . It shrank!"

"Don't look! Shut the bag! Quickly!" Raistlin ordered.

Caramon yanked on the drawstrings and the bag closed over the orb.

Raistlin knew he would have to take control of the dragon orb to use it in the final battle. But not yet. He dared not trust himself—or the orb. He took the bag from his twin and tied it securely to the belt around his robes. He decided to leave the book. He had no need for instruction. He knew—all too well—how to use the dragon orb.

"Let us rejoin the others and hope their mission ended as successfully as ours," said Raistlin.

They returned to Noble's Gate to find their friends waiting for them. Sturm had gone to stand at the entrance, keeping watch. Tasslehoff was seated on a large boulder, kicking his feet and recounting a story about gnomes and his uncle Trapspringer. Tanis and Flint were standing guard over several sheepskin bundles. The dusty rays of sunlight filtering through the broken walls gleamed on the silver tips of the dragonlances.

Tanis heard them coming and swiftly turned, his hand on his sword. Flint brandished his axe.

"Just us!" Caramon called.

"We found the dragon orb," Raistlin reported, indicating the bag that hung from his belt. "I have it in here. I see you found the drag-onlances."

"We met Gwyneth again!" Tas said excitedly. "Her spirit has been here all these years, guarding Huma's body. It was very sad. Even Flint got the snuffles, though he won't admit it. I asked Huma to forgive me because I couldn't save the song and Gwyneth gave us the dragonlances. And you brought back my hoopak! I really felt naked without it."

Caramon handed Tas the hoopak and he studied it closely, turning it over, upending it, and then sniffing at it.

"It's my hoopak, but it's different."

"No, it isn't," said Raistlin.

"Are you sure?" Tas asked. "It smells different."

"It is exactly the same," Raistlin said. He sank down wearily onto a large chunk of broken stone.

"Raist worked magic with it," Caramon told Tas. "You should have seen it! Your hoopak led us to the dragon orb, like that game, Hunt the Thimble."

"My hoopak *is* magic!" Tas said proudly. "I knew it!"

Flint thrust his axe into its harness. "We have what we came for. Let's get out of here."

"We haven't yet decided where we are going," said Tanis. "Now that we have the dragonlances and the dragon orb, what do we do with them? We were hoping you might have a suggestion, Raistlin."

"I do not know," said Raistlin. "But someone does."

He looked pointedly at Tas.

"You've known all along," Raistlin continued. "Fizban told you."

"Do you know, Tas?" Tanis asked.

"I know, but I had a good reason for not telling," said Tas. "At least, I thought I did. Kiri-Jolith made me see that I didn't. I met him in the temple. We had a good talk. The god says he knows you, Sturm. He knew me, too. He said I had the heart and soul of a knight. I asked if I could have his helm to go with it, but I guess I couldn't because he disappeared and took his helm with him."

"Where are we supposed to take the dragonlances, Tas?" Tanis asked patiently.

"Fizban told me to take them to Godshome," said Tas.

"Of course," said Raistlin, and Tanis nodded.

"Where?" Flint asked, frowning.

"Godshome. Where you died," said Tas. "That's why I didn't want to go."

"I'm not dead!" Flint said, stomping his foot. "I've never felt better in my life!"

"That's because I healed you," said Tas. "Kiri-Jolith reminded me. He said Lord Gunthar and the knights are going to travel there, along with the elves and the good dragons. They'll need the dragonlances."

"I never heard of this Godshome, but anywhere is better than here," said Flint. "Draw your circle, mage, or whatever you have to do to take us to this Godshome and away from here."

Tanis looked troubled. "A word with you, Raistlin. Alone," he added when he saw Caramon prepared to accompany them.

"Wait here with others, my brother," said Raistlin, who guessed what was coming.

He and Tanis walked down the corridor that encircled the temple. They could hear Tasslehoff giving various commands to his hoopak, ordering it to fly through the air or shoot fireballs, and Caramon asking if anyone had remembered to bring food.

Raistlin came to a halt. "What do you want, Tanis?"

"You said that in order to cast this journeying spell, you need to visualize your destination," Tanis replied. "But you were never in Godshome. You used the dragon orb to take you to Neraka."

"I was in Neraka, that is true. But I traveled to Godshome," said Raistlin. "Never mind why. It doesn't matter."

"I didn't see you there," said Tanis.

"Perhaps because you were committing murder, killing an innocent man," Raistlin returned coolly. "I know because I was there, Tanis, and I saw you run your sword through Berem Everman. Now do you believe me?"

Tanis was silent, remembering that terrible moment in Godshome when he thought Berem had struck down Flint. He had been blinded by rage, overcome with fury. And although he had slain Berem, he had not died. The Everman could not die, but that was a different story. Tanis remembered that moment and recoiled in horror from himself.

Raistlin waited for him to speak, but when he did not, Raistlin shrugged and continued.

"The only person who saw me in Godshome was Flint. I was with him when he died." Raistlin faintly smiled. "The grumpy old dwarf never liked me. Yet he was good to me, in his way. I could not save him when his heart gave out, but I could ease his pain and give him time to say goodbye to you and the others. I can take us to Godshome, Tanis. I can picture it in my mind. I will never forget it."

Tanis still didn't answer, and Raistlin grew impatient. "You can either trust me, Tanis, or you can walk to Godshome. And don't take long to make up your mind. If we're going to leave, we should do so before Kit arrives."

"Too late!" The sound of armor jingling and rattling and feet clumping heralded Flint, coming to find them. "Kit's already here. And so is her dragon."

CHAPTER
THIRTY-ONE

Raistlin and Tanis joined Sturm and the others, who were watching from the shadows inside Noble's Gate, as the blue dragon Skie landed on the battlements almost directly opposite them. Kitiara sat patiently in the dragon saddle waiting for Skie to secure his grip on the crumbling wall. He had to dig his front and back claws into the stone, dislodging chunks in the process, and flap his wings to balance.

"The gods will stop her if she tries to enter the temple," said Tas.

Flint shook his head. "Kitiara fears neither the living nor the dead or the gods. They won't stop her."

"We only need to delay her and give me time to cast the spell that will take us to Godshome," said Raistlin.

Skie finally managed to find purchase on the wall by balancing himself using his tail. Once he had dug in his claws and was steady, Kitiara unfastened the leather straps that held her into the saddle and climbed down off the dragon's back to stand on the wall. The sunlight glistened off her blue dragonscale armor and on the dragon rider's helm.

She removed the helm and shook out her black curls, then cast a sweeping glance around the tower, taking her time, studying the massive building above and the courtyard below. Kit's gaze stopped, fixing on Noble's Gate.

"Keep still, all of you," Tanis warned in a whisper. "Don't move."

"Look there," said Kitiara, pointing almost directly at them.

They crouched in the shadows, scarcely breathing, certain they'd been discovered.

"What am I looking at?" Skie asked.

"The gates have been torn down and part of the wall collapsed," said Kitiara. She was accustomed to shouting orders on a battlefield, and her voice carried in the crisp mountain air. Those hiding amid the ruins of the gate could hear the conversation quite clearly. If they could hear her, she and Skie would be able to hear them.

"The red dragon Immolatus attacked the tower during the Third Dragon War," Skie was saying. "He forced his way inside the temple, only to discover one of the foul knights and a silver dragon waiting for him, armed with dragonlances. That is the first we dragons knew of them. He was critically wounded and ended up fleeing back to the Abyss."

"And it is these same dragonlances that are in there now," said Kitiara.

"According to Queen Takhisis, they are," said Skie. "Cyan is supposed to be guarding them and not taking an afternoon nap."

"Wake up that lazy wyrm," Kit ordered.

Skie lifted his head and gave a ferocious roar.

A startled roar came in response.

"That is Cyan," said Raistlin softly. "He might appear to be a lumbering fool, but he is devious and dangerous, more dangerous than Skie. Cyan could kill us all with a single blast of his poisonous breath."

"So now we have to face two dragons—a blue and a green," Flint grumbled. "If you're going to cast your spell, mage, you'd better do it now."

"I will draw the circle around the dragonlances, so that the magic of the spell will transport them with us," said Raistlin. "But I need time to prepare it."

"I can buy you time. I will take one of the dragonlances and challenge Kitiara and her dragon," said Sturm.

"No, Sturm, you can't!" Tas cried, forgetting they were supposed to be quiet. "You died here once. You can't die here again!"

"No one is going to die or fight dragons!" Tanis said in a harsh whisper. "Kitiara may suspect we are in the tower, but she doesn't know for certain, and we are not going to confirm her suspicions by confronting her. Don't move yet. Wait until she's distracted."

Cyan had been napping, stretched out comfortably on the ground in front of the Knight's Spur, when Skie's roar roused him. He tried to leap into the air, but the green dragon had grown fat and bloated during the centuries of inactivity guarding the tower, and he struggled to lift his great bulk into the sky. He flew ponderously toward where Kitiara and Skie were waiting for him in front of the tower, barely clearing the battlements of the Knight's Spur.

Cyan coughed and wheezed. Green smoke trailed from his nostrils.

"Now, Raistlin!" Tanis said, seeing Kitiara's attention fixed on Cyan. "Go prepare your spell."

"Caramon, come with me," Raistlin said.

Raistlin was starting to draw the circle around the pile of dragonlances, tracing it in the dust, when he felt the familiar burning sensation in his chest. He seized his handkerchief and pressed it over his mouth, gagging and choking, doing his best to stifle his cough. Caramon started to hurry to his side, but Raistlin stopped him with a furious look.

"Do not step on the circle!" he whispered, choking.

"Sorry, Raist," said Caramon, and he backed away.

Fortunately, the coughing was not severe this time and it soon eased. He finished drawing the circle and hurried back to where Tanis and the others were keeping watch.

Cyan hung in the air above Kitiara, who glared at him from the battlements, her arms folded across her chest.

"Sorry to wake you," said Kitiara in a mocking tone.

"I was only pretending to be asleep, Highlord," Cyan said loftily. "A ruse to trick the enemy."

Kitiara laughed. "The enemy! You would not have noticed a legion of Solamnic Knights if they had marched across your snout!"

"I have guarded this tower for hundreds of years, Highlord, and no one has slipped past me!" Cyan said in offended dignity.

"And yet I am here because I received a report that thieves are likely inside the tower at this very moment to steal the dragonlances," said Kitiara.

"Your report is wrong! That is not possible," said Cyan. "The tower is guarded by . . . by undead. There's an evil spirit that won't let anyone pass."

"How do you know?" Kitiara asked, frowning. "Your orders were to stand guard over the tower, not go inside it. Did you try to enter?"

"I . . . uh . . . was going to try to recover the dragonlances, Highlord," said Cyan. "I knew Her Dark Majesty would be pleased if I did."

"Liar!" Skie growled. "You couldn't care less about dragonlances. You tried to enter because you thought there was treasure inside!"

"And a ghost frightened you away," Kit added, grinning.

"I wasn't frightened," Cyan said sullenly. "I just had second thoughts."

"Then if you are not afraid to go into the tower, fetch the dragonlances and bring them to me," said Kitiara.

Cyan bristled. "I am not your servant to fetch and carry, Highlord. I work for Her Dark Majesty."

"He is afraid," said Skie, his lips curling back to show his fangs.

Kitiara eyed the green dragon. "I believe you are right, Skie. The fat fool is afraid to go into the tower. Very well. I will go. Where are the dragonlances?"

"They are in the temple, and it is said that the god Paladine is inside there with them," said Cyan.

"Paladine!" Skie gave a derisive hoot.

"That puny, feeble, washed-up god! I do not fear him," said Kitiara. "Now that I know where to find the dragonlances, where is the dragon orb? Is it also in the temple?"

"Dragon orb?" Cyan repeated, alarmed. Puffs of green gaseous smoke escaped his jaws. "Her Dark Majesty said nothing to me about a dragon orb! Are you saying one of those terrible things is in there?"

"I have it on good information," said Kitiara.

"If I had known, I would have refused to come within a hundred miles of this place," said Cyan, shuddering. "The dragon orb could have seized me and made me its slave!"

Kitiara was exasperated. "Just tell me where it is. I'll find it myself."

But Cyan was clearly unnerved. "I did not come here to be enslaved by a dragon orb! I must take my leave, Highlord! I promised Her Dark Majesty that I would attend the Emperor's Summit in Neraka. I do not want to keep Her Majesty waiting."

Before Kitiara could stop him, the ponderous green dragon made a remarkably agile pivot in midair and flew off as rapidly as his leathery wings could carry his ungainly body.

"Should I go after him?" Skie asked.

Kitiara grimaced. "The fat coward. Takhisis is welcome to him. You and I can handle this."

"Speaking of the Emperor's Summit, the time draws near," said Skie. "We should be in position to march on Neraka."

"We will join our army when we have the dragonlances and I have found this dragon orb," said Kitiara. "Don't worry. I look forward to seeing Ariakas's face when I challenge him for the Crown of Power and launch my assault. Do you have any idea where this orb could be?"

"The orb is said to be adept at concealing itself, and there are a thousand places inside the tower where it could hide," Skie returned. "I've told you it is dangerous. Take these dragonlances, if you must, and be satisfied."

Kitiara did not appear pleased. "Do you think that what Cyan said is true, that Paladine guards the dragonlances and the dragon orb?"

"Takhisis herself could not destroy the dragonlances," said Skie. "Even a puny, washed-up god like Paladine is still a god. You might want to think twice before confronting him. As for the dragon orb, it guards itself."

Kitiara gazed at the tower in frowning thought. Skie eyed her, shook his mane, and settled down to wait for her to decide what to do.

"I am ready to cast the spell," Raistlin whispered. "We should go now!"

He was holding the words in his mind, tasting them on his lips, when Kitiara spoke.

"Skie, what would happen if you called to the dragon orb? Would it answer?" Kitiara asked. "If it does, we would know where to find it!"

Raistlin stared at Kitiara in horror. Tanis and the others were staring at him with the same expression.

"Will it answer if Skie calls to it?" Tanis asked urgently.

Raistlin hurriedly untied the bag containing the orb, opened it, and peered at the orb. It was still the size of a marble, but he could see the red mists inside restlessly stirring.

"It is already aware of Skie," said Raistlin. "The dragon in the orb will be constrained to answer. It cannot help itself."

"Then smash the damn thing!" said Flint.

"I broke a dragon orb once and everyone got mad at me," said Tasslehoff. "I'm used to people being mad at me, but never so many all at one time."

"I doubt if I could smash it!" said Raistlin. "The orb would not let me. And we must have the orb to defeat the Dark Queen's dragons at Neraka! Get inside the circle! Quickly!"

They could hear Skie arguing with Kitiara. "Have you considered that you will know where to find the orb, but the orb will know where to find me!"

"All the more reason for us to locate it. Or would you rather Tanis had hold of it," said Kitiara.

Skie grunted. "I will call to the dragon orb. But if it seizes me, you'll have to find another ride home."

The blue dragon raised his voice to a bellow that seemed to shake the walls. "Dragonlore holds that ancient wizards trapped five dragons inside the dragon orbs. One of these dragons is here within this orb. I ask you to respond to my plea, for my need is desperate. I call upon the white dragon, Tahina, Frostbite, daughter of Akis. I call upon the green dragon, Asphixia, Hissingdeath, daughter of Korril.

I call upon the blue dragon, Akasah the Meteor, son of Arkan. I call upon the black dragon, Musticallus the Corrosive, son of Corrozus. I call upon the red dragon, Inferno, daughter of Matafleur. Answer my call if one of you is trapped inside the dragon orb! Reveal your location to me so that I may set you free!"

Raistlin was holding the dragon orb in his hand, and he felt it come alive. The orb began to grow in size, expanding and enlarging. He held it in his palm, and then he required both hands. The red mists inside the orb whirled wildly, and he could see the eyes inside gazing at him, gleeful, malevolent.

"Can you stop it?" Tanis demanded.

"Too late . . ." Raistlin whispered.

The red dragon in the orb gave a wild, earsplitting, keening wail. The shriek pierced their brains, and they pressed their hands over their ears in a vain attempt to shut it out.

Raistlin was shaking so much he feared he might drop the orb. He opened the bag and thrust it inside, then cinched the drawstrings tight. He could no longer see the red eyes, and the dragon inside the orb stopped shrieking as it began tempting him to try to take control of it. The voice promised him his heart's desire.

You will wear the Crown of Power! Takhisis will bow before you. You have only to give yourself to me. . . .

Raistlin gritted his teeth and tried to ignore it.

Kitiara was shouting commands to Skie and pointing toward the ruins of Noble's Gate.

Sturm picked up one of the dragonlances from the bundle. "Cast your spell, Raistlin. I will gain you the time you need."

"Sturm, don't—" Tanis called after him, but the knight paid no heed.

"He has made his choice," said Raistlin. "The rest of you get into the circle!"

Tasslehoff took a firm grip on his hoopak and drew his knife. "I know you need my help, Raistlin, but you'll have to cast this spell on your own. I can't let Sturm die alone. Not this time."

Tasslehoff ran after the knight, shouting, "I'm coming, Sturm! Don't fight the dragon without me!"

"Fool kender," said Flint. "He's going to get himself killed."

The dwarf drew his axe from its harness and broke into a lumbering run.

Tanis turned to Raistlin. "I'll stay here with our friends. You and Caramon take the dragonlances and the orb to Godshome."

He drew his sword and ran to join the others.

"But if you and I leave, Raist, how will they get back?" Caramon asked.

"They're going to fight our sister and her dragon, my brother," said Raistlin. "They are not going to survive long enough to get back. Step into the circle."

Caramon hesitated, his hand on the hilt of his sword, gazing after his friends. "They need us!"

"The world needs us, Caramon," said Raistlin. "These weapons— the dragonlances and the dragon orb—will give us the chance to defeat the Dark Queen. We must take them to Godshome."

Caramon looked down at the dragonlances lying in the circle. Drawing a deep breath, he stepped inside.

Raistlin could feel the dragon orb squirming inside the bag, could hear its voice whispering promises. Making up his mind, Raistlin thrust the bag into Caramon's hands and stepped out of the circle.

Caramon regarded him in shock. "Aren't you coming?"

"I will stay with our friends. If they do manage to survive this encounter, they will need me to take them to join you," Raistlin replied. "I am not sending you directly to Godshome itself, for that would be too dangerous. I am sending you to someplace nearby, where you can remain hidden until—the gods willing—we can meet you there. Guard the dragonlances and the dragon orb with your life."

Caramon clutched the orb. "But what if it tries to suck me inside?"

"Do not worry, my brother," said Raistlin. "Your light is stronger than the orb's darkness. It cannot harm you."

Raistlin raised his hands. He felt the magic burning in his blood and spoke the words. *"Triga bulan ber satuan/Seluran asil/Tempat samah terus-menarus/Walktun jalanil!"*

The magic began to swirl around Caramon.

"Farewell, my brother," said Raistlin.

The magic swept Caramon up in a stardust cyclone—as Tas would have said—and carried him away. The fire of the magic in Raistlin's blood turned to ashes, leaving him alone in the darkness. The spell had utterly drained him. He could hear the battle raging outside, but he did not have the strength to come to their aid. After she had killed his friends, Kitiara would next come for him.

He sat down on the floor, leaned back against the broken wall, and waited.

CHAPTER
THIRTY-TWO

Sturm stood in the ruins of Noble's Gate, blocking the dragon's way into the temple. He knew he would not survive the encounter, and he bade his friends a silent farewell as he gripped the dragonlance. He had battled Skie before, defending the High Clerist's Tower, although not in this world or this time. Sturm did not let himself remember the shattered sun, the horrific pain of dying, the welcome release of death. He banished the memories to focus on the here and now.

Sturm tried to get inside the mind of his foe. Skie was hovering above the courtyard, staring down at him as though uncertain what to do. The dragon must have been surprised to see a knight walk out of the rubble, carrying a dragonlance. Did Skie know what the weapon was? Did he understand the danger it posed?

Sturm had no way of knowing. He gripped the dragonlance and judged the distance between himself and the dragon. The footman's lance was strong enough to be used as a thrusting spear, light enough to be thrown. Either way, Sturm would have to wait for the dragon to fly closer before he could attack.

Skie sucked in a breath, and Sturm realized he was going to attack with his breath weapon—deadly lightning bolts—and dove for cover beneath the gate, landing flat, keeping hold of the dragon-lance.

The lightning bolt exploded right where he had been standing, striking so close he could hear it and smell the sulphur. The blast tore up a chunk of the pavement and the resultant thunderclap shook the walls.

Sturm rose to his feet, still carrying the dragonlance, and walked back out into the courtyard. Skie growled in ire, realizing he'd missed. The dragon could not breathe another lightning bolt until his body rekindled the flame in his belly, so he continued his assault by un-leashing dragonfear—a debilitating weapon that would reduce his foes to whimpering puddles of unreasoning terror he could then de-stroy at his leisure.

Sturm felt the horrible sensation wash over him and his instinct was to flee. But he had experienced dragonfear before and knew that if he held fast, the fear would subside. He gripped the dragonlance tightly and prayed to the gods for strength.

Skie hovered above the courtyard, waiting for the knight to shrivel up in terror. Sturm stood his ground and the dragon grunted in surprise.

"Stop toying with him, Skie!" Kitiara ordered. She was standing on the battlements, watching the contest and growing restless. "Kill him and let us get on with our business."

Skie paid no heed to her, and Sturm could guess why. Skie had to contend with several issues when fighting this foe. If breath weap-ons and dragonfear failed, a dragon's next method of attack was to charge straight at his victim, catch him in powerful jaws, then crush and mangle him. But the walls surrounding the courtyard had been built to protect against such an assault. If Skie charged, he would risk smashing into the battlements.

Sturm kept a wary eye on Skie, uncertain what the dragon's next move would be. He knew better than to discount him. Skie was quick-thinking and intelligent and would be prepared to improvise.

Skie suddenly soared straight up into the air. The dragon flew higher and higher, beating his wings to gain speed and altitude. As Sturm watched, Skie drew back his wings, folded them close to his body, and went into a steep dive, slicing through the air, plummeting down on his foe.

Sturm flexed his hand on the dragonlance to make certain he had a firm grip and kept his gaze fixed on the dragon.

Skie dove with startling speed, then gradually slowed his descent as he drew near his victim. Lifting his wings, Skie extended his back claws like a stooping hawk, intending to use his front claws to seize hold of his prey.

Sturm had one chance and he could not squander it. He allowed the dragon to come as close as he dared, then hurled the dragonlance and struck Skie in his breast between his front claws.

The dragonlance plunged into Skie's chest, cleaving with ease through scales and flesh, muscle and bone. The dragon bellowed in pain and fury and his attack faltered. He flapped his wings in a desperate attempt to remain airborne, but he was flying too low, coming too close to the walls surrounding the courtyard. His tail and one of his wings clipped the wall. Thrashing and flailing, Skie tumbled, skidded, and rolled. The dragon crashed into the ruins of Noble's Gate in a flurry of wings and blood.

Sturm saw the wounded dragon hurtling toward him and he turned and ran back toward the shelter of the gate and flung himself forward, as far as he could manage. The ground shook beneath him. Walls cracked, and he heard the rumble of falling stone. Debris pelted him, shards of sharp rock cut him, and something struck him on the back of his helm.

He could hear, above the tumult, Kitiara cry out in shock and anger. Sturm scrambled to his feet and saw her running across the battlements toward the stairs that would take her down into the courtyard, where Skie lay, unmoving.

The dragon had taken down part of the wall, and his head and the upper part of his body were buried beneath chunks of rock. The dragon did not appear to be a threat, and Sturm turned his attention to Kitiara. He drew his sword, Brightblade—the sword that his father had carried and his father before him. Family legend held the sword would not break unless the one wielding it broke first, and that had never happened.

Sturm broke into a run and reached the bottom of the stairs

before Kitiara reached the top. Sturm dashed up them, taking them two at a time. Kitiara paid no heed to him. She was looking only at Skie, and she was grim-faced and pale with anger and fear.

Tanis had gone in pursuit of Tas, and Flint finally managed to catch up with them at the entrance to Noble's Gate. The dwarf arrived just in time to see the wounded dragon hurtling down on all of them.

"Take cover!" Tanis shouted.

Tas was standing transfixed, gaping in wonder at the astonishing sight. Flint grabbed him by the shirt collar and dragged him to the floor. Tanis threw himself down beside them, just as Skie slammed into the ruins of Noble's Gate.

The building shook. Walls crumbled. Stone, dust, and debris cascaded down around them with a loud rumble. Part of the ceiling collapsed and a wooden beam fell, narrowly missing them.

When the rumbling stopped, Tanis raised his head to check on his friends. Flint crawled out from beneath the beam. Tasslehoff was half-buried beneath the debris, and Tanis helped Flint dig him out. The kender was cut and bruised, but after checking his arms and legs, he stated that no bones were broken.

"What happened to the dragon?" he asked.

Tanis pointed to a large blue-scaled claw sticking out from beneath the rubble. The claw was no longer moving.

"Too much to hope that the beast is dead," said Flint.

Tanis thought the dwarf was probably right, but at least for the moment, they didn't have to worry about him. The dragon had brought down what remained of the wall, however, and an enormous mound of rubble and debris blocked the way out into the courtyard.

"Can anyone see what happened to Sturm?" Tas asked, trying to see through the rubble.

"The last I saw of him, Sturm was running across the courtyard trying to reach Kitiara," said Tanis. "We can't get out this way. We need to find another opening in the wall. Go back around."

They were starting to leave when Tas stopped, stricken.

"Where's my hoopak? I can't lose it! It's magic."

Flint dug the hoopak out of the debris and handed it to the kender. "It's not magic, you doorknob."

"It is so," said Tas, clutching it thankfully. "Raistlin said it was."

"You know you're going to lose that argument," said Tanis to Flint as they retraced their steps, going back the way they had come.

Flint growled and shook his head.

Clouds of dust hung in the air. Most of the wall facing the courtyard had collapsed and the corridor was choked with rubble. Worried about Sturm, the three were still trying to find a way into the courtyard when Tas suddenly stopped.

"I see a light over there in the corner."

"It's Raistlin," said Flint, startled. "I thought he left with his brother!"

Guided by the light gleaming from the staff, they found the mage slumped over on the floor, partially buried beneath chunks of rock that had fallen from the ceiling. He was unconscious, but his hand still gripped the staff. Tanis drew back his cowl and saw a bloody gash on the top of his head. He placed his hand on his neck to feel for the life beat.

"He's alive," Tanis said. "Any sign of Caramon?"

"If he was here, he'd be with Raistlin," Flint pointed out.

"True enough," said Tanis.

"The dragonlances are gone," Tas reported. "And the dragon orb isn't shrieking, so I guess it's gone, too."

"Raistlin must have sent his brother to Godshome with them while he stayed here," said Tanis. "He knew we couldn't travel there without him."

"Humpf!" Flint snorted. "More likely he found some treasure he won't leave."

Tanis smiled faintly. "I—Tas! Don't touch that!"

Tas had been reaching out his hand toward the Staff of Magius.

"I just wanted to hold it," said Tas. "I know the word to make it light up: *Shellac*. I'm sure Raistlin wouldn't mind—"

"But the staff might," said Tanis dryly.

Tas thought this over and reluctantly drew back his hand. "I guess I'll stick with my magic hoopak."

"It's not magic," Flint said dourly.

"We need to find Sturm," said Tanis hurriedly. "Someone should stay here with Raistlin."

"Flint can stay," Tas said promptly.

"Leave the kender," said Flint.

Before Tanis could make a decision, Tas made it for him. He dashed off, running down the corridor.

"I see daylight!" he cried.

"Doorknob," Flint muttered and hurried after him.

Tanis sighed. He couldn't let them go off on their own. He supposed Raistlin would be as safe here as anywhere, particularly since he had the Staff of Magius to keep watch over him.

"Over here! I found Sturm and Kitiara!" Tas was yelling. "*And the dragon!*"

Tas was peering out through a large hole in the wall that looked into the courtyard beyond. Tanis looked through and could see Sturm running up the stairs to reach the top of the battlements to confront Kitiara.

Flint sucked in a breath and pointed to where Skie was lying, half-buried in debris, not far from where they were standing. The dragon wasn't moving, but Tanis could hear the rasping breath and knew it wasn't dead.

Kitara barely seemed to notice Sturm. Her attention was fixed on her dragon.

She raised her voice. "Skie! Can you hear me?"

Tanis heard a groan and a snarl and a rumbling sound. Alarmed, he glanced over at the dragon and saw a blue-scaled claw clench. He heard another snarl and saw the enormous debris pile begin to heave and shift. Skie was attempting to crawl out from underneath the wreckage.

"I'm coming, Sturm!" Flint shouted, climbing over the rubble, heading for the courtyard. Tanis was about to follow when he realized Tasslehoff was starting to head off in the opposite direction. Tanis caught hold of the strap of his flour-sack pouch and dragged him back.

"Where are you going?"

"To kill the dragon," Tas replied solemnly. "With my magic hoo-pak."

Tas gave a wriggle and a twist, and Tanis was left holding the pouch, staring after Tas, who was wading through the debris, brandishing his hoopak as he advanced on the dragon.

STURM STOOD ON the stairs below Kitiara, blocking her attempt to descend. He had to watch his footing, for the stairs were cracked and crumbling. The battlements had already been in a dilapidated condition after centuries of neglect, and Skie had done more damage when he landed on them, crushing several of the merlons and knocking down others.

Kitiara was desperate to reach Skie and furious at the impediment blocking her way. She drew her sword and sprang at Sturm, sweeping her sword in a vicious arc intended to slice off his head and end this fight swiftly.

Sturm ducked her wild swing, and her sword whistled over him and struck one of the crumbling merlons. The blow jarred her sword hand and Kitiara swore in pain.

Sturm was about to press his advantage when he heard snarling and groaning and a rumbling sound, and he glanced over to see Skie crawling out from under the rubble, heaving chunks of stone off his back. The dragon was covered in dust and blood. He had a gaping wound in his chest, and he left a trail of blood behind when he moved, but he was alive.

Kitiara smiled in relief and lowered her sword.

"Well if it isn't Sturm Brightblade. I didn't know you at first. I should have recognized you by those scraggly mustaches. Where are your friends? Is Tanis with you? I'm sorry I'm late to the reunion, but I had other, more pressing matters to attend to first."

Sturm was not going to be lulled into complacency. He knew Kitiara of old. He had seen her fight in the days of their youth. One of her ploys was to flirt with an opponent, tease him, anger him—anything to distract—and then strike swiftly and unexpectedly.

"Was that a dragonlance you used to wound Skie?" Kitiara asked. "I'm impressed. What are you planning to do with the lances? If you were going to give them to your fellow knights, you're wasting your time. The knighthood is finished. Skie and I made sure of that. The cowards groveled before me, begging for their lives."

Sturm did not respond, and he could see his silence was starting to irritate Kitiara. He continued to wait, knowing she would grow impatient and make mistakes.

He watched her eyes, and when they shifted, Sturm was ready for her attack. She lunged at him, and he easily knocked aside her sword with his blade. Kitiara was angry, and she attacked him with a flurry of blows at his head and his body that he was hard-pressed to fend off. When she did not draw blood, she fell back, breathing hard, eyeing him warily. At that moment, Sturm heard someone shouting his name. He glanced back to see Flint running across the courtyard, his axe in his hand.

Sturm was astonished. He had assumed Flint and the others had gone with Raistlin to Godshome. His attention wavered, just for a second, but that was all Kitiara needed. She attacked him, aiming to cripple him by slashing at his thigh. Her blade bit deep into the muscle and when he stumbled, Kitiara slammed into him, trying to knock him off-balance and push him off the battlements.

Sturm was forced to fling aside his sword to grapple with her. They struggled until, using all his strength, he flung her away from him. Kitiara slipped on the loose gravel and fell, dropping her sword to catch herself. She landed on her hands and knees and made a grab for her sword, but Sturm kicked it out of reach.

"Hold!" Kitiara cried, raising her hand. "I yield!"

Sturm could not in honor strike a helpless foe, and Kitiara knew it. He could tell by her crooked smile. He threw her sword off the battlements, then picked up his own sword and stood over her. He heard, behind him, Flint running up the stairs.

"I'm coming!" Flint yelled.

Sturm saw Kit's eyes shift to the dragon.

"Skie!" she shouted. "I could use some help!"

"Flint, look out!" Sturm yelled, just as Skie shot a bolt of lightning, aiming for the dwarf.

The lightning missed Flint but struck the lower part of the staircase, pulverizing the stone, blowing apart the wall and knocking Flint off his feet. He clung to the stairs, but Sturm could see them starting to give way, and he reached out his hand to grab Flint's. Sturm was starting to haul him up when he heard footsteps behind him.

He turned, and Kitiara smashed him in the face with a broken paving stone.

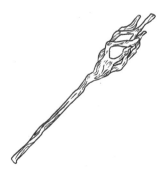

CHAPTER
THIRTY-THREE

Agenerally held belief on Krynn is that kender do not feel fear. Kender are a diverse people, however, and while this may hold true for some, it does not necessarily hold true for others. Tasslehoff had known lots of kender who could feel fear. One, in particular, had been positively terrified of turtles.

As for Tas, he was never afraid for himself. To his way of thinking, fear limited one's ability to enjoy life. He did occasionally try to follow Tanis's advice and consider whether a certain situation would be conducive to living a long life, but situations happened so fast that Tas generally didn't have time to work out whether a situation was conducive or it wasn't.

But while Tas was never afraid for himself, he did feel fear for his friends—particularly if they were in danger. When this happened, Tas had to take the bull by the horns and time by the fetlock—whatever that was—and spring into action, especially now that he was blessed with a magical hoopak.

Tasslehoff was not a knight like Sturm, so he couldn't fight Kitiara, but he could fight a dragon—especially one that had been whanged on the headbone by a large chunk of the High Clerist's Tower.

Tas considered making a frontal assault on Skie, but quickly abandoned that idea, mainly because he could see the dragon's frontal part trying to shake off rubble. Tas decided the best plan of attack was to sneak up on the dragon from behind.

Unfortunately, he was hampered by the lamentable fact that he had to crawl over, under, and around piles of rock and plaster and splintered wood to reach the dragon, with the result being that he made more noise than was required for sneaking. And to make matters worse, he heard Tanis chasing after him, calling out for him to stop.

Tas was highly annoyed. Here he was, trying to quietly sneak up on a dragon, and Tanis was raising all sorts of ruckus.

"After all these years of adventuring, he should really know better," Tas muttered irately, and he planned to give the half-elf a stern talking-to after all this was over.

As Tas sneaked toward the dragon, he kept an eye on Skie, expecting him to turn around to see what was sneaking up on him. But Skie was intent on the fight on the battlements. To give Skie credit (which Tas felt was only fair), the dragon probably thought no one would be bold enough to attack him from either the front or the rear.

Tas had been navigating a huge pile of stone, trying not to dislodge any of the chunks, when he had to pause because he was half blinded by a lightning bolt that streaked across the courtyard. The blast shook the walls, and he was worried about his friends. He rubbed his eyes and opened them just in time to see Flint almost fall down the stairs and Kitiara pick up a huge rock and smash it in Sturm's face.

Sturm was wearing his helm, but when you're smashed in the face with a large rock, a helm isn't much help. Sturm went down and lay sprawled on the stairs.

Tas was extremely angry and was tempted to rush out and smash Kitiara with a large rock, but then he remembered that he was in charge of attacking the dragon.

Skie's attack did offer Tas one advantage. Tanis had also seen and heard the lightning bolt streak across the courtyard, and he could see Flint clinging for dear life onto a broken staircase and Kitiara hitting Sturm. Tanis would have to stop chasing after Tas to go help those who certainly needed him a lot more than the kender did.

Tas returned to sneaking up on the dragon. He had to crawl under a big wooden beam, and when he came out the other side, he could see Tanis running toward the battlements, shouting Kitiara's name.

Tas noticed that he wasn't the only one watching what was happening on the battlements. Skie was staring straight at Tanis. The dragon snarled. His mane flattened, and he heaved himself to his feet.

Tas gave up on being sneaky. He dashed through the rubble as fast as he could, crunching on and tripping over and dislodging pieces of wall. If Skie heard him, he paid no heed.

The dragon was on his feet, his tail swishing back and forth, his attention focused on Tanis and Kitiara and whatever was happening in the courtyard.

Tas could hear people talking, but he couldn't take time to listen to what they were saying because he was now right behind Skie. Tas gripped his hoopak tightly, raised it above his head, and brought the hoopak down—*thump!*—on the dragon's tail.

Tas expected the magic to incinerate Skie's tail and Skie to roar with anger and howl with pain and whip around and bite off Tas's head.

But that didn't happen. Skie's tail didn't go up in flames. He didn't turn around, and Tas still had his head. Apparently, the dragon hadn't even felt the blow.

"Drat!" said Tas, annoyed. He eyed the hoopak, wondering what had gone wrong. "Maybe there are magic words I have to say to make it work, like Raistlin's staff."

Tas tried "*Shellac,*" which was the word Raistlin used, and then hit the dragon's tail again, to no effect. He was going to try Raistlin's other word, *Dewclaw,* but then Kitiara called out Skie's name and gave an order. Skie opened his mouth. Tas smelled brimstone, and he knew he had to act fast.

He dropped the magic hoopak—with considerable regret—and

drew his knife, which had been Rabbitslayer until his latest adventure, when he had renamed it Goblinslayer. Clutching his knife in his hand, Tas ran toward the dragon, intending to plunge the knife into Skie's tail.

Unfortunately, Skie happened to move his tail at that moment, but his hind leg and claw remained a tempting target. The thought popped into Tas's head that stabbing a dragon with a small knife was probably *not* conducive to a long life. Fortunately, the thought popped right out again.

Tas plunged Goblinslayer into Skie's foot.

CHAPTER
THIRTY-FOUR

Tanis had to make a decision. He could try to save Sturm and Flint, or try to stop Tasslehoff from attacking a dragon. He couldn't do both. Knowing Fizban had a special place in his heart for kender, Tanis consigned Tas to the care of the god and ran into the courtyard.

Sturm lay sprawled on the staircase, his face covered in blood, not moving. As Flint was trying desperately to crawl up the remains of the staircase to reach him, Kitiara picked up Sturm's sword from his limp hand and held it poised over the knight's face.

"Don't come any closer, old dwarf," she warned Flint.

Flint glared at her. "You're just coward enough to kill a wounded man. Fight me, if you dare!"

"I don't need to fight any of you," said Kitiara. "In case you hadn't noticed, I'm in charge here. Hand over the dragonlances and I'll be on my way."

"The dragonlances are gone, Kit!" Tanis shouted, calling up to where she stood on the top of the battlements. "Raistlin used his magic to send them away. Your dragon is wounded. Leave now, and we won't stop you."

"Wounded with a dragonlance!" Kitiara said angrily. "Hand over these accursed weapons and I might let you live!"

Tanis had hoped to be able to climb the stairs to reach Flint and Sturm, but the blast had destroyed most of the lower part of the stone staircase, leaving only the top relatively intact. Two sets of stairs led from Noble's Gate to the battlements—one on either side of the gate. The other staircase was not damaged. To reach it, Tanis would have to deal with the dragon. He looked at Skie and saw Skie looking at him.

The dragon snarled and rose to a crouch. Blood oozed from the wound in his chest where he'd been struck with the dragonlance, and he snarled again in pain. He probably found it painful to suck in a breath and let it out in a blast of lightning, but that wasn't likely to stop him.

Tanis saw Flint slowly and cautiously begin crawling up the broken stairs toward Kitiara, digging his fingers into cracks and crevices that only a dwarf could find. He was not carrying his axe, and Tanis guessed he had lost it in the blast. Sturm was moving, starting to regain consciousness. Tanis had to keep Kit's attention focused on him.

"You betrayed me and my friends, Kit," said Tanis. "I find it strange to think I ever loved you."

Kitiara gave a disdainful shrug. "I never loved you, half-elf. I merely kept you around for my own amusement. But now I grow weary of you and this conversation. When I give Skie the command, he will kill the dwarf. And after him, the knight. And after that he will kill you unless you tell me where to find the dragonlances."

Sturm was awake now. His eyes were open, and he was apparently aware of what was going on, for he kept still and did not try to rise. Tanis gauged the distance between himself and the dragon. He would never reach the stairs before the dragon incinerated him, but he had to try. Tanis drew his sword and broke into a run to reach the other staircase that led to the battlements.

Kitiara shouted at the dragon.

Skie lurched to his feet and sucked in a breath, only to let it out in a hideous howl of pain. He snaked his head around to see what had hit him, just as Tasslehoff came rushing out of the rubble, triumphantly waving a bloody knife in one hand and his hoopak in the other. Skie snapped viciously at the kender and took a swipe at him with his claw, but Tas was running as if a hundred sheriffs were in pursuit.

Flint took advantage of the distraction to scramble to his feet and clamor up the remaining steps. Kitiara heard him coming and whipped around to face him, wielding Sturm's sword.

Flint was unarmed, but that didn't stop him. The dwarf hunched his shoulders and lowered his head like a charging bull. Running straight at Kitiara, Flint rammed her in the midriff.

Kitiara reeled backward and crashed into one of the merlons. The crumbling stone parapet broke beneath her weight. She felt it give way and flailed wildly, trying to save herself. She lost her footing on the loose stones, slipped, and toppled off the battlements, disappearing amid a cascade of rock.

Skie gave a cry of rage and anguish and surged out of the rubble. His wings were battered and torn. Blood spewed from the wound in his chest and dribbled from a small wound on his hind foot. The dragon leaped into the air and flew over the battlements, spiraling down to find his Highlord.

Carried forward by his own momentum, Flint almost ended up going over the wall with Kitiara. Sturm made a grab for him and caught him by the heel of his boot. Flint landed hard on his belly, skidded forward, and now hung over the edge of the wall, staring in horror at the ground far below. Sturm had lost his grip on the dwarf, and Flint was too afraid to move. Tanis ran up the stairs to try to reach him, but Tasslehoff had already climbed them and was racing across the battlements.

"I'm coming, Flint!" Tas cried. "I won't let you die!"

The kender's shrill voice seemed to shake Flint out of his stupefied terror. Squinching his eyes tightly shut, he managed to crawl slowly back from the edge, propelling himself with his elbows, his knees scrabbling and slipping among the loose gravel. Tasslehoff caught hold of him by his harness and dragged him to safety.

Flint sat up, gasping for breath and mopping his face with his beard.

"I saved your life!" Tasslehoff said, squatting down beside him.

"This makes twice now. Maybe three times if you count me stabbing the dragon. And now I have to go see what happened to Kit."

He gave Flint a pat and then hurried over to peer down over the edge of the wall.

"Thanks, lad," Flint said, but he said it into his beard and then glowered at Tanis, who smiled at him. "Don't ever tell him I said so. Now go see to the knight!"

Sturm was groggy and dazed. His nose was broken. He had numerous cuts on his face, one eye was swelling shut, and he spit out a tooth. Blood ran down his leg, and he staggered when he tried to put weight on it and almost fell. Tanis knew better than to try to help him. Sturm grimaced, but he managed to stay upright.

"Where is my sword?" he asked.

Tanis searched for Brightblade and brought it to him. Sturm returned it thankfully to its sheath.

"I can see Kit!" Tas reported, leaning over the wall at a perilous angle. "She's down there and Skie is with her."

Kitiara lay crumpled amid the tall grass and weeds that had grown up around the base of the tower. Skie had landed beside her and was nudging her with a claw, rumbling deep in his chest, calling her name.

Kitiara stirred and moaned. Skie said something to her, and she nodded and tried to sit up, only to collapse with a cry. Skie gently and carefully clamped his teeth onto the back of her leather shirt, lifted her up, and hoisted her into the saddle. Kitiara fumbled at the straps, but then slumped forward and hung limp.

Skie cast her a worried look, then glared balefully at those standing on the battlements above him. He must have longed to blast them with lightning and thunder and death, but he was wounded as well; his fury and his strength were spent, and he had his Highlord to protect.

"Those two might be loyal to nothing and no one else in this world, but they are loyal to each other," Tanis remarked.

"What will happen to them, do you think?" Sturm asked.

"Dragons can heal themselves, and Takhisis's clerics will take care of Kit," said Tanis. "My guess is that both of them will be well enough to wreak havoc at the Emperor's Summit."

The dragon snarled defiance, then flew off. He was forced to fly slowly, for he was weak from loss of blood and he was afraid Kitiara might fall. He headed for the foothills, probably to search for some cave where they both could recover.

Tanis and the others watched until Skie was out of sight, then climbed down from the battlements. They had their own decisions to make.

Sturm rested his hand on Flint's shoulder. "You saved my life, old friend, and I am grateful."

"She just got what she's been deserving for a long time," said Flint gruffly.

Tas gave a wise nod. "No one expects a headbutt. Kit sure didn't."

"And you likely saved all of us, Tas," Tanis said. "Stabbing Skie was very brave. I am sorry I doubted you."

"I wasn't thinking about being brave," said Tas. "I was thinking that I couldn't let Flint and Sturm be dead again. Speaking of the dragon, could I call my knife Dragonslayer, even though I didn't actually slay the dragon?"

Tanis smiled. "The knife is yours, and you can call it whatever you want."

Tas thought this over.

"I guess I'll just keep calling it Goblinslayer. Otherwise, I'd have to name it Dragon-Footstabber, in order to be accurate, but that just doesn't have the same ring to it. Oh, and there's a dragonlance over there by the gate. I think it's the one Sturm used to skewer Skie. I was going to bring it with me, but I was too busy trying to keep the dragon from biting my head off. I first tried hitting him with the hoopak, but he didn't seem to notice so I guess it's not really magical. You can use it for a crutch, Sturm, if you'd like."

Sturm gravely thanked him, but said his wounds were not serious and that he could walk unaided. They crossed the blood-spattered courtyard, moving slowly to accommodate Sturm. On their return to Noble's Gate, Flint went to search for his axe among the rubble and Tas went along to help. Tanis checked on Raistlin and found him awake and standing, leaning on his staff.

"Are you all right?" Tanis asked.

"I have a splitting headache, but otherwise I am unharmed, so no need for some hypocritical show of affection," said Raistlin.

Tanis smiled ruefully. He motioned to Sturm and the two of them walked a short distance away. Sturm was wiping blood from his nose and forehead.

"I'll fetch the dragonlance and find water," said Tanis. "You could wait here with him and keep an eye on Flint and Tas."

"You are not trying to mollycoddle me, are you?" Sturm asked, frowning. "My leg has stopped bleeding. The pain is minimal, and I have suffered a broken nose before."

"I need you to stand guard," said Tanis. "After all, there might be bugbears."

Sturm took up his post at the gate, settling himself on a large chunk of broken stone, keeping his wounded leg outstretched. Tanis went in search of the dragonlance and found it lying in the courtyard in a pool of blood. He picked it up, reflecting on Sturm's courage, standing resolute and determined as he faced certain death, as he had done at the battle of the High Clerist's Tower in another war, another time.

He could hear Flint shouting from the courtyard.

"You have my axe, you doorknob! I can see the handle sticking out of your pouch!"

"I found it for you," said Tas. "I guess you must have dropped it. And it's polite to say 'thank you' when someone finds something you've lost."

Tanis smiled. The River of Time might overflow, sweep them away into unknown places, toss them and tumble them in its raging waters, and land them on unknown shores. But some things never changed.

Tanis decreed that they should spend the night in the temple. The spirit of the silver dragon was gone, as was the bier on which Huma had rested, but a sense of peace prevailed. Tasslehoff reported that Kiri-Jolith had left, as well, although his candle and those of the other gods still burned on the altar.

"Kiri-Jolith has probably gone back to Godshome, and I guess Caramon must be there, too, by now," said Tas. "I didn't want to go because that's where Flint died, but Kiri-Jolith told me that when we fall into the river we never know if we'll sink or swim."

"River?" Flint looked alarmed. "This Godshome doesn't have anything to do with boats, does it?"

"It doesn't," said Tanis. "Why don't you see if you can light the lantern?"

"So long as those dang spirits don't keep blowing it out," Flint muttered. He took out his tinderbox and struck the flint, and this time the spark caught. The candle flamed and nothing blew it out. Flint placed the glowing lantern on a rock and kept a wary eye on it.

Raistlin joined him, saying he felt better and that after a good night's sleep, he would be strong enough to work his magic. He crouched in the lantern's light, cupped his hand, and mixed herbs from his pouches with water in his palm. He dabbed the paste on the cut on his head and offered the rest of the mixture to Sturm.

"For the wound in your thigh," said Raistlin. "Dittany and pennyroyal, among other ingredients. The same I used to treat Destina's cut. Nothing magical, I assure you."

Sturm eyed the mixture dubiously, but reluctantly agreed. Raistlin instructed Flint to hold the lantern above the wound. The sword had sliced through Sturm's breeches, but so cleanly that no fragments of material remained in the cut. Raistlin poured water over the wound and washed away the dried blood.

"Kit must have struck in haste, for if she had hit the major arteries you would have bled to death," said Raistlin. "As it is, the bleeding has stopped. I should close the wound with stitches, but I have no needle or thread—"

"I might!" said Tas and he began to rummage through his pouch.

"That will not be necessary," said Sturm hurriedly.

Raistlin spread a thick layer of the paste on the wound.

"You will limp on that leg for a time," said Raistlin, "but the wound should heal cleanly."

"I must admit the pain has eased," said Sturm, sounding grudging.

"No need for thanks," said Raistlin.

"Good," said Sturm, but he smiled as he spoke.

They settled themselves as best they could in the temple. Tanis doled out the rest of the food. "This is the last of what I brought."

"No great loss," Flint stated.

"Our fate will be decided one way or the other tomorrow," said Raistlin. "I recommend a good night's sleep for everyone. I see no need to keep watch this night. The silver dragon and Huma may be gone, but the gods are with us, as we can tell by the unwavering flames of the candles on the altar."

He memorized his spells by the light of the lantern, then wrapped himself in a blanket, lay down on one of the pews, and sank into an exhausted sleep. Tas sat down to sort through the objects in his pouch. When Tanis went to check on him, he found the kender asleep on the floor with his treasures spread out around him.

Tanis picked up, among other things, a spoon that he recognized as coming from the Inn of the Last Home and a white chicken feather. He tucked them back into the pouch and returned to his friends.

Flint was shaking his head. "I don't care what the mage says. Ghosts. Candles that never go out. Gods that may be here or may not be here. I couldn't sleep if I wanted to. All the more reason to be on our guard, I say."

"I'll take the first watch this night," said Tanis.

"I will not argue," Sturm replied. "I am in need of rest. I will take second."

"Wake me for third," said Flint.

Tanis left the others sleeping and walked outside to stand guard. The Dark Queen's constellation seemed to fill the sky, but for the first time, he could see the dragon constellation of Paladine; the bison head of Kiri-Jolith; and the figure eight, symbolizing eternity, that was Mishakal.

Tanis felt heartened. He settled himself with his back against the wall and gazed at the stars. He did not mean to fall asleep, but when he woke, day was dawning. He looked up to see Flint standing over him, glaring down at him.

"Fine guard you are!" Flint scoffed. "You're lucky we didn't wake up dead. You'd best make haste. Raistlin is pacing back and forth, waiting for us. And that doorknob of a kender is complaining he's bored. You know what that means."

Tanis hurriedly scrambled to his feet. "How is Sturm this morning?"

"He's better," Flint reported. "He's down by the altar, praying." He flushed and added gruffly, "I said a prayer to Reorx myself. I figured it couldn't hurt."

Tanis found Raistlin drawing a circle in the dust on the temple floor.

"Today Takhisis will launch her assault on the High Clerist's Tower and Huma and Gwyneth will face her in battle. If Destina succeeds in changing time, Takhisis will be defeated and the River of Time will sweep us away—some to life in our former time, some, like Sturm and myself, to death."

Raistlin added with a shrug, "If Destina does not succeed, Takhisis will win and we will be stranded here. And we must arm ourselves for battle."

CHAPTER
THIRTY-FIVE

Tanis braced himself to return to Godshome, knowing he would have to revisit the place where he had committed an act so heinous that even now—years later and a world away—he writhed in shame to remember it. Acting in the throes of anger, he had slain an innocent man. He had not known that Berem Everman was immortal and that he would rise whole and alive from Tanis's deadly attack, and thus that was no excuse.

He had been forced to confront his own weakness and fallibility. Perhaps that was the purpose of Godshome—to look into a pool of darkness and see one's own face. And then to look up and see the blue, sunlit vault of heaven, promising understanding and forgiveness.

But when the magic of the journeying spell set them down on solid ground, Tanis looked around, puzzled. Thick mists shrouded a grove of spindly oak trees, clutching at them with trailing gray fingers of fog and blotting out the sunlight. The ground was covered in rotting leaves and soggy underfoot. Water dripped from the bare tree limbs. The air was chill and damp.

"This is not Godshome," Tanis stated.

"Interesting," said Raistlin. "The magic of Godshome must have blocked the journeying spell and prevented us from entering."

"Then where have you brought us?" Flint asked angrily.

"More importantly, where did you send Caramon and the dragonlances?" Sturm asked.

Raistlin gave a weary sigh and sat down on a fallen tree. Drawing his cowl over his head to protect from the water dripping from the branches, he looked about.

"I believe we are in what is aptly known as the Misted Vales, a wooded area surrounding Godshome. Two passages lead from the Vales into the sacred site, and then only if the gods permit you to find them."

"I remember!" said Tas excitedly. "Fizban took us to one of the passages and it was so narrow that Caramon wouldn't fit and we had to pull him through and he got all scraped and bloody."

"Do you remember the way?" Tanis asked.

Tas batted irritably at the fog, then pointed. "I think that's the way. No, wait a moment. That's not the way. This is the way, I am sure of it. Unless it isn't . . ."

"I know the way."

Caramon appeared, emerging from the mists, his boots squelching through the mud.

"There's an opening in the rock wall. Like Tas says, it's a tight fit. But how did you know about it?" Caramon asked, with a puzzled look at the kender. "Have you been here before?"

"Yes, once," said Tas. He caught Raistlin's baleful eye. "I mean, no, never."

"Whether the kender was here or wasn't doesn't matter," Raistlin said impatiently. "Where are the dragonlances? Are they safe?"

"The dragonlances are with the knight inside Godshome," said Caramon.

"Knight? What knight?" Sturm asked, intrigued.

"I'll take you to him," said Caramon. "He led me to the entrance. I heard a man's voice calling for help and I called back that I was here, but I didn't know where he was or how to reach him. He told me to follow the sound of his voice and I did. It led me to the entrance to Godshome, which is back this way."

"How can you tell where we are in this murk?" Flint grumbled. "I can't see my beard in front of my nose!"

Caramon pointed to the ground. "Follow my tracks."

He had left deep imprints in the mud, and he led the way, keeping his gaze on the ground. The rest slogged after him through the muck, which was so deep that when Flint took a step, he sank up to his knees and couldn't move. Caramon and Tanis hauled him out by the shoulders.

"This is the last time I come with you on any fool venture, half-elf," Flint muttered.

"Don't say that," said Tanis quietly, remembering that this had been the last time Flint had come with him.

They continued on through the oppressive mists. Caramon's footprints were still visible, though they wouldn't be for long, for they were filling up with water. Perhaps because of the shrouding mists, Tanis had the feeling that the world beyond this vale had ceased to exist. He heard no sounds of life, only the incessant drip of water from the denuded branches of the stunted oaks. And yet, he knew that eyes were watching and ears were listening. The others must be feeling the same, for when Sturm spoke, his voice was low and muffled.

"Tell me about this knight, Caramon," he said as they walked.

"He's in a bad way," said Caramon somberly. "His armor is smashed and broken. He is covered in blood, so that I can't see where he's hurt. I was going to take off his armor, to try to stop the bleeding, but he said he needed to remain vigilant. He had driven off his foe, but not for long."

"What is his name?" Sturm asked.

"Kind of a strange one for a Solamnic," said Caramon. "Sir Kiri or something like that."

Sturm halted to stare at him. "Kiri-Jolith?"

"That's the name," said Caramon. "Do you know him?"

"I have long honored him," said Sturm, his voice reverent. "Kiri-Jolith is the god of honorable and just battle, for those who fight to protect the innocent. But what foe does he fight?"

"Kiri-Jolith told me he was fighting the Dark Queen because she was trying to seize Godshome," said Tas.

"I don't know anything about this Kiri-Jolith being a god or fighting the Dark Queen," said Caramon. "But I do know he's in a bad way. I think he's dying."

"And we are told to bring the dragonlances here, to Godshome, to ensure their safety," said Tanis. He shook his head. "To a place the Dark Queen is trying to seize."

Raistlin had remained silent, trudging over the muddy ground by his brother's side, leaning on the Staff of Magius. He kept his cowl over his head, his face concealed. He paused, leaning on the staff.

"I remind you, Half-Elven, that our task is to draw the Dark Queen's attention to us. Takhisis is now ruler of all of the world except this one bleak and barren plot of land that consists of a couple of hundred square feet and an obsidian pool, and is to all appearances worthless. Yet Godshome frets her like a patch of missing scales on her hide, for it is her single weak spot. The gods may be wounded and close to death, but they continue to defy her. And now the Heroes of the Lance and the dragonlances arrive in the one place in all the world where she knows she is vulnerable. She will descend on Godshome in all her fury."

"You talk like this is a good thing!" Flint growled.

"So long as we keep the Dark Queen's eyes on us, she will not be looking somewhere else," said Raistlin.

"She won't be looking for the—" Tas sneezed. "Drat!"

Tanis shook his head. "And we must do this without getting ourselves killed because that would change the future in the past."

"Unless our future is here," said Sturm. "In that instance, we will need the dragonlances. We have to risk dying in this time in order to keep Takhisis from seizing them."

"And thus you see Chaos at work," said Raistlin. "In saving one future that may never come to pass, we may well change another that already has."

"Moonstruck mad," Flint muttered. "The lot of you."

"How long do we have to hold out?" Tanis asked. "Huma and the silver dragon battle the Dark Queen this day. Do we know when?"

"The morning of the assault, or so legend holds," said Sturm.

"Chaos will have a say in that," said Raistlin.

A pale and watery sun appeared, breaking through the mists. The sunlight glistened on the smooth gray wall of a cliff that seemed to spring up suddenly out of nowhere. They could not see the top of the cliff, for it was lost in the clouds. The rock wall extended on either side of them for as far as they could see.

Caramon's footprints led up to the side of the cliff and disappeared.

"Now what?" said Flint.

Caramon pointed to a fissure in the rock. "We go through this passage. I know it looks narrow, but this is how I got inside Godshome. When I heard the knight call for help, I found this crack, and since it seemed to be the only way to reach him, I ran through it and it led to a narrow passage. He told me to carry the dragonlances in here and I did."

Sturm put his hand on the hilt of his sword and stepped into the passage.

Flint followed and immediately got stuck.

"I'll help you," said Tas. "Only you have to promise me you're not going to die."

Tas got behind Flint and pushed. Tanis heard the dwarf's armor scrape against the rock and his helm bang into something, and Flint protesting and Tas telling him to suck in his breath, and then loud swearing in dwarven.

"We're here!" Tas called from the other side.

"I'll go next," Caramon offered.

"Wait!" said Raistlin. "You spoke of the dragonlances. Where is the dragon orb?"

Caramon thrust his hand into a pouch on his belt and drew out the velvet bag. "I have it with me. Do you want it?"

"No!" Raistlin drew back. "Now is not the time. Keep it safe a while longer, my brother."

"Sure, Raist," said Caramon. He entered the narrow passage with seeming ease.

Tanis glanced up at the sun, which was almost directly above them, drifting in and out of wispy, trailing scarves of mist.

"The time is midday and Takhisis attacked the High Clerist's Tower in the morning. If Destina had succeeded, we would not be here. And yet here we remain in this world, in this time," said Tanis.

Raistlin said nothing, for there was nothing to say. Leaning on the Staff of Magius, he entered the passage. Tanis paused, then plunged in after him.

CHAPTER
THIRTY-SIX

He and the others found themselves in a bowl in the center of a nameless mountain. Tall cliffs surrounded the bowl, seeming to press down on them, as Tanis remembered. The land was desolate and barren, again as he remembered. But there the memories ended.

The sky above had been azure, clear, and cold, like an eye in the heavens. Looking up now, Tanis saw darkness, the pupil of an empty, soulless eye.

He recalled the twenty-one gigantic, misshapen pillars that formed a circle in the center of the bowl. They had fit so close together that he had not been able to see between them, to find out what they guarded.

Twenty of the pillars were destroyed, smashed and pulverized, struck down in rage. One pillar alone remained, towering over the destruction, almost—but not quite—triumphant. In the center of the broken ring, the pool of shining black obsidian was now laid bare for all to see.

Tanis had looked into that black pool and been startled to see the stars and the three moons, although blue sky had shown above.

Now he gazed down into the pool and saw the empty eye staring back at him.

"This is not the Godshome I remember," said Tanis, shocked.

"According to Sir Kiri, Takhisis vented her fury on it when she tried to take it and failed," said Caramon.

"She has not yet given up, nor will she." Raistlin drew back the cowl from his head to look searchingly about. "Caramon, what did you do with the dragonlances?"

"Sir Kiri told me to put them in the middle of that black pool of rock. I carried them over and set them down—"

Caramon blinked. The black pool of obsidian was empty except for scattered pieces of broken rock from the crushed pillars.

"Caramon ..." said Raistlin severely, his voice grating. "What have you done with the dragonlances?"

"I swear, Raist, I put them down on that black rock!" said Caramon. "Like Sir Kiri told me. Look, there he is! Sturm's with him. We could ask him."

Sturm was kneeling beside a knight in dented and bloody armor lying on the barren ground. The knight's black hair was matted in blood and his face was bloody and battered. His broken sword lay at his side. Sturm said something to him in Solamnic, but Kiri-Jolith did not respond. He lay unmoving.

Tas stood beside Sturm, cradling Kiri-Jolith's battered helm close to his chest and gazing down on him sadly.

"Can you help him, Raistlin?" Tas asked. "Maybe you could smear some of that bad-smelling green stuff on him."

"Kiri-Jolith is a god, Tas," said Raistlin. "He clothes himself in flesh and blood so that he may interact with a mortal world, but his true nature is of the heavens."

"Then he can't die?" Tas asked hopefully.

"Not as you know death, kender," said a voice that shook the ground like booming thunder. "When mortals die, they go on to the next stage of their life's journey. A god will dwindle to nothingness and be forever lost."

The voice came from the other side of the cliff. They were nearly deafened by a clanging sound, as of metal striking a mighty blow against solid rock, and the passage split asunder.

An enormous minotaur wielding a gigantic war hammer strode into Godshome. His horns seemed to scrape the sky. The ground trembled beneath his feet, and his bellowing voice echoed through the heavens. He wore belted armor studded with steel and inlaid with gold.

Sturm drew his sword and rose to stand protectively over Kiri-Jolith.

"Stand aside, Sir Knight," said the minotaur. "I mean him no harm. I've come to speak to my old foe."

Sturm looked uncertain, but he sheathed his sword and moved away, though not far. The minotaur paid no heed to him, but squatted down on his haunches beside the fallen god.

"For centuries you and I—Kiri-Jolith and Sargonnas—have fought, our battles resounding throughout eternity. We heaved back and forth, swinging sword and hammer, striking blow upon blow. We trampled mountains beneath our feet and split the ground. Most of the time I was victorious, though sometimes you bested me. But always we fought with honor."

Sargonnas turned his horned head and saw the ruins of the ring of pillars. His brows came together. His snout quivered in anger.

"We created Godshome in rejoicing, to celebrate the forging of the world. All of us aligned: the light and the dark and the gray that lay in between. I was the Dark Queen's consort, her equal, and I stood proudly at her side. But now she expects to see me on my knees, groveling at her feet. She has enslaved my people and dishonors them, ordering them to butcher and kill the weak and the helpless."

Sargonnas laid down the war hammer to take hold of the knight's limp hand. Engulfing it in both of his own, he clasped him tightly.

"I am not a healer, as you well know," said Sargonnas. "But I am strong. I raised up mountains with my bare hands and scooped out rock to form the seas. I impart my strength to you, old foe. Rise and do battle with me once more. Only this time you and I will stand side by side and not toe to toe."

Kiri-Jolith groaned and opened his eyes. He looked at Sargonnas and faintly smiled. "What do you mean 'sometimes I bested you'? I was the victor in the majority of our contests, as you well know."

Sargonnas gave a thundering laugh and heaved himself to his feet and then hauled Kiri-Jolith to his. The minotaur picked up the knight's broken sword and clasped his hand around the naked blade, paying no heed to the pain or the blood that dripped to the ground. When Sargonnas opened his palm, the blade was whole, though covered in the minotaur's blood.

Kiri-Jolith took back his sword and wiped it clean on his breeches.

"Here's your helm," said Tas, holding it out. "I kept it safe."

"Thank you, Master Burrfoot," said Kiri-Jolith. He took the bloodstained helm and eyed it ruefully, then smoothed out the dents with a touch of his hand and placed the helm on his head. "As for the dragonlances, Paladine keeps them safe as Huma Dragonbane stands with Gwyneth the silver dragon and the Knights of Solamnia, prepared to defend the High Clerist's Tower."

"What does that mean?" Tanis asked Raistlin. "If Destina succeeded in restoring time, we wouldn't be here."

"It means that thus far, history has not changed," said Raistlin. "Takhisis has not found the Graygem."

"But Her Dark Majesty is searching for it up and down the River of Time," said Sargonnas. "We must lure her to this place and this time."

Sargonnas strode over to the single pillar that remained standing triumphantly amid the ruins of the others. Clasping his war hammer in both huge hands, the minotaur swung it at the pillar and struck a blow that pulverized it. He struck again and again until he had reduced the immense pillar to dust and then he shook his hammer at the sky and gave a defiant roar.

"I am no longer your slave, my queen! My people and I will join forces with Kiri-Jolith and the Knights of Solamnia and together we will march to the gates of your glorious city of Neraka. We will batter the gates to the ground and then tear the walls down stone by stone and bury your armies and your Highlords and their foul dragons beneath them."

Sargonnas lowered his war hammer and gave an enormous grin. "I think that should catch her attention."

The minotaur strode out onto the obsidian pool, planted his legs in a firm stance, and clasped his war hammer in both hands. Kiri-Jolith took his place at his side, holding his sword. Sturm drew his sword and was about to join them, when Kiri-Jolith stopped him with a gesture.

"You and your companions must leave Godshome now. Go back out through the passage. You do not have much time. Already the sky above darkens with her rage."

"I will not run from danger, Lord!" Sturm said angrily.

Kiri-Jolith smiled in understanding. "Your duty is to your companions, Sturm Brightblade, to the world we are trying to save, and to a battle you have yet to fight. The Heroes of the Lance have done their part. Now it is up to us, the gods, to do ours."

"A duty we have long neglected out of fear," Sargonnas growled. "But we are afraid no longer."

A twisting mass of boiling black revolved around the empty, soulless eye, and it was transformed into the reptilian eye of an enormous dragon. And then ten eyes glittering with fury rose like hideous suns above the mountain as the dragon's gigantic body smashed through the cliff that crumbled around her. Vast wings filled the dome of the heavens, blotting out the sun and sweeping aside the moons. Five heads writhed and twisted as they dove to attack, striking at the two gods.

The red maw spewed fire and the blue spit jagged bolts of lightning. Sargonnas blew out the fire with a puff of breath and knocked aside the lightning bolt with his hammer. Kiri-Jolith struck the blue dragon's head with his sword, slicing open a gaping wound.

The red dragon tried to seize hold of Kiri-Jolith. Sargonnas smashed the head in the side with his hammer, shattering the jaw, as Kiri-Jolith ducked and then leaped to plunge his sword into the dragon's throat.

Tanis realized that this, indeed, was not their fight.

"Run for the passage!" he cried, as blood splattered down on them.

Flint was already racing in that direction, his head down, his legs pumping. But Sturm lingered, his hand on his sword. And Tas was dashing toward the knight, flourishing his hoopak.

"I'm coming, Kiri-Jolith!" Tas cried.

Tanis grabbed hold of the kender's topknot as Tas raced past him and jerked him to a halt.

"Ouch! My hair!" Tas wailed.

"I need you to scout ahead!" Tanis told the squirming kender. "See what's on the other side of the passage. I don't want to escape Godshome just to find the Dark Queen's army on the other side. Besides, you have to help Flint through the passage."

Tas ran off, yelling for Flint to wait. Sturm hesitated only a moment longer, then he saluted Kiri-Jolith, bowed to Sargonnas, and ran to join his friends.

The blow from the god's hammer had widened the passage but had started a small rockslide that was partially blocking it. Flint was shifting debris in an effort to clear it, as Caramon picked up huge rocks with ease and tossed them aside. Tasslehoff crawled over the debris pile and peered through the passage.

"It's safe!" he reported. "No army. Or bugbears!"

Raistlin had fallen behind and was trying to catch up to them when he suddenly began to cough. Clutching his chest, he sagged to his knees, unable to breathe. Caramon heard his brother's distress and dropped the rock he was holding to start to go back to him.

"Keep working!" Tanis shouted. "I'll go back for your brother!"

"I will cover you," Sturm offered.

The battle continued to rage in the center of Godshome. Takhisis lashed out with her claws as her five heads darted to the attack, one after the other, striking with their fangs. Sargonnas fell, driven to his knees by the relentless assault. Kiri-Jolith stood guard over the minotaur, fending off the dragon, his shining sword cutting bloody swaths through the writhing necks, until Sargonnas managed to regain his feet. Tanis did not think the battle could last much longer.

He put his arm around Raistlin and helped him to his feet.

"Can you walk?" Tanis asked urgently.

Raistlin nodded. His lips were frothed with blood. He pressed his handkerchief over his mouth. Leaning on his staff and on Tanis, he staggered toward the passage. Sturm followed, guarding their backs.

The noise was horrendous. The five heads roared in fury. Jagged lightning blasted the ground; thunder shook the cliffs and sent rocks cascading down the side of the mountain. Blood from the wounded dragon pelted them in a frightful rainstorm as another head swooped to the attack. Tanis felt a painful burning sensation on his hand and saw drops of green acid, drool from the maw of the black dragon. The pain was excruciating, and he frantically wiped his hand on his leather armor as he ran.

Tanis could feel Raistlin flinch and saw green drops on the hand holding the staff. The burns must have been painful, but Raistlin stubbornly clasped the staff, refusing to drop it.

Tanis blinked the blood from his eyes and looked ahead to see that Caramon and Flint had managed to clear a path through the rubble. Flint was continuing to work as Tasslehoff stood in the passage, keeping watch and motioning for them to hurry. Beyond lay the gray fog of the Misted Vale. Tanis had no idea if they would be safe there, but at least they would be able to take cover in the fog instead of being caught in the open.

"Stay with Raistlin," said Sturm, close behind them. "I'll bring the others."

Caramon had reached out his hand to his brother and Tanis was helping Raistlin climb among the rocks when they heard a loud hissing sound and saw the head of the white dragon snake down from the sky. Its tongue flicked between its teeth, its white eyes fixed on them with malevolent intent.

Takhisis had found them.

"Look out!" Flint bellowed.

Caramon flung himself on top of Raistlin, dragging him to the ground and shielding him with his body. Flint grabbed Tasslehoff, and the two of them skidded and slid among the rocks. Tanis and Sturm both flattened themselves on the ground.

The white dragon spewed a fierce blast of frost at the passage, blocking it with a barrier of ice, sealing it shut. Frigid cold penetrated their lungs so that they struggled to breathe.

Tanis was covered in ice that turned a hideous pink from the dragon's blood. He could not speak or move. His facial muscles were frozen. He watched green acid drip onto the frost and saw the black head hanging above him. The green head dipped down, breathing a noxious cloud. He had no idea if the others were dead or alive, for they were buried beneath mounds of white, like a graveyard in the winter.

Death would not be long in coming.

And then suddenly Takhisis paused. Her five heads shifted as though she were searching. The heads were silent as though she were listening. The frost thawed; the acid sizzled and disappeared. The lightning stopped; the thunder ceased.

"What is happening?" Tanis asked, afraid that this presaged some new and more horrific attack.

Raistlin was lying next to him, gazing up at Takhisis. His hourglass eyes were shadowed.

"She sees her peril," he said quietly.

As one, the five heads stared down through the centuries, searching for what had caught the Dark Queen's attention—perhaps nothing more than a flash of gray light glimmering on the surface of the river.

Takhisis shrieked in outrage, then spread her massive wings and took flight through time, disappearing into the storm. Tanis lay flat, not daring to move, unable to believe he was still alive. He was about to ask if everyone was all right when Tas gave a frantic cry.

"Come quick!" Tas was digging among the rocks with his hoopak. "Flint was buried in the rockslide! We can't let him die again!"

All Tanis could see was a pile of rock and the heel of the dwarf's boot, but he was relieved to hear Flint swearing.

Caramon was already flinging aside the rocks covering the dwarf, and Sturm stood ready to haul Flint out from under the pile. The dwarf emerged, sputtering and complaining and spitting dirt. He was unharmed, save for a few bruises.

Raistlin was sitting up. He was breathing heavily, rasping. He was still holding fast to his staff and he leaned on it to slowly regain his feet, flinching away from Caramon when he would have helped him.

"Are you all right, Raist?" Caramon asked.

"Considering that you came down on top of me like half the mountain, I am mercifully unharmed," said Raistlin irritably.

The clouds had boiled away, leaving the sky azure, cold, and empty. Tanis looked back at the obsidian pool where only moments before Kiri-Jolith and Sargonnas had been battling the Dark Queen. All traces of the gods and the desperate battle they had waged had disappeared. The obsidian pool glistened in the unseen sunshine beneath the azure sky. The blood that had poured down in a gruesome rain had vanished. The icy barrier that had blocked the passage had melted away.

Tanis could hear nothing except the wind sighing among the cliffs, and it had the sound of a lament.

"The gods are gone," said Raistlin. "All the gods."

"I thought *we* were goners," said Tas. "Did we scare Takhisis away?"

"Takhisis saw her peril. She has gone back to try to prevent Destina from restoring time."

"As the Measure says, '*Ahn fax Paradon sec baranis Charadon,*'" Sturm quoted. "'The fate of the world balances on the edge of a knife.'"

"Are you talking about Tully's knife, the one that's poisoned?" Tas asked unhappily. "Destina's back in time with that bad man and his poisoned knife and I'm not there to be her bodyguard!"

He sighed deeply and glanced at Flint. "I guess I'm needed here. That's the fourth time I've saved your life. Or maybe the fifth."

Flint glared at him, but he was spitting out bits of rock and couldn't answer.

"At least we kept Takhisis distracted for a short while," said Raistlin. He cast an irritable glance at Caramon, who was hovering near him, shifting uncomfortably from one foot to the other and looking guilty. "What is wrong, my brother? Don't stand there fidgeting! You know that annoys me."

Caramon flushed. "I'm sorry, Raist. It's the dragon orb. It's ... uh ... broken. I guess I must have crushed it when I fell. It's smashed all to bits. I don't think you're going to be able to fix it this time."

Shamefaced, Caramon opened the velvet bag in which the orb had been stored.

Raistlin snatched the bag from him and looked inside, then upended the bag. Glittering shards, no bigger than grains of sand in an hourglass, covered the ground, sparkling in the sunshine.

"I hope you're not too mad at me," said Caramon.

"If anything, I am relieved," said Raistlin. He glanced at Tanis as he crumpled the bag in his hand. "Now I will not be tempted."

"What do we do?" Sturm asked.

"We wait," said Raistlin. "If it is any comfort, we should not have to wait long."

"What are we waiting for?" Caramon asked.

"To find out if we drown in the River of Time," Raistlin replied.

"How long will that take?" Caramon asked.

"I do not know," said Raistlin. "A moment. A century. Time has no meaning here."

Flint gave Caramon a nudge and asked in a low voice, "Do you know what he's talking about?"

"No, but then I rarely do," said Caramon cheerfully. His stomach rumbled and he grimaced. "All I know is that I'm really hungry. I can't remember the last time I ate. If we're going to be stuck here, we need to eat. I wonder if the gods left any food."

"Maybe there's sausages!" Tas said excitedly. "Let's go look!"

"I think we should stay together," Tanis began, but he spoke too late. Caramon and Tas had already walked off and Flint was stumping along behind them.

"Gods and Graygems and rivers," the dwarf was grumbling. "This place shivers my skin."

"I will go with them, see that no harm comes to them," Sturm offered. He held out his hand to Tanis. "I am glad the gods gave us a chance to meet again."

"I have missed you, my friend," said Tanis. He clasped Sturm's hand and then embraced him. "More than I can say."

He watched Sturm leave. The knight soon caught up with Caramon. The two fell into step, walking companionably together.

"It's good to see you again," Caramon was saying. "Do you remember that time you got hit on the head and thought you saw a white stag? You said it had something to do with some song about a knight who followed a stag and it led him somewhere. I forget. Anyhow, you made us traipse after it."

"I remember the time we were in that rickety old fishing boat, and you tried to catch a fish with your hands and tipped over the boat and threw Flint into the water," said Sturm.

"That's the day we found out the dwarf couldn't swim," said Caramon. His laughter boomed among the cliffs, and the sky above seemed to grow lighter.

Raistlin gazed after him. "I remember that laugh. When I was so ill as a child, Caramon would make those silly shadow puppets to try to cheer me and he would laugh like that. He gave me the will to keep living. Tasslehoff tells me that Caramon still grieves when he thinks of me, after all this time, even after the terrible things I did to him."

"He does," Tanis affirmed. "Tika scolds him and tells him you don't deserve his sorrow, but Caramon has a heart as big as his body."

"Tasslehoff says I should tell him I am sorry," said Raistlin.

"He wouldn't know what you meant," said Tanis. "And according to you, he wouldn't remember anyway, for if Destina succeeds in changing time back to what it was, none of this will have happened."

Raistlin rested his hand gently on the Staff of Magius and ran his fingers over the wood. "That is true, although as I once told Sturm, perhaps the heart will remember what the head does not. Maybe the good I did in my past life stemmed from memories of Magius that I do not remember."

"As Tas would say," said Tanis with a smile.

He looked out across the strange landscape of Godshome. Tas and Flint and Sturm and Caramon had reached the obsidian pool. Tas was shouting excitedly that there were sausages and that they must be magical sausages. Flint was saying he would sooner starve to death than eat a magical sausage, and Caramon said that was fine, he'd take his share. Sturm was laughing. Tanis did not know when or if he had ever heard Sturm laugh.

Tanis hoped that Raistlin was right, that somehow he would remember what had never happened. His memories of Godshome were steeped in blood and shame, shadowed by sorrow. He wanted to look back and see what he saw now, his friends together in life, no longer parted by death.

"What will happen if Destina succeeds?" Tanis asked. "How will we know? Will we know?"

"Perhaps we won't. Or perhaps we will experience a fleeting moment when we will see our reflections in the River of Time before the waters rise and we are swept away," Raistlin answered. "You will meet the dwarf and the kender on the road to Solace in the autumn when the leaves of the vallenwood are turning gold and you will travel together to the Inn of the Last Home to be reunited with old friends after five years apart. You will be amazed at the sight of my golden skin and hourglass eyes, and Flint will ask me if I am cursed. Sturm will find two wandering Plainsfolk carrying a blue crystal staff and bring them inside to warm themselves by the fire."

"Fizban will ask Goldmoon to sing her song, and we will go out through the kitchen," said Tanis, smiling.

"A fate that now depends on the courage and resolve of Destina Rosethorn," said Raistlin.

"May the gods be with her," said Tanis.

"One of them will be," said Raistlin grimly.

CHAPTER
THIRTY-SEVEN

The blaring of enemy war horns woke those few in the High Clerist's Tower who had been able to sleep. Destina had not been one of them. She had been sitting at the window of her bedchamber, watching for the dawn and reflecting sadly on the ill-fated choices that had led her here. Choices that had affected many others, whether in this time or stranded in another.

The Measure says: *Do not dwell on regret. Looking back helps no one and prevents you from looking forward. Be remorseful, ask forgiveness of the gods, and walk with your gaze straight ahead into the future.*

But for the moment, regret and remorse were all Destina had to offer. That and a firm resolve to make things right, no matter the cost.

The clarion call of the horns in the High Clerist's Tower sounded defiantly in answer, summoning its defenders to arms. The sun had not risen, though a sliver of red slashed across the eastern sky. Most were already at their posts, braced to face the foe, knowing this might be their last sunrise. Destina could hear them talking. Some were jesting to ease the tension. Others were grim and silent as they strode along the battlements. She gazed out at the Solamnic plains and saw it alive with a roiling sea of the enemy, eager for blood.

She went over again, in her mind, all that would happen this day, according to Astinus.

Blue dragons sent by the Dark Queen appeared as the sun was rising over the High Clerist's Tower. Huma and Gwyneth determined to challenge them in the skies. As Huma took his place in the saddle and armed himself with a dragonlance, the assassin, Mullen Tully, emerged from the crowd, planning to attack Huma with a magical greatsword given to him by Immolatus. Commander Belgrave had been keeping watch on him and challenged him. Belgrave killed Tully, thus preventing him from assassinating Huma, although the commander himself died in the fight.

But Chaos had intervened and history had changed. Commander Belgrave was dead. She had warned Sir Reginald and others about Tully, and they had promised to be on the lookout for him, but since they were concentrating on the approaching battle, she doubted if they would give Tully a thought. And that left it up to her and the gods.

"Destina, are you awake?" Kairn called, gently knocking on her door.

"I could not sleep," she said, joining him in the hall.

The two were alone on the sixth floor. She and Kairn were the only guests. Most of the servants had taken up arms. Magius's room was empty, the door locked. Huma had given orders that nothing should be disturbed—an unnecessary command. No one would have dared touch anything in that dread room.

Destina greeted Kairn with a gentle kiss and clasped his hand. "I have spent the night thinking, and I want you to know that I am sorry for all that has happened, especially to you. I shamelessly used you for my own ends. I dragged you into my schemes and plots."

Kairn tried to stop her rush of words, but she would not let him.

"I was nearly responsible for your death at the hands of the Gudlose, and now, once again, because of me, you are in peril of your life. I never should have involved you. . . ." She blinked tears from her eyes, her words failing her.

Kairn took hold of her hands and clasped them tightly.

"You could not have stopped me, Destina," Kairn said with a smile. "Before I set out on this journey, I sat at my desk day in and day out, recording the stories of the lives of others but never living a life of my own until I met you. Once, I wrote about love, but you filled me with love. Huma and Raistlin Majere and Sturm Brightblade were words on a page, and now I have met them and they are flesh and blood. And today, I will be present at one of the most decisive battles in history—a scholar's dream!"

Kairn added with a smile, "Who knows, someday some young monk may write about me! I have the Device of Time Journeying in this rucksack. I could leave this moment and take you with me. I could keep us both safe—at least as safe as we are ever safe in this life. But I will not do so, because you must fulfill your destiny and I love you enough to risk losing you to destiny. And that is how much I hope you love me."

Destina raised her eyes to his. "Undoing the wrong I have caused is my duty. *You* are my destiny."

They found comfort in each other's embrace. Their lips met, then they separated reluctantly, aware of time passing, the river flowing.

"We need to go to the courtyard," said Kairn. "The sun is not yet risen, and Huma and Gwyneth are in the temple, asking Paladine's blessing. They will not take flight until the day has dawned. But men are outside, preparing for battle, and Tully might be among them. You know the plan we discussed."

"If we see him, we do not confront him," said Destina. "We summon Sir Reginald or one of the officers to have him arrested."

"He tried to kill you once," Kairn reminded her, regarding her anxiously. "And remember, he carries a poisoned dagger as well as a greatsword."

"And as Raistlin warned me, I must not use the Graygem," said Destina. "Takhisis is searching for it and she would know where to find it."

The two were leaving when they were met by an elderly man, hale and strong and dressed for battle, approaching them. Destina recognized him as Will, Commander Belgrave's loyal retainer.

"I am glad to see you two awake," said Will gruffly. "I came to tell you that Lord Huma is in the courtyard with the silver dragon, preparing to ride to battle. If you want to help defend the tower, you had best go to your posts."

"But we heard Lord Huma would not attack until dawn!" said Kairn, startled.

"My lord Huma has decided to take the fight to the enemy, not wait for the enemy to come to him," said Will.

He turned on his heel and clomped off, as Destina and Kairn turned to each other in dismay.

"Day has not dawned! It is not yet time!" Destina said. "Huma should be in the temple, not preparing for battle."

"Perhaps Will is mistaken," said Kairn.

"He isn't," said Destina bitterly. "Remember what Raistlin said? 'Chaos is our hope, as it is our despair. That is the paradox.' The Graygem has changed time. And while we need the Graygem to change time, Chaos cannot be allowed to change it for the worst. Tully might be with Huma now!"

She saw the Graygem flare, mocking, and felt it hot against her skin. Overwhelmed with anger, frustrated and afraid, Destina grabbed hold of the jewel and gave it yank.

The chain broke and slithered down her neck.

The Graygem came off in her hand. The gray light had died, but she saw a tiny flash of green coming from the emerald, the ring of Chislev.

Kairn was staring at her. "Destina . . ."

"No time," she said urgently. She slipped the Graygem into her pocket. "We have to find Tully!"

The sun struggled to lift above the mountains. Night refused to relinquish the field, and the courtyard was in shadow. Soldiers lined the battlements. They could not see the vast numbers of the foe arrayed against them, but they could hear them beating their swords against their shields and promising death. They could hear the war horns blaring in the distance, and the shrieking and howling of the Dark Queen's dragons, certain of victory.

But then a single ray of sunlight from a defiant sun pierced the darkness and shone through the Westgate pass, where the ground was still red from the blood of innocents cut down by Immolatus, and drove the shadows from the courtyard.

The sunlight gilded Huma's armor and glistened on Gwyneth's silver scales. The dragonlances lay on the stones at the dragon's feet, shining like the river of molten dragonmetal from which they had been forged.

Huma was seated in the dragon's saddle, adjusting the straps that would hold him securely in place as the dragon flew to battle. He had designed the dragon saddle himself. Centuries later, during the War of the Lance, leatherworkers would craft saddles based on the same design, to be used by the Knights of Solamnia when they rode into battle on the backs of dragons.

Destina and Kairn ran into the courtyard, only to stop, dismayed by the number of soldiers that were crowded around Huma and Gwyneth. Some were buckling the thick leather straps that bound the saddle around the silver dragon's body, as others stacked the dragonlances against a tall wooden rack designed to hold them for easy access. Still more were there to forget their fear of the upcoming battle, to gape in wonder at the dragon, and to wish their lord god-speed.

Destina searched frantically among the yeomen wearing armor and helms, the squires in canvas jackets and breeches, and the servants in woolen tunics and stockings.

"Do you see Tully?" Destina asked, clutching at Kairn.

"He could be any one of those men," said Kairn hopelessly.

"But I don't see any of them carrying a greatsword!" said Destina.

"He might not wear it in this crowd, fearing it would draw too much attention," said Kairn. "And remember, if Tully has the poisoned knife, he does not need it."

"He will have to get close to Huma to use it," said Destina. "Keep watch on those near Huma."

Huma was making the final adjustments to the straps on his saddle, cinching them tight, and talking to Sir Reginald, who was standing at his side, the two of them going over final plans for the defense of the tower. Gwyneth was staring fiercely at the blue dragons of the Dark Queen that wheeled in the sky above the vanguard of the army.

Destina noticed a man wearing the leather armor of a yeoman standing at the knight's stirrup, on the dragon's right flank, as though prepared to obey any final orders. He wore a helm that partially covered his face, but Destina knew him. She would never be able to forget him.

"There he is! The yeoman at Huma's side!" said Destina.

"I see him," said Kairn. "But what can we do?"

Destina could scarcely breathe for fear. Tully was standing near Huma, and if he had the knife in his hand, he could kill Huma with a flick of his wrist.

Destina gave a frantic shout, but the trumpets were blaring, summoning men to arms. The crowd around Huma was dispersing as the soldiers ran to their posts. No one could hear her above the tumult.

Destina sought to push her way through the milling soldiers to reach Sir Reginald, who was standing on the dragon's left flank, but the guards barred her way.

The sun rose higher in a blaze of purple and blood red. The courtyard was now bathed in sunlight. Gwyneth's scales shone silver. Huma's armor seemed washed in gold. The crowd in the courtyard quickly dispersed, to give the dragon room to spread her wings. Only Sir Reginald remained. And Mullen Tully.

Destina watched the River of Time flow past her, and she was helpless to stop it.

Sir Reginald grasped Huma's hand. "May the gods fight at your side, my lord."

"And with you, my friend," said Huma. He turned to Tully and held out his hand. "Give me the dragonlance."

"Yes, my lord," said Tully, his voice muffled by the helm.

He bent as though to pick up one of the dragonlances, but then he paused to stare, frowning, at a buckle on the dragon saddle near where Huma was loosely grasping the reins.

"This strap is too long, my lord," he said. "I fear it might impede the dragon's flight. I will cut it off for you."

Tully drew the knife he wore in his belt. Destina recognized it as the same knife he had held to her throat, the same knife that had nicked her skin.

Even this tiny amount of poison has sickened her, Raistlin had said. *She would already be dead if the knife had gone deeper.*

Tully was holding the poisoned blade near Huma's hand. Huma

was wearing leather gloves, but the knife would slice through the leather easily. Tully had only to jab the knife into Huma's flesh and the poison would enter his body. Tully could swear the cut had been an accident and Huma would likely pass it off, for the poison was slow acting and he would not feel the effects immediately.

He would be in the air, holding the dragonlance, when he would start to feel death coursing through his body. He might die before he ever met Takhisis in battle.

Destina felt the ring of Chislev tighten on her finger and saw the emerald shine and heard her mother's voice.

The ring is a blessed artifact of Chislev and has sacred powers. If you are ever lost anywhere—in field, cave, or forest—you have only to clasp the ring and call upon the goddess, and she will guide you to safety.

Destina was lost. She had been lost ever since the day she had decided to steal the Graygem and use it to alter time. Since that day, Chaos had used her. But that was going to change.

Destina took firm hold of the Graygem and drew it from her pocket. The gem squirmed and grew hot, trying to escape, but she held it tightly. The gem blazed with blinding light, trying to daunt her. But its gray light was now eclipsed by the green glow of the emerald.

"Chislev is with me," said Destina. "Chaos is with me, whether it wants to be or not."

Kairn was by her side. She could feel his love supporting her and she remembered what Paladine had told Gwyneth, *The most powerful weapon you have against evil is love.*

She looked at Kairn. "I must break my promise and I need your help."

"I understand," Kairn said.

He shifted the quarterstaff to a horizontal position and gripped it with both hands. He gave Destina a nod and then, shouting Gile-an's name, Kairn struck two of the guards with the staff and shoved them backward.

Destina darted past them and ran toward Huma, shouting a warning.

"Lord Huma, look out! That man is an assassin. The knife is poisoned!"

Her voice carried above the shrieks of dragons and the cries of men. Destina pointed directly at Tully. Light from the Graygem welled out from between her fingers. Instead of trying to hide it, as she had done in the past, she opened her palm. A beam of gray light struck Tully, illuminated his face, and gleamed in his startled eyes.

Tully raised his hands, still holding the knife.

"The woman is mad, my lords!" he protested. "You both know me . . ."

"Now that I see you in the light of day, I *do* know you! You are Mullen Tully," Sir Reginald said grimly. "He is an agent of the dragon, Immolatus, my lord!"

Gwyneth snaked her head around to fix Tully with a baleful gaze. The silver dragon could have decapitated him with a snap of her teeth, but Huma rested his hand on her neck.

"He protests his innocence. He will stand trial, as the Measure states," Huma said.

Gwyneth obeyed him but her eyes glinted in warning.

"Surrender the knife," Sir Reginald ordered. "Drop it on the ground."

Tully lowered his hand, appearing to obey. Destina watched his eyes, as her father had taught her. She saw his gaze glance sideways at Noble's Gate and she guessed he was going to bolt. Then, without warning, he turned and raised the knife, intending to stab Gwyneth.

Chaos is our hope, as it is our despair.

Destina struck at Tully with the only weapon she had—the Graygem.

The blast was loud and silent—dazzlingly bright, impenetrably dark. Everyone saw it and no one saw it—with the exception of Takhisis, who had been searching for it up and down the River of Time. She knew now where to find it.

Destina blinked her eyes, half-blinded, and when the dazzling light faded, she saw Tully staring stupidly at the handle of the knife protruding from his rib cage. He grasped the knife and yanked it out, bringing with it a gush of blood.

But he was too late. The blade had penetrated deep into his body, and the poison was already coursing like fire in his veins. He flung the knife away and sagged to his knees. Then he shuddered and pitched forward, writhing in agony on the pavement. He gave a howling wail, his body jerked and twitched, and then he lay still.

Destina clasped her hand tightly over the Graygem and dropped it into her pocket.

Sir Reginald was kneeling beside Tully. He put his hand on Tully's neck.

"He is dead," he reported.

"You said you knew him," said Huma.

"Commander Belgrave suspected him of being an assassin, sent by the dragon. Are you all right, my lord?" Sir Reginald asked.

"Neither Gwyneth nor I have taken any harm, thank the gods and this young woman," said Huma. "What is your name, Mistress?"

"Destina Rosethorn, my lord," she replied faintly.

"I thought I saw a flash of light, right before this man fell," said Huma. "The light was strange in color. I have never seen the like. What was it?"

Destina clasped her hand tightly around the Graygem, hiding it in the folds of her skirts. She had no idea what to say, and yet she had to say something, for everyone was staring at her.

And then Destina became aware of Gwyneth intently observing her. If the dragon did not understand everything, she understood enough.

"Do we question the gods who have given us a miracle?" Gwyneth asked. The dragon bowed her head in grateful acknowledgment to Destina. "I recognize the knife. It belongs to Immolatus, and the blade is infused with deadly poison."

Gwyneth blasted Tully's knife with her breath, freezing it with such bitter cold that it shattered. She breathed on it again and the particles withered away to nothing. Sir Reginald ordered men to drag Tully's corpse away and dump it in the refuse pit.

"I ask your pardon for questioning you, Mistress Rosethorn," said Huma. "The Measure speaks truly when it says good redeems its own and evil turns upon itself. You have my grateful thanks and the gratitude of all those gathered here."

Sir Reginald raised his voice in salute and the soldiers joined in, clashing their swords against their shields, shouting Destina's name.

She smiled in acknowledgment, but her lips were stiff. She

searched for Kairn and saw him trying to reach her, pushing his way through the crowd.

The sound of the war horns grew louder. The enemy was marching closer.

As the sun climbed above the mountain peaks and shone full and bright in the cloudless blue sky, the defenders of the High Clerist's Tower prepared for battle. They could hear the shrieks of the dragons and the howls of their foes. They could feel the ground shake with the rumbling of siege engines and the pounding thunder of thousands.

Sir Reginald picked up the dragonlance and handed it to Huma.

"Go with the gods, my lord," said Sir Reginald.

Huma took firm hold of the dragonlance and held it high.

"No matter the outcome of this day, the courage and bravery of those who stand ready to give their lives in the defense of their country will shine down through the ages," Huma called. "The bards will long sing of your deeds, and I am proud to fight at your side."

Huma reached out his hand to touch the dragon's neck. Gwyneth turned her head, and he said something to her that only she could hear. Then he straightened in the saddle and lowered the visor on his helm. Gwyneth spread her wings, leaped into the air, and took flight. The sun glistened on her silver scales and blazed on the tip of the dragonlance as those watching cheered.

Destina reached out to Kairn and thankfully caught hold of him. She watched Gwyneth and Huma flying toward the dragons that wheeled in the sky.

"I did not want to use the Graygem. Raistlin warned me not to, but I had to stop Tully from harming Gwyneth," said Destina. "And now I fear Takhisis is aware of it. I can almost feel her eyes on me! We have to leave this time and return to our own!"

The Graygem flickered. It was listening, watching. Destina might have gained control of it, but it would always try to escape. She fastened the chain around her neck again, for safekeeping.

"We should go into the temple," said Kairn. "No one will be there, and we can use the Device and disappear without anyone noticing."

But before they could reach Noble's Gate, the enemy launched the initial assault, using infernal machines to lob huge globs of molten lava over the battlements.

The lava splashed down onto the pavement and spread across the courtyard in blazing rivulets, sending men fleeing in terror.

Kairn and Destina got caught up in the panic. Soldiers shoved and jostled them in an effort to escape. Kairn almost lost his hold on the rucksack, and he struggled to keep it from being torn from his grasp. Destina pressed against him, clinging to his arm to keep from being separated.

The fiery globs continued to rain down from the sky. Men carried buckets of sand to dump on them when they fell, in an attempt to put them out. Those struck by the lava screamed as the molten fire flowed over their bodies.

The crowd heaved and surged around them. Kairn was caught in a press of bodies and torn from Destina's grasp. He vanished, as though he had been sucked under raging water.

Destina was desperately searching for Kairn when someone shouted a warning. She looked up to see an enormous ball of lava hurtling down on her, trailing fire like a comet.

Destina tried to run, collided with someone else trying to run, and fell, striking her head on the stone. Pain jabbed through her skull. The terrible heat of the lava and fear of burning to death drove her to her feet. She staggered a few faltering steps and then collapsed, and darkness closed over her.

She woke to find herself lying on cold stone. She sat up, disoriented, her head throbbing. She did not know where she was and she was frightened, at first. Then she saw the reassuring light of candle flames, burning on the altar of Paladine.

"Kairn?" she called, hoping he might have found her.

But there was no answer. She looked around to see that the temple was empty.

The battle raged outside, for she could hear the clash of arms and men shouting and fighting and dying. But the sounds were far away. She wondered what was happening and did not know how long she had been unconscious.

Destina touched the Graygem, hanging again around her neck. The jewel was cool to the touch, its light dimmed. She pulled herself to her feet, holding fast to the back of a pew as a wave of dizziness assailed her. When that passed, she felt better and walked toward the ruins of Noble's Gate.

The figure of a woman materialized out of the darkness.

Or perhaps the darkness materialized into the figure of a woman.

Takhisis wore armor made of dragon scales that were all colors and none. Her black hair was alive, coiling and twining about her head. Her face was white as the bleached bones of the dead. Her eyes were triumphant. Her voice was soft and sibilant.

"I have been searching through the centuries for you, Destina Rosethorn. I knew, sooner or later, you would lead me to the Graygem."

CHAPTER
THIRTY-EIGHT

estina nearly suffocated from fear. She couldn't breathe or
speak. She shrank back from the terrifying apparition,
thinking to run, even as she knew she had nowhere to go.
For there was nowhere the god could not find her.

"You have long wanted to be rid of the Graygem," Takhisis said
softly. "And now you will be free of the burden."

The Dark Queen stretched out her hand. Her fingers were the
claws of a dragon. She delicately snagged the chain forged by Reorx
in a claw. But at her touch, the flames of the candles on the altar
flared with light as bright and blinding as the sun.

Takhisis snarled in pain and averted her eyes, and in that moment, Destina grabbed hold of the Graygem, tore the chain from her
neck, and dropped the jewel into her pocket.

Takhisis roared in anger and blasted the candles, dousing the
flames. She looked back at Destina and saw that the Graygem was
gone.

"Where is it?" Takhisis hissed. "Tell me or I will tear apart your
living body until I find it."

Destina could not speak for terror. She could only give a small shake of her head.

Takhisis raved in anger, grabbed Destina by the hair and yanked her head back, forcing her to look into the hideous eyes. Nails sharp as talons dug into her neck.

Destina moaned. The pain was agonizing. Her wounds burned with searing fire as though flames were consuming her flesh. Dimly, through the rush of blood in her ears, she heard a hollow voice calling from the darkness.

"Queen Takhisis! Are you here? I bear an urgent message!"

A messenger on horseback galloped into the temple. He was wearing black armor and riding a demonic horse that might have sprung from the Abyss, for its mane was fire and flames flared from its steel hooves. The messenger reined in the beast, causing it to rear and stamp the floor. It stood still, quivering, snorting flames from its nostrils.

Takhisis appeared annoyed at the interruption.

"What is your message?" she demanded churlishly. She spoke over her shoulder, not releasing her hold on Destina. "Be quick about it."

"Commander Bhatt bids me say these words," said the messenger. "'If Her Dark Majesty does not want to lose this war, she will immediately come to our aid.'"

"Lose the war?" Takhisis hissed in anger. She threw Destina to the floor and swung around to face him. "What does the fool mean?"

"The knight, Huma, and the silver dragon have killed your blue dragons, Cyclone and Sandstorm. The knight wounded them with a fey weapon and the silver dragon attacked with claw and tooth and breath. The blues fell from the sky, and when the Solamnics saw this victory, they opened the gate and charged into the midst of our troops, wielding death!"

"Where is Immolatus?" Takhisis demanded. "He was ordered to slay this knight and the silver dragon before the battle started!"

"Immolatus has fled the field, Your Dark Majesty. An infernal gnomish device blew up in his camp. The blast wiped out his army and wounded him. He cursed your name and flew back to the Abyss. When our forces saw him flee and the blue dragons fall, they turned tail and ran, and now they are in full flight across the plains. Commander Bhatt says that if you do not come in person to rally your forces, my queen, the battle is lost."

Takhisis gave a scoffing laugh. "Victory is mine! I cannot lose! My armies vastly outnumber the Solamnics. My warriors are more ferocious. Ogres, kobolds, goblins—they revel in slaughter, devour the bones of their victims! My dragons rule the skies. A lone knight and an army of farmers will never defeat me!"

"Yet, Your Dark Majesty, they do," said the messenger.

Destina crawled across the floor through her own blood. She grasped hold of one of the pews and slowly and agonizingly pulled herself up. She shuddered with pain, but she would not die on the floor, a piteous object lying at the feet of the Dark Queen.

"You do not understand," Destina said, her whisper loud in the stillness of the temple. "We are fighting for our homes and our families. Our weapons are freedom and hope, and against those, fear and darkness cannot prevail."

Takhisis regarded her with a contemptuous smile. "Enjoy your victory while you can, for it will be short-lived. You will soon see it perish in blood and death."

Takhisis raised her hands to the shadows and they swelled and shifted and transformed into an immense dragon. Five heads sprouted hideously from the gigantic body, reared up, and cracked the dome ceiling. Huge leathery wings brushed the walls of the temple and reduced the altars of the gods to dust. The dragon's enormous tail thrashed, smashing pews to kindling. Her five heads roared in a fury that shook the walls of the High Clerist's Tower.

"Keep watch on the human, but do not touch her or go near her," Takhisis ordered the messenger. "I will deal with her after I have slain this knight and his dragon."

The darkness embraced the goddess, and she vanished from the temple. The demon horse snorted fire and restlessly pawed the floor with its steel hooves, striking sparks. The messenger dismounted and walked over to Destina. He was a human, dressed in black leather armor with a leather helm, and he carried a short sword. He loomed over Destina, viewing her impassively, seeming to relish her pain.

"What do you possess that is of such interest to Her Dark Majesty?" the messenger asked. "You'll never survive those wounds she inflicted. Her touch kills, but she can make the pain last hours, days, years—even an eternity, if she chooses."

He drew closer, his breath touching her cheek. "Tell me what she is after and I will end your suffering. I'll be quick. A single slash across your throat. You'll never feel it."

Destina recoiled from him in horror and despair. He spoke the truth. The pain was like fire consuming her flesh, but the chill of death was in her blood. She closed her eyes to banish the sight of the messenger's leering face, so close to hers, and saw Kairn, as he had come to her in Commander Belgrave's office, come to take her home....

The demon horse suddenly shrieked a warning and Destina opened her eyes. She could not believe what she was seeing and feared perhaps this was some cruel trick, meant to deceive her. Kairn stood at the entrance to the temple, holding his quarterstaff.

"I have come to take you home, Destina," he said quietly.

The demon horse rose up on its hind legs and lashed out at Kairn with its fiery hooves.

"Gilean, stand by me!" Kairn called.

He ducked beneath the slashing hooves and thrust his staff between the horse's hind legs, causing the beast to founder. The horse crashed to the floor, and Kairn smashed the staff into its flaming head. The demon horse vanished in a swirling cloud of fire-tinged night.

Kairn turned on the messenger. The man drew his sword with a grim smile and charged at Kairn, swinging the blade in a sweeping arc meant to behead a foolish monk.

Kairn countered the vicious attack with his staff and knocked the blade aside, then rapped the man on the head. He stumbled back and Kairn struck his sword arm with a blow that cracked the bone. The man howled and Kairn advanced, whirling his staff. Attacking with a flurry of blows, he pummeled the man on his head and shoulders.

The man staggered beneath the onslaught, trying to escape but not knowing which way to turn, for the staff was always there to batter him. Finally, Kairn drove the staff into the man's gut. He groaned and pitched forward, and Kairn slammed the staff down on his head.

The messenger lay sprawled on the floor in a pool of gore. Kairn jabbed him with the staff, but the man did not move. Assured that he was no longer a threat, Kairn dropped his staff and sank down on his knees beside Destina. Kairn regarded her in shock, and she knew she must be almost unrecognizable, for she was covered in blood, her body slashed, her face ravaged.

"You are badly injured!" Kairn said, his voice shaking. "Rest here! I will bring a healer—"

He started to stand, but Destina clutched at him.

"Takhisis inflicted these wounds, and they are death blows. A healer could do nothing, and I must see the battle!" Destina struggled to rise. "I must know that time has been restored!"

Kairn could undoubtedly see for himself that what she was saying was true, for he grew very pale.

"Do not carry me," said Destina. "If Takhisis sees me, she will see me standing on my own."

Kairn did not argue but put his arm around her waist and lifted her to her feet. The pain coursed through her body, as though Takhisis were still tormenting her, and Destina almost collapsed.

"Take hold of my staff," Kairn said, handing it to her. "Gilean will aid you."

Destina clasped the staff and death receded, though she could see it lurking not far away, biding its time, aware that she could not escape. She put her hand in her pocket and clasped hold of the Graygem as she had done so many times before. It squirmed and grew hot to the touch, but the little ring with the emerald tightened around her finger. She gripped the Graygem firmly and would not let it go.

Kairn assisted her to walk and, leaning on his staff, she limped down the aisle and out into the courtyard.

The sun was at its zenith in a blue and cloudless sky. The sounds of battle could still be heard on the plains, but those gradually ceased as friend and foe alike stopped the struggle to watch Huma Dragonbane and Gwyneth, the silver dragon, challenge Takhisis.

The Queen of Darkness had taken up her position on the battlement of the High Lookout, as though the tower was already in her possession. She planted her enormous body, her feet firmly grasping the stone. She could survey the field of battle, on the ground below and in the heavens above.

A single knight and a silver dragon stood between her and victory.

Huma rode on Gwyneth's back, holding the dragonlance, wet with the blood of dragons, in his hand. As Gwyneth circled above Takhisis, her five heads writhed and twisted and snapped at them. Flame crackled and lightning thundered. At Huma's command, Gwyneth dove down on Takhisis and blasted the heads with her icy breath.

Ice encased the head of the red, flame-breathing dragon, and it sagged and flopped about, impeding the attacks of the other heads. The black dragon managed to shove the red out of its way and spit a stream of deadly acid into Gwyneth's face.

The acid melted her eyes, ate into her scales, and dissolved her flesh. Blind and in terrible pain, Gwyneth was yet mindful of Huma, and she made an attempt to land so that he could safely dismount. But she could not see, and she floundered, missing her footing.

Takhisis struck. Four of her dragon heads attacked Gwyneth. Huma impaled one of them—the black dragon—with the dragonlance, but before he could fight off the others, the enormous green dragon, the largest of all of Takhisis's heads, sank its teeth into Gwyneth's neck.

The silver dragon fought to free herself from the terrible grip, slashing at the green dragon with her talons and striking with her tail. Huma struck the green head with the dragonlance again and again, trying to force it to let go. Blood flew from the wounds he inflicted, but the green dragon held fast.

Gwyneth collapsed onto the battlements but managed, with her failing strength, to twist her body so that she would not land on Huma. They crashed into the wall and he lost his hold on the dragonlance. It fell, clattering, to the stone.

He tried to reach it, but he was trapped in the saddle, held fast by the straps. He drew his sword, cut himself free, and jumped.

He caught up the dragonlance and stood protectively over Gwyneth. He lunged at Takhisis, but she batted him aside. Her powerful jaws closed over Gwyneth's neck, snapping it. The silver dragon's blood ran down the walls of the High Clerist's Tower. Gwyneth looked at Huma and kept him in her vision until death closed her eyes.

Huma knelt grieving by her side, still holding the dragonlance. The sun shone on his face, wet with tears. Takhisis was mad with fury, suffering from the wounds he had inflicted with the lance forged of metal from Silver Dragon Mountain. She saw the knight alone and on his knees and she determined to end this battle swiftly. She hurled herself at Huma, claws extended, tail thrashing, wings beating.

Huma rose to his feet to stand beside the body of his beloved. The Dark Queen's claws raked him, ripping through his armor, slashing through his flesh. He braced his hand on Gwyneth's body to steady himself, gripped the dragonlance, and plunged it deep into Takhisis's chest, impaling her.

Her heads howled and wailed. Takhisis fought frantically to free herself, but Huma kept hold of the lance, and her own furious struggles drove it still deeper. She struck him a savage blow in the head with her claws, smashing his helm and crushing his skull. She hit him again and Huma crumpled. He slumped over Gwyneth. His blood mingled with hers, silver and steel.

Takhisis clung to the wall. Her dragon heads sagged and twitched and moaned in agony. She seized hold of the dragonlance that was still embedded in her chest, to try desperately to free herself from the terrible pain, but the lance had cleaved through her immortal flesh, and was buried deep, piercing eternity.

She could not fly, for her wings were broken, the membrane shredded from beating against the walls. The sunlight shone through them and the wind shriveled them, and her wings flapped and flailed.

Takhisis toppled off the battlements and plummeted to the ground. The Abyss opened to receive her, swallowed her up, and closed over her.

The war horns of the enemy bleated in panic and then were silent, as those who carried them fled or were cut down where they stood. The Solamnics, grieving as they fought, drove the last of the Dark Queen's forces from the field.

Destina stood in the courtyard of the High Clerist's Tower outside the ruins of Noble's Gate, braced by Gilean's staff and supported by Kairn's love and strong arms.

"The day is ours," said Kairn, holding her close. "You kept your vow, Destina. The knights have won the Third Dragon War. Takhisis has been banished to the Abyss."

Destina was growing weaker and knew that she must soon slip beneath the water and let the River of Time flow on without her. She clasped her hand around the Graygem and took it from her pocket. The Graygem had lost its luster and looked as drab and ordinary as a pebble on a riverbank, but she was not fooled. She had one more mission.

"Take me to Astinus," she said to Kairn. "Before I die, I must give the Graygem into the care of the gods."

Kairn took the Device of Time Journeying from the rucksack. The jewels glittered in the light of the victorious sun, and Destina placed her hand on it.

"If you see Tasslehoff," she told Kairn with a smile, "tell him we saved the song!"

CHAPTER
THIRTY-NINE

K airn held Destina tightly in his arms, as though he could keep her from slipping away into death. She had lost consciousness and was growing weaker. She would cling to life until she gave the Graygem into the care of the gods. Kairn had only to say the words to the spell, and the device would take them to Astinus.

But Kairn kept hearing Destina's last words. *Tell Tasslehoff we saved the song.* And Kairn realized that the song was not Huma's song or Gwyneth's song. Every soul sang its own song. He knew what he had to do, and he brought another destination to mind—another time, another place. He spoke the verse as Alice Ranniker had taught him.

"'And with a poem that almost rhymes, now I travel back in time.'"

He held Destina in his arms, and the River of Time lifted them up and bore them through the centuries as gently as autumn leaves floating on a placid stream and set them down beneath the trunks of an enormous vallenwood tree.

The ground was blanketed with the golden leaves of the vallenwoods. The sun was setting. Night was falling, and light from the stained glass windows in the front of the Inn of the Last Home filtered down through the branches of the enormous tree in which it was built. Stairs leading to the front entrance wound round the trunk of the tree.

Kairn prayed to Gilean that he had come on the right night, even though he was taking a risk. If this was the night of the reunion in 351 BC, goblin soldiers, searching for a blue crystal staff, would be barging through the front door.

Tanis Half-Elven and his friends and Riverwind and Goldmoon would be forced to flee by the back, through the kitchen.

Destina was still warm to the touch, but her breathing was growing faint.

"Do not leave me!" he whispered.

He carried her to the back of the inn until they were beneath the kitchen, as he could tell by the thick, stout rope securely knotted around a large tree limb. He could see people silhouetted against the light of the kitchen fire and hear their voices. As he watched, someone flung open a trapdoor. Light flooded down through the hole and a kender appeared in the opening. The kender was festooned with pouches, carried a hoopak, and had a long, flowing topknot.

"Ah!" said Tasslehoff Burrfoot, pointing to the rope hanging from the tree limb. "Here the ale comes up and the garbage goes down."

Kairn breathed a sigh of relief and whispered a prayer.

Tas shinnied down the rope and landed lightly on the ground. Kairn looked up through the trapdoor and saw the light shining on red curls. He saw a woman standing beside her with silver-golden hair, carrying an ordinary looking wooden staff.

"I'm sorry about this," Tika was saying, "but it is the only way out of here."

"I can climb down a rope," Goldmoon told her. "Though I admit it has been many years."

She handed her staff to the tall, thin man at her side and began to skillfully descend. Once she was safely on the ground, Riverwind tossed the staff down to her, then caught hold of the rope and dropped to the ground. Two more people appeared in the opening.

One was wearing the red robes of a mage, and the other was big and burly.

"How are you going to get down, Raist?" Caramon asked. "I can carry you on my back—"

"I can get down myself!" Raistlin hissed.

The crystal atop the Staff of Magius shone brightly. Gripping the staff, Raistlin jumped into the hole, floated through the air, and drifted to the ground. A dwarf stood at the trapdoor, peering through the darkness after them. His friend, a man with elven features and a human beard, stood behind him.

"He shivers my skin," Flint said dourly.

"Hurry!" Tanis said, giving the dwarf a shove.

Flint took hold of the rope and climbed down slowly. Caramon followed, causing the stout limb to creak from his weight.

"I will go last," Sturm said.

"Very well," said Tanis. He started to climb down the rope, only to slip. He landed heavily on the ground and stood gazing grimly at the palms of his hands, which were skinned raw.

Sturm descended hand over hand. The light from the kitchen shone on the breastplate that was his legacy and on his sword, Brightblade. As he landed on the ground, Tika stood in the opening, peering down at them. "Go to my house!"

She shut the trapdoor and the light vanished.

"I know the way!" Tasslehoff said eagerly. "Follow me!"

He started confidently through the vallenwood forest, guiding the others. They followed, weapons drawn. Goblins might be lurking in the shadows of the trees, but Kairn had to risk calling to them, otherwise no one would see him.

"Help, friends! Please!" Kairn implored.

Sturm heard him and turned around, his sword raised. Light shone from the windows in the kitchen, and by that light Sturm could see Destina and Kairn.

"Tanis!" Sturm called. "Over here!"

"What is it?" Tanis asked, turning back.

"A woman, badly injured. She is covered in blood," said Sturm.

Tanis knelt swiftly by Destina's side and looked at Kairn. "Who did this to her? How did this happen?"

Kairn could think of only one response. "We were attacked by goblins. I fear she is grievously hurt. Can you help us?"

By this time, the others had hurried over to see what was wrong. Sturm stood guard, holding his sword, keeping watch. Tasslehoff squatted down beside Destina and gazed at her anxiously. Flint stood nearby, shaking his head and looking grim. Raistlin spoke a word—"*Shirak*"—and the crystal on his staff started to glow, shining on his golden skin, reflected in his hourglass eyes. At the sight of her dreadful wounds, he looked grave.

"Raist, can you help her?" Caramon asked.

Raistlin knelt by her side and placed his fingers on her neck. He shook his head.

"Her life beat is faint. She has lost too much blood. There is nothing I can do to save her." Raistlin rose to his feet. "But we have among us one who can."

He shifted his strange gaze to Goldmoon and the wooden staff she held in her hand. Riverwind glowered at him, and Goldmoon appeared bewildered.

"I don't understand. How can I help her?"

"Raistlin's right! Your staff healed Hederick when he fell into the fire," Tas said excitedly. "His hands were burnt to a crisp and then that old man told me to hit him with your staff to put out the flames and it turned bright blue—your staff, not the old man. And Hederick's hands were all pink and pudgy again!"

"But . . . I don't know how or why that happened. . . ." Goldmoon faltered.

"Just hit her with the staff like I hit Hederick," Tas urged. "Well, maybe not *hit* her. But you could try touching her very gently."

"Whatever you do, be quick about it," Sturm warned. "Goblin patrols will soon have the inn surrounded."

"Please help the lady, Goldmoon!" Tas begged. "I don't want her to die!"

Goldmoon knelt down beside Destina and smoothed back her blood-gummed hair to see her face. "She is so grievously hurt. I wish I could help her, but I do not know how, except offering my prayer that she might find ease."

As Goldmoon spoke, the staff began to shine with a blue radiance, illuminating Destina with soft blue light. Destina sighed and seemed to sink into a deep and restful slumber. Her body went limp in Kairn's arms, and he knew he was too late. He had lost her. His heart ached with grief, but he was glad that she was free from pain and fear.

He kissed her forehead. "Walk with the gods, my love . . ."

"So she will, but not this night," Raistlin said. He placed his hand again on Destina's neck. "Her life beat is strong. Her wounds have vanished. I doubt if she will even bear the scars."

He stared intently at the staff in Goldmoon's hand. The blue light had faded. The staff appeared to be an ordinary walking stick, trimmed with feathers. Raistlin would have added something, but he began to cough. Swiftly he drew his handkerchief and pressed it over his mouth. Caramon hovered near him.

Destina stirred and opened her eyes. She looked at Goldmoon, kneeling beside her, and gave a little gasp. Kairn stopped her before she could say anything. "Hush, my love, you must rest. Thank you, Mistress Goldmoon. By saving Destina's life, you saved my own. For she is my life."

"I do not understand this mystery," said Goldmoon. "But I am thankful she is well."

Riverwind reached out his hand to her. Goldmoon clasped hold of him, and he helped her rise. She smiled into his eyes. "For I know what it is to love."

"Are we going to Tika's house, or are we planning to wait for the goblins to catch us?" Flint growled.

"Keep close to me," said Sturm.

Riverwind and Goldmoon fell into step beside him, and he led them deeper into the forest. Flint stumped after them, his armor clanking. Raistlin and Caramon followed the dwarf.

"Can your staff do that, Raist?" Caramon was asking. "Heal someone?"

"Try not to be any stupider than you can help, my brother," Raistlin said caustically, dabbing blood from his lips.

Tasslehoff was still squatting beside Destina and Kairn.

"Hurry up, Tas," Tanis said impatiently. "We should be going."

But Tas was not to be rushed. He held out his hand. "Hullo. My name is Tasslehoff Burrfoot, but you can call me Tas. Everyone does."

Destina took hold of Tas's hand and gravely shook it. "I am Destina. And this is Kairn. We are both so glad to meet you."

"This is my friend Tanis. And those were my other friends," Tas added with a wave of his hoopak. "We're going to Tika's house. You can come with us, if you'd like. Can't they, Tanis?"

"We are seeking refuge from the goblins," said Tanis. "You and your lady are welcome to come with us."

"Thank you, but we will go to my own house," said Kairn. "It is not far from here."

"Are you certain?" Tanis asked. "It is not safe to be in the woods this night."

"I am certain," said Kairn.

"Very well," said Tanis. "Come along, Tas."

Tasslehoff gave Destina a pat, then stood up. He was about to dash off, when Tanis suddenly grabbed hold of his topknot.

"Ouch! My hair!" Tas wailed.

"What are you holding?" Tanis demanded.

The kender's closed fist was strangely glowing.

Tanis pried open Tas's fist. The Graygem fell to the ground and lay among the golden leaves of the vallenwood, faintly glimmering.

Tas swooped down to pick it up. "Look at this interesting jewel! I guess someone must have dropped it."

"I did," said Destina. "It is very valuable. I am glad you found it."

Tas handed the Graygem to Destina, along with a lecture. "You should really be more careful of your belongings. There are a lot of bad people in this world."

Destina closed her hand over the Graygem. The gem flared defiantly, then the light dimmed, as though sulking.

"Thank you, Tas," Destina said, smiling through her tears. "Thank you for everything."

"Safe journey, friends," Tanis said to Kairn and Destina, then he put his hand firmly on Tasslehoff's shoulder and marched him off.

Tas was talking as they disappeared into the shadows. "That

jewel was awfully ugly. It gave me a squirmy feeling. Not the good kind. The bad kind."

Destina fastened the chain around her neck.

"We should leave before the Graygem finds some other way to escape."

Kairn pointed to the stars in the night sky, visible through the limbs of the vallenwood. "We know for certain the River of Time is flowing in the proper channel. Two constellations are missing. The one known as the Queen of Darkness and the one called Valiant Warrior. The War of the Lance has started."

Destina took hold of the Graygem. She gave Kairn a kiss, then placed her hand on the Device of Time Journeying.

"'And with these words that almost rhyme, now we travel back in time. . . .'"

CHAPTER
FORTY

Dalamar and Justarius were once again in Solanthas, walking along the road that led to Alice Ranniker's house. Dalamar had slowed his pace to accommodate Justarius, who was limping on his crutch. Justarius was in a bad mood. He had not wanted to return to this place, for he did not like Mistress Ranniker. But they had received a message from Astinus, telling them that Destina had completed her mission and she and Brother Kairn would be returning to the Great Library with the Graygem.

"I have asked Alice Ranniker to design a repository for the dangerous jewel," Astinus had told them. "And since it is magic, I thought you two should be the ones to pick it up and bring it to the Great Library."

"Does this mean time has been restored?" Dalamar had asked.

Astinus had gone back to his writing and did not answer.

Justarius was grumbling. He had been grumbling since they had left Astinus's study.

"I will have to report to the Conclave, and if anything goes wrong, the members will blame me," Justarius stated. "Given the unorthodox behavior of this obstreperous female, I am certain something will go wrong."

"Mistress Ranniker did an excellent job creating a new Device of Time Journeying," said Dalamar, concealing his smile in the cowl of his black robes. "Astinus remains tight-lipped about what has occurred, but since he asked Alice to design this box according to his specifications and asked us to bring it to him, I think we can assume that Destina's journey has ended in success. The master has the Graygem in hand, and the River of Time is restored."

"Astinus should have commissioned *us* to design a repository for this fey gem," Justarius said grimly.

"I would have turned him down," said Dalamar. "I would not want the responsibility. Would you?"

Justarius was silent, limping on his crutch, then said grudgingly, "No, I would not."

The house belonging to Mistress Ranniker was screened from view of the road by a thick stand of fir trees, and just when Justarius and Dalamar thought they had taken a wrong turn and were certain they were not going to find it, they found it.

Alice was not at work in the forge today apparently, for the forge fire was cold and no dark cloud of soot rained down on them, for which Justarius was grateful. He had taken the precaution of wearing a cloak to cover his red robes.

"They were black as yours by the time I returned to the tower last time," he said to Dalamar.

They could hear the clanking of the mechanical water well as they approached, and Dalamar paused to watch, fascinated, as the small buckets attached to a chain traveled down into the well and then emerged filled with water.

"It really is ingenious," he remarked, as the mechanical hand tipped each bucket, spilling its contents into a trough. "Despite her other failings in magic, she has a true gift as an artificer."

Justarius snorted. "The racket is giving me a pounding headache. Let's get this over with."

They climbed the stairs that led to the front door of the cottage, only to find it adorned with a new and formidable-looking door knocker—a full-sized iron fist attached to an iron arm. Since the fist appeared quite capable of punching a hole in either the door or those knocking, neither wizard was inclined to touch it. Dalamar rapped on the door with his knuckles and called out Alice's name.

"In the back!" Alice shouted. "I'm hanging out my laundry!"

They circled the cottage and came to the backyard, where they found Alice frowningly observing one of her inventions, which was busily at work.

"Since you gents were last here, I built this to dry my drawers," Alice explained, jotting down notes in a leather-bound book. She was wearing the same sprigged dress and had her hair wrapped up in a scarf. She was short and compact, with the strong, muscular arms of a blacksmith.

A large, iron, treelike contraption with numerous limbs stood over a laundry basket filled with wet clothes. As Justarius and Dalamar watched, one of the limbs swooped down, picked up a pair of long, wet, lace-trimmed drawers from the basket, and flung them in the general direction of a clothesline. The drawers landed on the roof of the cottage.

Alice looked up at the drawers on the roof, looked at the limbs of the tree, looked down at the basket filled with laundry, and shook her head. She continued furiously writing notes as one of the tree limbs made another grab for the wet clothes.

"Greetings, gents," she said, glancing at them. "I wasn't expecting you today. I told Astinus next week."

"Given the urgency of the dire situation, we were hoping you might have completed your work early," said Justarius, coldly polite.

Alice chuckled. "You mean you came to make certain I am actually working, and you were planning to lean on me if I wasn't."

Justarius drew himself up. "I assure you, Madame, I have no intention of 'leaning' on you or any—"

Alice interrupted him. "You gents might not want to stand too close. My clothes dryer is still in the development phase."

Justarius and Dalamar hastily backed up as another pair of lace-trimmed drawers went sailing up to the roof.

"As it happens, you're in luck. I finished constructing your box," Alice continued. "I just added the final touches this morning. I was going to let you know by means of this new invention that sends messages along a wire through a series of charged particles. Unfortunately, it has two drawbacks. First, you would have to have a receiving wire in your towers, which you don't, and second, I have yet to figure out how to stop the wire from melting and ruining the kitchen table—"

"Mistress, look out!" Dalamar warned.

Alice turned in time to see one of the iron arms swooping down on her instead of the laundry. She ducked the grasping hand, shook her fist at it, then walked to the side of the contraption and pulled down on a brass lever. The limbs clanked to a halt and hung, drooping, as though they knew they were in disgrace.

"Still needs work." Alice stood gazing disconsolately at her drawers on the roof. "Could one of you gents magic those down for me? Otherwise, you'll have to wait for your box until I fire up the mechanized ladder."

Dalamar saw Justarius go red in the face and hastily spoke a few words of magic. With a sweep of his hand, he caused the drawers to float down gently from the roof and land on the ground.

Alice retrieved them, tossed them in the laundry basket, then led the way into the cottage through the back door. They entered the well-remembered kitchen, with its large stone table littered with glass beakers and cannisters, phials and tubes, and, in the center, an object shrouded in a dish towel.

A fire burned in the large fireplace. The last time they had been here, a mechanical hand in the fireplace had been turning a spit on which Alice had been roasting a chicken. This time, the hand was holding a wooden spoon, stirring a viscous red liquid bubbling in a pot.

"Is that blood?" Justarius asked, horrified.

Alice gave him a strange look. "Tomato soup. I don't suppose you gents would like to stay for lunch?"

"We must be getting back," Dalamar said hurriedly.

"I understand. Dire situation, utmost urgency, world in peril," said Alice with a wink. "Well, it's your loss. I put those little crackers in it. Here's what you came for."

She sat down on a stool in front of the table and whisked away the dish towel to reveal a beautiful, ornately painted box. She regarded it proudly.

"As you can see, it's a heptagon, which means it has seven sides," said Alice. "I made it in honor of Zivilyn, the seventh god in the pantheon of neutrality."

"Why Zivilyn?" Dalamar asked curiously.

"If you recall the story of the barbarian prince who trapped the Graygem, Gargath was a follower of Zivilyn. The god represents wisdom and balance and favored Gargath, who followed his precepts. According to legend, Zivilyn helped Gargath create the magical traps that held the Graygem. If you look closely, you'll see that six sides are painted to tell the story of Gargath and the Graygem," Alice explained. "Sit it down, gents. You'll want to examine it. You'll find chairs in the parlor."

Justarius leaned his crutch against the fireplace as Dalamar brought two chairs from the parlor and placed them at the table. He and Justarius sat down to study the box.

"This side portrays Reorx being tricked by Hiddukel into capturing Chaos inside the Graygem," said Alice. "On the second side, you see a gnome armed with a butterfly net climbing a magical self-extending ladder to steal the Graygem from Lunitari. The third side portrays the Graygem circling the world, creating and destroying. The fourth side pictures Gargath's tower with a gray light shining from the top, and the fifth side shows gnomes besieging the tower to steal the Graygem. On the sixth side, the gnomes battle each other and the Graygem escapes. The seventh side portrays the world tree of Zivilyn."

"These paintings are beautiful, Mistress Ranniker," said Dalamar, impressed.

"Did you paint them yourself?" Justarius asked.

"Not me," said Alice with an airy wave toward the fireplace. "The mechanical hand. It is quite talented."

"Incredible!" said Justarius, amazed.

"By my gears and garters, you are gullible!" Alice laughed and slapped Justarius on the back. "Of course I painted the box, you ninny! I'm not just another pretty face. The illustrations are just for show, mind you. They don't really do anything. The magic's inside the box itself. It's based on a theory I developed about Chaos. I have another theory regarding relativity and one involving string, in case you'd like to hear those."

"Just tell us how the box works, Mistress, so that we may take it and depart," said Justarius coldly.

"You put the Graygem in the box and shut the door," said Alice.

"Then what?" Dalamar prompted.

"That's it," said Alice. "The Graygem can't escape."

"But how is that possible?" Justarius demanded, frowning.

"I drew the mathematical diagram here on the tablecloth," said Alice. She brushed off some breadcrumbs to reveal a series of numbers interspersed with lines and squiggles. "If you take a look at these equations . . ."

"Madame, we do not have time for mathematics!" Justarius said, almost shouting.

"You were the one who asked," said Alice. "See that gold leaf on the world tree? Touch that and the hinged door will pop open."

Dalamar gingerly touched the gold leaf, then swiftly snatched back his hand as the side of the box sprang open.

"Look inside," said Alice.

He peered into the box and was astounded to see seven mirrors, one on each side of the box. But these were not ordinary mirrors. Dalamar could see his face reflected in the seven mirrors and then again in mirrors that mirrored those mirrors and then again in mirrors that mirrored those mirrors and on and on forever.

The effect was unnerving, and Dalamar drew back, startled.

"I call them infinity mirrors," Alice explained. "When you put the Graygem inside the box, its gray light will be reflected an infinite number of times. The Graygem will see itself seeing itself seeing itself and so on into infinity. Shut the door on it, touch this other leaf, and it will lock."

She raised a warning finger. "But make certain the Graygem is inside, for once it's locked, the door can never be unlocked."

"So this will remove Chaos from the world?" Justarius asked.

"You can remove the *Graygem* from the world," Alice clarified, wagging her finger at him. "You can't remove Chaos, for it was there before everything. Remember the story of creation. 'Reorx, the Forging God, struck his hammer amidst the Chaos. Chaos slowed, and the sparks from his hammer became the stars.' If the Graygem broke and freed Chaos, the effect would be devastating."

"I saw what happens when Chaos is released," said Dalamar in a low voice.

"You did?" Alice stared at him. "How?"

Dalamar gazed at the box in silent thought. He could hear the mechanical arm stirring the soup and the water well clanking outside. He sighed and looked at Justarius.

"We need to tell her what I learned from Ranniker's clock," Dalamar said.

"Great-great-great grandfather's clock?" Alice asked.

"I suppose we must," Justarius muttered.

"You remember that I told you I saw the clock Ranniker had created—a clock that foretold the future," said Dalamar. "I said it had been destroyed."

"I remember," said Alice. "I told Ranniker about it when I went back in time to see him. He said he never meant to cause all this trouble, and perhaps it's just as well the clock was destroyed. It was only a prototype—"

"Please, allow me to finish, Mistress," said Dalamar. "I am afraid I succumbed to the temptation to use the clock to see the future. I saw a strange creature with blue skin crack open the Graygem and free Chaos into the world. The effects, as you predicted, were devastating. Takhisis stole the world and carried it to a distant place in the universe inhabited by cruel, hideous dragons."

"Well, that's a kick in the head," said Alice, impressed.

"Our question is this," said Justarius. "If we capture the Graygem and place it in the Infinity Box, can we prevent that future from coming to pass?"

"Mmmm," said Alice. "I need to think about that."

Her thought process apparently involved taking off her scarf and rumpling her hair with both hands until it stood straight up. "Helps cool my brain."

After a moment's vigorous rumpling, she reached a conclusion. "According to my calculations, the River of Time will carry us where it will, gents. All we can say with certainty about the future is that none of us will live to see it."

"Is that a threat?" Justarius demanded.

"Common sense,' said Alice. "Today is the present. Tomorrow is the future. When we reach tomorrow, it will be the present. Since the future is always one step ahead of us, we'll never live to see it."

"I suppose that is true," Dalamar murmured.

Justarius snorted.

Alice slid off the stool. "And now, as much as I've enjoyed this visit, gents, I have to be getting back to work. My laundry isn't going to hang itself."

"How much do we owe you for the box?" Justarius asked.

Alice did the math in her head and ticked the numbers off on her fingers. "You owe me for the materials I used making the box—wood, paint, brushes, turpentine, gold leaf, latches, and hinges. Oh, and I had to pay a traveling circus a pretty hefty sum for those mirrors."

"Circus?" Justarius repeated in alarm.

Dalamar nudged him with his elbow. Justarius sighed and handed over the amount Alice named. Dalamar picked up the box. They politely declined to stay for soup, even with the little crackers, and Alice escorted them to the front door.

"By the way, I drew up designs for that mechanical leg brace I promised you, Mister Justarius. I've worked out the kinks and, in nine tries out of ten, it won't run away with you. I'll send it to you once it's finished. And remember, Mister Dalamar, you promised me a tour of your Tower of High Sorcery. Do you sell souvenirs? If not, I was thinking I could make you little miniature towers to put on key chains."

Dalamar thanked her, but said he had no use for souvenirs, and he and Justarius managed to escape at last. Arriving at the end of the lane, they paused to talk before they traveled their separate paths of magic. Justarius was returning to Wayreth Tower, to report to the Conclave. Dalamar would travel to the Great Library to present the Infinity Box to Astinus.

"Let me know when this is ended," said Justarius. "I will sleep soundly for the first night in months."

"I will do so," Dalamar promised.

"May the gods walk with you," Justarius said.

He cast his spell, set foot on the paths of magic, and disappeared.

Dalamar paused a moment, holding the box in his hands. Thinking back over the strange events of the past, he devoutly hoped that the saga of the Graygem was finally nearing its end.

"May the gods walk with us," he murmured.

He stepped upon the paths of magic and traveled to the Great Library of Palanthas.

Upon arriving, he incurred the wrath of Bertrem by interrupting the master at his work.

CHAPTER
FORTY-ONE

The River of Time carried Destina and Kairn to the Great Library of Palanthas, where they materialized outside the office of Astinus, much to the great astonishment of Bertrem.

He stared at them, shocked and appalled.

"What are you doing here, you . . . you cutthroat hooligans?" Bertrem demanded indignantly, eyeing their torn and blood-stained clothes, covered with mud and autumn leaves. He caught sight of the Device of Time Journeying in Kairn's hands and gasped.

"The Device is supposed to be in the Artifact Room! Help! Thieves have broken into the Artifact Room!"

His cries were interrupted by the cool voice of the master.

"Bring them into my office, Bertrem," Astinus called through the closed door. "I am expecting them."

Bertrem eyed Kairn and Destina askance and ventured a rare and agonized protest. "But, Master, are you certain? They appear to be footpads!"

"And fetch two chairs," Astinus continued as though Bertrem had not spoken.

Bertrem gave a long-suffering sigh, opened the door, and ushered Kairn and Destina inside. He then placed two chairs in front of the master's desk and departed, closing the door behind him.

Astinus sat in his chair with his hand resting on the Sphere of Time, writing, recording. He did not look up from his work. Destina approached the master's desk. Kairn stood behind her, offering strength and silent support, but knowing she had to walk the last few steps of this journey alone.

Destina closed her hand over the Graygem, which she wore on the chain around her neck. The jewel was burning cold to the touch, but she took hold of it, unfastened the clasp of the chain, removed the Graygem, and laid it on the desk in front of Astinus.

She did not, however, let go of it.

Astinus said nothing. He continued writing.

Destina held fast to the Graygem—held fast to Ungar and Wolfstone, Mari and Tas. She held fast to Sturm and Magius and Raistlin, Huma and Gwyneth. She held fast to her father. She held fast to pain and sorrow, guilt and remorse. The gods had healed her of the wounds inflicted by the Dark Queen. As Raistlin had said, she would not even bear the scars. But she would always bear the scars of the wounds she had inflicted on herself and on others.

Astinus ceased writing and looked up at her. "The Measure says, 'Forgiveness begins with ourselves.'"

Destina let go of the jewel and drew back her hand.

The Graygem lay on the master's desk amid the papers, near the master's inkwell. It pulsed with sullen gray light, defiant, ugly. Plotting. Scheming.

"Archmage," said Astinus and he beckoned to the Graygem with the quill pen.

A figure clothed in black emerged from the shadows. Destina was startled to see Dalamar. He carried in his hands a seven-sided box, beautifully painted, and placed the box on Astinus's desk.

Astinus touched the golden leaf on the front of the box and a door opened. Astinus laid down his pen, ceased writing. He picked up the Graygem as nonchalantly as he might have picked up a rock from the riverbank and placed it in the center of the box. Gray light glowed, reflected in the mirrors, reflected in the mirrors, reflected in the mirrors . . .

Astinus shut the panel and touched the gold leaf that locked the box. They heard a click.

Astinus picked up his quill pen, dipped it in the inkwell, and returned to his writing.

This day, as above Afterwatch rising five, the Graygem of Gargath is trapped in Infinity.

Dalamar lifted the box with reverent care, bowed to Astinus, stepped onto the paths of magic, and vanished.

Astinus continued writing. "Your journey has ended, Mistress Rosethorn. If there is nothing further, Bertrem will escort you and Brother Kairn out—"

"I have a question, Master," said Destina. "Raistlin said that if I restored time, we would not remember what happened because those events would have never happened. Yet I remember, and so does Kairn."

"You remember because you were the bearer of the Graygem," said Astinus. "Brother Kairn remembers with Gilean's sanction, as would any of my aesthetics who had gone back in time to record what they saw."

"Will Raistlin and Sturm and Tas remember?" Destina asked anxiously. "If they do, won't that alter history?"

"You saw them just now at the Inn of the Last Home. They saw you," said Astinus. "Did they recognize you, Mistress Rosethorn?"

"No, they did not," said Destina. She felt relieved, but also a little sad. "Not even Tas knew me."

"You have your answer," said Astinus and he continued to write. "Bertrem!"

The door opened, and Bertrem stepped inside.

Astinus gestured to the Device with his quill pen. "Return the Device of Time Journeying to the Artifact Room. Then bring me the book on the Third Dragon War."

Brother Kairn handed the Device of Time Journeying to Bertrem. The jewels sparkled and glittered in the perpetual light that shone on the master's work.

Bertrem held the Device close, as though fearing it would be wrested from his grasp. "I trust its return will now mean an end to the chaos we have endured around here, Master."

"Let us pray that it does, Bertrem," said Astinus gravely.

As Bertrem departed, Destina and Kairn both sat down in the chairs across from the master's desk and waited in silence, watching Astinus's pen scratch across the page.

The book in which Astinus had recorded the history of the Third Dragon War had provided the first indication that the Graygem had changed history, for it had named Sturm Brightblade and Huma on the muster roll of those knights defending the High Clerist's Tower. Raistlin Majere and Magius had both been listed as war wizards. And instead of recording the victory of Huma over Takhisis, the pages following had been blank.

"The Third Dragon War," Bertrem announced and placed the immense tome on the desk.

Astinus opened the book with a touch of his hand to a page that was covered with his own neat, concise handwriting.

Astinus pointed to a notation halfway down. Kairn and Destina both rose to read it.

"As you see," said Astinus. "Huma Feigaard is listed among the knights. Sturm Brightblade's name does not appear. Magius was the only war wizard. Raistlin is not mentioned. Read the third paragraph aloud, Brother."

"'As the battle begins, and the sky is darkened by the wings of Takhisis and her evil dragons, Huma and the silver dragon, Gwyneth, prepare to ride. Huma reaches out his hand to take the dragonlance from a man disguised as a squire, but who is in truth Mullen Tully, an agent of the dragon Immolatus, sent to assassinate Huma.

"'Commander Belgrave discovers the plot, but he is badly wounded by Immolatus in the dragon's attack on the temple. As he lies dying, the commander reveals the plot to a young woman, believed to be a refugee from Palanthas.

"'Tully tries to kill Huma with a poisoned dagger, but he is stopped by the young woman, who accosts him and attempts to take the knife from his hand. During the encounter, Tully accidentally cuts himself with the dagger and falls victim to the poison. Huma takes up the dragonlance. . . .'"

Kairn stopped reading. He and Destina exchanged worried glances.

"But this account is different from the original, Master," said Destina. "Commander Belgrave recovered from his wounds and killed Tully."

Astinus paused in his writing. He held the pen poised above the sheet of paper and regarded Destina with his gray eyes, vast and endless and emotionless as the sea.

"Are you saying I made a mistake in my account, Daughter?" Astinus asked.

"No, Master, of course not," Destina murmured, stricken. "It's just—"

A single drop of ink fell on the page. Astinus frowned at it, reached for the blotter, and continued to write. "Proceed, Brother Kairn."

Destina did not dare utter another word. Kairn continued reading.

"'Huma and the silver dragon Gwyneth defeat the Dark Queen at the cost of their lives. Silver dragons carry the bodies of Huma and Gwyneth to Silver Dragon Mountain, where they will lie throughout eternity. The gods join together to imprison Takhisis in the Abyss, dooming her to remain there, though they well know that she will never cease scheming and plotting to return to the world.'"

"Read the footnote at the bottom of the page," said Astinus.

"'The identity of the young woman who saves Huma from the assassin's blade is never known,'" Kairn read. "'The knights search for her after the battle ends, but they do not find her and come to believe she was killed in the battle, although they do not recover her body. To pay tribute to her courage, they confer upon her an honorary knighthood. Since they do not know her family, they design a special device in her honor—a single red rose on a white background.'"

"How extraordinary!" said Destina. "The young woman cannot have been me, for now that time is restored, I was not there. Who was she, Master?"

"A drop in the river, Mistress Rosethorn," said Astinus. "Yet one that turned the tide of time."

He came to the end of the page, set it aside, took another sheet of blank paper, and began again to write.

CHAPTER
FORTY-TWO

When Dalamar returned to the Tower of High Sorcery, carrying the Infinity Box, he closed the tower to everyone—the living and the dead. He sent away the apprentices and the students. He ordered the specters, spirits, phantoms, and wraiths who served as guardians to reinforce the Shoikan Grove. Last, he set free the sole inhabitant of the dungeons: the wretched Ungar.

The Conclave had charged Ungar with a variety of crimes, including fraud, blackmail, selling counterfeit artifacts, stealing a book from the Great Library, and, most egregious, destroying Ranniker's Clock. As punishment, the Conclave recommended to the gods of magic that they strip him of his power. Since he had been a Red Robe, Lunitari was responsible, and she decreed that if he tried to utter a single word of magic, it would change into a toad and fall from his mouth. When Dalamar set him free, Ungar bolted out of his cell and ran as fast as he could into the night. Dalamar had no idea where he went or where he was planning to go, nor did he care.

When the last being had departed, Dalamar locked and sealed the tower with powerful magicks he had learned from his *Shalafi*,

Raistlin Majere. Dalamar then climbed the winding stairs to the very top of the center spire and entered the Chamber of the Three Moons.

Dalamar lit the three pillar candles—one black, one red, and one white—that adorned the altar.

Solinari appeared, robed all in white. Lunitari in red stood at his side. Nuitari hung in the shadows, a disembodied face, round as a moon.

"You know what has occurred," said Dalamar.

"Gilean placed the Graygem in the Infinity Box, where it is captivated by itself," said Lunitari.

"Paladine closed the door on it," said Solinari.

"And Takhisis locked it," said Nuitari.

"I am amazed your mother gave up the fight to try to take the Graygem for herself," said Solinari.

"She claims that since she is all powerful, she has no need of it," said Nuitari. "In truth, I think she came to fear that in the end, it would devour her."

Dalamar placed the beautifully painted box containing the Graygem on the altar. "I give this into your care. What will you do with it?"

"We have prepared its repository," said Solinari.

"A magical vortex that is vaster and deeper than time," said Lunitari. "Not even light can escape it. The Graygem will never do harm again."

The gods of magic gathered around the altar. Solinari and Lunitari and Nuitari lifted the box containing the Graygem. A breath of air blew out the flames of the candles on the altar, and the gods vanished.

Dalamar remained standing by the altar in the darkness lost in thought, until he eventually realized he was shivering with the cold. Leaving the chamber, he sealed and locked it, and made the long trek down the spiral staircase to his own study.

The tower was eerily silent without its complement of apprentices and students. Dalamar found that he missed them. He missed their laughter, their arguments over theories of magic, and even the occasional explosion when a spell went awry. He would bring back the tower's residents—living and dead—tomorrow. But tonight he was glad to be alone.

He lit a fire with a word, sank down in his chair, and poured himself a glass of elven wine. He was particularly fond of this year's vintage, and he savored the taste on his tongue. Still cold, he drew near the fire and wrapped his black velvet robes closely around him.

He thought of the Graygem, imprisoned in infinity. He knew in his head, in his heart, in his soul, that it could not escape. The gods rested secure this night, and he should do so, too.

But in the profound silence, Dalamar could hear, once again, the ticking of Ranniker's Clock. . . .

CHAPTER
FORTY-THREE

estina had no idea what became of the Graygem after she gave it to Astinus and Dalamar had taken it away. She had no need to know. She was blessedly free of the gem, and quiet joy filled her heart. But even as she thought that, she found herself putting her hand reflexively to her throat, as though the chain were still around her neck.

"I will never be free of its shadow," said Destina, sighing as she lowered her hand.

Kairn clasped her hand in his. "The Measure says, 'Shadows exist because of sunlight.'"

Bertrem had hustled them out of Astinus's office and then stood upon the stairs of the Great Library, watching to make certain they left.

"I suppose we should be planning our wedding," said Destina.

Kairn's reply was to take her in his arms on the steps of the Great Library and kiss her, leaving the scandalized Bertrem to purse his lips in disapproval and hasten back inside.

"I wish I knew where my mother was, so that she could perform the ceremony," said Destina as they walked aimlessly, hand in hand, through the streets of Palanthas. "But I have no idea where she is or how to contact her. She was planning to travel to Ergoth to find her people, but that land is vast, and the Ackal are nomads. I wouldn't even know where to start searching."

"Ask Chislev to help you," Kairn suggested. "You said your mother was a cleric of the goddess."

Even as he spoke, the small emerald ring on Destina's finger began to tighten, as it did when serving as a guide. The emerald sparkled in the sunlight.

"You are right," said Destina, marveling. "It seems the goddess is trying to guide me, though I have no idea where she wants me to go. Certainly, it cannot be to Ergoth."

She looked around, puzzled, and suddenly realized they were on a street she knew.

"We are near the house I own in Palanthas!" said Destina. "My odious cousin permitted me to keep it when he took everything else, including Castle Rosethorn. Perhaps we could sell it. The house is far too large for us, and the upkeep is expensive. We could buy a more modest dwelling closer to the Great Library, so that you could continue your work for Astinus."

"Librarians rarely grow wealthy," Kairn said ruefully.

"And you are marrying the daughter of an impoverished knight," Destina said. "But we have each other."

"And that makes us as rich as the Lord of Palanthas," said Kairn, laughing. "Perhaps that is what Chislev is trying to tell us."

Destina had left the key to the house with a neighbor—the same one, as it happened, who had tumbled over Tasslehoff Burrfoot on his door stoop. The neighbor was pleased to see her.

"So you're planning to sell it? I'd be willing to take the house off your hands," he said as he handed her the key.

"Truly?" Destina asked, startled.

"My son is getting married, and he'd like to settle near me," said the neighbor. "That house would be ideal."

Destina named a price. The neighbor named a lower price but added that he had the cash on hand to pay for it. Destina agreed.

They shook hands, and the neighbor went off to fetch a strong box. He paid her the money and also handed her an envelope that bore her name.

"A man named Captain Peters left this letter in my keeping only last week, Mistress Rosethorn," said the neighbor. "He said if you returned, I was to give it to you."

The letter was very brief. Destina read it and crumpled it in her hand.

"Bad news?" Kairn asked, observing her anxiously.

"My cousin has sold Castle Rosethorn," said Destina. She had to pause to steady her voice. "Captain Peters bids me come to finalize the sale, although I am not certain why I need to be there. The castle belongs to my cousin."

"Captain Peters would not have asked you to come unless it was important," said Kairn. "I think we should go, unless returning to the home that was your father's legacy would be too painful for you."

Destina felt the little ring on her finger tighten. She felt a longing to visit her home at least one last time before it passed into the hands of strangers.

"My journey has taught me that my father's true legacy lives in my heart, not in brick and mortar," said Destina. "He would want me to be there."

She and Kairn hired horses for their journey and purchased clothes and supplies needed for traveling. Her home was on the Vingaard River, east of the Habakkuk mountain range, and they had to ride through Westgate Pass to reach it. When they sighted the spires of the High Clerist's Tower in the distance, they stopped their horses to remember before riding on.

Destina spent the long journey steeling herself to see her home in the hands of strangers.

"I fear Castle Rosethorn itself will be a stranger," she told Kairn. "I have not seen it since I heard my cousin tore down the Rose Tower and sold my father's books. But perhaps that is for the best. I will find it easier to say goodbye."

When they rode through the village of Ironwood, Destina kept the hood of her cloak over her head to avoid recognition. She could not bear for people to stop her to commiserate or view her with pity.

She would return when all was settled and she did not fear she might break down in tears.

They passed the Berthelbochs' shop and saw people bustling in and out. Business must be good. She wondered suddenly if they were the new owners of Castle Rosethorn. As they rode on to the well-remembered road that would take them to her home, Destina abruptly turned her horse's head.

"We will visit Saber first," she said to Kairn. "The dragon loves to gossip. He will tell me about the new owners. I need to be prepared."

As they approached the dragon's lair, Destina was pleased to see a horse she recognized tied up some distance from the cave. The horse belonged to Captain Peters. He and Saber had long been friends, and he often visited the dragon.

"I am glad the captain is here, for I want you to meet him," she said to Kairn as they dismounted. "He has been a true and loyal friend to me. He will tell me why he insisted that I come."

Destina had spoken calmly, but she held very tightly to Kairn's hand as they walked to the cave.

The time of year was spring. The grass was new and shiny green. The trees were leafing out, welcoming the migrating birds that had returned to fill the air with song and bicker over nesting rights. They found Saber stretched out full length on the rocks, basking in the sunshine that shone on his copper scales with an almost blinding light.

Captain Peters sat on a boulder near the dragon. He was laughing over something Saber had said, and the dragon was the first to hear someone approaching.

"Visitors," Saber announced, pleased. He clambered ponderously to his feet and hooted joyously when he recognized Destina. "Captain Peters, it is our Destina! We were just speaking of you, weren't we, Captain?"

The dragon was in a flutter of excitement, flapping his wings and thrashing his tail about with such wild enthusiasm he nearly knocked over Kairn.

"Welcome home, Mistress," said Captain Peters.

He extended his hand, but his glad smile and warm greeting touched her heart. Remembering his kindness, his loyalty, and especially his friendship, Destina embraced him as she would have her father.

Destina introduced Kairn to her friends as her future husband. Saber was ecstatic. He fussed over Kairn, making certain he sat on the most comfortable boulder and that he was neither too hot nor too cold, and offered him something to eat. He asked Kairn about the Great Library, and if it was true that Astinus was really a god, and if the library had books on copper dragons, and if so, what did the books say about copper dragons, and a great many other questions, and then never gave Kairn a chance to answer.

Captain Peters shook hands politely with Kairn, but Destina was touched to see the captain reserve judgment until he had determined that Kairn was worthy of the young woman the captain had watched over since her father's death.

Destina had remembered to bring Saber a gift—a string of multicolored glass beads interspersed with little bells. The beads sparkled, and the bells jangled, delighting the dragon. He was entranced with the bauble, particularly by the bells.

"This will be the centerpiece of my collection!" Saber said, and to do honor to the occasion, he kept shaking it, to hear the bells ring.

Destina gathered her courage.

"Tell me about the new owners of Castle Rosethorn, Captain," she said, determined to be cheerful.

"I have no need to tell you, Mistress, because you know the new owner. I can introduce you right now," said Captain Peters.

He turned to Saber, who was bobbing his head up and down enthusiastically and thumping his tail on the ground. "I am honored to present the owner of Castle Rosethorn."

"Who is it?" Destina asked, looking around, puzzled.

"Me, my lady!" Saber said excitedly. "*I* am the new owner of Castle Rosethorn! Or rather, you are. It's yours! A wedding gift!"

The sun must have been too hot, for when Destina came to herself, she found Kairn holding her in his arms, Captain Peters offering her a cup of water, and Saber fanning her with his wing.

"I am sorry," said the dragon remorsefully. "I shouldn't have sprung it on you like that, but I've been so eager to tell you that I couldn't contain myself any longer!"

"I don't understand," Destina said faintly.

"You rest and drink your water and I'll explain," said Saber. "I would invite you into my lair where it is shady, but my treasure is strewn about the cave so that the appraiser could evaluate it, and I have no room for entertaining. I barely have a place to sleep. I am doing my best to set my dwelling to rights, but it's taking longer than I expected."

"Appraiser?" Destina repeated, sitting up. "Why did you have your treasure appraised? And how did you come to own Castle Rosethorn?"

"You should start at the beginning, Saber," said Captain Peters.

"Sorry. It's just that I'm so excited," said Saber. "You know I've always been extremely proud of my treasure hoard. One day I had a visit from a brass dragon I met during the war. His name is Heatstroke, and he was boasting about his treasure and how much it was worth. When I showed him mine, he hooted in derision. He said my treasure was a lot of 'cheap gimcrackery,' as he put it, and dared me to have it appraised. Dares among dragons are matters of honor. I could not refuse, especially since the dare came from a brass, who are notorious braggarts. And so I accepted and Captain Peters found an appraiser."

Destina could guess what was coming next, and she was sorry for the dragon. "You know, Saber, that it doesn't matter what this Heatstroke or the appraiser or anyone else says about your treasure. Its value lies in what it means to you."

"Oh, I know most of my treasure is junk," Saber said serenely. "I figured Heatstroke would win the dare. I just wanted to show him that I didn't care what he thought. But, in the end, you see, I made that brass eat his words. My treasure was worth a king's ransom, as the saying goes. In fact, I could ransom several kings."

Saber bristled with triumph. "At the very bottom of my treasure pile, the appraiser found the largest diamond she said she had ever seen. I don't know much about diamonds, but according to her it is a great many carats, and is of 'remarkable cut, color, and clarity,' whatever that means. You can be certain I let Heatstroke know! He nearly shed his scales in envy."

Destina found this hard to believe and looked to Captain Peters for confirmation.

"I took the diamond to a jeweler in Palanthas," Captain Peters said. "He confirmed its value."

"I had no idea it was worth anything," Saber said. "The diamond was pretty, but it was in a very ugly setting, and I can't think why I picked it up. I must have been newly hatched when I found it. It certainly isn't as lovely as this."

Saber shook the string of sparkling beads and jangling bells with immense satisfaction.

"The diamond was set in a gold headpiece, very elegant in its simplicity," Captain Peters explained. "The jeweler said the work dated back to the time of the Kingpriest and made me an offer. Saber granted me permission to sell."

"I had a plan to buy Castle Rosethorn," said Saber. "I am sorry to have to say this about one of your relatives, Destina, but your cousin is a reprehensible human being. I found out that he was going to murder me."

"What?" Destina asked, shocked.

Captain Peters hastened to explain. "Your cousin was trying to sell Castle Rosethorn, and he thought the dragon's presence was driving away buyers. He hired mercenaries to kill him."

"I am so sorry, Saber, but I cannot say I am surprised," said Destina, stroking the dragon's neck. "I hope they didn't hurt you."

"Actually, it turned out rather well," said Saber. "When Captain Peters found out about your cousin's scheme, he told the townsfolk, and they came to my rescue!"

"Saber has been doing odd jobs for the people of Ironwood," Captain Peters added. "He drove off a band of marauding bandits, helped raise barns, and lifted a tree that fell onto a house during a storm. The townsfolk have become attached to him, and they lined up in front of Saber's cave and told the mercenaries they'd have to go through them to get to Saber. Even Bertie Berthelboch was there. When the mercenaries saw the crowd, they said they weren't getting paid enough to fight an entire town and beat a retreat."

"I was going to melt your cousin into pudding, but Captain Peters persuaded me that revenge was a dish best served cold, so I decided to get even with him by buying Castle Rosethorn myself and giving it to you," said Saber. "Captain Peters handled the sale. Your cousin sold the castle for a lot less than it is worth."

"Your cousin and his wife were eager to sell," said Captain Peters. "They had blazed through his wife's fortune and were in considerable debt. They fled in the middle of the night, pursued by their creditors."

"And so I have a lot of money left over, which Captain Peters said you could use to make repairs and renovations," said Saber.

Destina was close to tears. She rubbed the dragon's snout. "Your gift is more than generous, Saber. I am deeply touched by your kindness, but I cannot accept it. You are the rightful owner of Castle Rosethorn."

Saber looked truly alarmed. "Me? But what will I do with a castle? I can't possibly live there. All those rooms and they're all so small and the hallways are confusing. And I don't like windows. You can see out, but did it ever occur to you that total strangers can see in? I like to be surrounded by stone. Dark and comfortable. And I would have to constantly mind my manners. I couldn't ever relax. I would always be worried about spilling deer guts on the carpet and dripping acid on the floor. My wings would smash the furniture and my tail would knock over the servants and I'd hit my head on the chandeliers."

Saber reached out a claw to gently touch Destina's hand. "The castle is yours, dearest friend. It could not belong to anyone else. Your mother has hired workmen to start rebuilding the Rose Tower."

"My mother!" Destina gasped. "But Atieno is in Ergoth!"

Captain Peters cast an exasperated glance at Saber, who fluttered his wings in distress.

"Oh, dear! She was supposed to be a surprise," said Saber. "And here I promised your mother most faithfully I wouldn't tell you about her or the tower or the books."

"But how did my mother know I was coming home?" Destina asked, bewildered.

"Chislev told her, and your mother returned to celebrate your wedding," said Captain Peters. "She is rebuilding the Rose Tower. And you recall that your cousin sold your father's books? Your mother and I located the buyer and Saber purchased them. You will find them in boxes in the library."

Destina was overcome with emotion. She turned to Kairn. "As my future husband, you should be involved in this decision. What do you think I should do?"

"I think we should unpack your father's books and put them back on the shelves of his library," said Kairn, putting his arm around her. "I will catalog them for you."

Destina held on to him tightly for a few moments to calm herself and hide her happy tears against his shoulder. Then, wiping her eyes, she rested her hand on Saber's snout.

"I accept your gift, dear friend, but only on the condition that you accept a gift from me. I declare this cave and the land surrounding it are now yours," said Destina. "No one will ever be able to drive you away, Saber, for you will be the landowner."

"This cave will be mine?" said Saber, his mane quivering with happiness. "I can live here forever and always?"

"I will have my attorney draw up the deed of ownership," said Destina gravely.

"A deed!" Saber exclaimed, awed and overwhelmed. "My very own deed! I will build a shrine for it right inside the entrance. If you will excuse me, I must go find a suitable location. Wait until Heatstroke hears about this!"

The dragon ducked back into his cave, and they could soon hear the sound of thudding and thumping, rocks breaking, and a crash as though something had fallen from the ceiling.

Destina and Kairn and Captain Peters left Saber to his work and rode companionably on to Castle Rosethorn. The captain had questions, naturally, about where Destina had been all this time, what she had been doing.

"I went on a search for my father's legacy," Destina replied.

"Did you find it?" Captain Peters asked, somewhat puzzled.

"I did," Destina answered. She placed her hand on her heart. "It is here, where it has always been."

Destina longed to see her mother, to thank her for the ring that had given her faith in herself and in the gods, to beg for her forgiveness, and to introduce her to Kairn. Atieno would find it difficult to understand a man who spent his life among books, but the fact that he served the god Gilean—the In Between God, as she had once said—would count in his favor.

As Destina rode toward her home, she thought about the future. She was under no illusions. She and Kairn would not live a life of ease or luxury. The castle had been long neglected and would require a considerable amount of work. She had a duty to her tenants and to the people of Ironwood, and her first task would be to supply their needs. She would help them before she helped herself.

But such work would bring her joy. She would ask Captain Peters to hire and train men-at-arms to ensure the castle's defense, and she would lay in a store of supplies as her mother had done, so that if war threatened, people could take refuge in the castle.

Kairn would have her father's library. He could do his writing there and complete his work on the Third Dragon War. Their children would visit him in the library, as she had done with her father, and Kairn would hold them in his lap and read them stories of Huma and Gwyneth, the silver dragon who loved him. They would listen wide-eyed and play at being Huma and fight imaginary dragons with dragonlances made of wood, but which in their minds were forged of shining dragonmetal.

Atieno would visit, but she would never stay long, preferring to roam the woods she loved. She would perform the wedding ceremony, and the goddess Chislev would bless their union. Her mother would instruct her grandchildren in her own unique views on the Measure and teach them how to use a bow and set traps.

One cloud dimmed Destina's bright sunshine.

"I understand what Astinus is saying and that Sturm and Raistlin would have no memory of me and being transported back through time," Destina said. "Raistlin said the same thing. That is as it should be. But I am sorry that Tas won't remember. Do you agree?"

"You ask a question that involves Chaos and kender," said Kairn. "I am not certain even the gods would know."

Every year on the anniversary of the fall of the High Clerist's Tower, Destina and Kairn and their children, together with Captain Peters—by then Sir John Peters—and his family, would make a pilgrimage to visit those buried in the tower's sepulcher. Destina would tell them the story of the battle and of Gregory Rosethorn and Sturm Brightblade and all the heroes who had given their lives at the Battle of the High Clerist's Tower.

"Individual drops of water," she would say, "but they became a mighty river."

Destina would dedicate much of her time and money to the funding, educating, training, and equipping of aspiring young people who wanted to join the Knights of Solamnia. She would especially champion the cause of women entering the knighthood, citing the example of the "unknown" woman who was knighted at the end of the Third Dragon War.

All female knights would wear a badge on their armor: a single red rose set against a white background, bearing the motto that came from the Measure.

A true knight's worth springs from the beating heart.

She and Kairn and Captain Peters continued along the road and stopped when they saw Castle Rosethorn, rising proud and steadfast from the tor where it had stood for so many generations. Destina could see the battlements where she had fought the goblins. She could see the gate where she had bid her father farewell as he rode off to war, never to return. She could see the forest where she and her mother had hunted deer and laid snares for rabbits.

She saw Atieno standing at the entrance, dressed in leather tunic and trousers, waiting to meet her daughter, as Chislev had foretold.

"Welcome home, Destina!" Atieno shouted in the voice of the Akal warrior-woman, which could be heard above the howls of goblins and the roaring of ogres. "Welcome home!"

And Destina heard her father's voice in her heart.

Welcome home, the Lady of Castle Rosethorn.

CHAPTER
FORTY-FOUR

Tasslehoff Burrfoot stood on the steps of the Great Library of Palanthas and pondered what to do. He had traveled all the way to the Great Library to speak to Astinus on a matter of considerable importance, but the placard saying "No kender allowed" was still posted on the door.

Tas had asked Brother Kairn about this rule during a lull in their adventuring.

"I am quite fond of reading books," Tas had told him. "Or at least I would be if I didn't have to keep going on adventures to save my friends. I've been thinking about it, and I consider it unfair for me and all kender to be banned from the Great Library."

"I understand," Brother Kairn had said. "Unfortunately, some kender have a tendency to walk off with the books."

"That could be because the books fall in our pouches when we're not looking," Tas had suggested helpfully.

"That may be so," Kairn had said. "But if that happened every time people entered the library, we would soon have no books."

Tas had thought this over and conceded the point. He could see that if he were Astinus in charge of running a library, having your books disappear would be an annoyance. But that didn't help matters. Kender were still not allowed. The aesthetics were still standing guard outside, and Tas still needed to talk to Astinus.

He considered sneaking into the Great Library like he had been forced to do the last time he was here. Hiding in the bushes, crawling through a window, lurking beneath tables, and dodging among the bookshelves had been very exciting, though his sneaking hadn't exactly turned out as planned. He had found Mari (who hadn't really been Mari) and he'd taken her to meet his friends in the inn and that had led to time blowing up and so on and so forth.

Tas didn't want to risk it and decided that, before resorting to sneaking, he would first ask politely if he could talk to Astinus. He had been taught as a young kender that honey caught more flies than vinegar, and he could attest to the fact this was true, for he'd conducted the experiment.

He'd poured honey all over a table in the inn and counted the flies that landed in it, then he had done the same with vinegar. Tika had been extremely angry when she caught him, even though he had tried to point out that he was doing this in the interest of science. She had said she'd give him science and had thumped him on his headbone.

Tasslehoff walked up to one of the aesthetics, who took one look at him and said immediately, "No kender allowed."

"I know that, and I have to tell you I consider this rule discriminatory," Tas said, extremely proud of the big word. "I intend to register a complaint about it when I have time, only now I have to talk to Astinus. It's Very Important."

The aesthetic opened his mouth and Tas could see his lips start to form the word no in giant letters when he suddenly changed his mind. "What is your name?"

"Tasslehoff Burrfoot," Tas replied. "That's spelled with two *s*'s and one *hoff*."

"Wait here," said the aesthetic and hurried away.

Tas considered this a promising development, so he waited.

The aesthetic returned shortly, bringing with him another aesthetic who was short and pudgy, with a bald head and sandals that flapped when he walked. Tas recognized him as Bertrem, Astinus's assistant.

The first aesthetic pointed to Tas. "This is the kender the master was asking about, Bertrem."

"Tasslehoff Burrfoot," said Tas, holding out his hand.

"Are you certain?" Bertrem asked in hopeless tones.

"Pretty certain," said Tas, who had honestly never stopped to think about it. "I've been called Tasslehoff Burrfoot ever since I was a little kender. Actually, you and I have met before, Bertrem. I was with my friend Caramon, and we—"

"I was not talking to you!" said Bertrem crossly. "Are you certain, Brother, that the master said he wanted to speak to a . . . a kender?"

"I am, sir," said the aesthetic. "The master gave instructions to those of us standing guard that if a kender named Burrfoot requested admittance, we were to admit him. I didn't think I should let him wander about without an escort—"

Bertrem went quite pale and ran his hand over his head as though he had hair, which he didn't.

"I will ask the master, just to make certain there has been no misunderstanding. Wait here," Bertrem said, then added, "Although if you want to leave, please feel free to do so."

"I'll wait," said Tas. "It's Very Important."

Bertrem sighed and walked off, his sandals flapping. Tas and the aesthetic both waited. He smiled at Tas, who smiled back.

"You look like an extremely nice person," Tas told him. "Any other time I'd be glad to tell you all about my interesting adventures, but I'm on an Important Mission and I have to concentrate my thoughts."

"I understand," said the aesthetic sympathetically.

They waited some more, and pretty soon Bertrem came back. He was dragging his sandals and looking even more unhappy.

"The master said he would see you," Bertrem stated in the same doleful tones he might have used to announce the end of the world. "I will take you to him. But first you must remove your pouches and the knife, and leave them here, along with the stick."

"First of all, it's not a stick," said Tas indignantly. "It's a hoopak. Second of all, Goblinslayer is magic and I can't leave it anywhere."

"Take it off," said Bertrem.

"It will just come back to me," Tas argued.

Bertrem was adamant. Tas shook his head and divested himself of his pouches and Goblinslayer and handed them and his hoopak to the nice aesthetic, who promised to look after them for him.

"Don't worry if you lose Goblinslayer," said Tas. "It won't be your fault."

He announced to Bertrem that he was ready.

"You must stay with me and not wander off," Bertrem instructed. "And keep your hands where I can see them at all times."

Tasslehoff had no idea why Bertrem wanted to see his hands, except perhaps to make certain he had scrubbed under his fingernails, but he obligingly extended them. Bertrem grabbed Tas by the shoulder and marched him into the Great Library.

They passed by rows and rows of bookshelves filled with rows of books, and rows of tables where rows of aesthetics sat reading and writing. The room was sunny and very quiet.

"You certainly do have a grip like a vise, Bertrem," Tas said, because his shoulder was starting to ache. "What sort of monsters are vise exactly? I've always wondered. Do they have talons or claws?"

Several of the aesthetics raised their heads to glare at him.

"No talking!" Bertrem scolded in a loud whisper.

"Sorry!" said Tas, adding loudly, "Sorry!"

Bertrem, looking grim, hustled him through the library until they came to a closed door.

"Wait here while I announce you," said Bertrem.

I'm being announced, Tas thought with pride. He had never been announced before, and he wanted to do justice to the occasion, so he smoothed his topknot (which was growing back quite nicely) and washed his face with kender spit. While not magical, like elf spit, it worked well on grime.

Bertrem gave a gentle knock and then opened the door. "Tasslehoff Burrfoot to see you, Master."

"On an Important Mission!" Tas added, poking his head around Bertrem.

"Bring him inside, Bertrem," said Astinus.

Tas started to enter, but Bertrem pulled him back.

"Stand up straight," Bertrem instructed. "Don't slouch. Don't speak until you are spoken to. Don't sit down. Don't pester the master with foolish questions. And, above all, keep your hands to yourself!"

"Who would I give them to?" Tas asked curiously, being fairly certain that this was not a foolish question.

Whether it was or not, Bertrem didn't answer it. He escorted Tas into the office and planted him in front of the desk. Astinus was sitting where he always sat, with his hand on the Sphere of Time, writing away.

"You may leave, Bertrem," said Astinus, not looking up.

Bertrem was in agony. "Are you certain, Master? A ... kender ..."

"That will be all," said Astinus.

Bertrem departed and, after one more pleading look, as though hoping Astinus would change his mind, closed the door behind him.

"Hullo," said Tas and he held out his hand. "You and I have met before, although maybe you don't recall—"

"I recall," said Astinus, ignoring the kender's outstretched hand.

Tas stood in front of the master's desk trying to remember everything he wasn't supposed to do.

"You may be seated, Master Burrfoot," said Astinus.

"I don't mean to be rude, sir, but could I stand?" Tas asked. "Being short, I'm even shorter when I sit down, and it's hard to see you over the desk."

"Very well," said Astinus. "How may I be of assistance?"

Tas plunged ahead with his tale. "I guess since you're a god, you know all about where I've been and what I've been doing and Lady Destina and the—" Tas sneezed. "Drat!"

"Graygem," said Astinus. "I am aware."

"So I was with Tanis and Sturm and Raistlin and Caramon and my friend Flint, who wasn't dead anymore, in the High Clerist's Tower, and Kitiara was there and Flint gave her a headbutt, and I stabbed Skie in the foot and we took the dragonlances to Godshome and we were fighting the Dark Queen when she left quite suddenly. We had worked up an appetite and I had just found some sausages, but then Raistlin said that me and Flint and Tanis and Sturm were going back to where we needed to be and suddenly I wasn't in Godshome anymore. But what with jumping from the present to the past and the future that wasn't the right future, even though it seems like now it is, I am so muddled I don't know where I need to be. So what I came to ask is how do I get there? Where I need to be?"

Tas paused to draw a breath and wait for Astinus to say something. Astinus didn't say anything, however. He only kept writing, and so Tas ploughed on.

"I found Tanis in Palanthas with Laurana and a lot of knights. I tried to ask Tanis where I needed to be, but he didn't remember finding the dragonlances or that Flint and Sturm and Raistlin were alive when they were dead. He told me I certainly did have a vivid imagination and that he would love to hear more about it, but he and Laurana were negotiating with the Knights of Solamnia and didn't have time. Which wasn't much help.

"I decided to visit Tika and Caramon and tell them about my adventures and see if they could help me figure out where I'm supposed to be. I went to the inn and I had just reached the point in the story where I was describing how that bad man, Tully, killed Huma and Gwyneth and ruined the song, when Tika said that Sturm would be turning over in his grave to hear me talk like that, because everyone knows the story about Huma and Gwyneth and how they were heroes who drove the Dark Queen back into the Abyss.

"So then I told Tika and Caramon about Mari and how I brought her to meet Tanis and Flint and her and Caramon the night of the reunion when we met Goldmoon, only the magic exploded because of the Graygem and carried us back into the past. Tika asked me if I had a fever and put her hand on my forehead. Caramon told me that I never brought anyone named Mari or anyone else to the reunion and I thought back and I knew he was right. I didn't remember bringing Mari to our reunion even though I know I did and at the same time I know I didn't."

Astinus stopped writing and laid down his pen.

"What you are saying is that you remember the past that was and the past that wasn't and the future that will not happen," said Astinus.

"I knew you'd understand!" Tas said, relieved. "No one else does. I was hoping you could explain why I'm remembering things that everyone tells me I shouldn't be remembering."

"It is called a paradox," said Astinus.

"What does that mean?" Tas asked.

"It means that the gods love you, Tasslehoff Burrfoot," said Astinus.

"So I can believe myself?" Tas asked cautiously, not certain that he did.

"You can," said Astinus. "But you must understand that other people such as Tika and Caramon and Tanis might not."

"They might if I could tell them about Destina and the—" Tas sneezed. "Drat!"

And it was then, with the sneeze, that Tas understood.

"I sneezed!" he said excitedly. "Gwyneth scrubbed my face with magical elf spit and after that every time I start to talk about the—" Tas sneezed. "I sneeze! And I'm still sneezing! So I *did* meet Gwyneth and Huma and Magius.... And I *did* meet Knopple and the gnomes and the dragonlance that belched and whistled! I guess that if you take everything into account, I did save the song! Thank you, Master! You've taken a load off my mind."

Astinus gave the ghost of a smile and went back to his work.

Tas was about to leave, but then he had another thought. "I was meaning to ask. Brother Kairn said he was going to bring the Device of Time Journeying back to you. I know where it is. It's in the Artifact Room. Could I borrow it sometime? I was thinking of visiting the Kingpriest—"

"No," said Astinus, and he sounded like he meant it.

Tas decided, on second thought, that perhaps visiting the Kingpriest again wasn't such a good idea, because the last time he'd visited the Kingpriest, a fiery mountain had nearly landed on his headbone, and it might not miss the second time. He thanked Astinus, who kept writing. Tas was opening the door to leave when Bertrem pounced on him.

"I can show myself out," said Tas.

Bertrem paled at the thought and hauled Tas out of the office. He shut the door, searched Tas's pockets, and took away a handkerchief, which he angrily said belonged to him.

"You must have dropped it," said Tas. "Good thing I found it for you."

Bertrem marched him back through the library and the rows of shelves, books, and aesthetics and pushed him out the front door.

"It's polite to say 'thank you' when someone finds something that you lost," Tas said, but by that time Bertrem had firmly shut the door.

Tas found the nice aesthetic still guarding his pouches and his hoopak.

"I'm sorry, but your knife has gone missing," said the aesthetic. "I'm not sure what happened to it."

Tas looked and, sure enough, Goblinslayer was in his belt.

"It came back to me," said Tas. "It always does, which is good because I have a tendency to misplace things. I misplaced a wife once. Not even Uncle Trapspringer can say that!"

Tas picked up his pouches and his hoopak, thanked the aesthetic, and then left the Great Library. He felt immensely better after talking with Astinus. He had saved the song and found a paradox. And if Tika and Caramon and Tanis didn't believe him when he told them his stories about Huma and Gwyneth and Magius and Destina and Mari and the—

Tas sneezed. "Drat!" But he said *drat* happily, because even though they didn't believe those stories or any of his other stories about the woolly mammoth or going to the Abyss or the teleporting ring or the Kender Spoon of Turning, they were still his friends.

A friend is someone who listens to stories they don't believe and calls you a doorknob and yells at you about spoons that somehow manage to fall into your pouch and worries about you when you are off adventuring and gives you a hug and a plate of spiced potatoes when you come back safe.

Tas wondered where he should go from here. Destina and Brother Kairn would be getting married soon, and of course he would go because all the best stories end with a wedding. But in the meantime, he had Goblinslayer and his hoopak and his pouches and a new road that stretched out in front of him.

"New roads demand a hoopak," said Tasslehoff, getting a firm grip on his.

And as every kender will tell you, no road is ever old.

ACKNOWLEDGMENTS

Tracy and I would like to acknowledge Shivam Bhatt, our Astinus, whose help with all things Dragonlance has been indispensable. Perhaps more than that, we both value his friendship, which has only grown stronger through the years.

REFERENCES

DRAGONLANCE CHRONICLES
By Margaret Weis and Tracy Hickman
TSR, INC., 1984–1985

Dragons of Autumn Twilight
Dragons of Winter Night
Dragons of Spring Dawning

DRAGONLANCE LEGENDS
By Margaret Weis and Tracy Hickman
TSR, INC., 1986

Time of the Twins
War of the Twins
Test of the Twins

DRAGONLANCE LOST CHRONICLES
By Margaret Weis and Tracy Hickman
WIZARDS OF THE COAST, 2006–2009

Dragons of the Dwarven Depths
Dragons of the Highlord Skies
Dragons of the Hourglass Mage

The Second Generation
By Margaret Weis and Tracy Hickman
TSR, INC., 1994

Dragons of Summer Flame
By Margaret Weis and Tracy Hickman
TSR, INC., 1995

The Soulforge
By Margaret Weis
WIZARDS OF THE COAST, 1998

Brothers in Arms
By Margaret Weis and Don Perrin
WIZARDS OF THE COAST, 1999

Dragonlance Adventures
By Tracy Hickman and Margaret Weis
TSR, INC., 1987

Atlas of the Dragonlance World
By Karen Wynn Fonstad
TSR, INC., 1987

Dragons of War
By Tracy and Laura Hickman
WIZARDS OF THE COAST, 1985

ABOUT THE AUTHORS

Margaret Weis and Tracy Hickman published their first novel in the Dragonlance Chronicles series, *Dragons of Autumn Twilight*, in 1984. More than thirty-five years later they have collaborated on over thirty novels set in many different fantasy worlds. Hickman is currently creating new realms of adventure on the cutting edge of global entertainment. Weis and Hickman are working on future novels in the Dragonlance series.

MARGARET WEIS

margaretweis.com

Facebook.com/Margaret.weis

X: @WeisMargaret

TRACY HICKMAN

trhickman.com

Facebook.com/trhickman

X: @trhickman

ABOUT THE TYPE

This book was set in Caslon, a typeface first designed in 1722 by William Caslon (1692–1766). Its widespread use by most English printers in the early eighteenth century soon supplanted the Dutch typefaces that had formerly prevailed. The roman is considered a "workhorse" typeface due to its pleasant, open appearance, while the italic is exceedingly decorative.